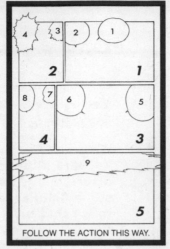

THIS IS THE END OF THIS GRAPHIC NOVEL!

FOLLOW THE ACTION THIS WAY.

To properly enjoy this Perfect Square graphic novel, please turn it around and begin reading from right to left.

AUTHOR BIO

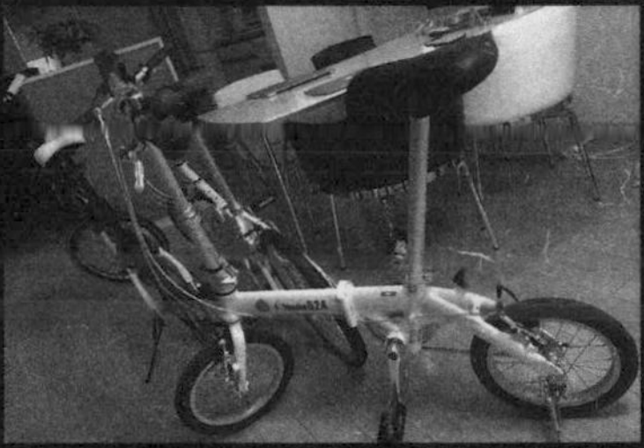

The meeting space at my office is also the bicycle shed.

—Noriyuki Konishi

Noriyuki Konishi hails from Shimabara City in Nagasaki Prefecture, Japan. In 2014, he received the 38th Kodansha Manga Award. He debuted with the one-shot *E-CUFF* in *Monthly Shonen Jump Original* in 1997. He is known for writing manga adaptations of *AM Driver* and *Mushiking: King of the Beetles*, along with *Saiyuki Hiro Go-Kū Den!*, *Chōhenshin Gag Gaiden!! Card Warrior Kamen Riders*, *Go-Go-Go Saiyuki: Shin Gokūden* and more.

Little Battlers eXperience

LBX
LITTLE BATTLERS EXPERIENCE

Story and Art by
HIDEAKI FUJII

Welcome to the world of Little Battlers eXperience! In the near future, a boy named Van Yamano owns Achilles, a miniaturized robot that battles on command! But Achilles is no ordinary LBX. Hidden inside him is secret data that Van must keep out of the hands of evil at all costs!

All six volumes available now!

YO-KAI WATCH

4

STORY AND ART BY
NORIYUKI KONISHI

ORIGINAL CONCEPT AND SUPERVISED BY LEVEL-5 INC.

YO-KAI WATCH
Volume 4
DANCE FIGHT
Perfect Square Edition

Story and Art by Noriyuki Konishi
Original Concept and Supervised by LEVEL-5 Inc.

Translation/Tetsuichiro Miyaki
English Adaptation/Aubrey Sitterson
Lettering/William F. Schuch
Design/Izumi Evers
Editor/Joel Enos

YO-KAI WATCH Vol. 4
by Noriyuki KONISHI
© 2013 Noriyuki KONISHI
© LEVEL-5 Inc.
Original Concept and Supervised by LEVEL-5 Inc.
All rights reserved.
Original Japanese edition published by SHOGAKUKAN.
English translation rights in the United States of America,
Canada and the United Kingdom arranged with SHOGAKUKAN.

Printed in the U.S.A.

Published by VIZ Media, LLC
P.O. Box 77010
San Francisco, CA 94107

10 9 8 7 6 5 4 3 2
First printing, March 2016
Second printing, April 2016

www.perfectsquare.com   www.viz.com

YO-KAI WATCH

4

STORY AND ART BY
NORIYUKI KONISHI

ORIGINAL CONCEPT AND SUPERVISED BY LEVEL-5 INC.

CHARACTER INTRODUCTION

NATHAN ADAMS

AN ORDINARY ELEMENTARY SCHOOL STUDENT. WHISPER GAVE HIM THE YO-KAI WATCH, AND THEY HAVE SINCE BECOME FRIENDS.

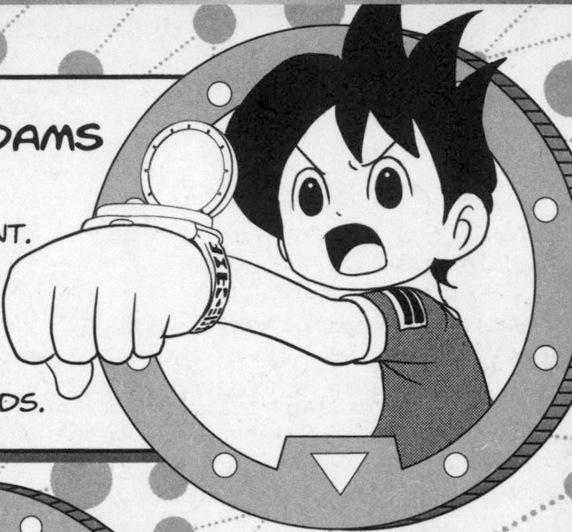

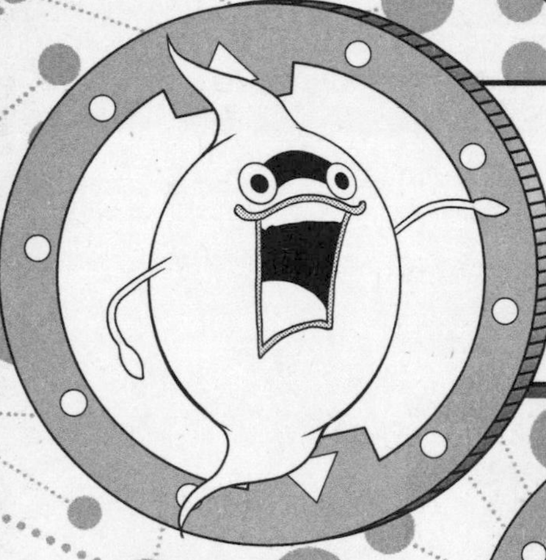

WHISPER

A YO-KAI BUTLER FREED BY NATE, WHISPER HELPS HIM BY USING HIS EXTENSIVE KNOWLEDGE OF OTHER YO-KAI.

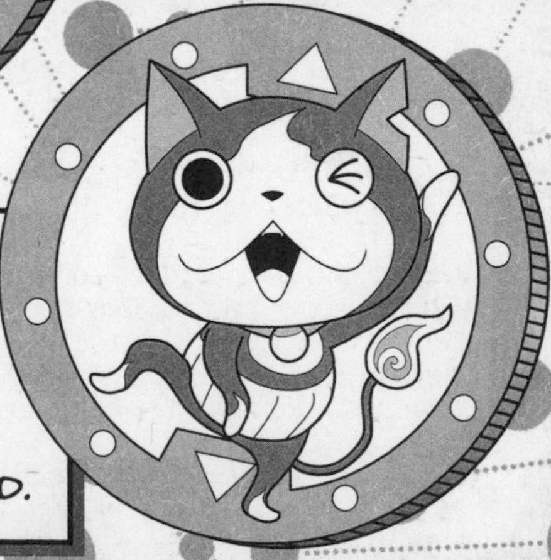

JIBANYAN

A CAT WHO BECAME A YO-KAI WHEN HE PASSED AWAY. HE IS FRIENDLY, CAREFREE AND THE FIRST YO-KAI THAT NATE BEFRIENDED.

EDWARD ARCHER
NATE'S CLASSMATE. NICKNAME: EDDIE. HE ALWAYS WEARS HEAD-PHONES.

BARNABY BERNSTEIN
NATE'S CLASSMATE. NICKNAME: BEAR. CAN BE MISCHIEVOUS.

TABLE OF CONTENTS

Chapter 25: I Want Girls to Like Me!!
featuring Cupid Yo-kai Cupistol 6

Chapter 26: Banish the Cold with Your Burning heart!
featuring Hot-Blooded Yo-kai Blazion 29

Chapter 27: Who can you Trust?!
featuring Skeptical Yo-kai Suspicioni 39

Chapter 28: Protect the Yo-kai Watch!
featuring Yo-kai Gargaros 64

Chapter 29: Dance Fight!♪
featuring Dance Lover Yo-kai Steppa 91

Chapter 30: Too Lazy to Fight?!
featuring Lazy Yo-kai Cutta-nah 100

Chapter 31: Stay Out of the Way!
featuring Blocking Yo-kai Blowkade 117

Chapter 32: Behold: The Jibanyan of the Future?!
featuring Robot Yo-kai Robonyan 125

Chapter 33: Don't Play with Weapons!
featuring Low Profile Yo-kai Blandon 155

Chapter 34: More than Meets the Eye?!
featuring Illusion Yo-kai Illoo 163

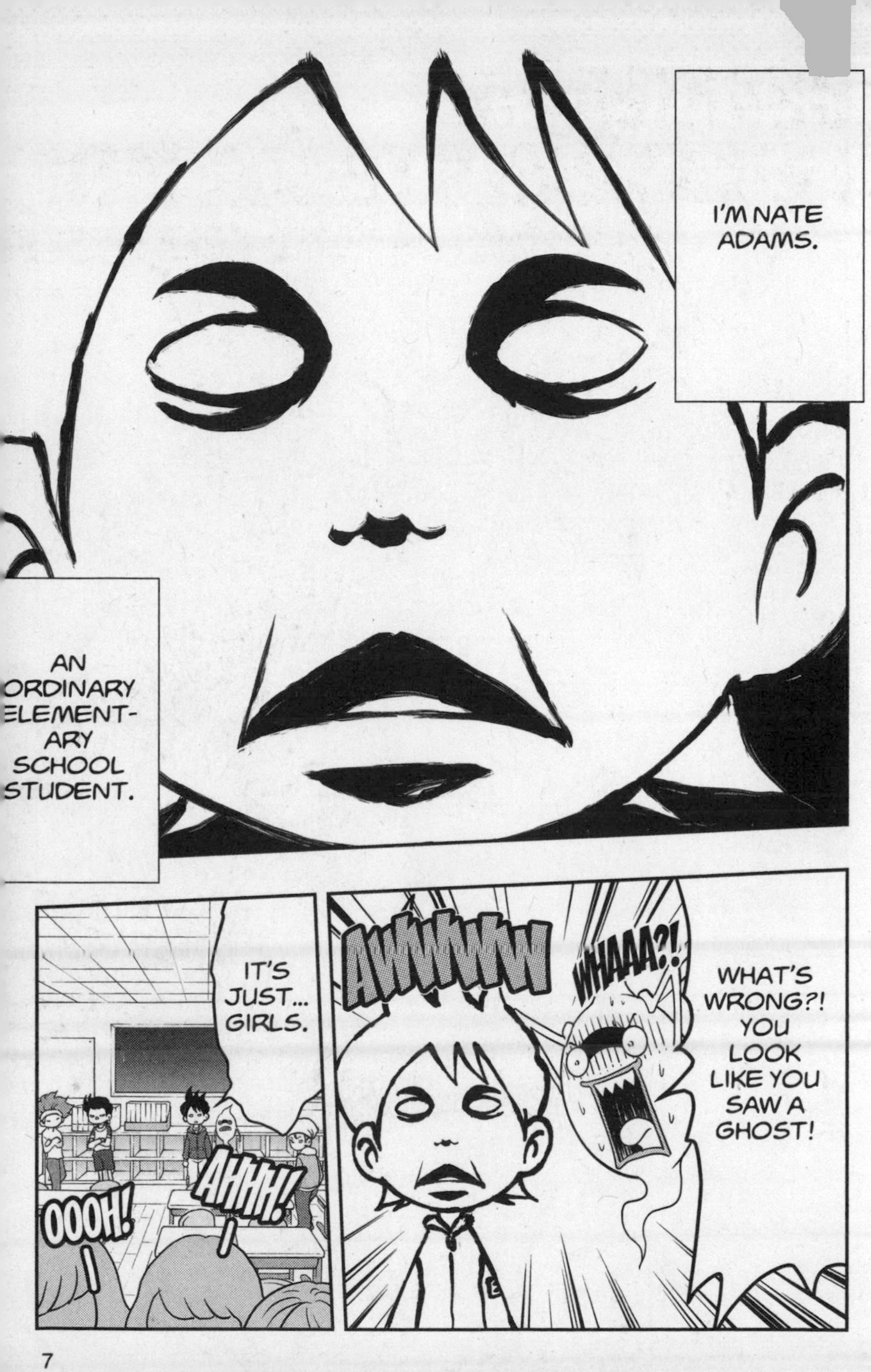
I'M NATE ADAMS.
AN ORDINARY ELEMENT-ARY SCHOOL STUDENT.
WHAT'S WRONG?! YOU LOOK LIKE YOU SAW A GHOST!
WHAAA?!
AWWWWW
IT'S JUST... GIRLS.
AHHH!
OOOH!

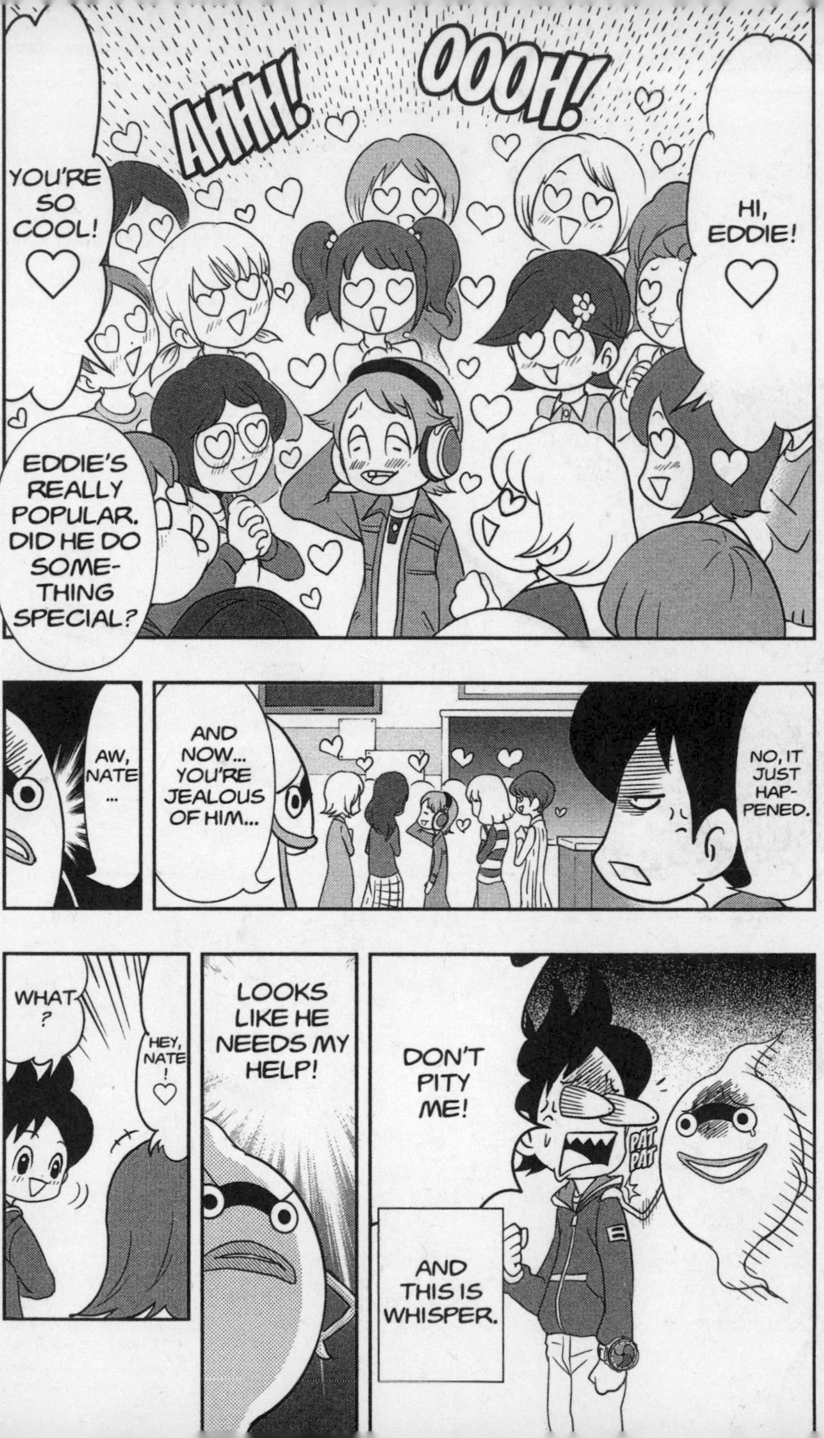
OOOH!
AHHH!
HI, EDDIE! ♥
YOU'RE SO COOL! ♥
EDDIE'S REALLY POPULAR. DID HE DO SOME-THING SPECIAL?
NO, IT JUST HAP-PENED.
AND NOW... YOU'RE JEALOUS OF HIM...
AW, NATE ...
DON'T PITY ME!
PAT PAT
AND THIS IS WHISPER.
LOOKS LIKE HE NEEDS MY HELP!
HEY, NATE! ♥
WHAT?

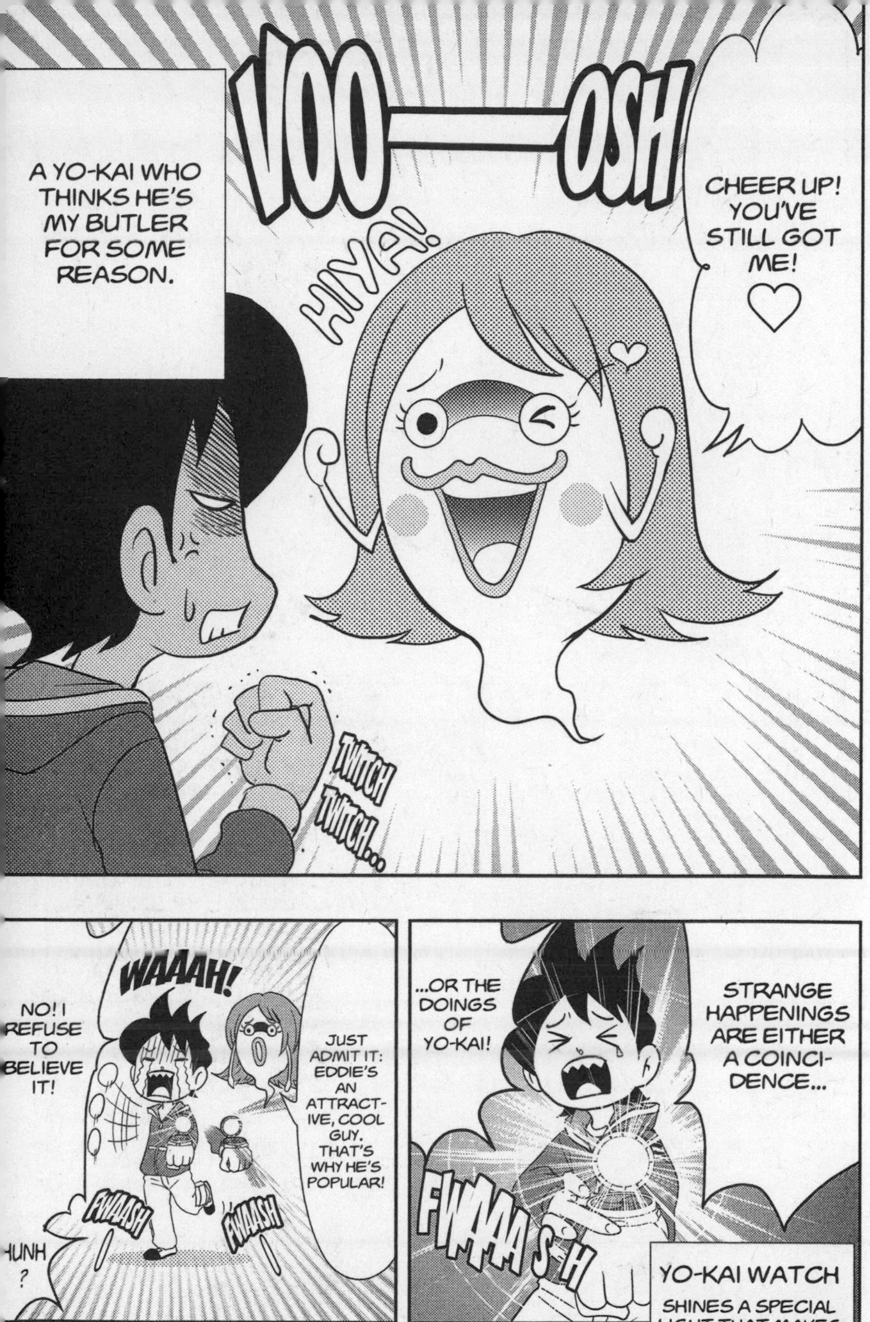
VOO—OSH
CHEER UP! YOU'VE STILL GOT ME! ♥
HIYA!
A YO-KAI WHO THINKS HE'S MY BUTLER FOR SOME REASON.
TWITCH TWITCH...
STRANGE HAPPENINGS ARE EITHER A COINCI-DENCE...
...OR THE DOINGS OF YO-KAI!
FWAAASH
YO-KAI WATCH
SHINES A SPECIAL LIGHT THAT MAKES YO-KAI VISIBLE.
JUST ADMIT IT: EDDIE'S AN ATTRACT-IVE, COOL GUY. THAT'S WHY HE'S POPULAR!
WAAAH!
NO! I REFUSE TO BELIEVE IT!
FWAASH
FWAASH
HUNH?

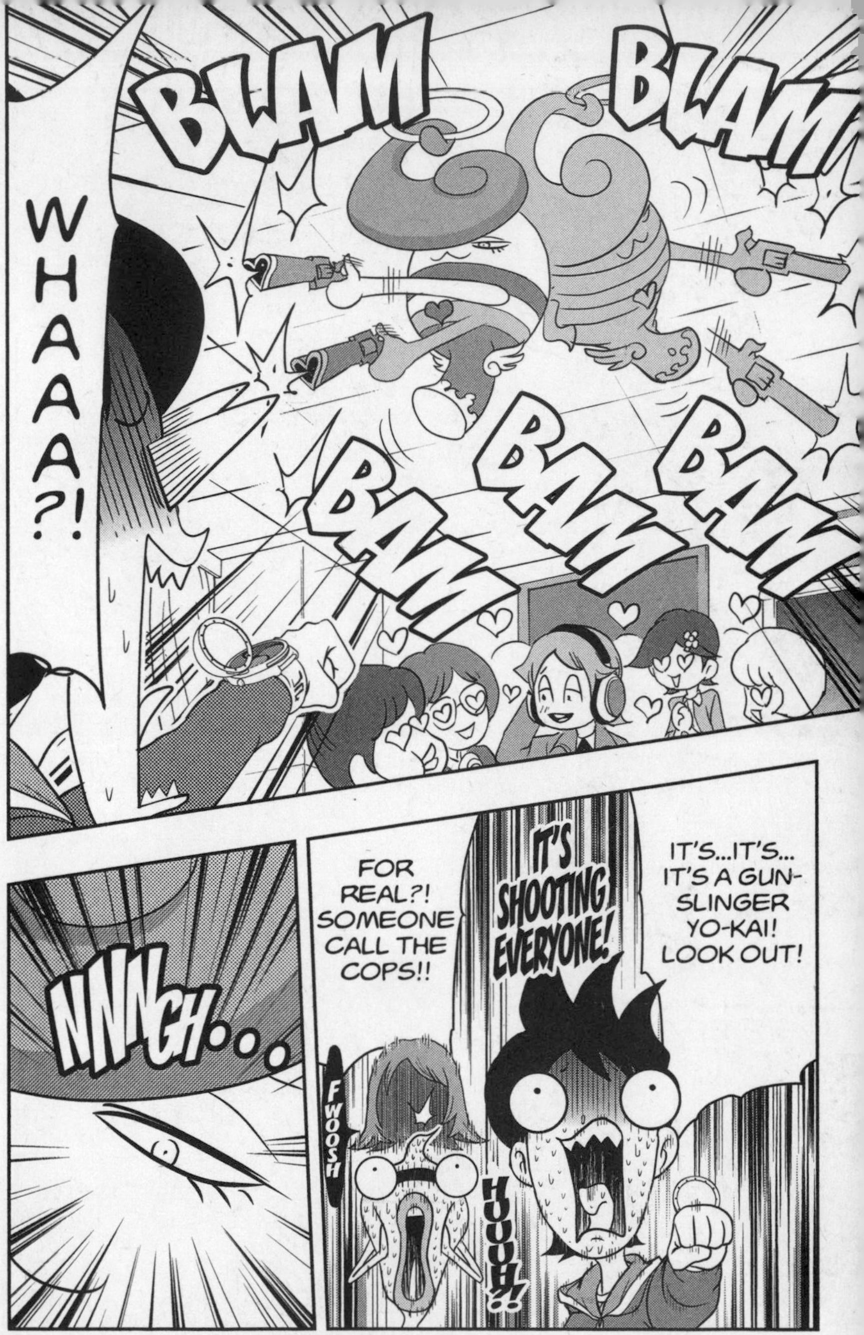
BLAM
BLAM
WHAAA?!
BAM
BAM
BAM
IT'S...IT'S... IT'S A GUN-SLINGER YO-KAI! LOOK OUT!
IT'S SHOOTING EVERYONE!
FOR REAL?! SOMEONE CALL THE COPS!!
HUUUH!!
FWOOSH
NNNGH...

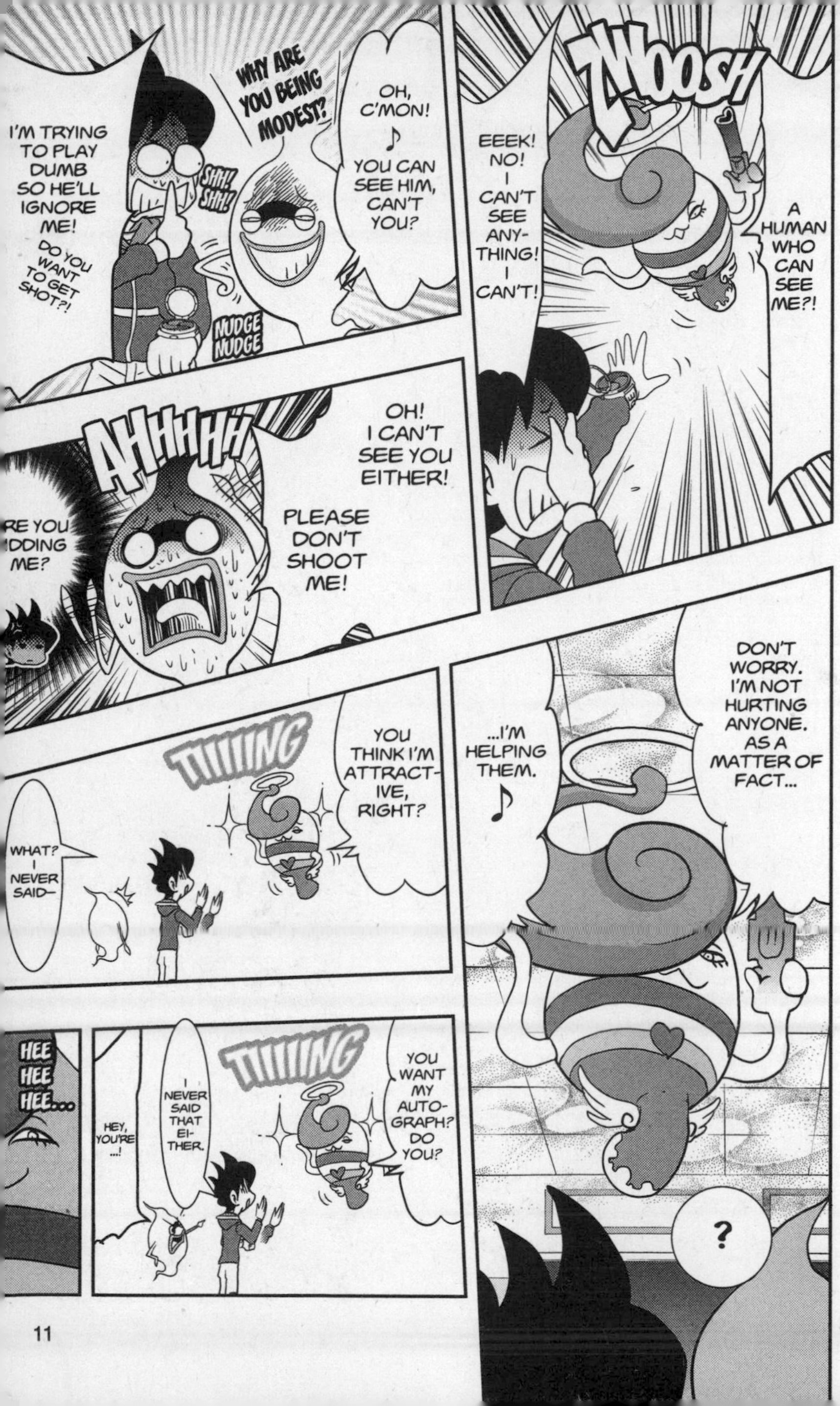
ZWOOSH
A HUMAN WHO CAN SEE ME?!
EEEK! NO! I CAN'T SEE ANYTHING! I CAN'T!
OH, C'MON! ♪ YOU CAN SEE HIM, CAN'T YOU?
WHY ARE YOU BEING MODEST?
SHH! SHH!
I'M TRYING TO PLAY DUMB SO HE'LL IGNORE ME!
DO YOU WANT TO GET SHOT?!
NUDGE NUDGE
OH! I CAN'T SEE YOU EITHER!
PLEASE DON'T SHOOT ME!
AHHHHH
RE YOU DDING ME?
DON'T WORRY. I'M NOT HURTING ANYONE. AS A MATTER OF FACT...
...I'M HELPING THEM. ♪
?
THIIING
YOU THINK I'M ATTRACTIVE, RIGHT?
WHAT? I NEVER SAID—
THIIING
YOU WANT MY AUTOGRAPH? DO YOU?
I NEVER SAID THAT EITHER.
HEY, YOU'RE ...!
HEE HEE HEE...

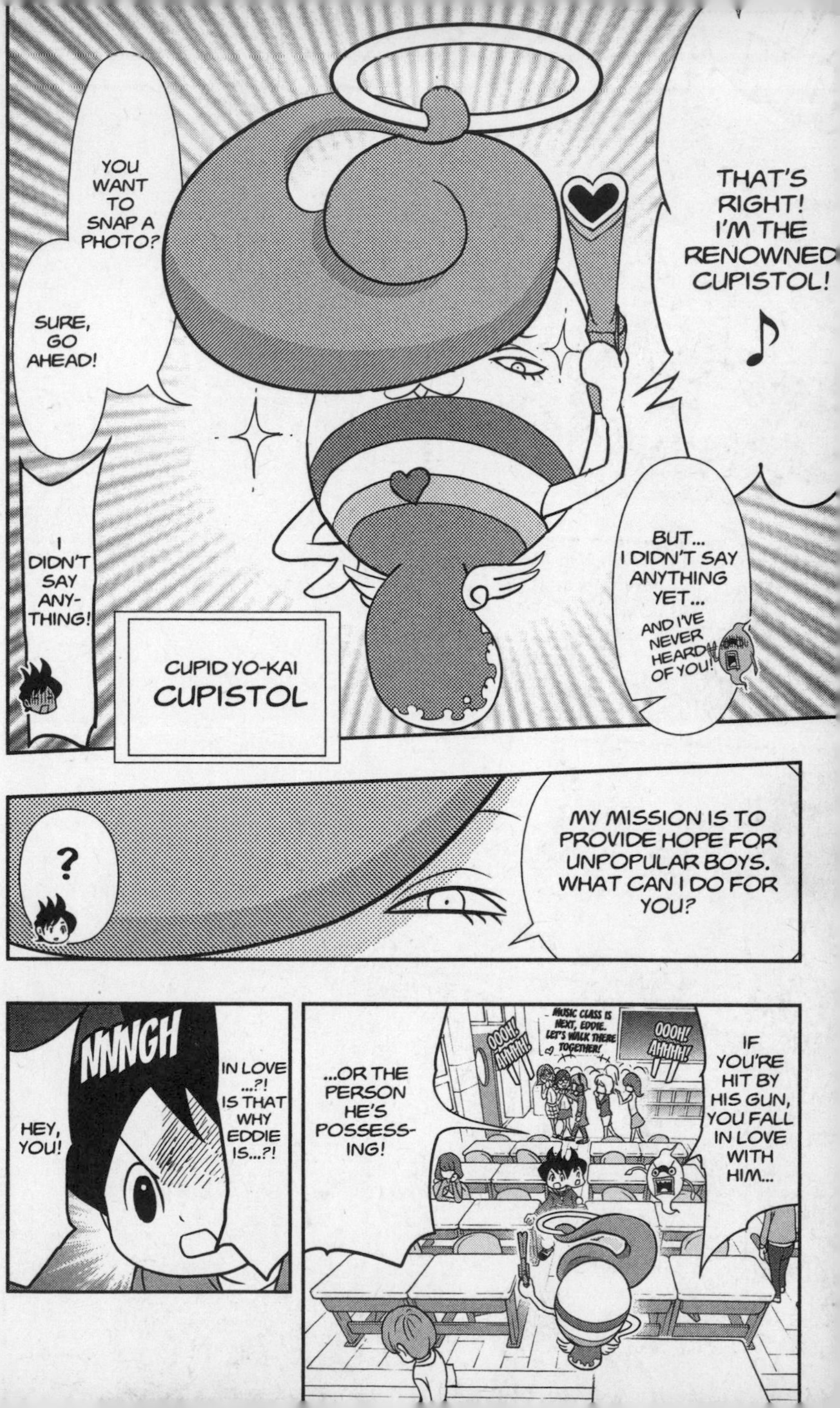
THAT'S RIGHT! I'M THE RENOWNED CUPISTOL! ♪
YOU WANT TO SNAP A PHOTO?
SURE, GO AHEAD!
BUT... I DIDN'T SAY ANYTHING YET...
AND I'VE NEVER HEARD OF YOU!
I DIDN'T SAY ANY-THING!
CUPID YO-KAI CUPISTOL
MY MISSION IS TO PROVIDE HOPE FOR UNPOPULAR BOYS. WHAT CAN I DO FOR YOU?
?
IF YOU'RE HIT BY HIS GUN, YOU FALL IN LOVE WITH HIM...
...OR THE PERSON HE'S POSSESS-ING!
OOOH! AHHHH!
MUSIC CLASS IS NEXT, EDDIE. LET'S WALK THERE TOGETHER!
OOOH! AHHHH!
IN LOVE ...?! IS THAT WHY EDDIE IS...?!
NNNGH
HEY, YOU!

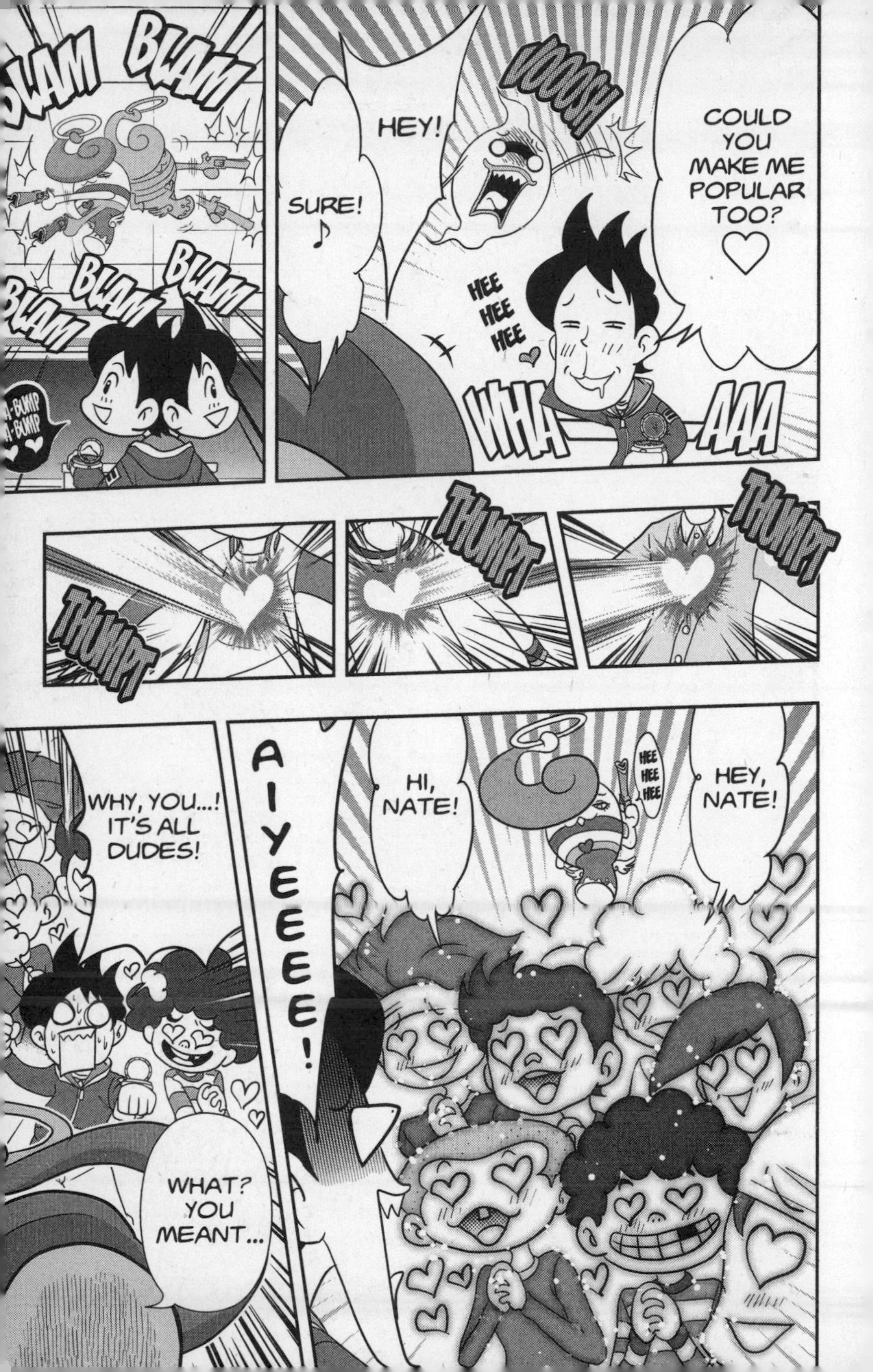
VOOOSH
COULD YOU MAKE ME POPULAR TOO? ♡
HEY!
SURE! ♪
HEE HEE HEE
WHAAAA
BLAM BLAM
BLAM BLAM BLAM
THWIPT
THWIPT
THWIPT
HEY, NATE!
HEE HEE HEE
HI, NATE!
AIYEEEEE!
WHY, YOU...! IT'S ALL DUDES!
WHAT? YOU MEANT...

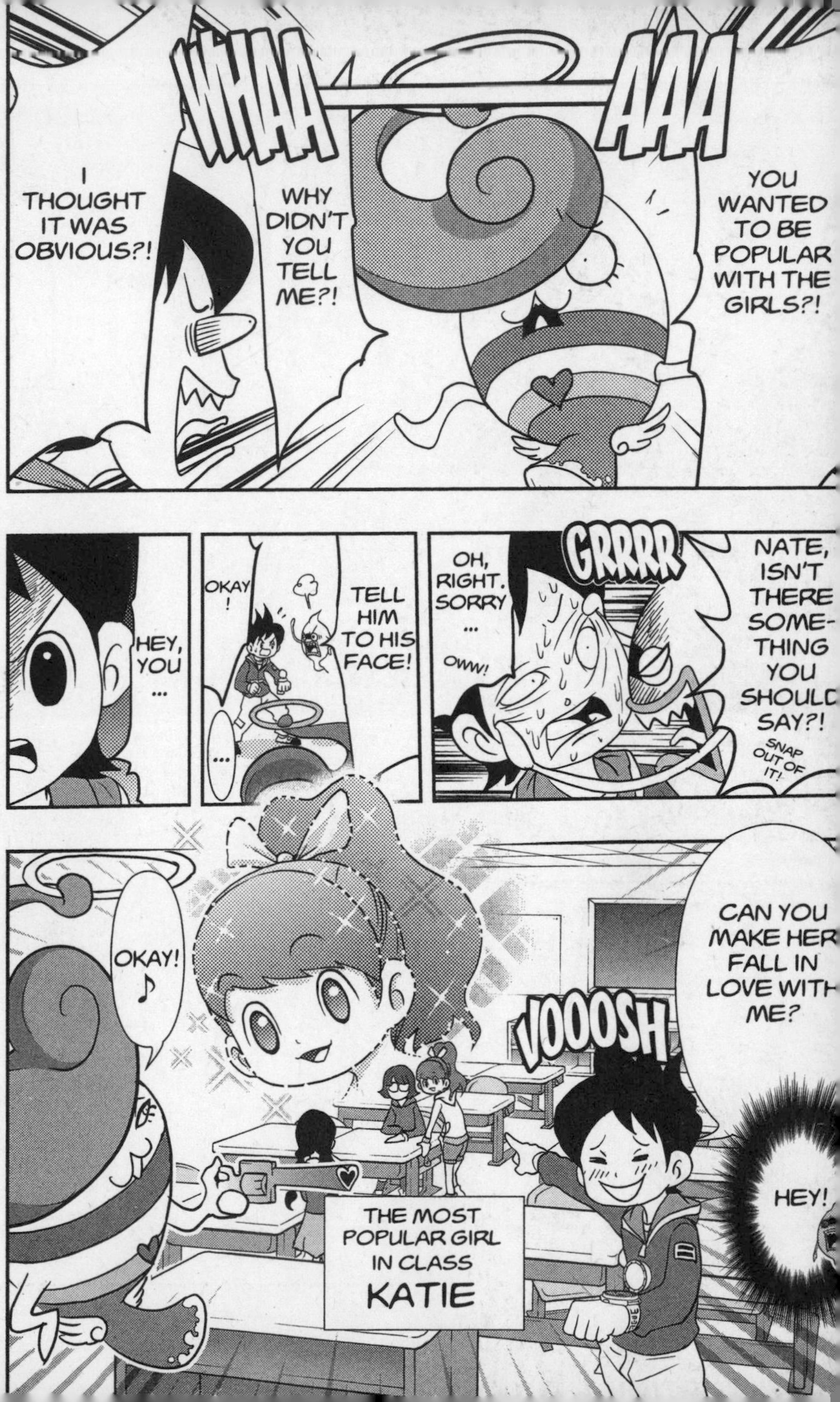
WHAA AAA
YOU WANTED TO BE POPULAR WITH THE GIRLS?!
WHY DIDN'T YOU TELL ME?!
I THOUGHT IT WAS OBVIOUS?!
GRRRR
NATE, ISN'T THERE SOME-THING YOU SHOULD SAY?!
SNAP OUT OF IT!
OH, RIGHT. SORRY ...
OWW!
TELL HIM TO HIS FACE!
OKAY!
...
HEY, YOU ...
CAN YOU MAKE HER FALL IN LOVE WITH ME?
HEY!
VOOOSH
OKAY! ♪
THE MOST POPULAR GIRL IN CLASS
KATIE

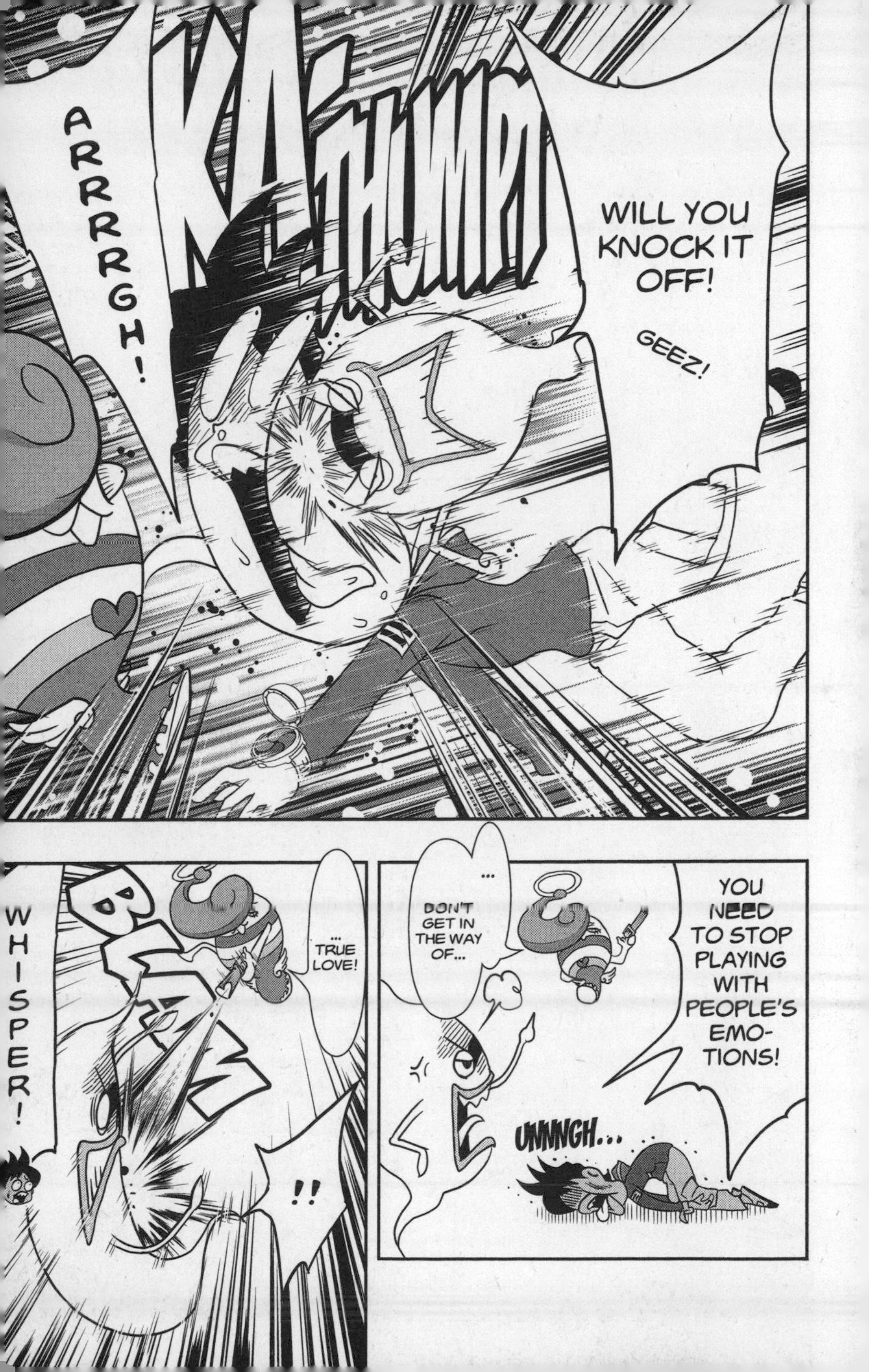
WILL YOU KNOCK IT OFF!
GEEZ!
KA-THUMP
ARRRRGH!
YOU NEED TO STOP PLAYING WITH PEOPLE'S EMO-TIONS!
...
DON'T GET IN THE WAY OF...
UNNNGH...
... TRUE LOVE!
WHISPER!
!!

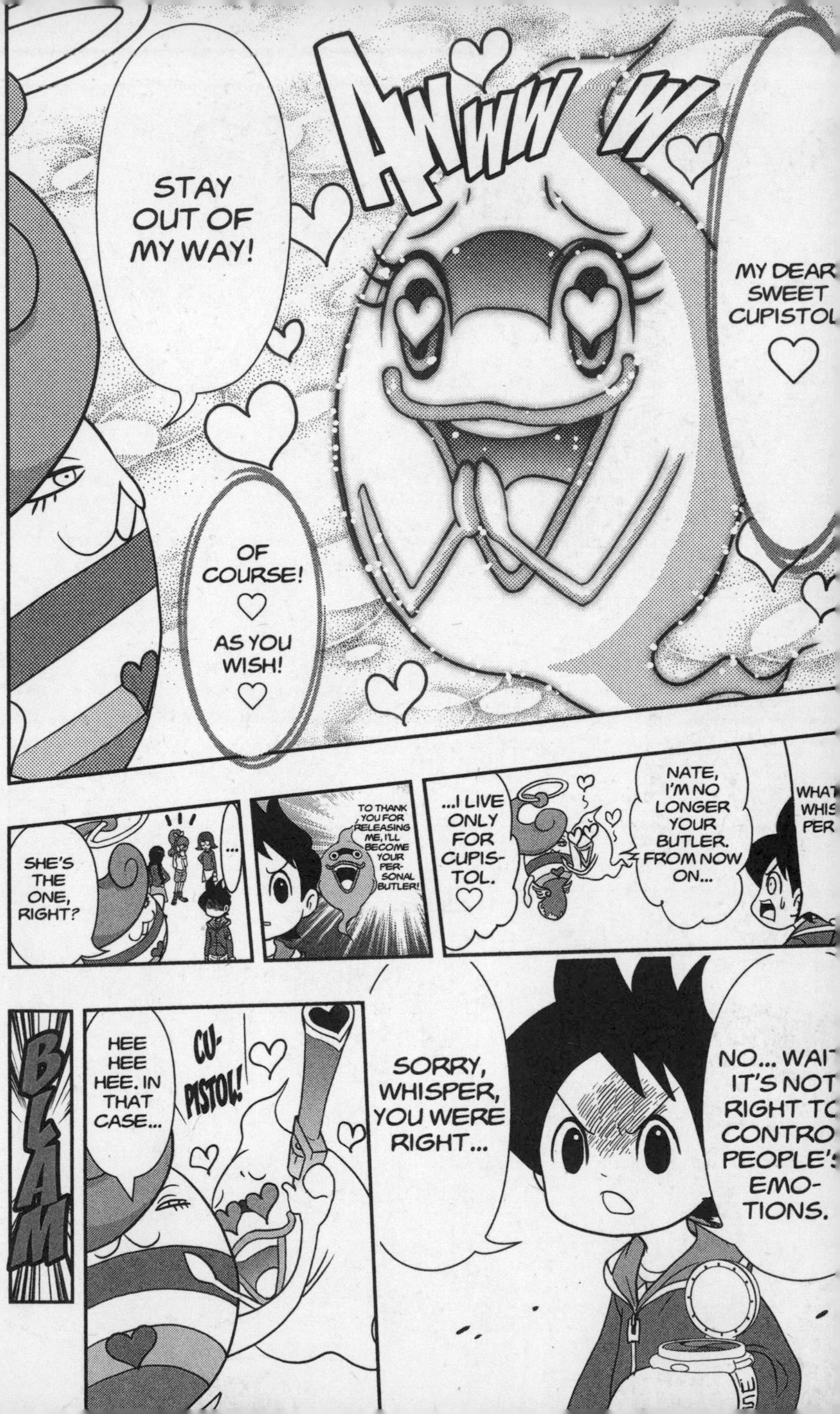
MY DEAR SWEET CUPISTOL ♡
AWWWW W
STAY OUT OF MY WAY!
OF COURSE! ♡ AS YOU WISH! ♡
WHAT WHIS PER
NATE, I'M NO LONGER YOUR BUTLER. FROM NOW ON...
...I LIVE ONLY FOR CUPIS-TOL. ♡
TO THANK YOU FOR RELEASING ME, I'LL BECOME YOUR PER-SONAL BUTLER!
...
SHE'S THE ONE, RIGHT?
NO... WAI IT'S NOT RIGHT TC CONTRO PEOPLE'S EMO-TIONS.
SORRY, WHISPER, YOU WERE RIGHT...
CU-PISTOL!
HEE HEE HEE. IN THAT CASE...
BLAM

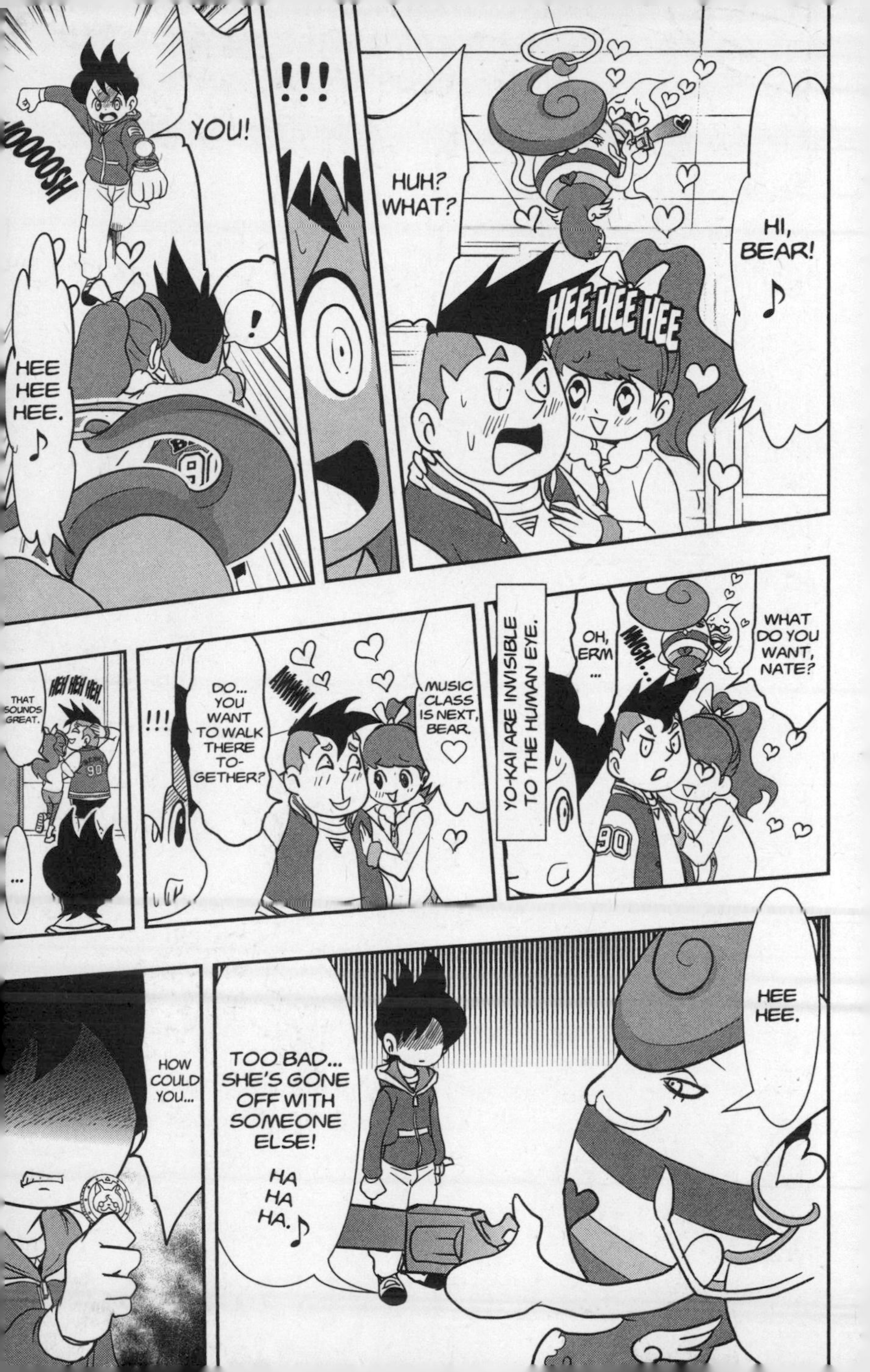
HI, BEAR! ♪
HEE HEE HEE
HUH? WHAT?
!!!
YOU!
WHOOOSH
!
HEE HEE HEE. ♪
WHAT DO YOU WANT, NATE?
MMGH...
OH, ERM ...
YO-KAI ARE INVISIBLE TO THE HUMAN EYE.
MUSIC CLASS IS NEXT, BEAR.
AWWW
DO... YOU WANT TO WALK THERE TO-GETHER?
!!!
HEH HEH HEH.
THAT SOUNDS GREAT.
...
HEE HEE.
TOO BAD... SHE'S GONE OFF WITH SOMEONE ELSE!
HA HA HA. ♪
HOW COULD YOU...

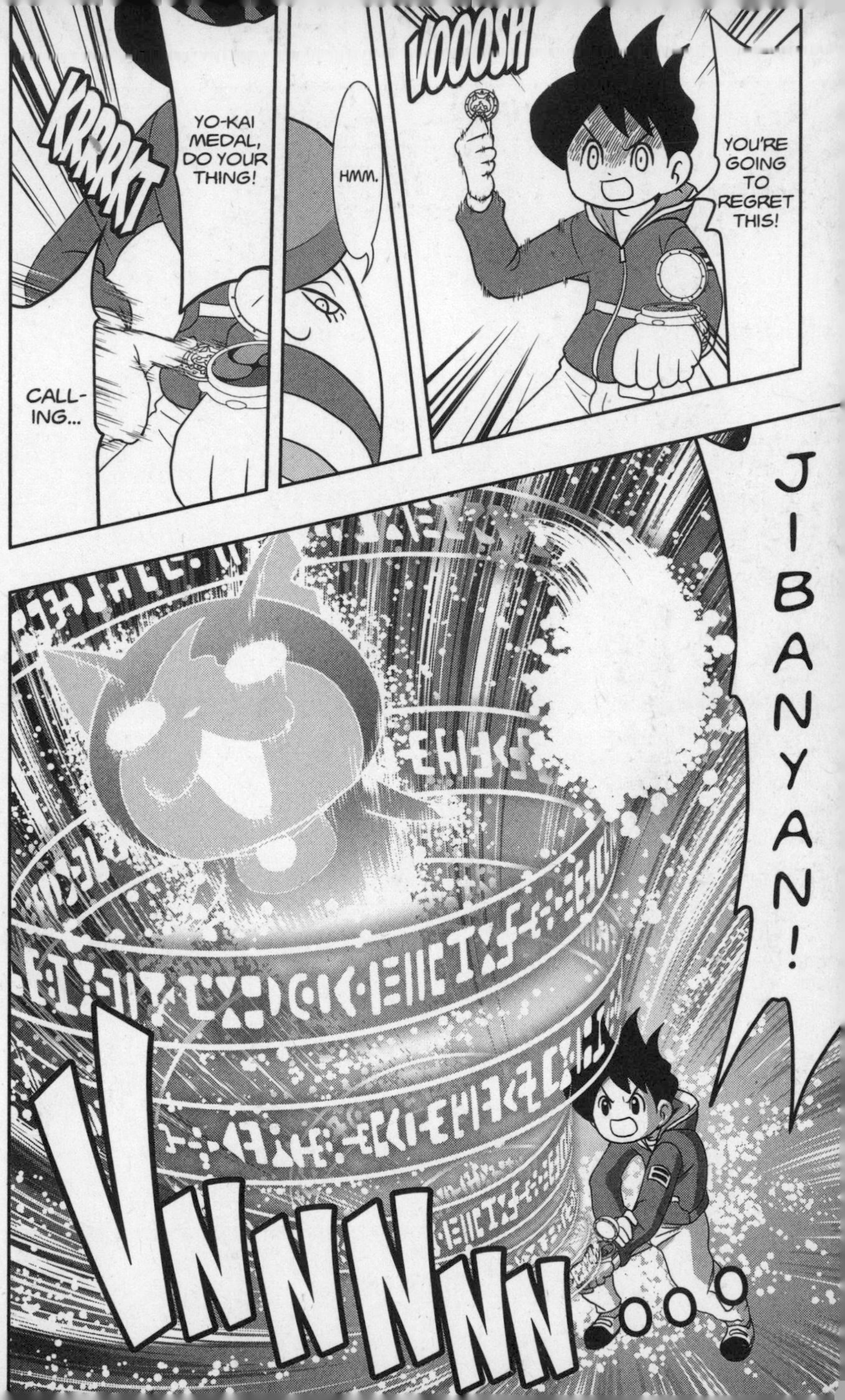
VOOOSH
YOU'RE GOING TO REGRET THIS!
HMM.
YO-KAI MEDAL, DO YOUR THING!
KRRRKT
CALL-ING...
JIBANYAN!
VNNNNNN...

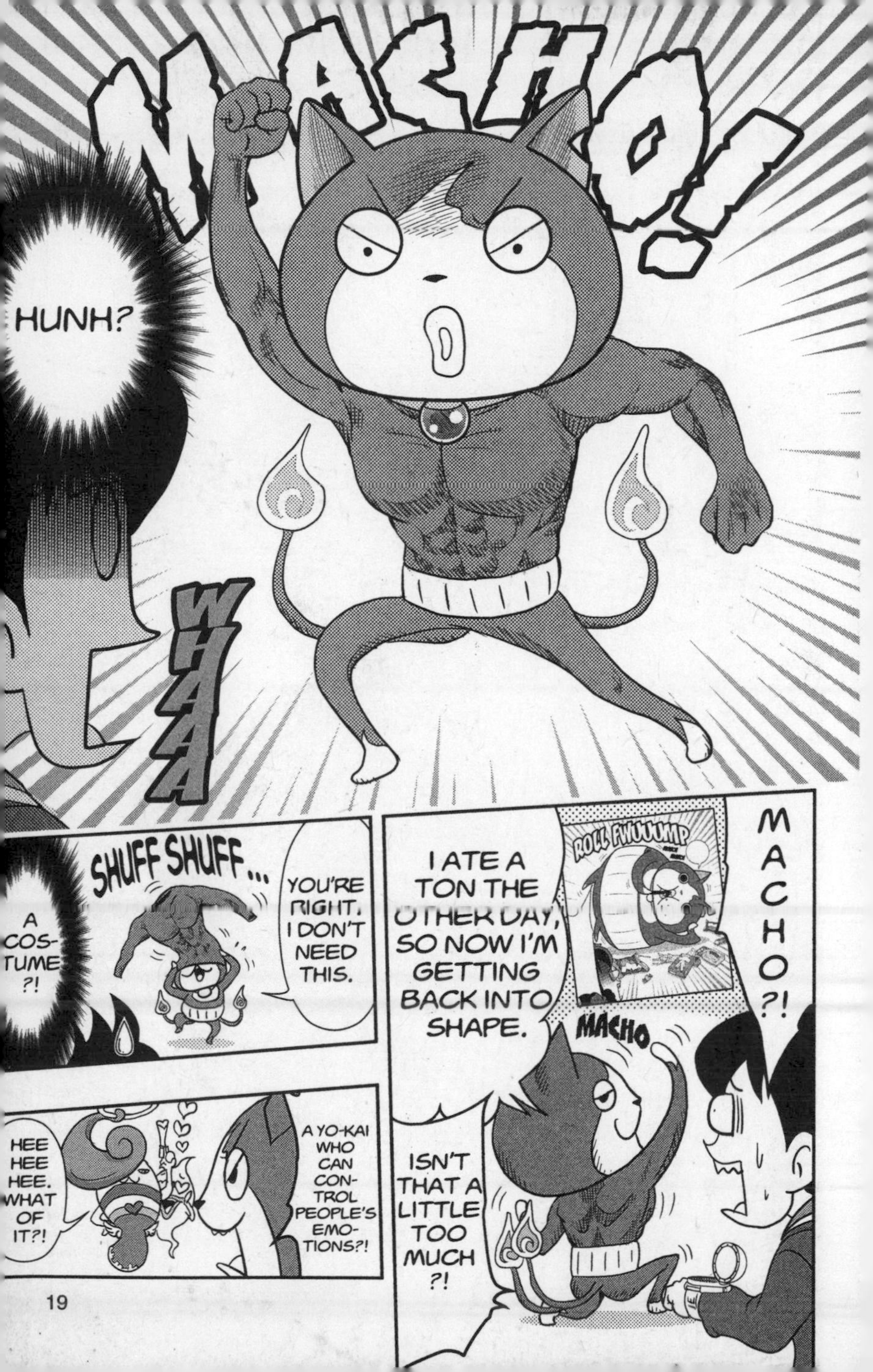
MACHO!
HUNH?
WHAAA
MACHO?!
ROLL FWUUUMP
I ATE A TON THE OTHER DAY, SO NOW I'M GETTING BACK INTO SHAPE.
MACHO
ISN'T THAT A LITTLE TOO MUCH?!
YOU'RE RIGHT. I DON'T NEED THIS.
SHUFF SHUFF...
A COSTUME?!
A YO-KAI WHO CAN CONTROL PEOPLE'S EMOTIONS?!
HEE HEE HEE. WHAT OF IT?!

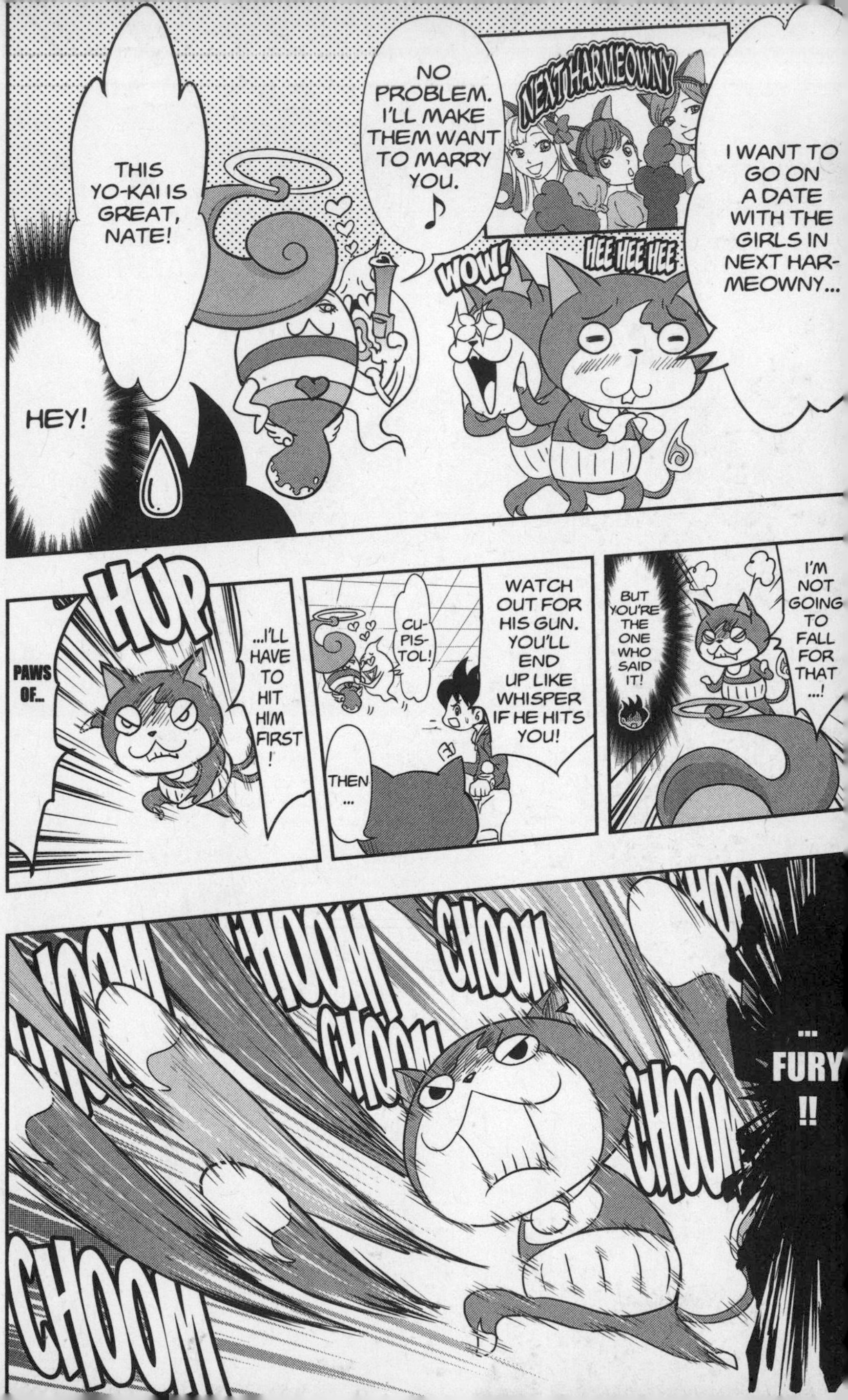
I WANT TO GO ON A DATE WITH THE GIRLS IN NEXT HAR-MEOWNY...
NEXT HARMEOWNY
HEE HEE HEE
WOW!
NO PROBLEM. I'LL MAKE THEM WANT TO MARRY YOU. ♪
THIS YO-KAI IS GREAT, NATE!
HEY!
I'M NOT GOING TO FALL FOR THAT...!
BUT YOU'RE THE ONE WHO SAID IT!
WATCH OUT FOR HIS GUN. YOU'LL END UP LIKE WHISPER IF HE HITS YOU!
CU-PIS-TOL!
THEN...
...I'LL HAVE TO HIT HIM FIRST!
HUP
PAWS OF...
...FURY!!
CHOOM
CHOOM
CHOOM

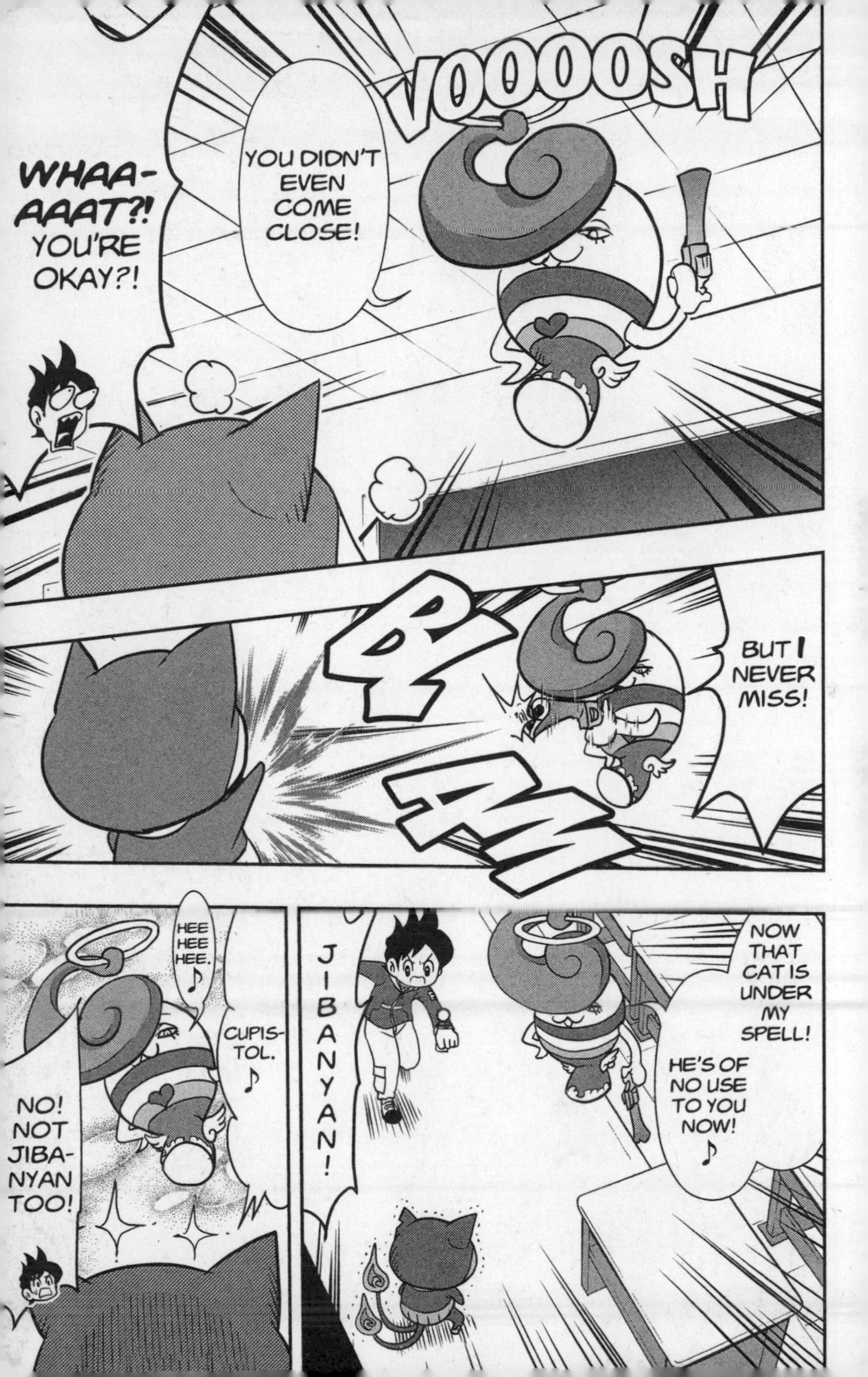
VOOOOSH
YOU DIDN'T EVEN COME CLOSE!
WHAA-AAAT?! YOU'RE OKAY?!
BUT I NEVER MISS!
BAM
NOW THAT CAT IS UNDER MY SPELL!
HE'S OF NO USE TO YOU NOW! ♪
JIBANYAN!
HEE HEE HEE. ♪
CUPIS-TOL. ♪
NO! NOT JIBA-NYAN TOO!

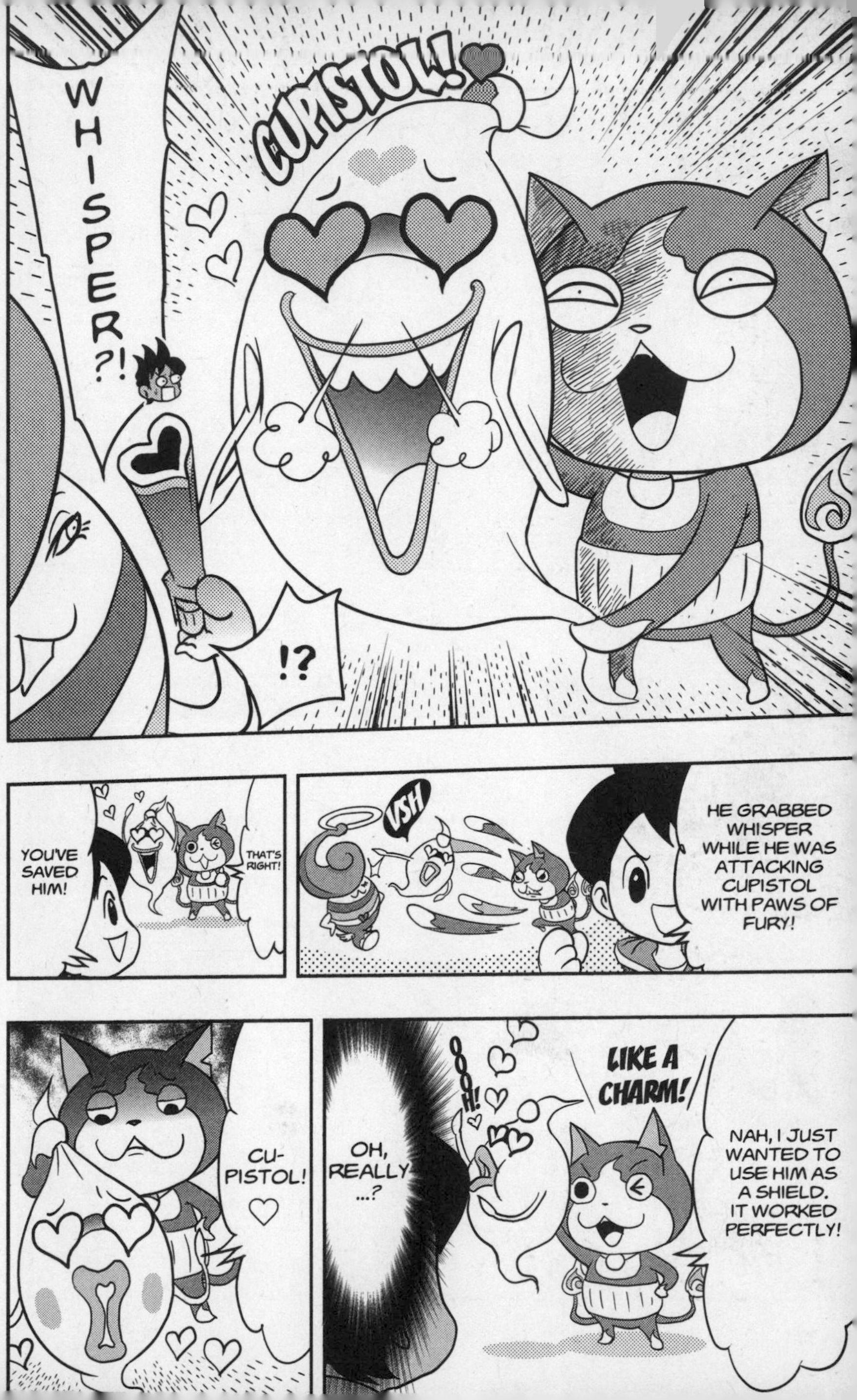
CUPISTOL!
WHISPER?!
!?
HE GRABBED WHISPER WHILE HE WAS ATTACKING CUPISTOL WITH PAWS OF FURY!
VSH
THAT'S RIGHT!
YOU'VE SAVED HIM!
NAH, I JUST WANTED TO USE HIM AS A SHIELD. IT WORKED PERFECTLY!
LIKE A CHARM!
OOOH!
OH, REALLY...?
CU-PISTOL!

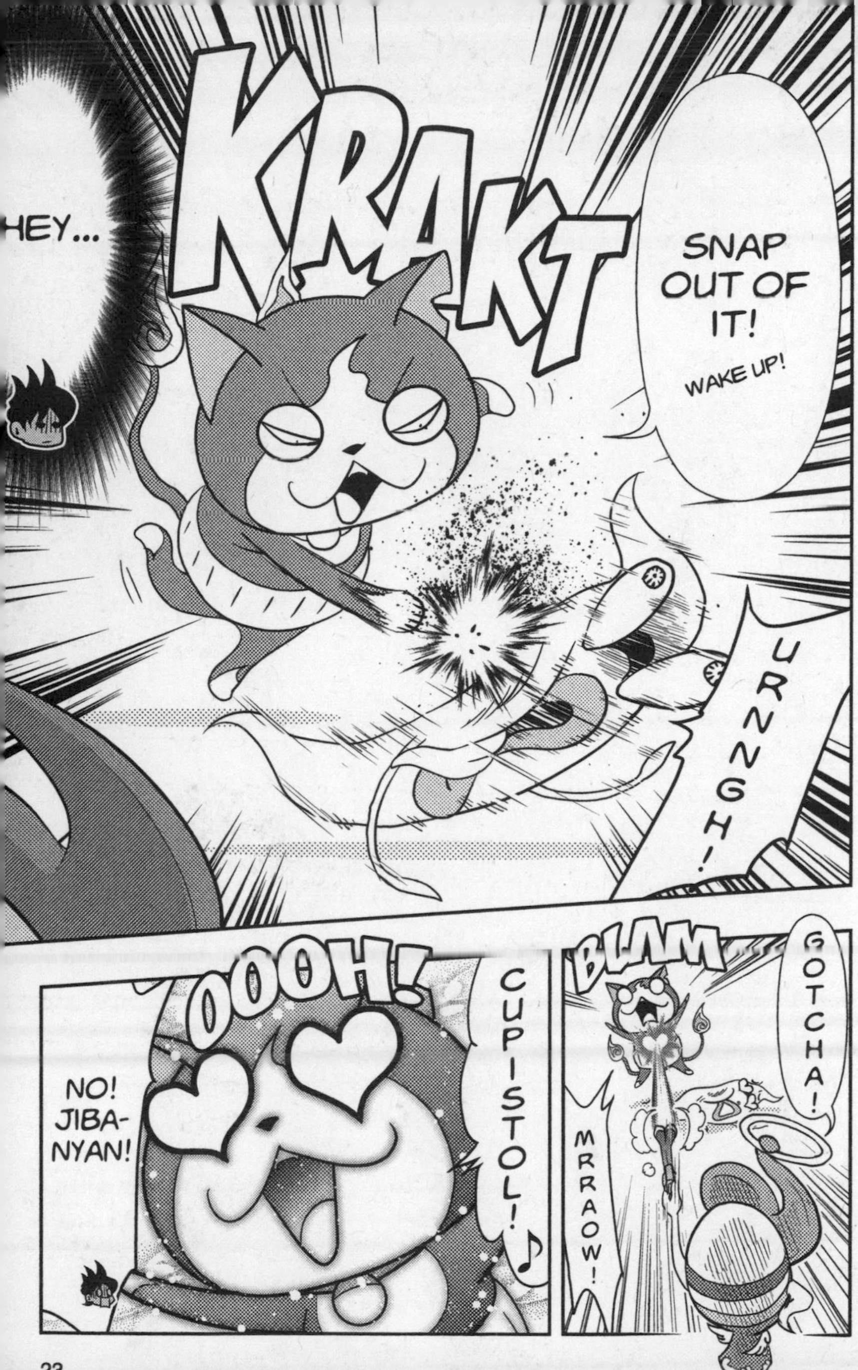
SNAP OUT OF IT!
WAKE UP!
KRAKT
HEY...
URNNGH!
GOTCHA!
BLAM
MRRAOW!
CUPISTOL! ♪
OOOH!
NO! JIBA-NYAN!

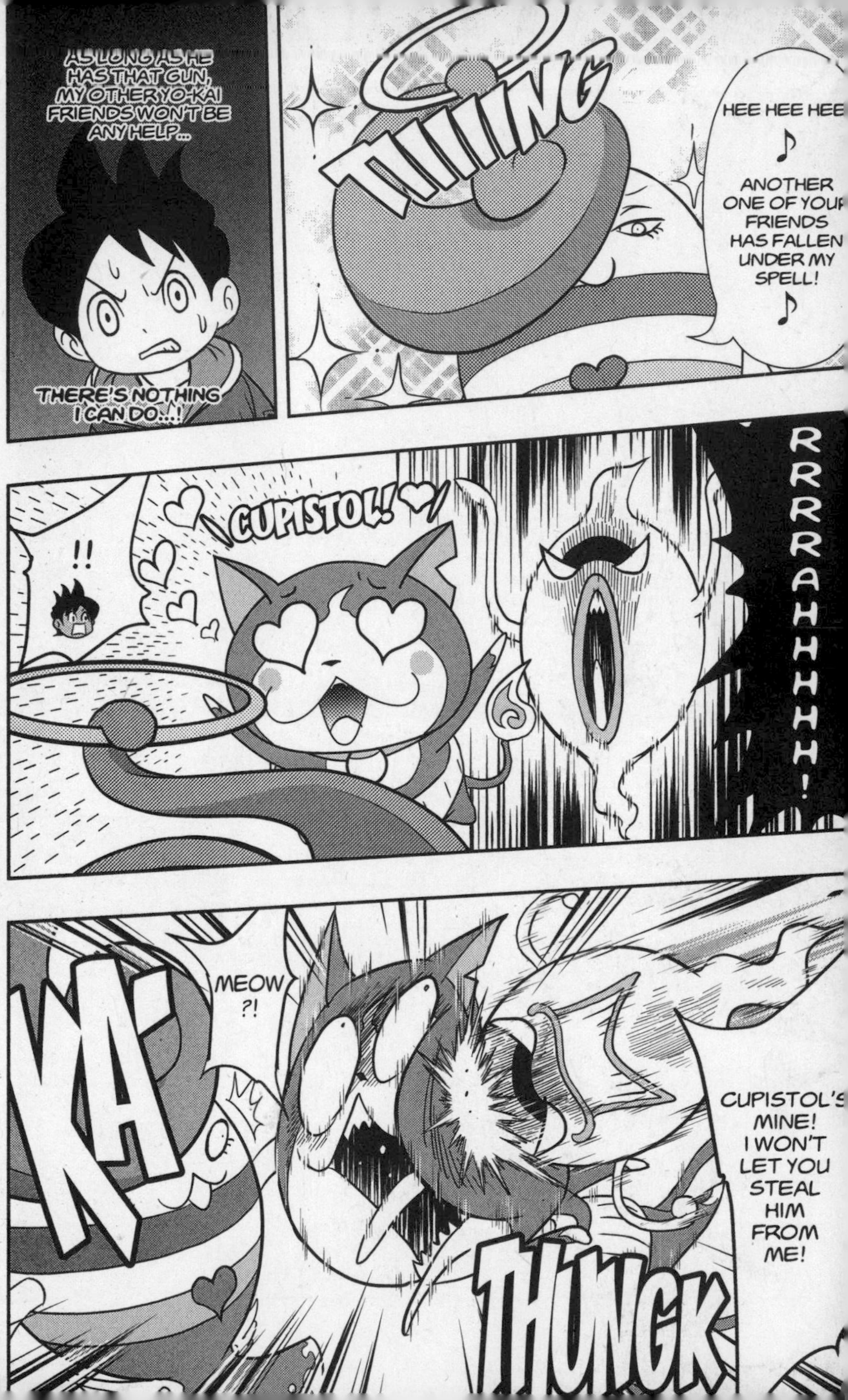
TIIIING
HEE HEE HEE ♪
ANOTHER ONE OF YOUR FRIENDS HAS FALLEN UNDER MY SPELL! ♪
AS LONG AS HE HAS THAT GUN, MY OTHER YO-KAI FRIENDS WON'T BE ANY HELP...
THERE'S NOTHING I CAN DO...!
RRRRAHHHHHH!
CUPISTOL!
!!
CUPISTOL'S MINE! I WON'T LET YOU STEAL HIM FROM ME!
THUNGK
MEOW ?!
KA

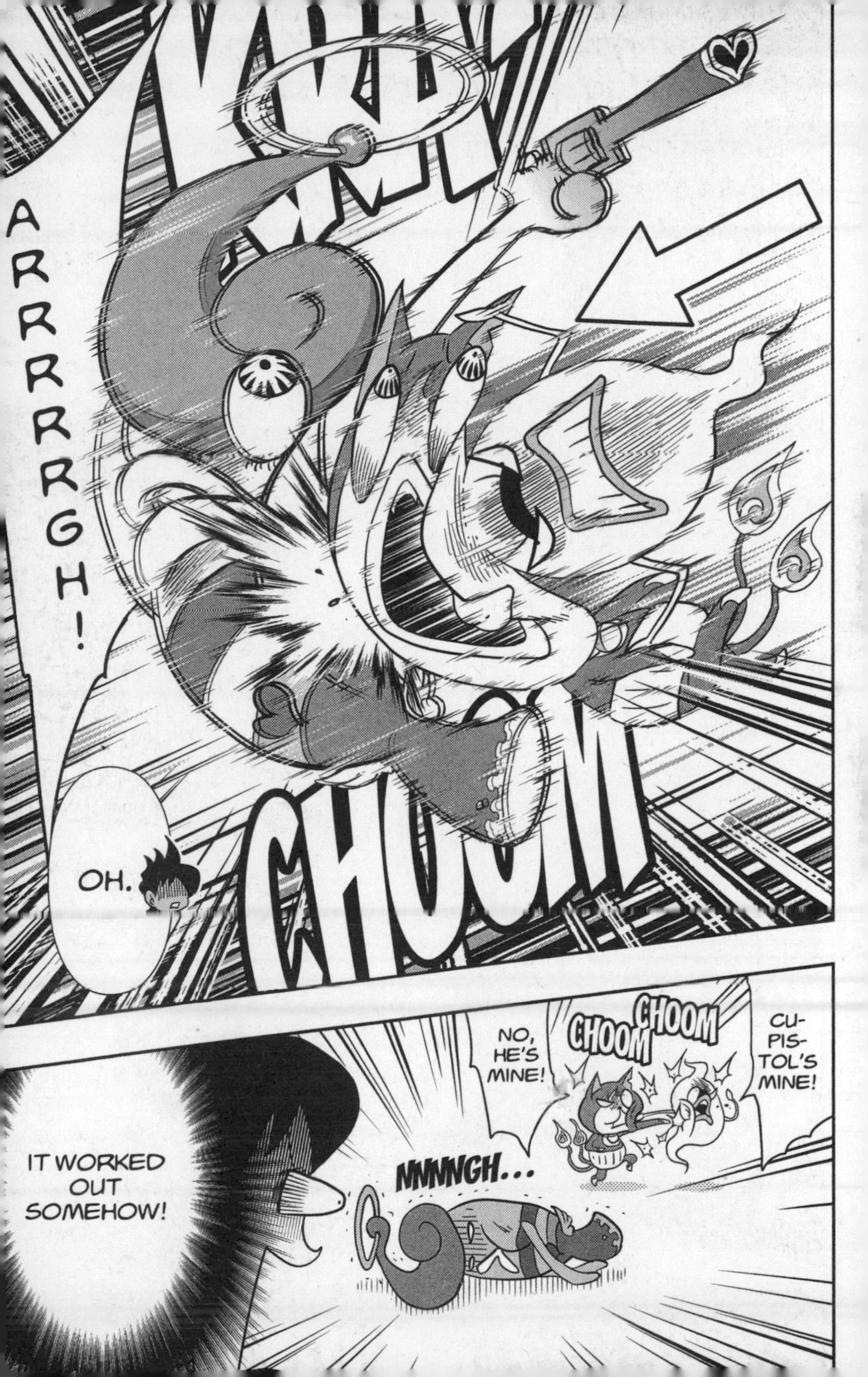
ARRRRRGH!
CHOOM
OH.
CU-PIS-TOL'S MINE!
CHOOM CHOOM
NO, HE'S MINE!
MNNNGH...
IT WORKED OUT SOMEHOW!

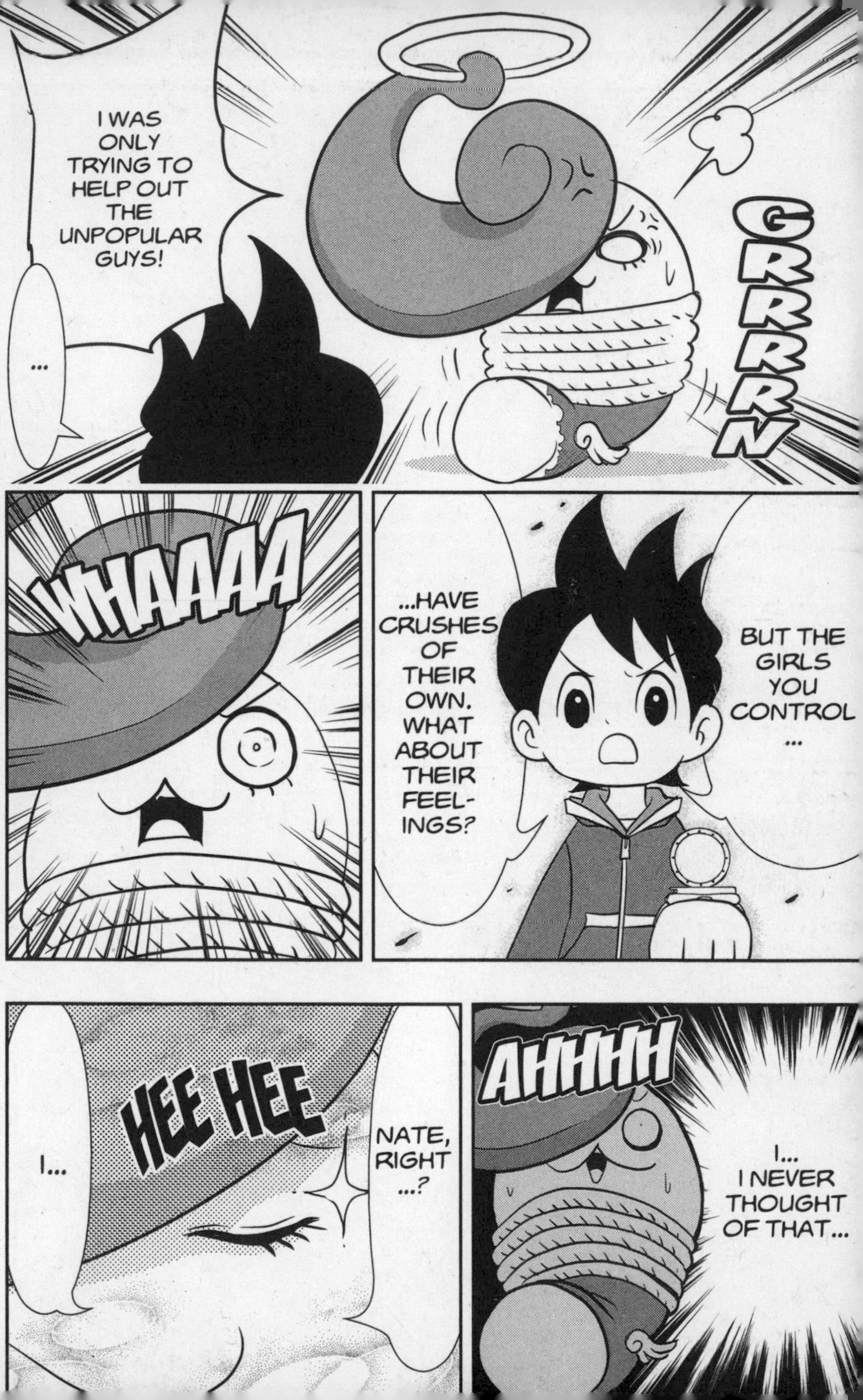
GRRRRN
I WAS ONLY TRYING TO HELP OUT THE UNPOPULAR GUYS!
...
BUT THE GIRLS YOU CONTROL ...
...HAVE CRUSHES OF THEIR OWN. WHAT ABOUT THEIR FEEL-INGS?
WHAAAAA
AHHHHH
I... I NEVER THOUGHT OF THAT...
NATE, RIGHT ...?
HEE HEE
I...

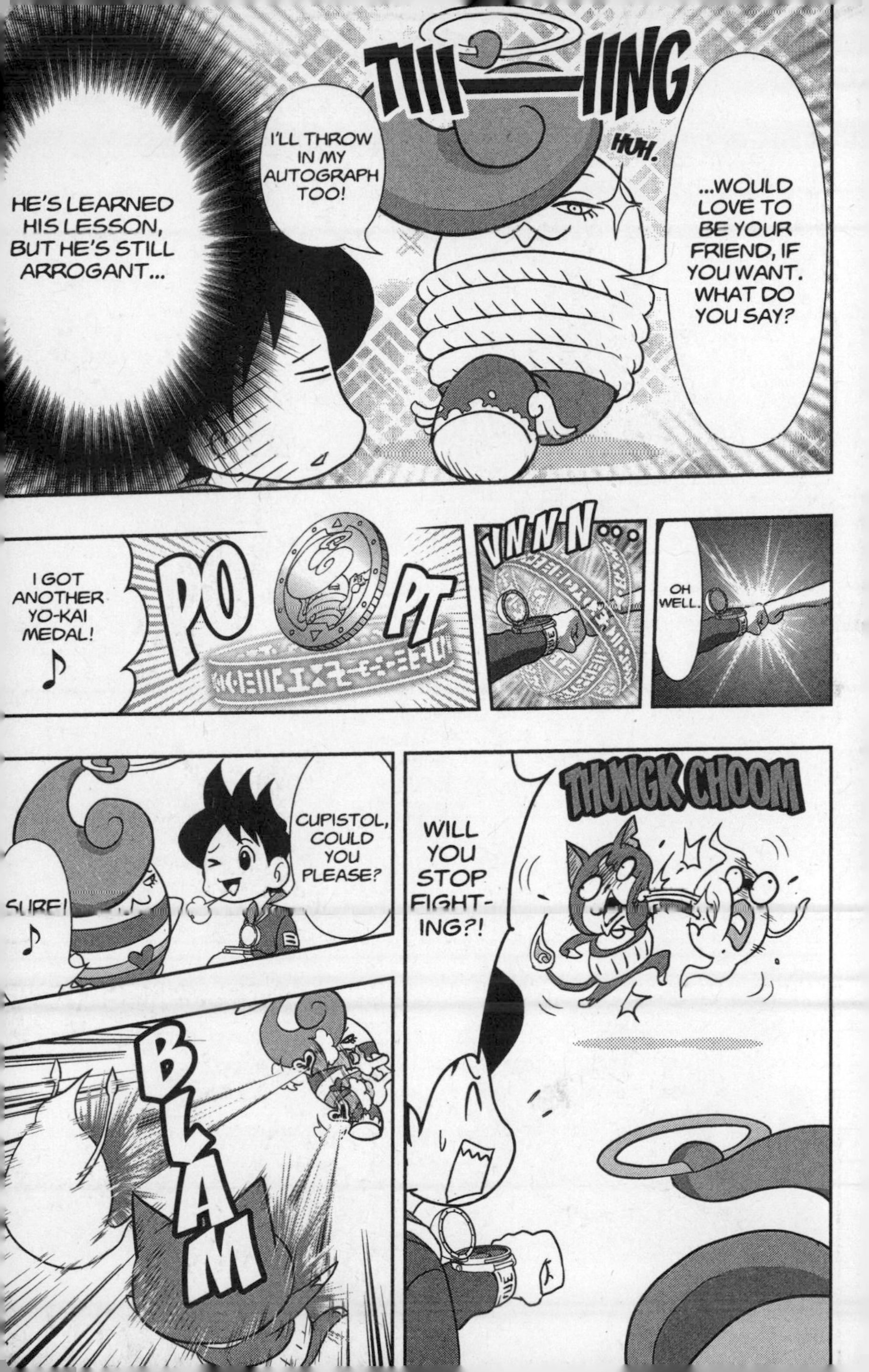
...WOULD LOVE TO BE YOUR FRIEND, IF YOU WANT. WHAT DO YOU SAY?
HUH.
TIII—IING
I'LL THROW IN MY AUTOGRAPH TOO!
HE'S LEARNED HIS LESSON, BUT HE'S STILL ARROGANT...
OH WELL.
VNNN...
POPT
I GOT ANOTHER YO-KAI MEDAL! ♪
WILL YOU STOP FIGHT-ING?!
THUNGK CHOOM
CUPISTOL, COULD YOU PLEASE?
SURE! ♪
BLAM

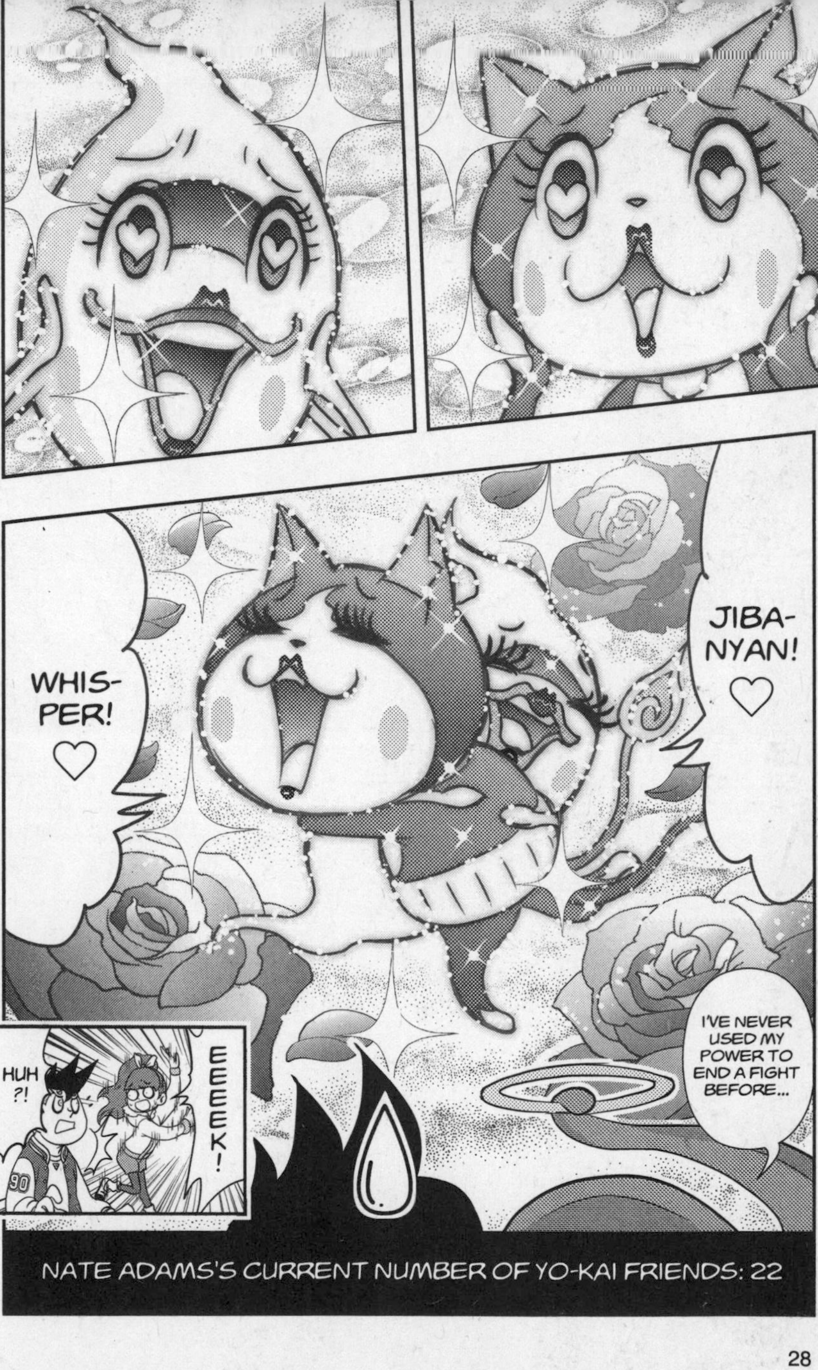
JIBA-NYAN! ♡
WHIS-PER! ♡
I'VE NEVER USED MY POWER TO END A FIGHT BEFORE...
EEEEEK!
HUH ?!
NATE ADAMS'S CURRENT NUMBER OF YO-KAI FRIENDS: 22

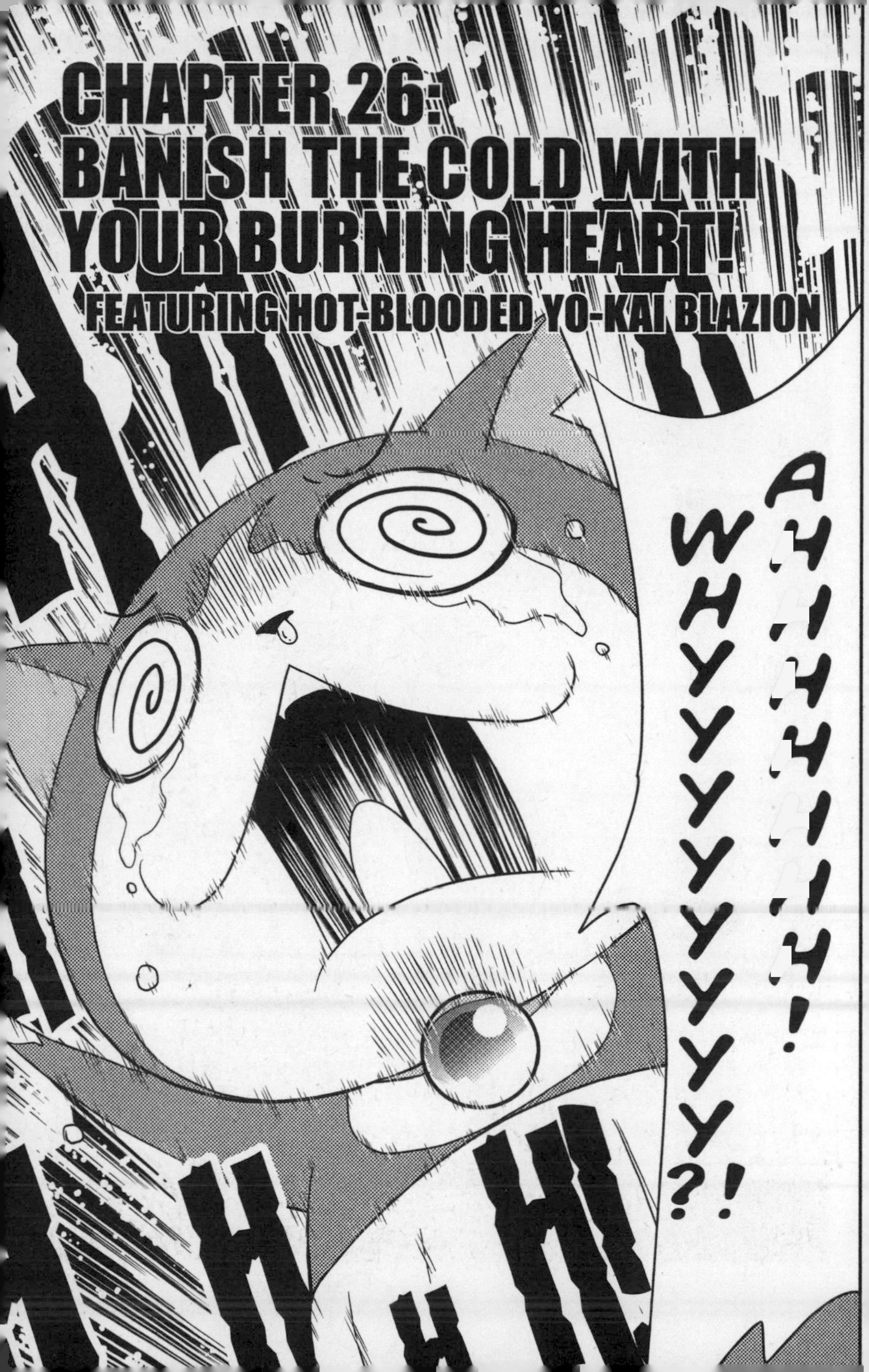
CHAPTER 26:
BANISH THE COLD WITH YOUR BURNING HEART!
FEATURING HOT-BLOODED YO-KAI BLAZION
AHHHHHHH!
WHYYYYYYYY?!

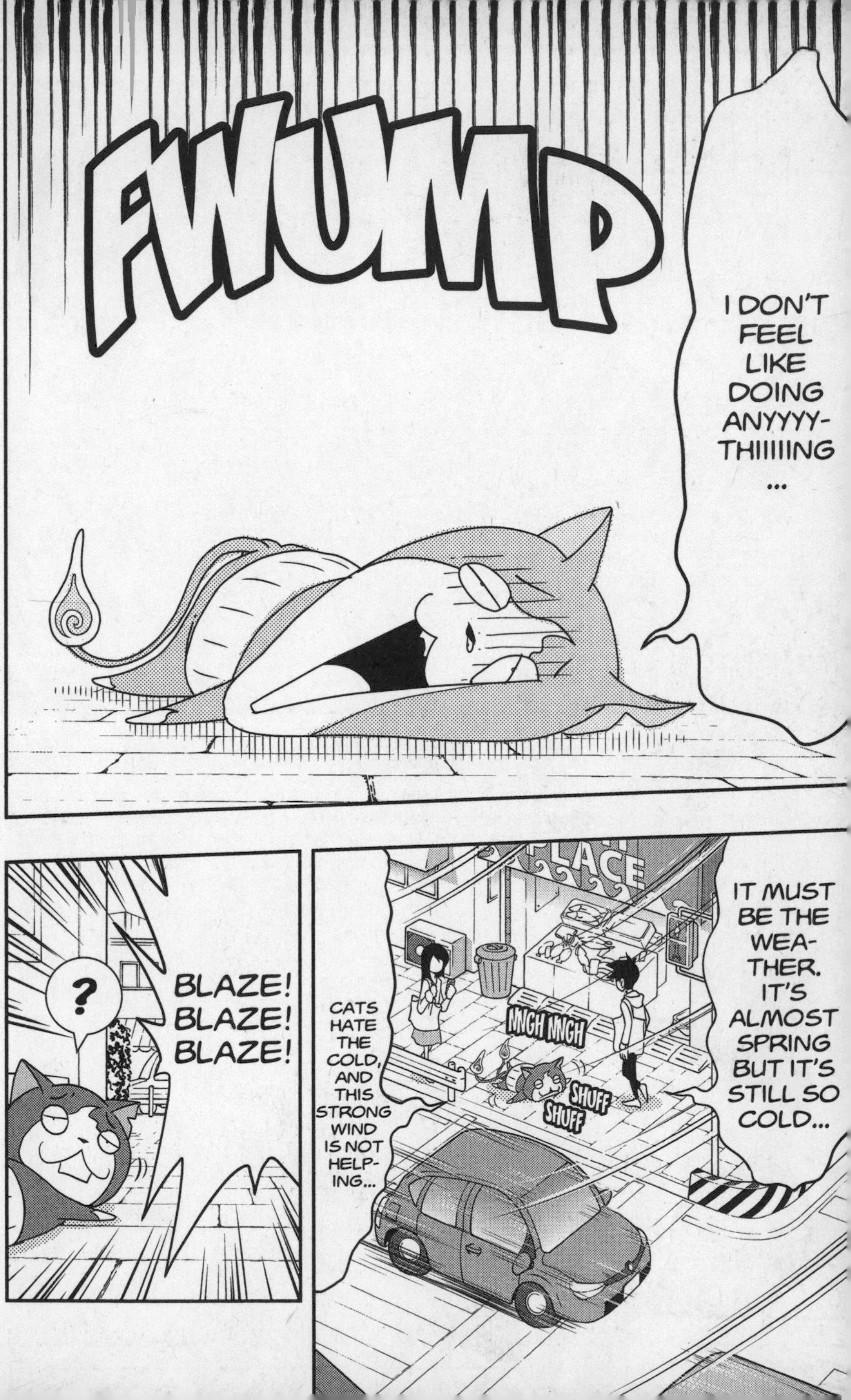
FWUMP
I DON'T FEEL LIKE DOING ANYYYY-THIIIIING...
IT MUST BE THE WEA-THER. IT'S ALMOST SPRING BUT IT'S STILL SO COLD...
PLACE
CATS HATE THE COLD, AND THIS STRONG WIND IS NOT HELP-ING...
NNGH NNGH
SHUFF
SHUFF
BLAZE! BLAZE! BLAZE!
?

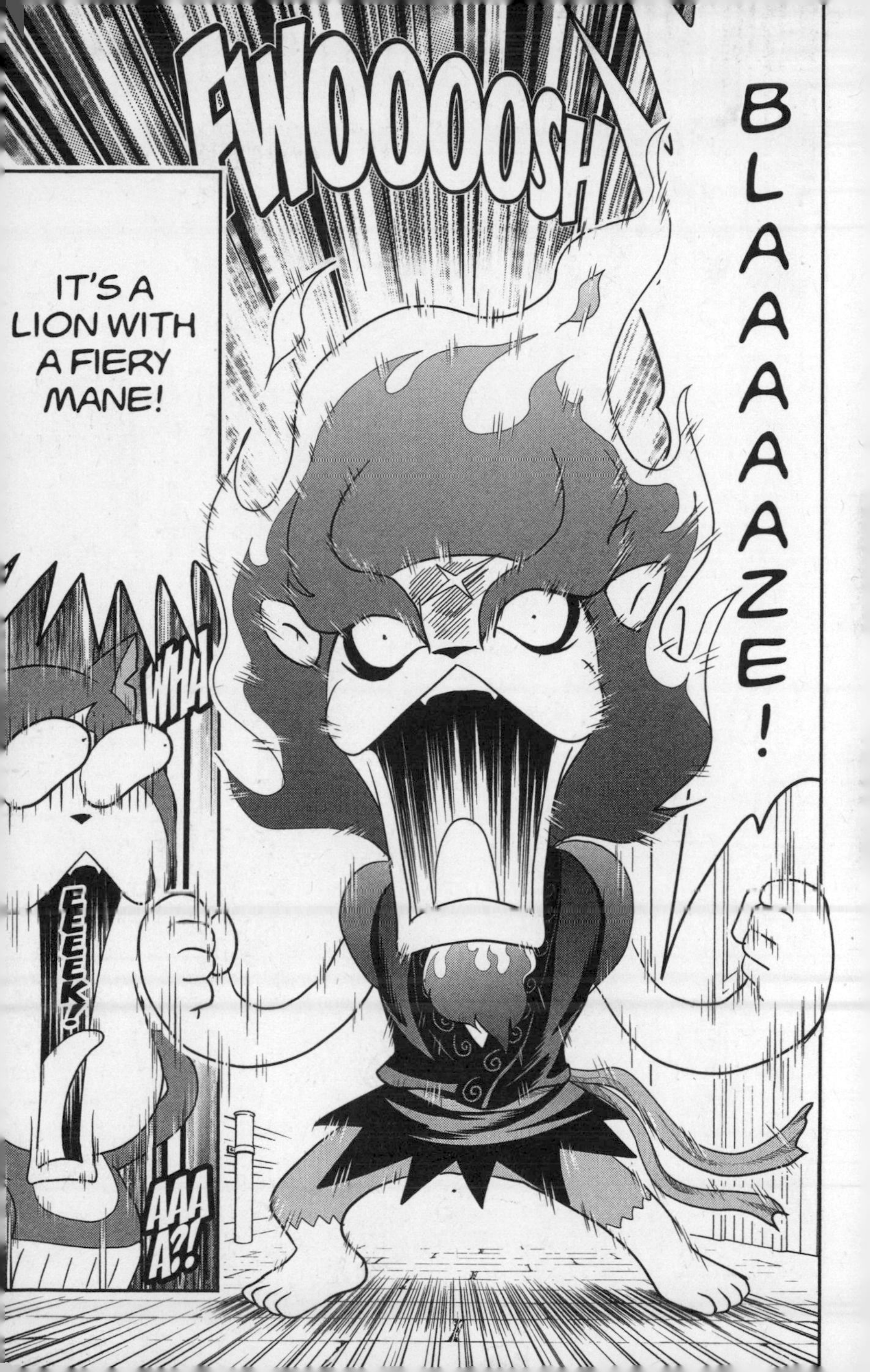
FWOOOOSH
BLAAAAAZE!
IT'S A LION WITH A FIERY MANE!
WHA
EEEEK!
AAAA?!

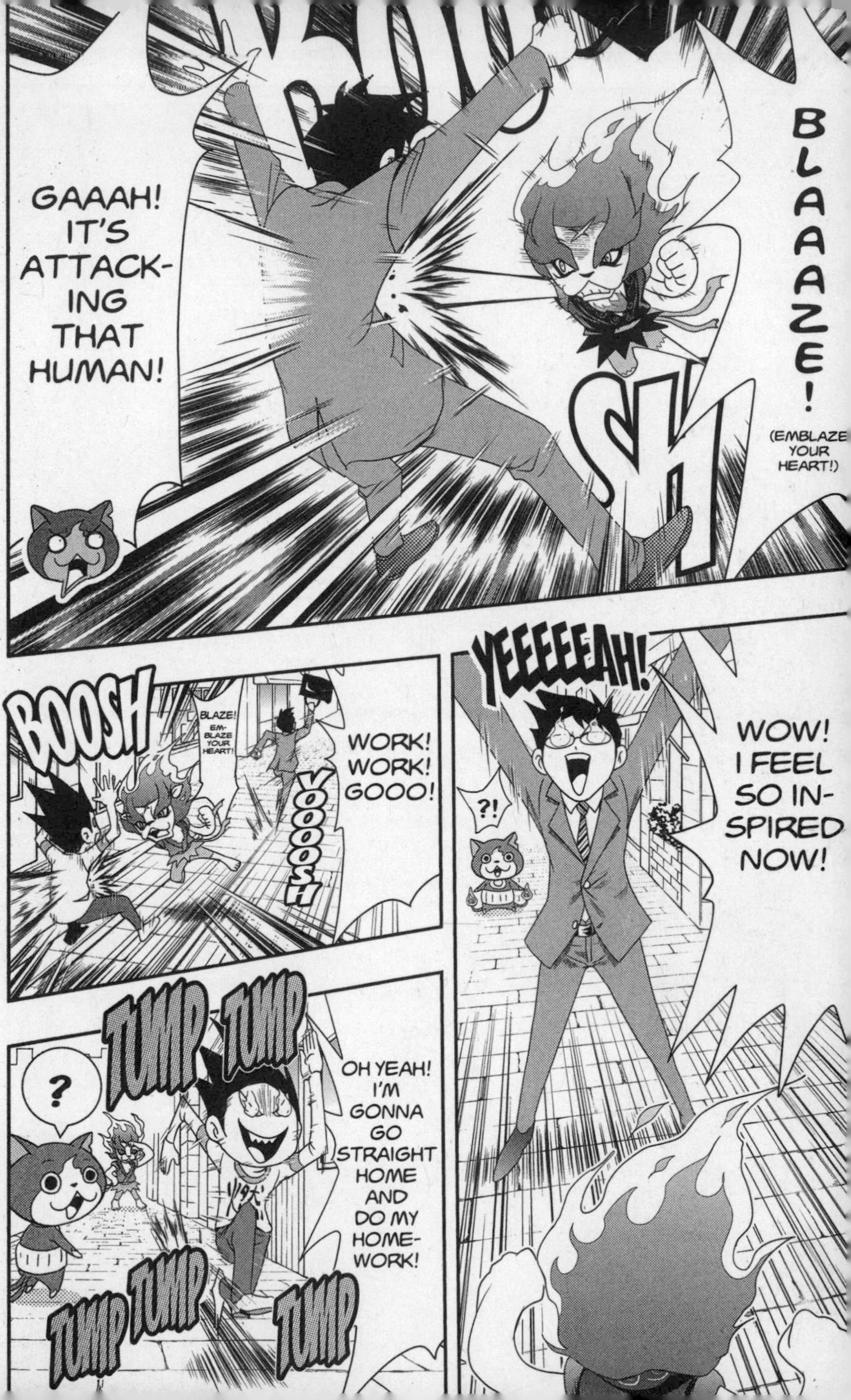
BLAAAAZE!
(EMBLAZE YOUR HEART!)
SH
GAAAH! IT'S ATTACK-ING THAT HUMAN!
YEEEEEAH!
WOW! I FEEL SO IN-SPIRED NOW!
?!
WORK! WORK! GOOO!
VOOOOOSH
BLAZE! EM-BLAZE YOUR HEART!
BOOSH
TUMP TUMP
OH YEAH! I'M GONNA GO STRAIGHT HOME AND DO MY HOME-WORK!
?
TUMP TUMP TUMP

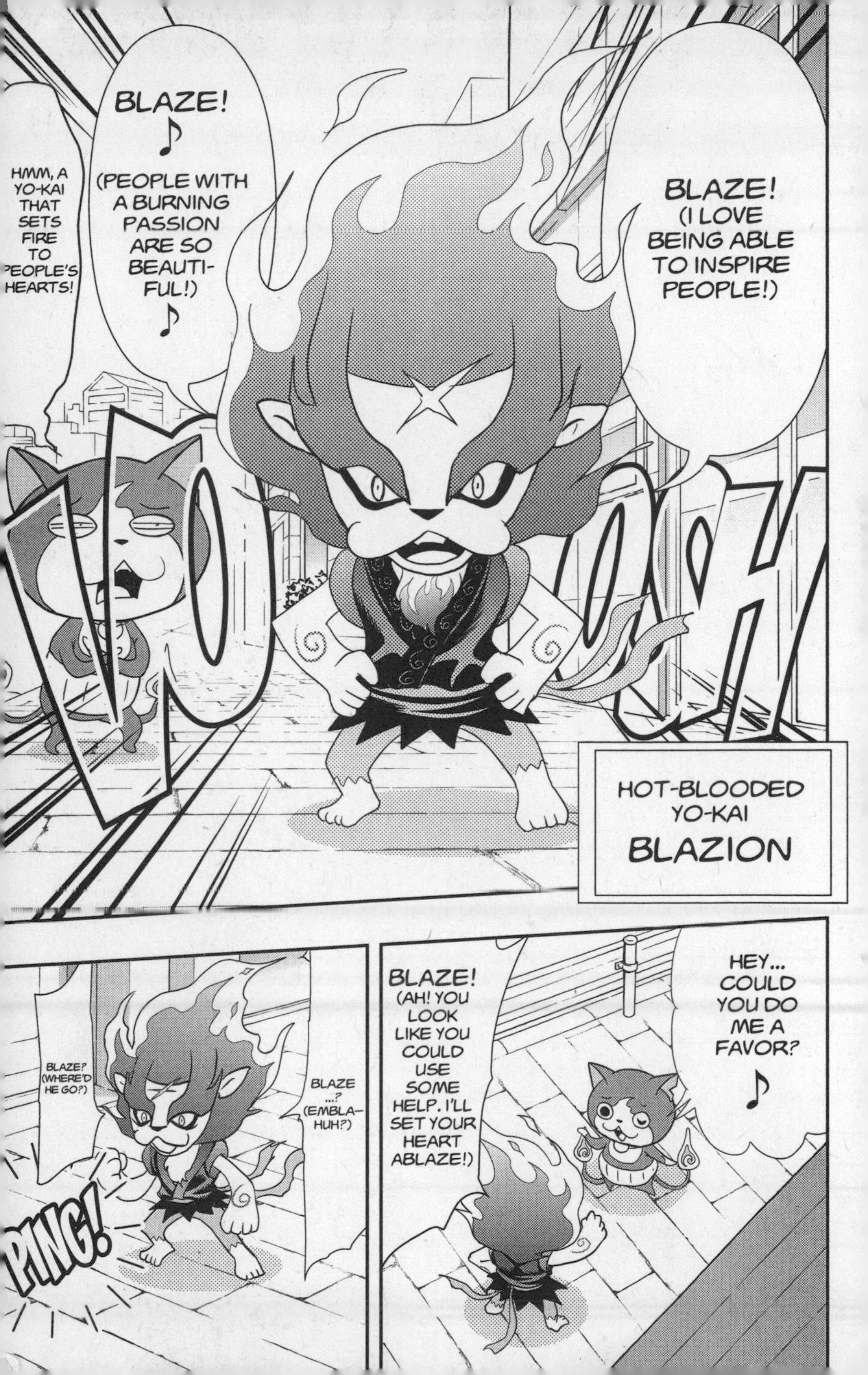
BLAZE! (I LOVE BEING ABLE TO INSPIRE PEOPLE!)
BLAZE! ♪ (PEOPLE WITH A BURNING PASSION ARE SO BEAUTI-FUL!) ♪
HMM, A YO-KAI THAT SETS FIRE TO PEOPLE'S HEARTS!
HOT-BLOODED YO-KAI BLAZION
HEY... COULD YOU DO ME A FAVOR? ♪
BLAZE! (AH! YOU LOOK LIKE YOU COULD USE SOME HELP. I'LL SET YOUR HEART ABLAZE!)
BLAZE ...? (EMBLA-HUH?)
BLAZE? (WHERE'D HE GO?)
PING!

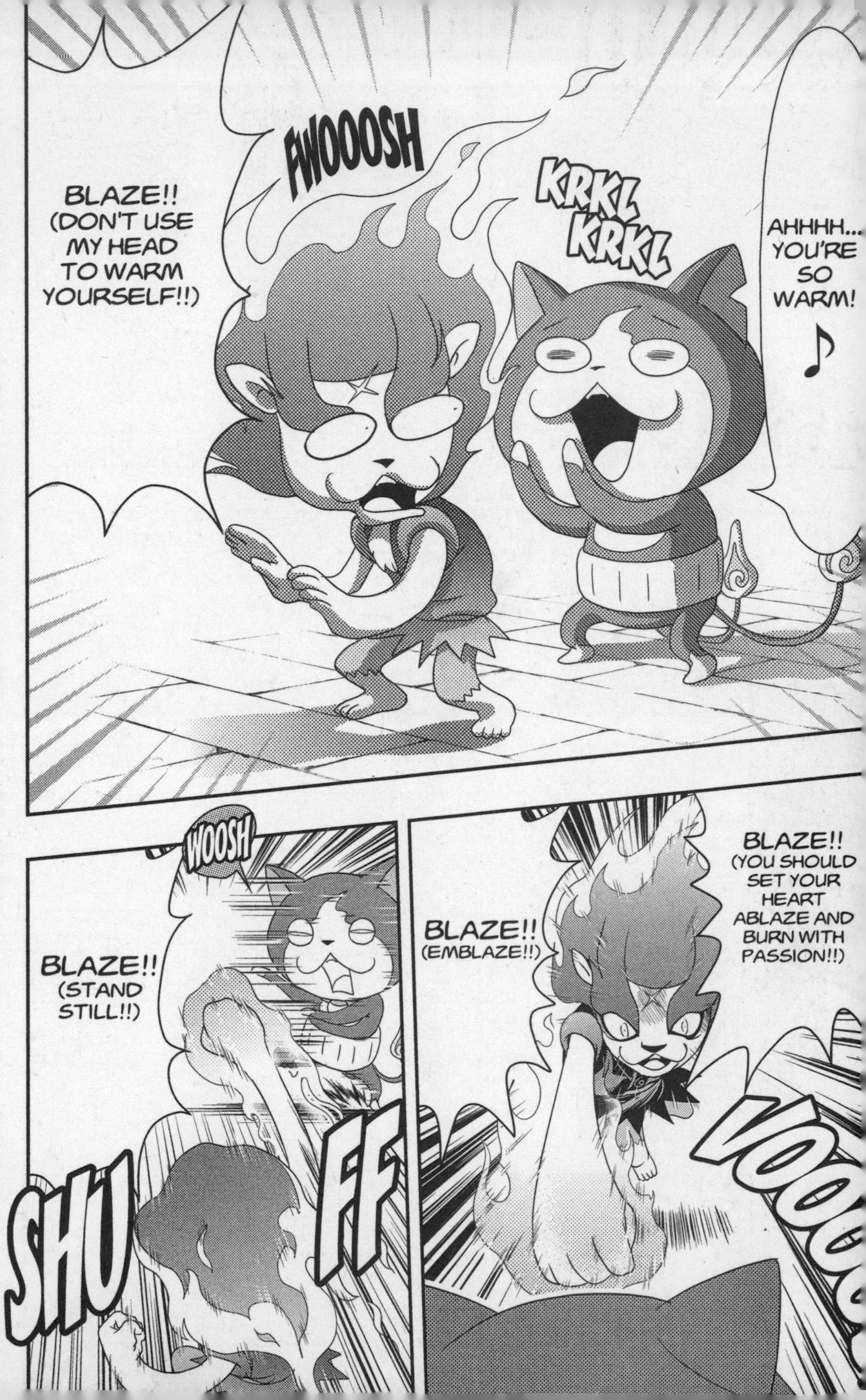
AHHHH... YOU'RE SO WARM! ♪
KRKL KRKL
FWOOOSH
BLAZE!! (DON'T USE MY HEAD TO WARM YOURSELF!!)
BLAZE!! (YOU SHOULD SET YOUR HEART ABLAZE AND BURN WITH PASSION!!)
BLAZE!! (EMBLAZE!!)
VOOOO
WOOSH
BLAZE!! (STAND STILL!!)
SHUFF

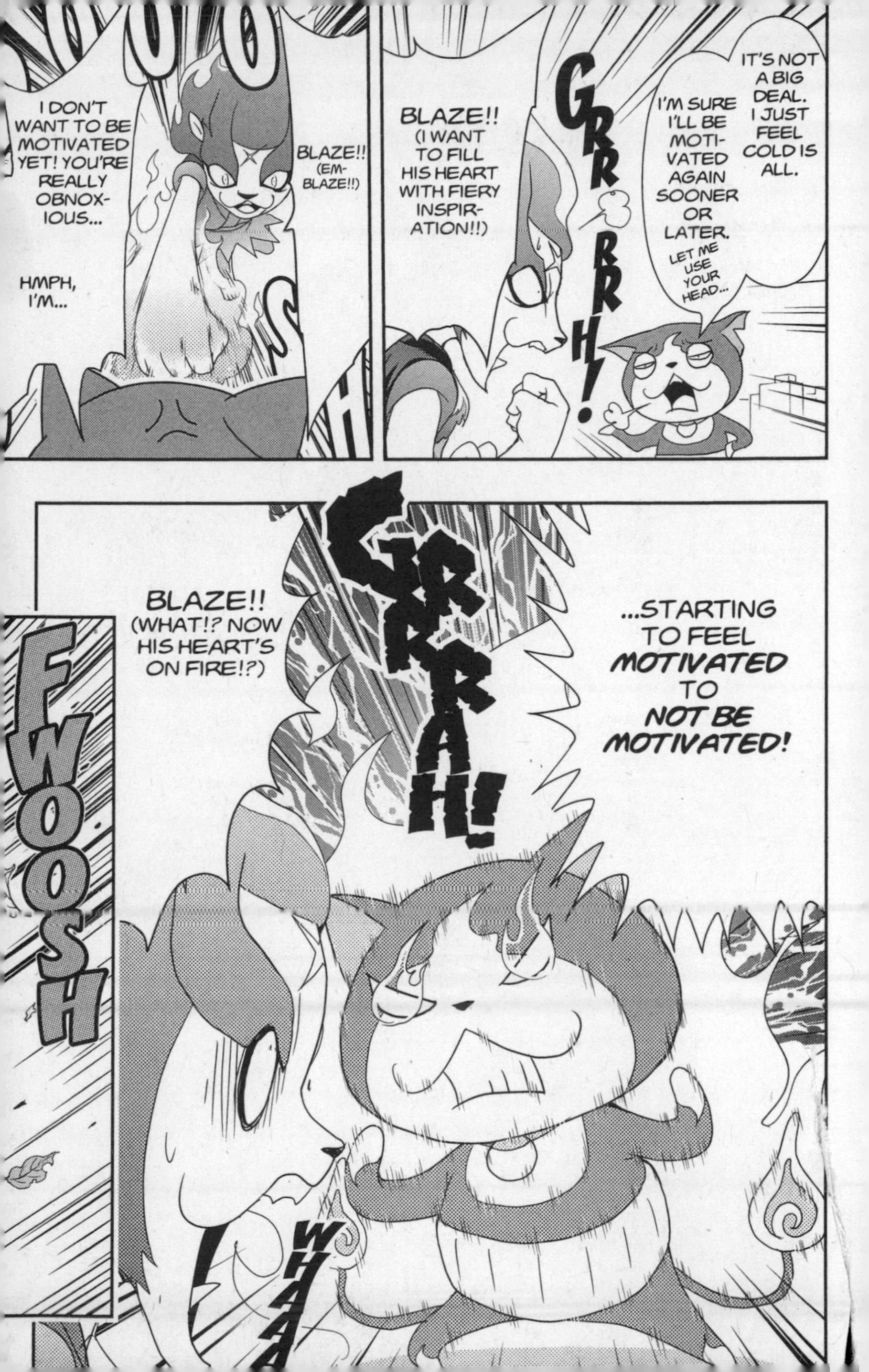
IT'S NOT A BIG DEAL. I JUST FEEL COLD IS ALL.
I'M SURE I'LL BE MOTI-VATED AGAIN SOONER OR LATER. LET ME USE YOUR HEAD...
GRRRRH!
BLAZE!! (I WANT TO FILL HIS HEART WITH FIERY INSPIR-ATION!!)
BLAZE!! (EM-BLAZE!!)
I DON'T WANT TO BE MOTIVATED YET! YOU'RE REALLY OBNOX-IOUS...
HMPH, I'M...
...STARTING TO FEEL *MOTIVATED* TO *NOT BE MOTIVATED!*
GRRRRAH!
BLAZE!! (WHAT!? NOW HIS HEART'S ON FIRE!?)
FWOOSH
WHAA

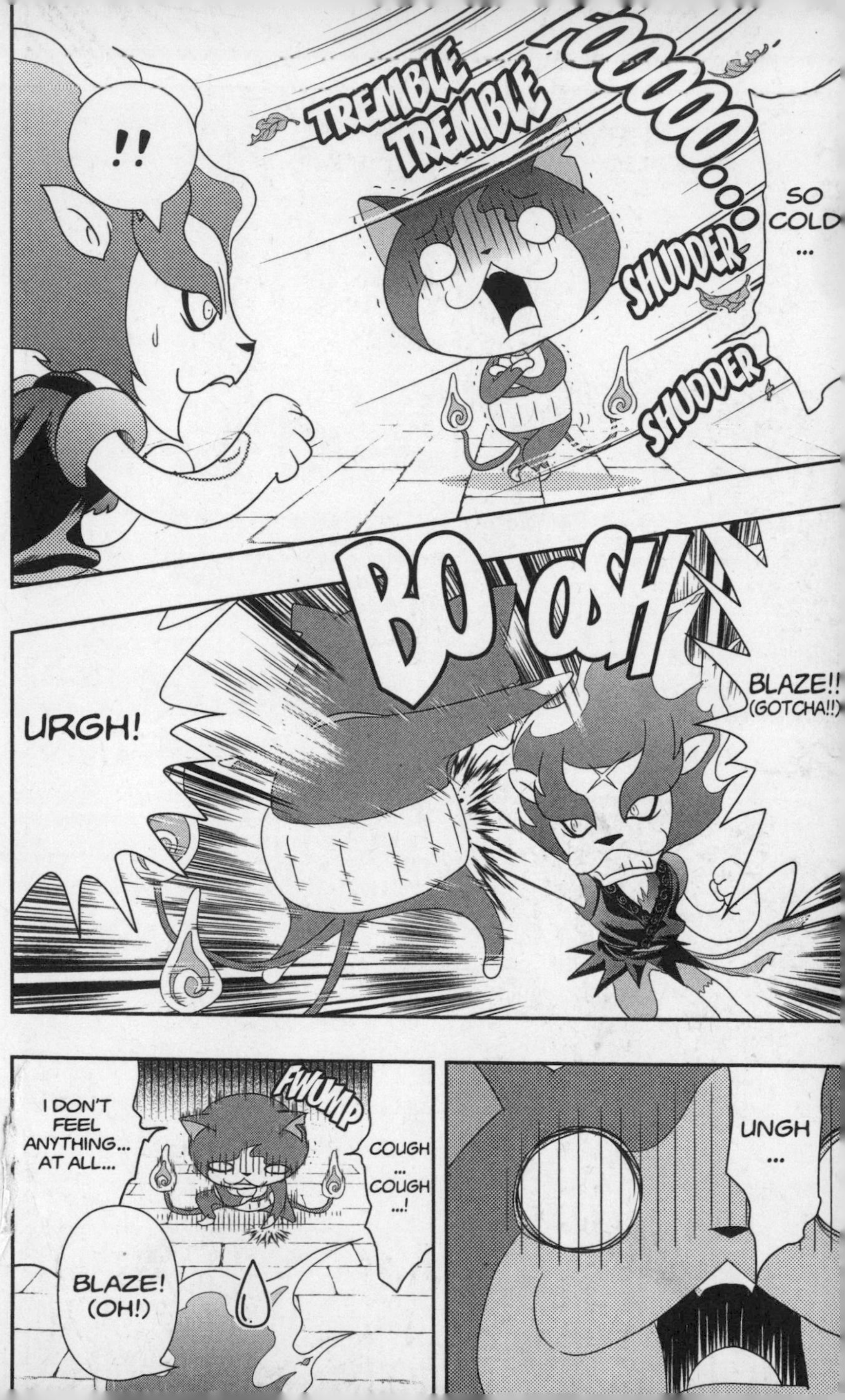
SO COLD ...
SHUDDER
SHUDDER
-OOOOO...
TREMBLE TREMBLE
!!
BLAZE!! (GOTCHA!!)
BOOSH
URGH!
UNGH ...
COUGH ... COUGH ...!
FWUMP
I DON'T FEEL ANYTHING... AT ALL...
BLAZE! (OH!)

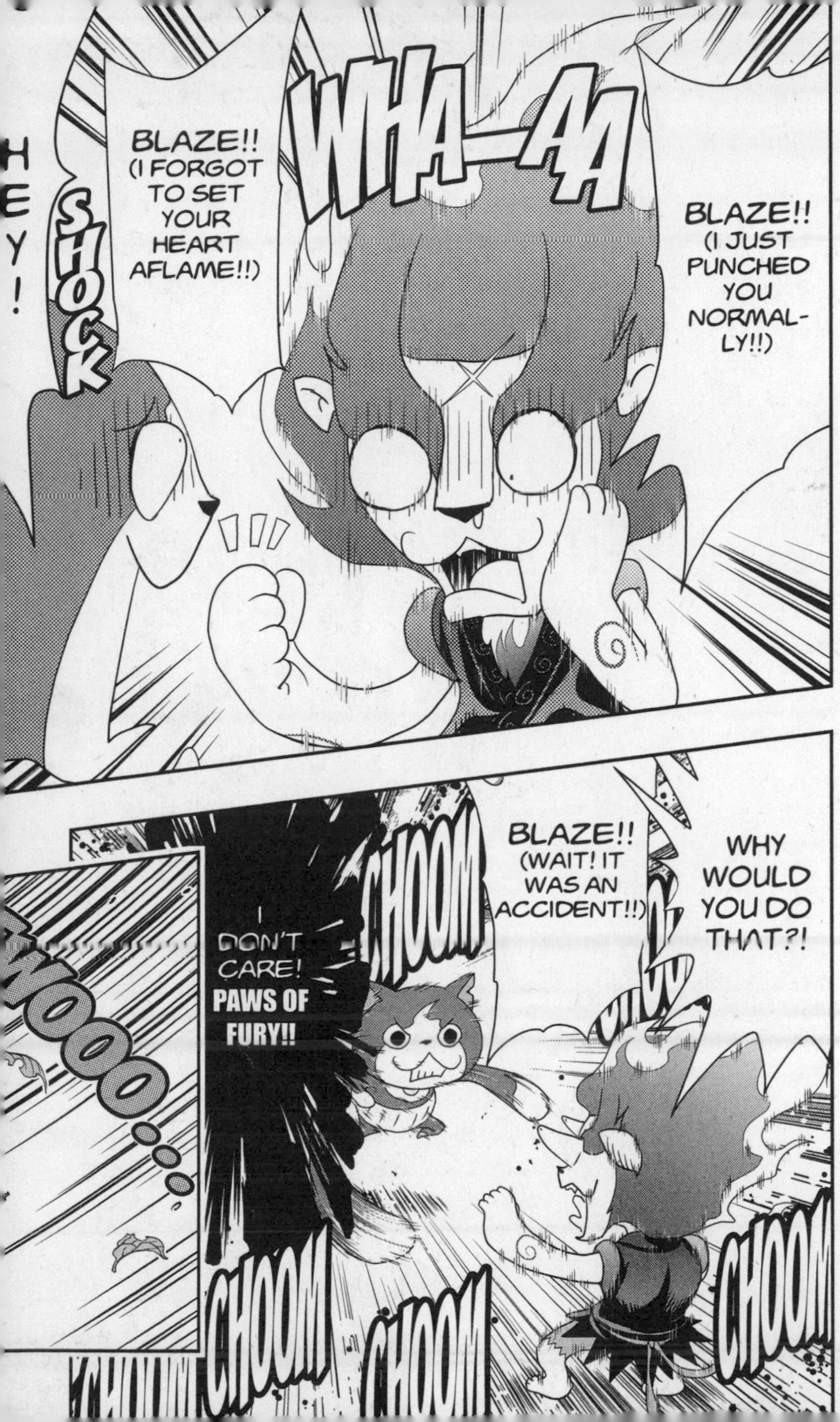
BLAZE!!
(I JUST PUNCHED YOU NORMALLY!!)
WHA-AA
BLAZE!!
(I FORGOT TO SET YOUR HEART AFLAME!!)
SHOCK
HEY!
WHY WOULD YOU DO THAT?!
BLAZE!!
(WAIT! IT WAS AN ACCIDENT!!)
CHOOM
I DON'T CARE!
PAWS OF FURY!!
WOOOO...
CHOOM
CHOOM
CHOOM
CHOOM

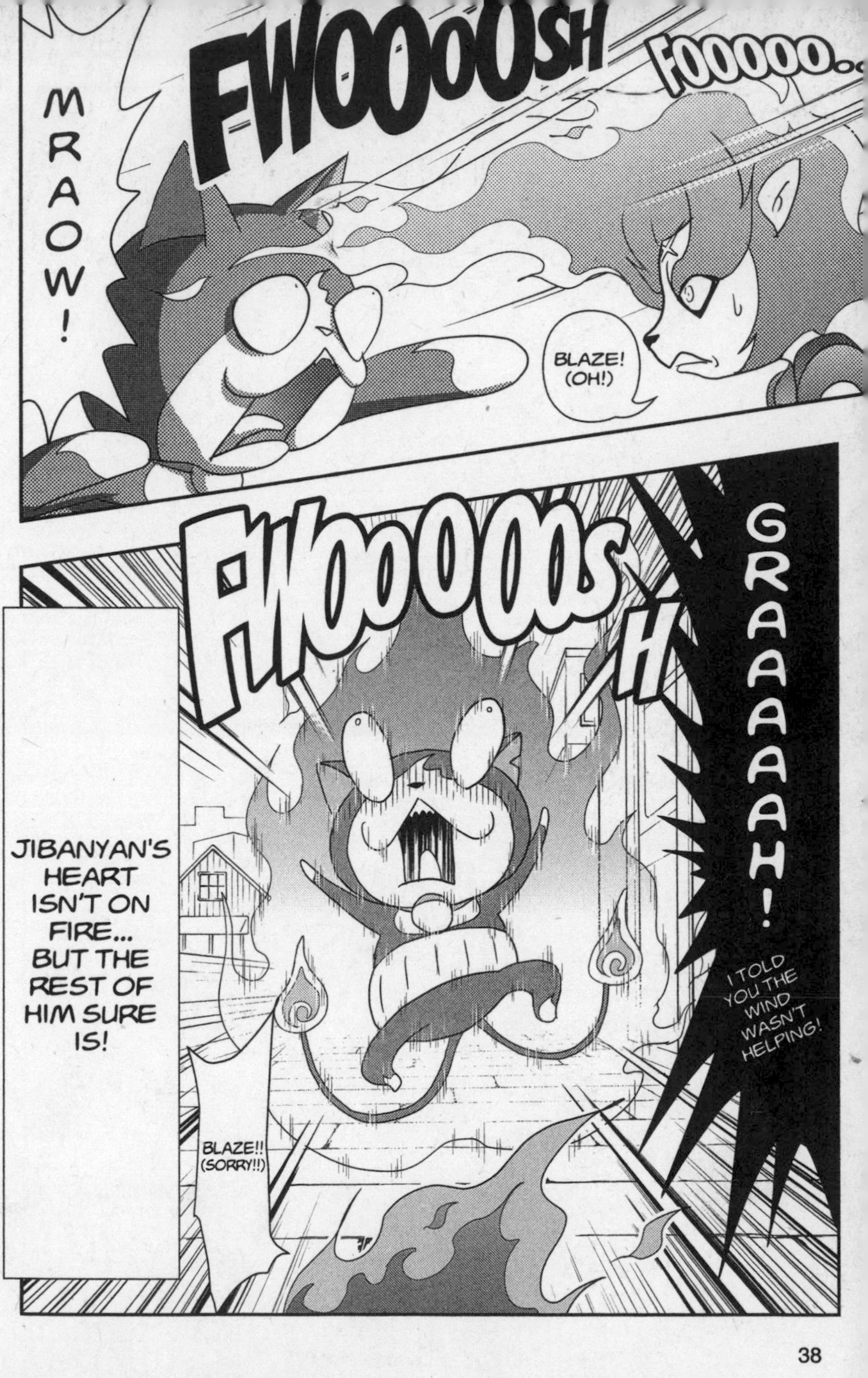
FOOOOO..
FWOOOOSH
BLAZE! (OH!)
MRAOW!
GRAAAAAH!
FWOOOOOSH
I TOLD YOU THE WIND WASN'T HELPING!
JIBANYAN'S HEART ISN'T ON FIRE... BUT THE REST OF HIM SURE IS!
BLAZE!! (SORRY!!)

CHAPTER 27: WHO CAN YOU TRUST?!

FEATURING SKEPTICAL YO-KAI SUSPICIONI

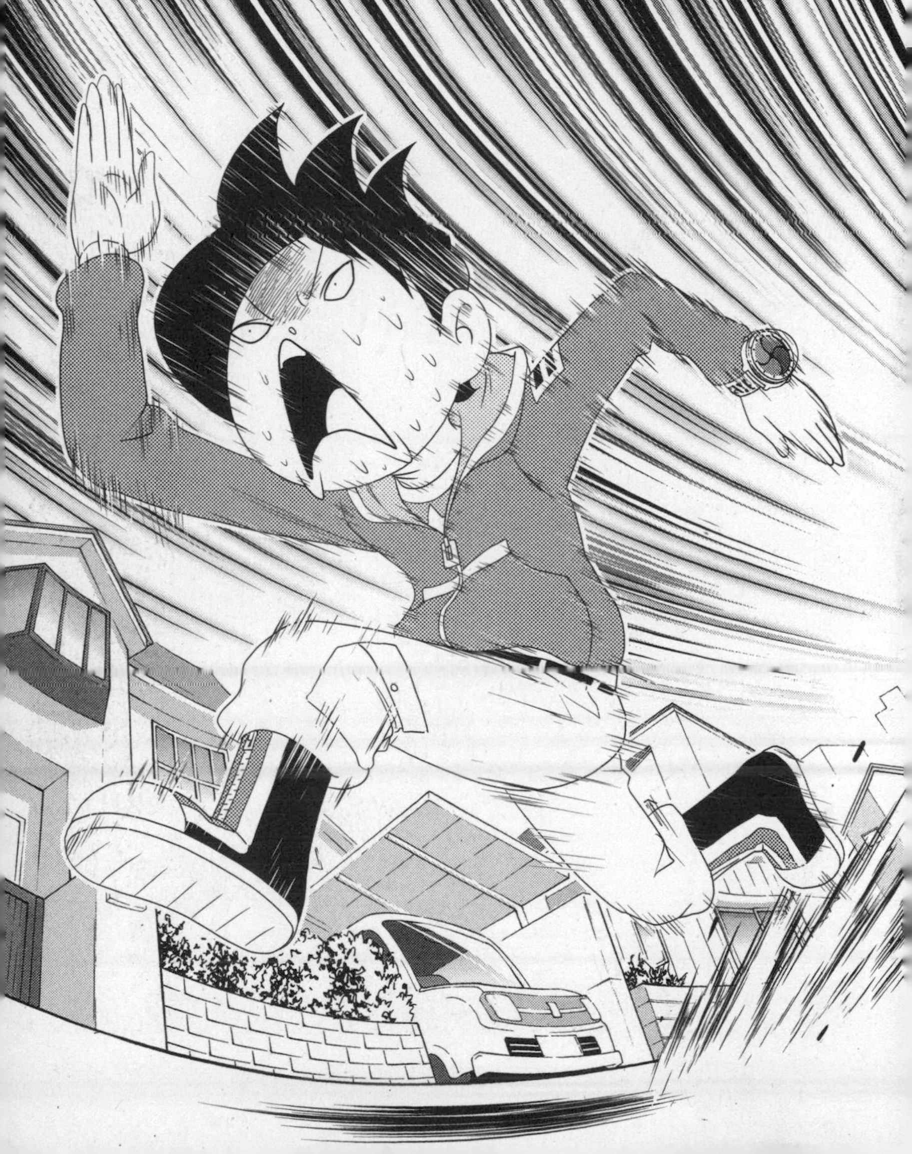

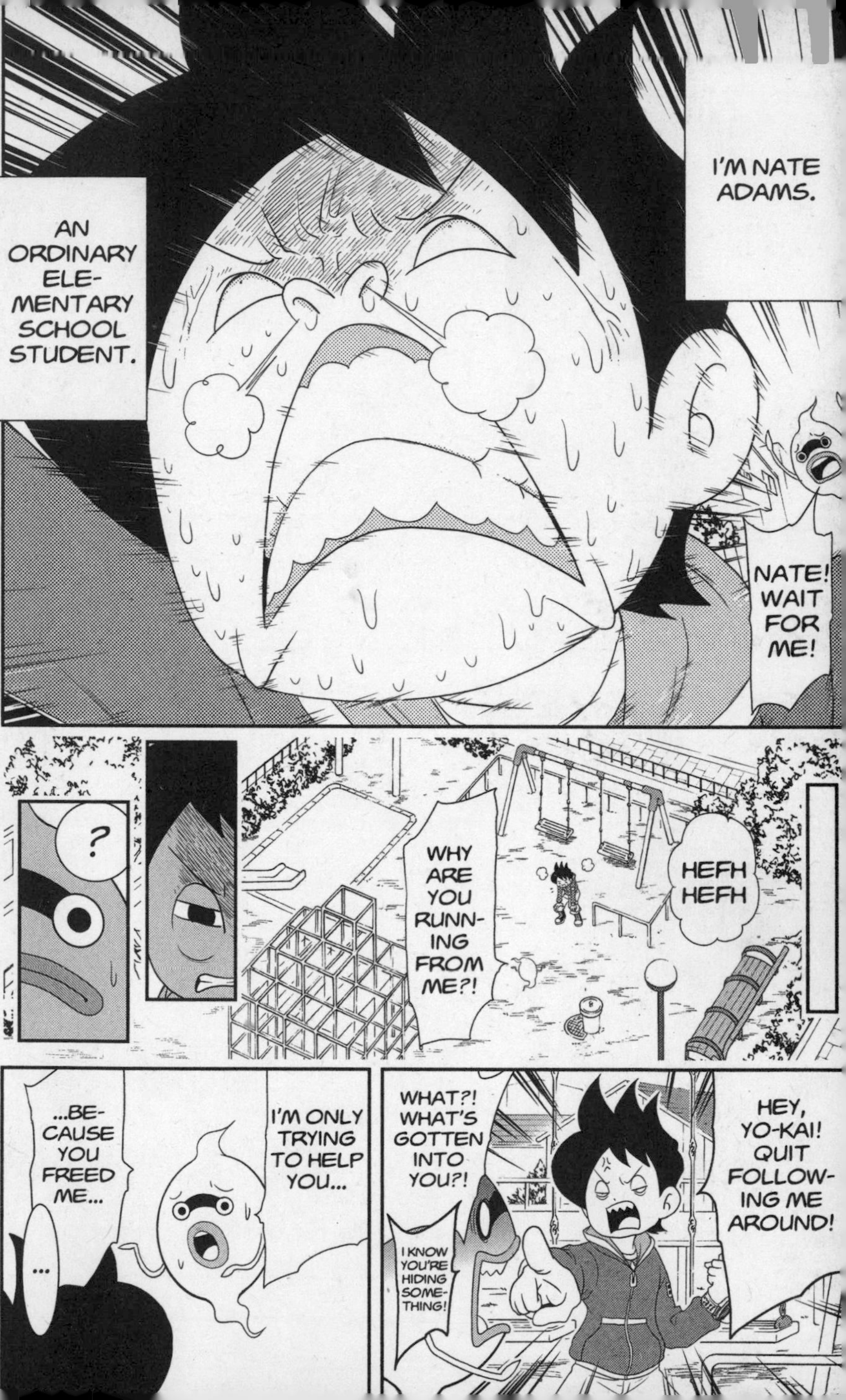
I'M NATE ADAMS.
AN ORDINARY ELE-MENTARY SCHOOL STUDENT.
NATE! WAIT FOR ME!
HEFH HEFH
WHY ARE YOU RUNN-ING FROM ME?!
?
HEY, YO-KAI! QUIT FOLLOW-ING ME AROUND!
WHAT?! WHAT'S GOTTEN INTO YOU?!
I KNOW YOU'RE HIDING SOME-THING!
I'M ONLY TRYING TO HELP YOU...
...BE-CAUSE YOU FREED ME...
...

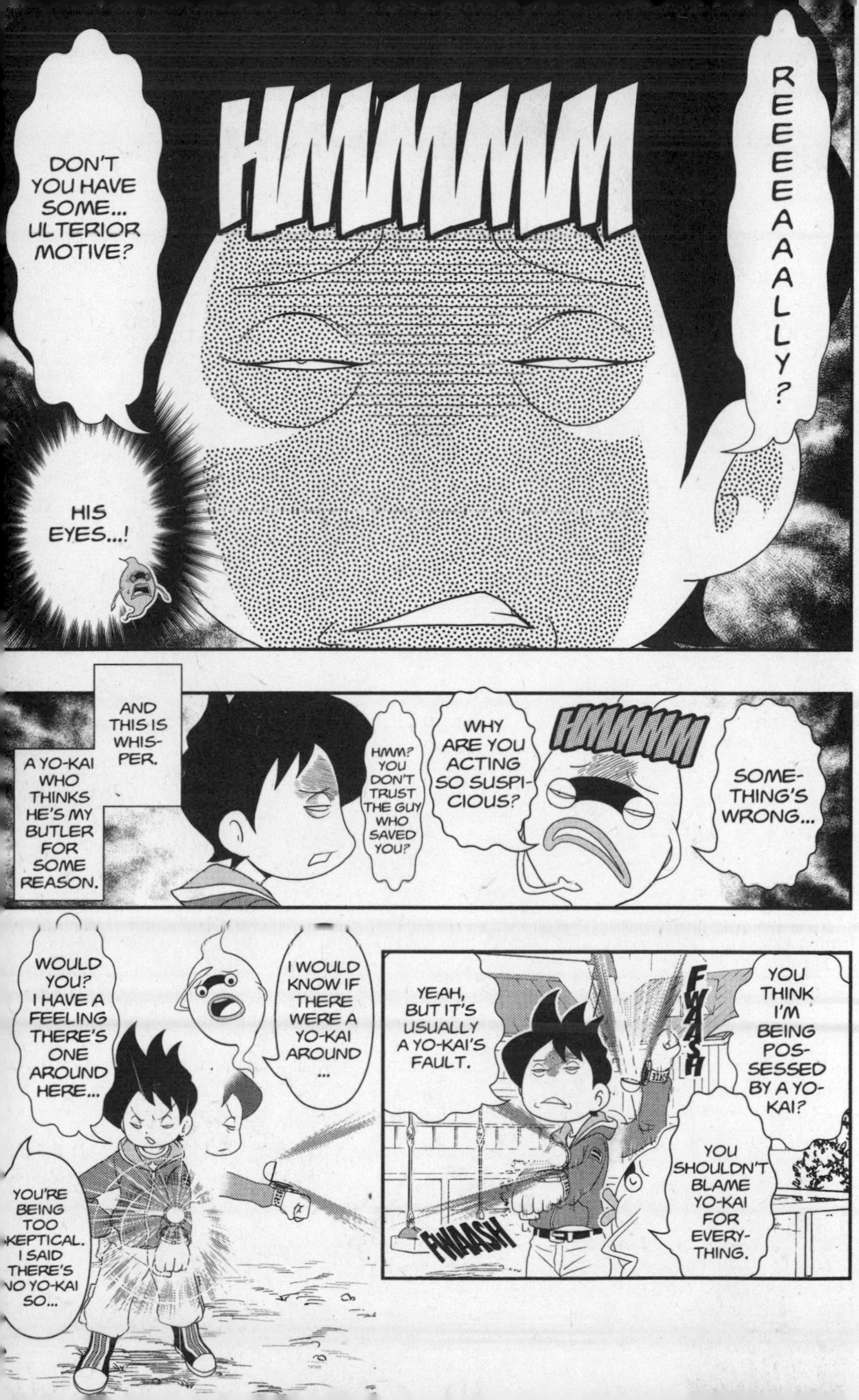
REEEEAAALLY?
HMMMMM
DON'T YOU HAVE SOME... ULTERIOR MOTIVE?
HIS EYES...!
SOME-THING'S WRONG...
HMMMM
WHY ARE YOU ACTING SO SUSPICIOUS?
HMM? YOU DON'T TRUST THE GUY WHO SAVED YOU?
AND THIS IS WHIS-PER.
A YO-KAI WHO THINKS HE'S MY BUTLER FOR SOME REASON.
YOU THINK I'M BEING POS-SESSED BY A YO-KAI?
FWAASH
YEAH, BUT IT'S USUALLY A YO-KAI'S FAULT.
YOU SHOULDN'T BLAME YO-KAI FOR EVERY-THING.
FWAASH
I WOULD KNOW IF THERE WERE A YO-KAI AROUND ...
WOULD YOU? I HAVE A FEELING THERE'S ONE AROUND HERE...
YOU'RE BEING TOO KEPTICAL. I SAID THERE'S NO YO-KAI SO...

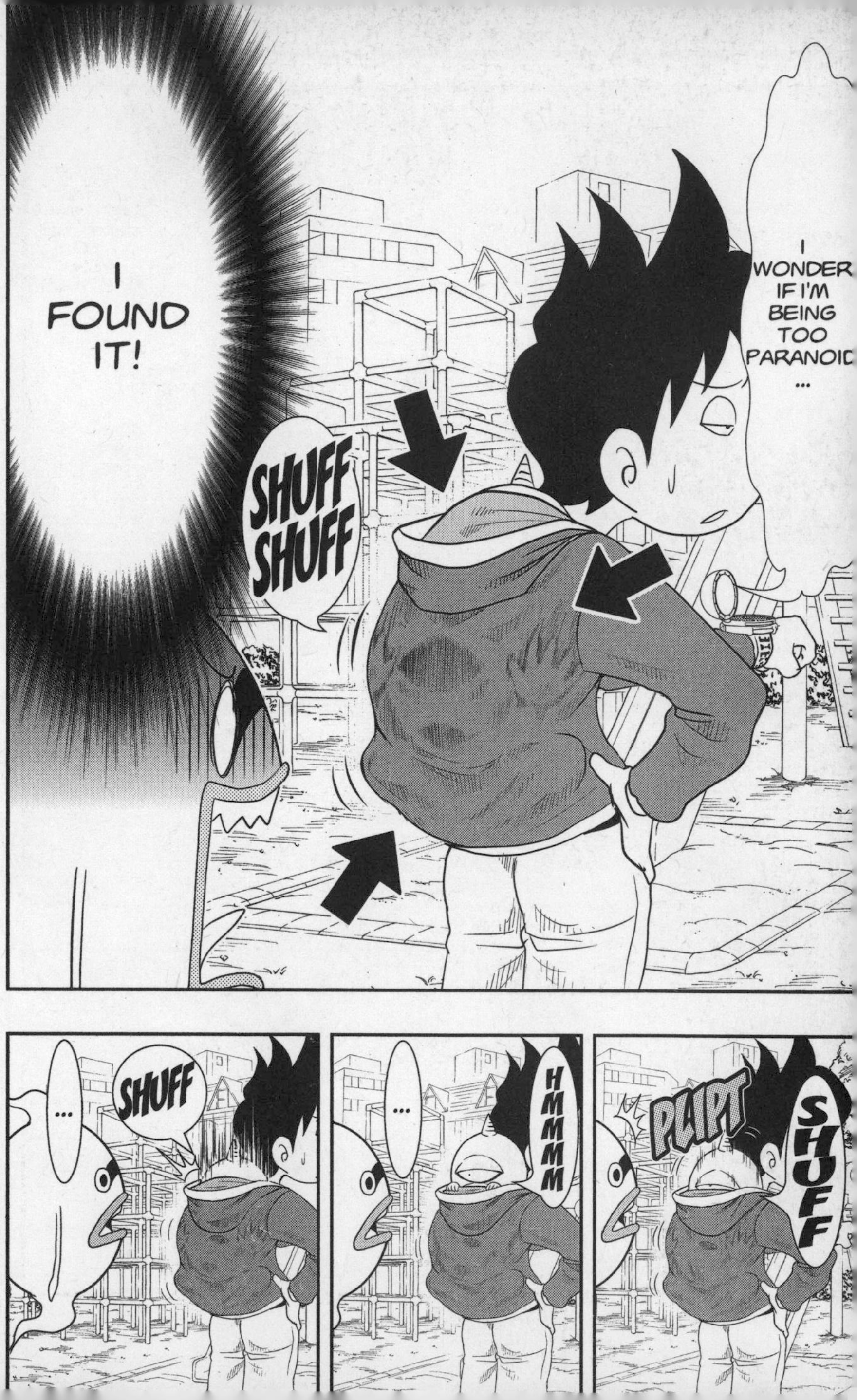
I WONDER IF I'M BEING TOO PARANOID...
SHUFF SHUFF
I FOUND IT!
SHUFF
PLIPT
HMMMM
...
SHUFF
...

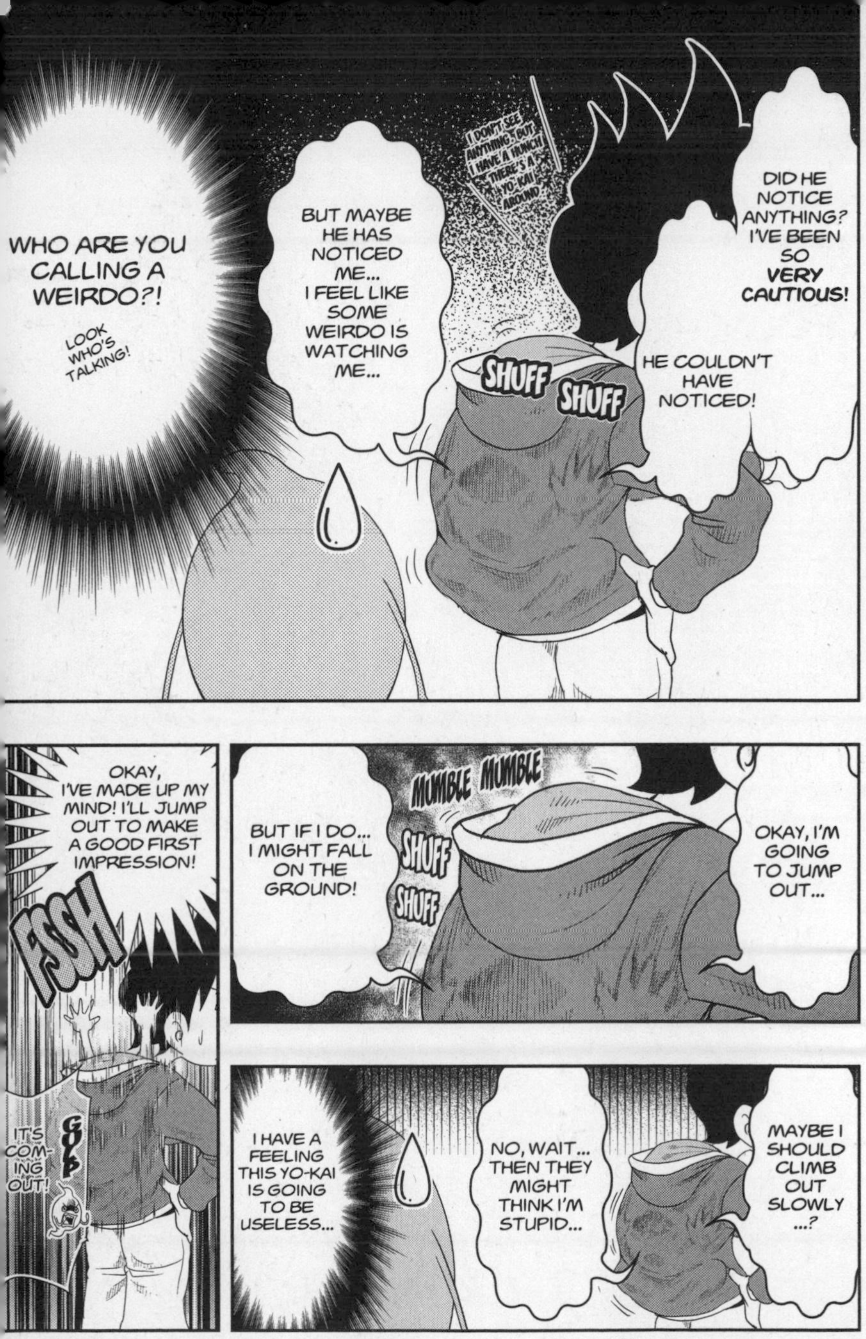
DID HE NOTICE ANYTHING? I'VE BEEN SO **VERY CAUTIOUS!**
HE COULDN'T HAVE NOTICED!
SHUFF
SHUFF
I DON'T SEE ANYTHING, BUT I HAVE A HUNCH THERE'S A YO-KAI AROUND
BUT MAYBE HE HAS NOTICED ME... I FEEL LIKE SOME WEIRDO IS WATCHING ME...
WHO ARE YOU CALLING A WEIRDO?!
LOOK WHO'S TALKING!
OKAY, I'M GOING TO JUMP OUT...
MUMBLE MUMBLE
SHUFF
SHUFF
BUT IF I DO... I MIGHT FALL ON THE GROUND!
MAYBE I SHOULD CLIMB OUT SLOWLY ...?
NO, WAIT... THEN THEY MIGHT THINK I'M STUPID...
I HAVE A FEELING THIS YO-KAI IS GOING TO BE USELESS...
OKAY, I'VE MADE UP MY MIND! I'LL JUMP OUT TO MAKE A GOOD FIRST IMPRESSION!
FSSH
GULP
IT'S COM-ING OUT!

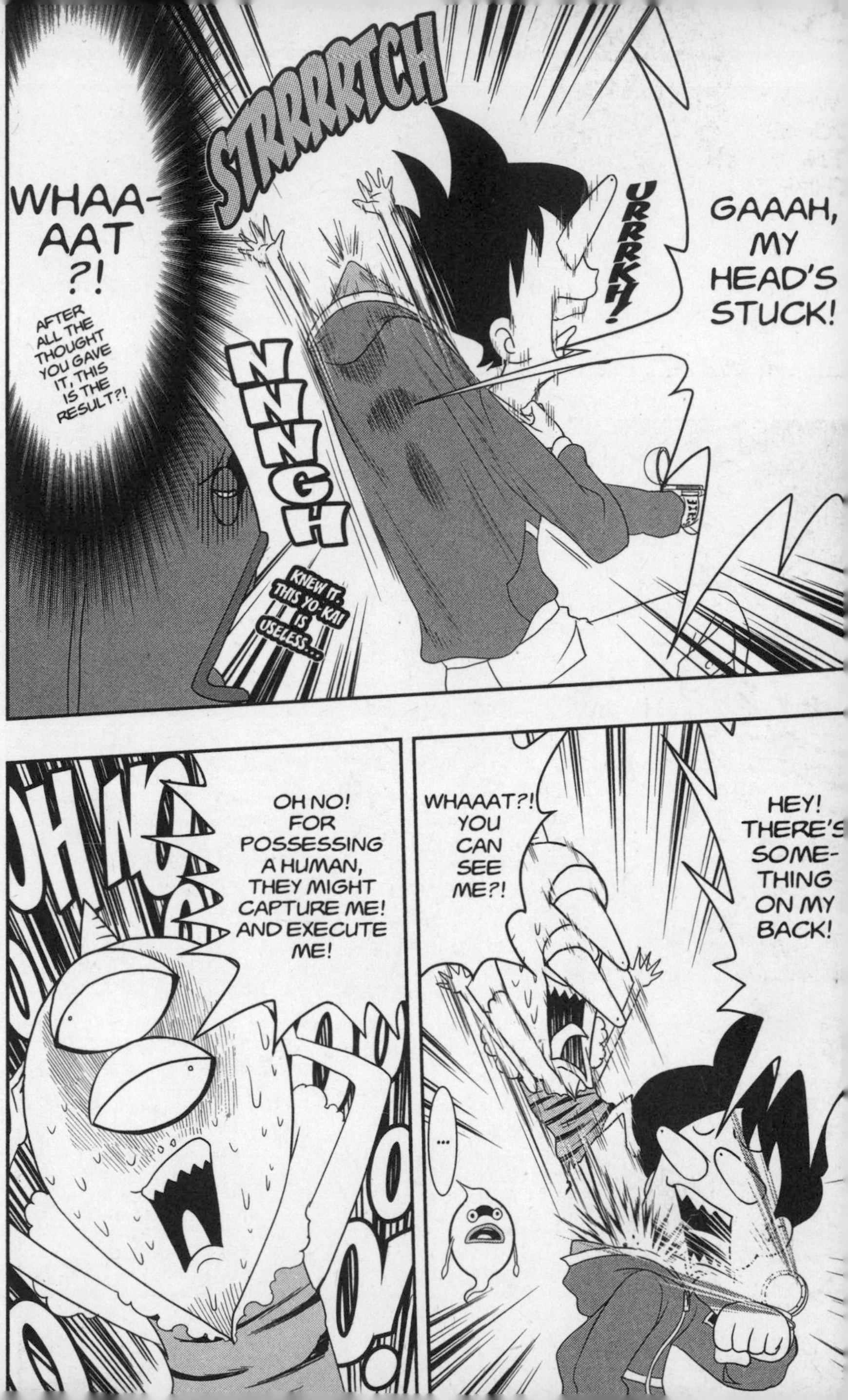
GAAAH, MY HEAD'S STUCK!
URRRKH!
STRRRRTCH
WHAA-AAT?!
AFTER ALL THE THOUGHT YOU GAVE IT, THIS IS THE RESULT?!
NNNGH
KNEW IT. THIS YO-KAI IS USELESS...
HEY! THERE'S SOME-THING ON MY BACK!
WHAAAT?! YOU CAN SEE ME?!
...
OH NO! FOR POSSESSING A HUMAN, THEY MIGHT CAPTURE ME! AND EXECUTE ME!

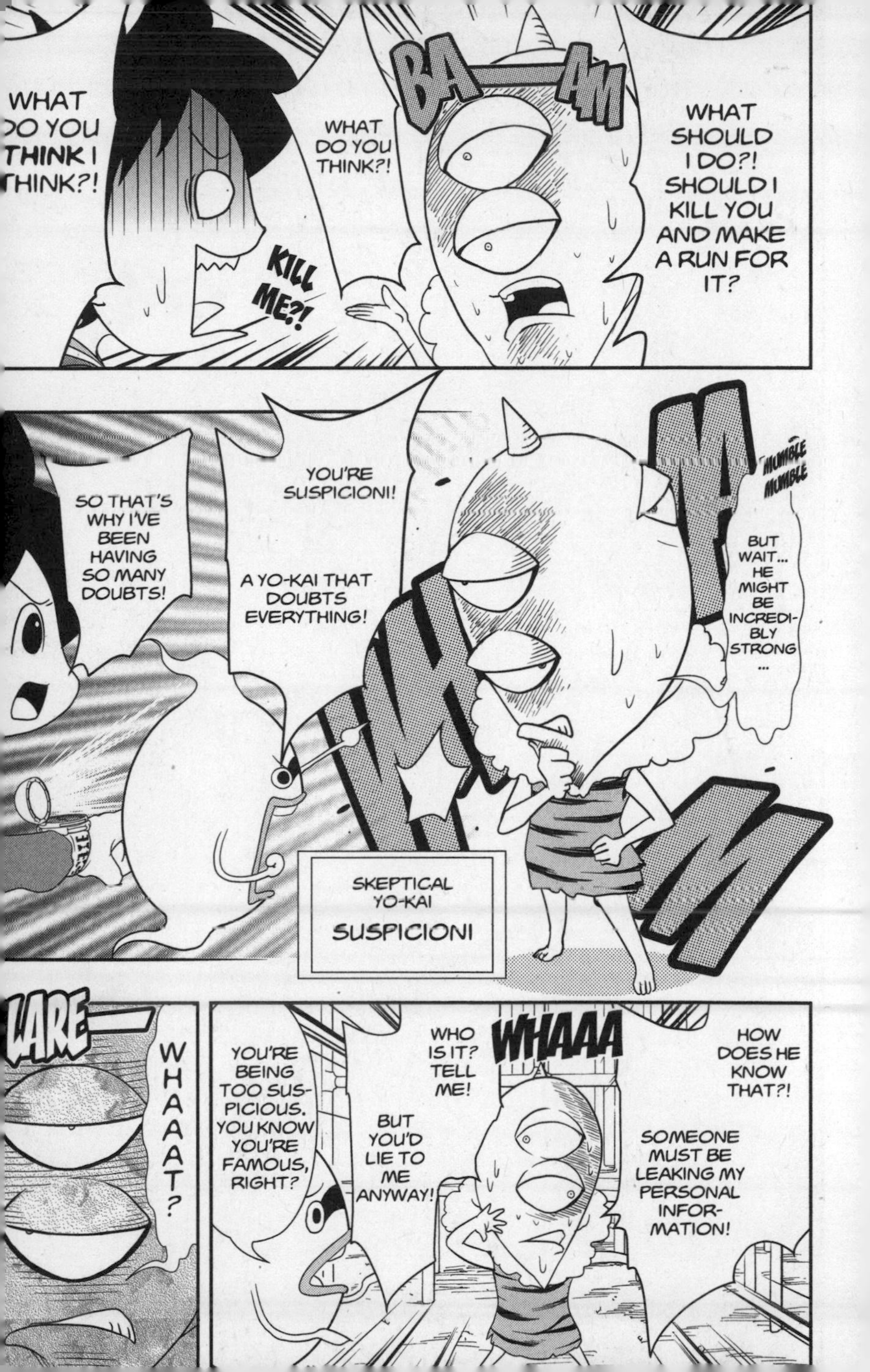
WHAT SHOULD I DO?! SHOULD I KILL YOU AND MAKE A RUN FOR IT?
BA-AM
WHAT DO YOU THINK?!
KILL ME?!
WHAT DO YOU THINK I THINK?!
MUMBLE MUMBLE
BUT WAIT... HE MIGHT BE INCREDI-BLY STRONG...
WHAM
YOU'RE SUSPICIONI!
A YO-KAI THAT DOUBTS EVERYTHING!
SO THAT'S WHY I'VE BEEN HAVING SO MANY DOUBTS!
SKEPTICAL YO-KAI
SUSPICIONI
HOW DOES HE KNOW THAT?!
SOMEONE MUST BE LEAKING MY PERSONAL INFOR-MATION!
WHAAAA
WHO IS IT? TELL ME!
BUT YOU'D LIE TO ME ANYWAY!
YOU'RE BEING TOO SUS-PICIOUS. YOU KNOW YOU'RE FAMOUS, RIGHT?
WHAAAT?
LARE—

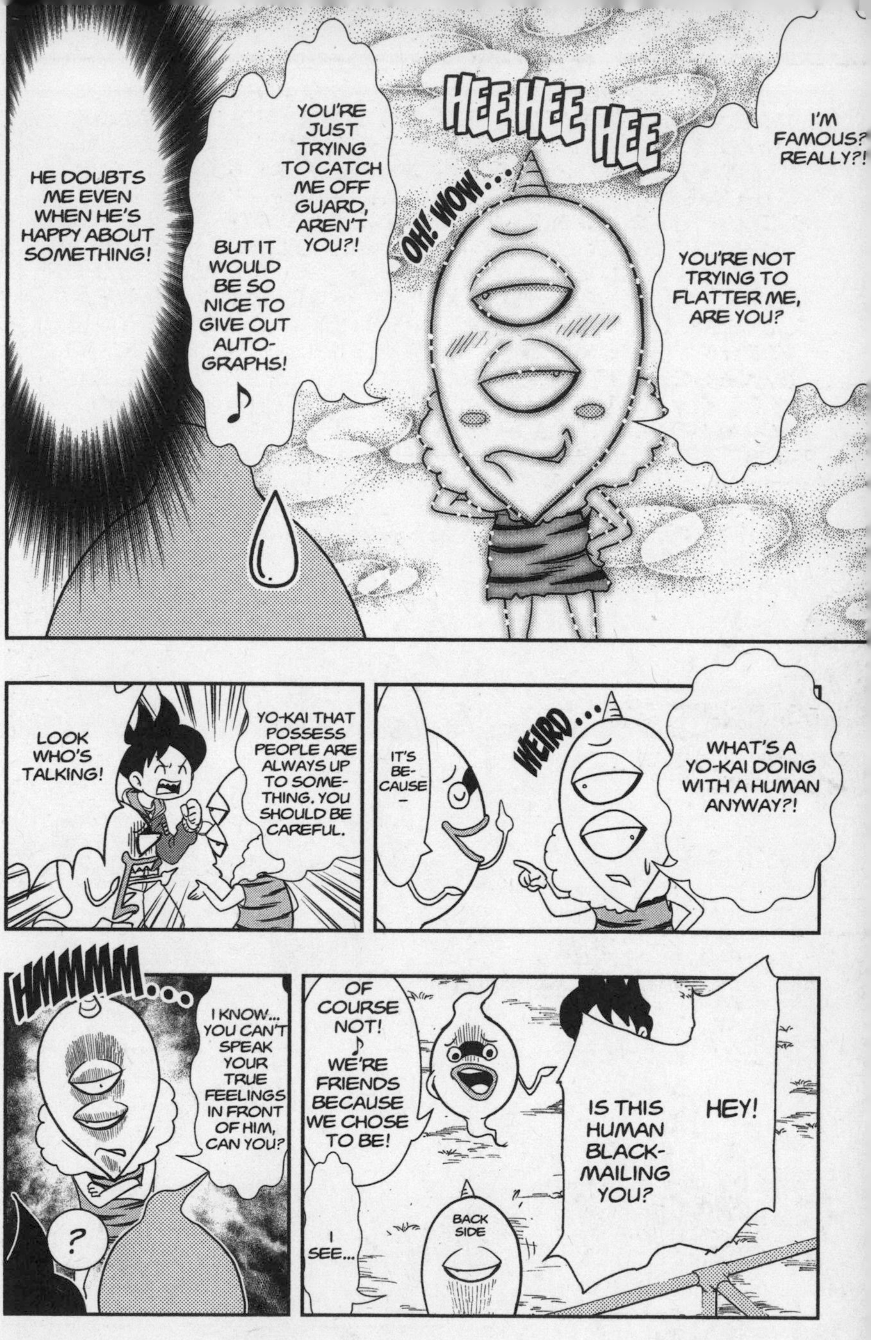
I'M FAMOUS? REALLY?!
HEE HEE HEE
YOU'RE NOT TRYING TO FLATTER ME, ARE YOU?
OH! WOW...
YOU'RE JUST TRYING TO CATCH ME OFF GUARD, AREN'T YOU?!
BUT IT WOULD BE SO NICE TO GIVE OUT AUTOGRAPHS! ♪
HE DOUBTS ME EVEN WHEN HE'S HAPPY ABOUT SOMETHING!
WHAT'S A YO-KAI DOING WITH A HUMAN ANYWAY?!
WEIRD...
IT'S BECAUSE—
YO-KAI THAT POSSESS PEOPLE ARE ALWAYS UP TO SOMETHING. YOU SHOULD BE CAREFUL.
LOOK WHO'S TALKING!
HEY!
IS THIS HUMAN BLACKMAILING YOU?
OF COURSE NOT! ♪ WE'RE FRIENDS BECAUSE WE CHOSE TO BE!
BACK SIDE
I SEE...
HMMMM...
I KNOW... YOU CAN'T SPEAK YOUR TRUE FEELINGS IN FRONT OF HIM, CAN YOU?
?

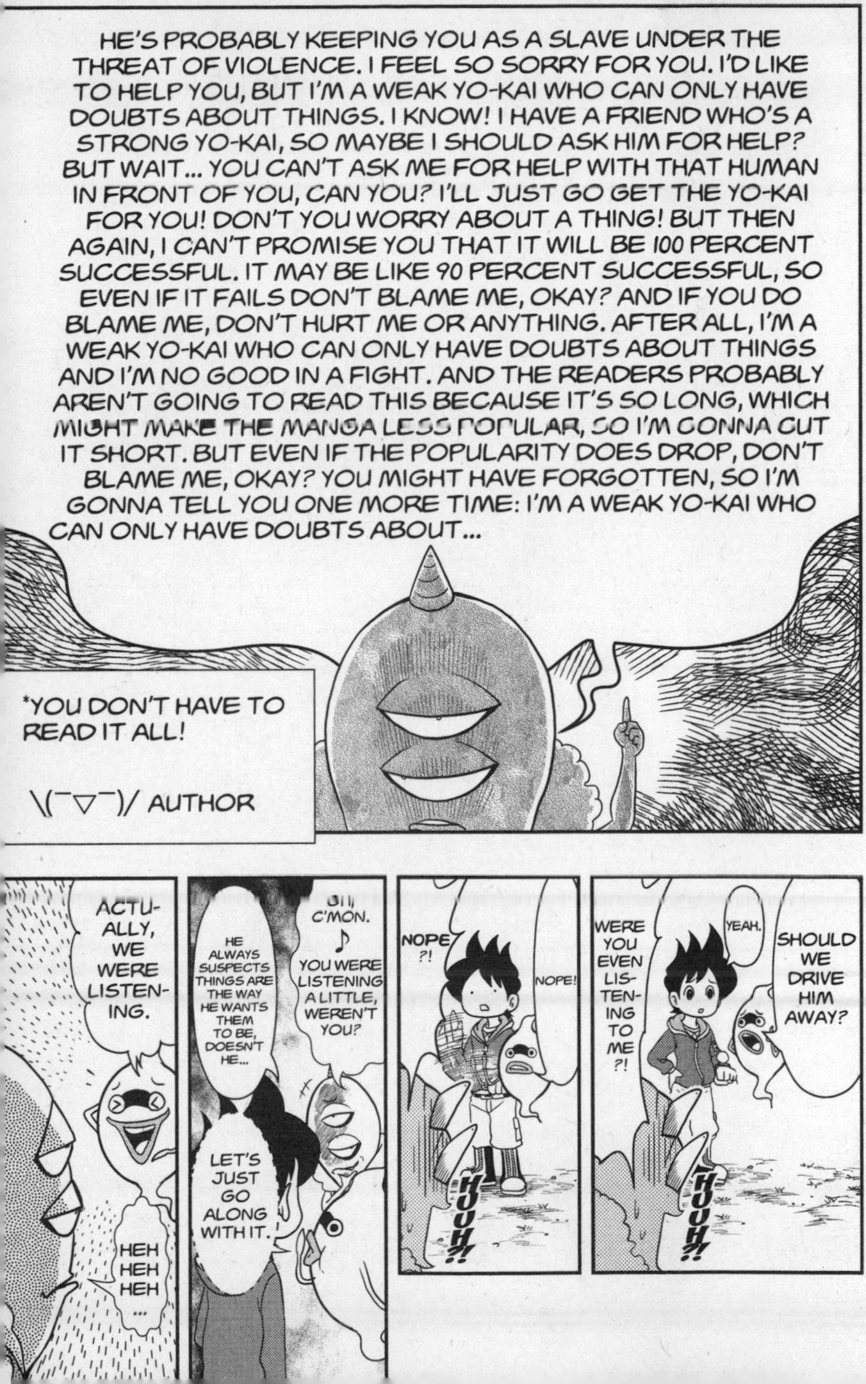
HE'S PROBABLY KEEPING YOU AS A SLAVE UNDER THE THREAT OF VIOLENCE. I FEEL SO SORRY FOR YOU. I'D LIKE TO HELP YOU, BUT I'M A WEAK YO-KAI WHO CAN ONLY HAVE DOUBTS ABOUT THINGS. I KNOW! I HAVE A FRIEND WHO'S A STRONG YO-KAI, SO MAYBE I SHOULD ASK HIM FOR HELP? BUT WAIT... YOU CAN'T ASK ME FOR HELP WITH THAT HUMAN IN FRONT OF YOU, CAN YOU? I'LL JUST GO GET THE YO-KAI FOR YOU! DON'T YOU WORRY ABOUT A THING! BUT THEN AGAIN, I CAN'T PROMISE YOU THAT IT WILL BE 100 PERCENT SUCCESSFUL. IT MAY BE LIKE 90 PERCENT SUCCESSFUL, SO EVEN IF IT FAILS DON'T BLAME ME, OKAY? AND IF YOU DO BLAME ME, DON'T HURT ME OR ANYTHING. AFTER ALL, I'M A WEAK YO-KAI WHO CAN ONLY HAVE DOUBTS ABOUT THINGS AND I'M NO GOOD IN A FIGHT. AND THE READERS PROBABLY AREN'T GOING TO READ THIS BECAUSE IT'S SO LONG, WHICH MIGHT MAKE THE MANGA LESS POPULAR, SO I'M GONNA CUT IT SHORT. BUT EVEN IF THE POPULARITY DOES DROP, DON'T BLAME ME, OKAY? YOU MIGHT HAVE FORGOTTEN, SO I'M GONNA TELL YOU ONE MORE TIME: I'M A WEAK YO-KAI WHO CAN ONLY HAVE DOUBTS ABOUT...
*YOU DON'T HAVE TO READ IT ALL!
\(¯▽¯)/ AUTHOR
SHOULD WE DRIVE HIM AWAY?
YEAH.
WERE YOU EVEN LISTENING TO ME?!
HJUH?!
NOPE!
NOPE?!
HJUH?!
C'MON. ♪ YOU WERE LISTENING A LITTLE, WEREN'T YOU?
HE ALWAYS SUSPECTS THINGS ARE THE WAY HE WANTS THEM TO BE, DOESN'T HE...
LET'S JUST GO ALONG WITH IT.
ACTUALLY, WE WERE LISTENING.
HEH HEH HEH...

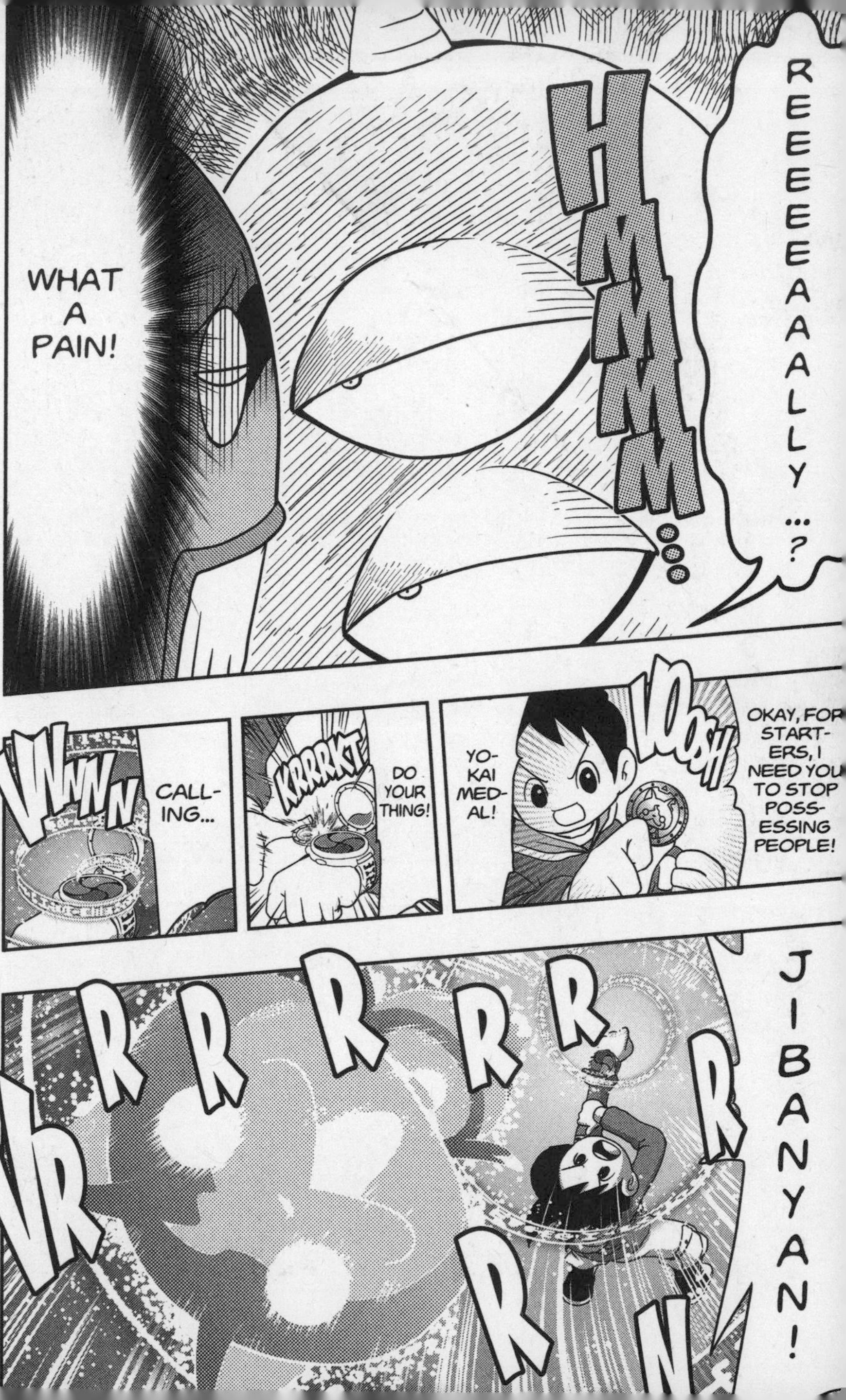
REEEEEAAALLY...?
HMMMM...
WHAT A PAIN!
OKAY, FOR STARTERS, I NEED YOU TO STOP POSSESSING PEOPLE!
VOOSH
YO-KAI MEDAL!
DO YOUR THING!
KRRRKT
CALLING...
VWNNN
JIBANYAN!
VRRRRRRRN

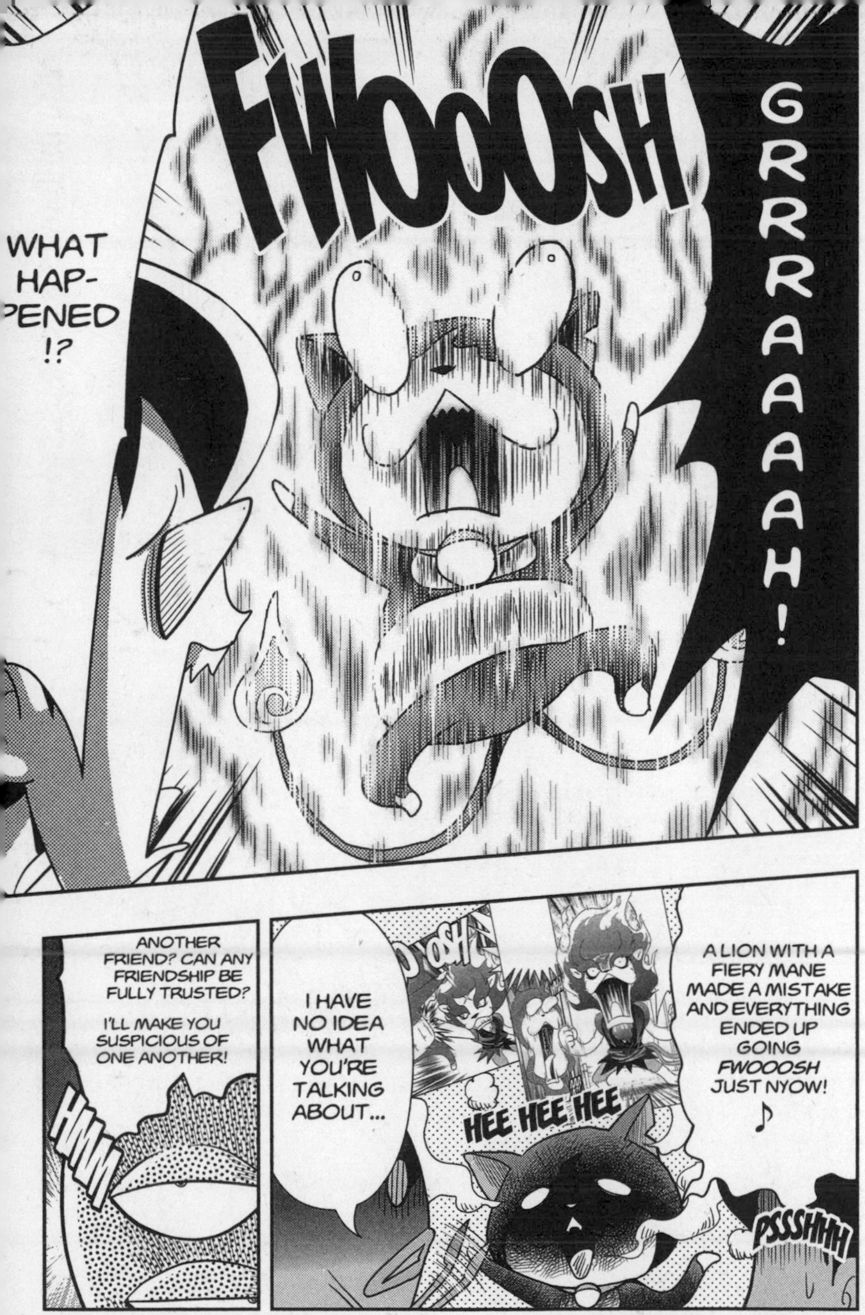
FWOOOSH
GRRRAAAAAH!
WHAT HAP-PENED!?
A LION WITH A FIERY MANE MADE A MISTAKE AND EVERYTHING ENDED UP GOING FWOOOSH JUST NYOW! ♪
HEE HEE HEE
PSSSHHH
I HAVE NO IDEA WHAT YOU'RE TALKING ABOUT...
ANOTHER FRIEND? CAN ANY FRIENDSHIP BE FULLY TRUSTED?
I'LL MAKE YOU SUSPICIOUS OF ONE ANOTHER!
HMM

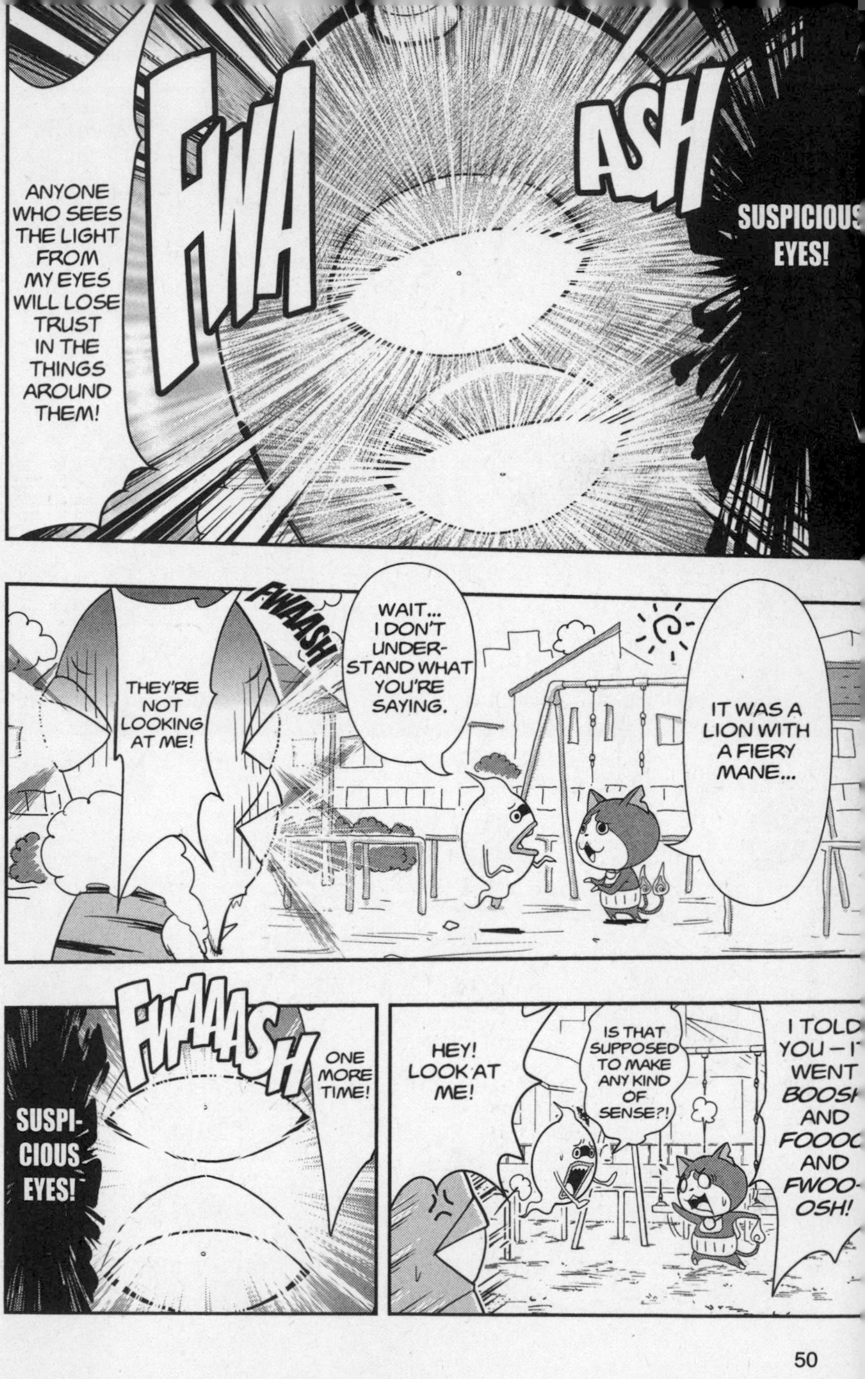
FWA ASH
SUSPICIOUS EYES!
ANYONE WHO SEES THE LIGHT FROM MY EYES WILL LOSE TRUST IN THE THINGS AROUND THEM!
IT WAS A LION WITH A FIERY MANE...
WAIT... I DON'T UNDER-STAND WHAT YOU'RE SAYING.
FWAASH
THEY'RE NOT LOOKING AT ME!
I TOLD YOU — I WENT *BOOS* AND *FOOO* AND *FWOO-OSH!*
IS THAT SUPPOSED TO MAKE ANY KIND OF SENSE?!
HEY! LOOK AT ME!
FWAAASH
ONE MORE TIME!
SUSPI-CIOUS EYES!

GRAAAAH!

KA— THUNGKT

SHUT UP!

THE CHARACTERS IN MANGA AND ANIME NEVER GET ATTACKED WHEN THEY'RE DOING THEIR SPECIAL MOVES, SO I THOUGHT THAT I WOULD BE OKAY...

I SHOULD HAVE... BEEN MORE... SUSPI-CIOUS...

WHISPER CAN'T HEAR ME BECAUSE YOU KEEP BABBLING!

NNGH NNGH

NO... I JUST DON'T UNDER-STAND WHAT YOU'RE TALKING ABOUT!

HUNH?

WHAT?

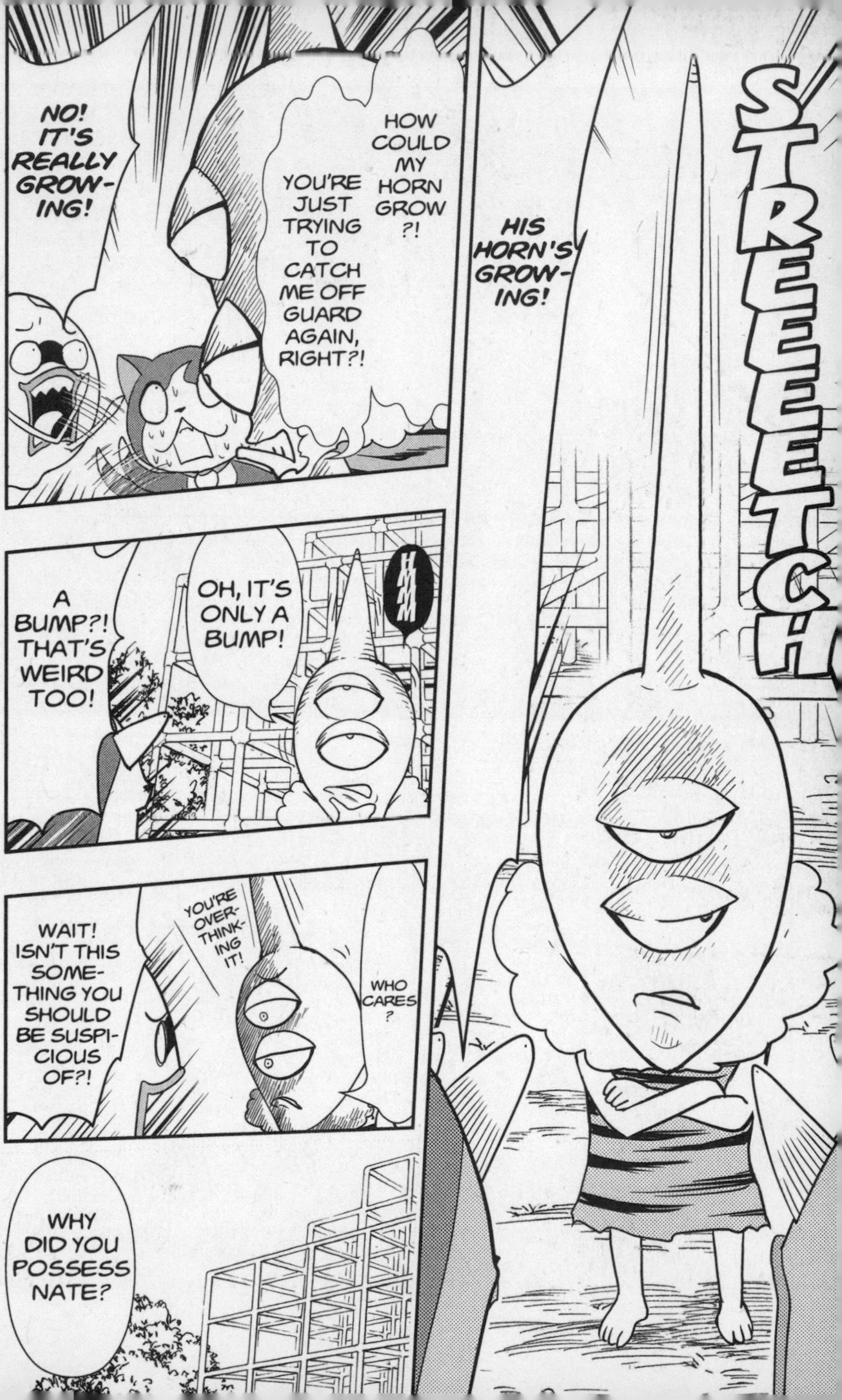
STRETCH
HIS HORN'S GROWING!
HOW COULD MY HORN GROW?!
YOU'RE JUST TRYING TO CATCH ME OFF GUARD AGAIN, RIGHT?!
NO! IT'S REALLY GROWING!
HMM
OH, IT'S ONLY A BUMP!
A BUMP?! THAT'S WEIRD TOO!
WHO CARES?
YOU'RE OVERTHINKING IT!
WAIT! ISN'T THIS SOMETHING YOU SHOULD BE SUSPICIOUS OF?!
WHY DID YOU POSSESS NATE?

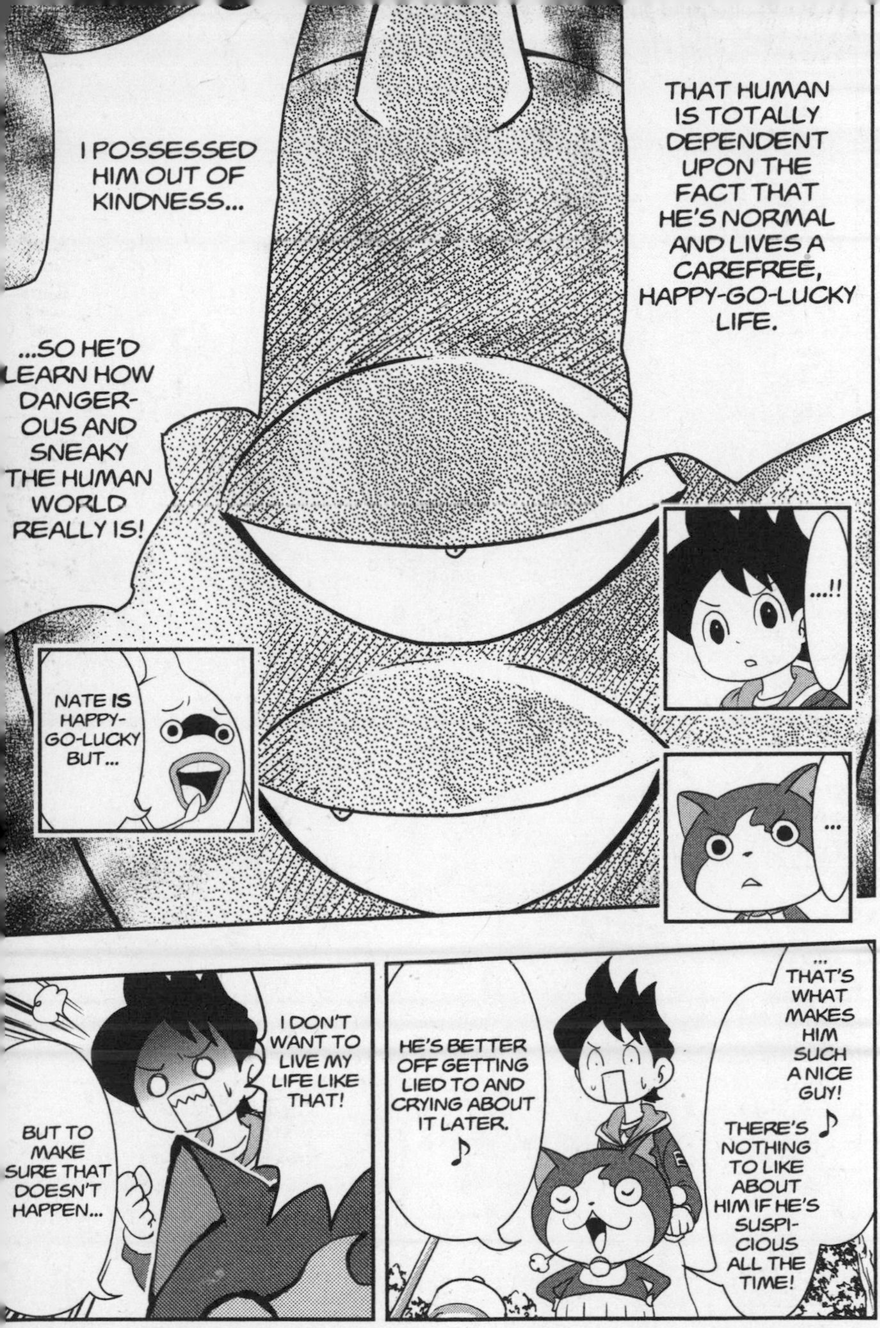
THAT HUMAN IS TOTALLY DEPENDENT UPON THE FACT THAT HE'S NORMAL AND LIVES A CAREFREE, HAPPY-GO-LUCKY LIFE.
I POSSESSED HIM OUT OF KINDNESS...
...SO HE'D LEARN HOW DANGER-OUS AND SNEAKY THE HUMAN WORLD REALLY IS!
...!!
...
NATE IS HAPPY-GO-LUCKY BUT...
...THAT'S WHAT MAKES HIM SUCH A NICE GUY! ♪
THERE'S NOTHING TO LIKE ABOUT HIM IF HE'S SUSPI-CIOUS ALL THE TIME!
HE'S BETTER OFF GETTING LIED TO AND CRYING ABOUT IT LATER. ♪
I DON'T WANT TO LIVE MY LIFE LIKE THAT!
BUT TO MAKE SURE THAT DOESN'T HAPPEN...

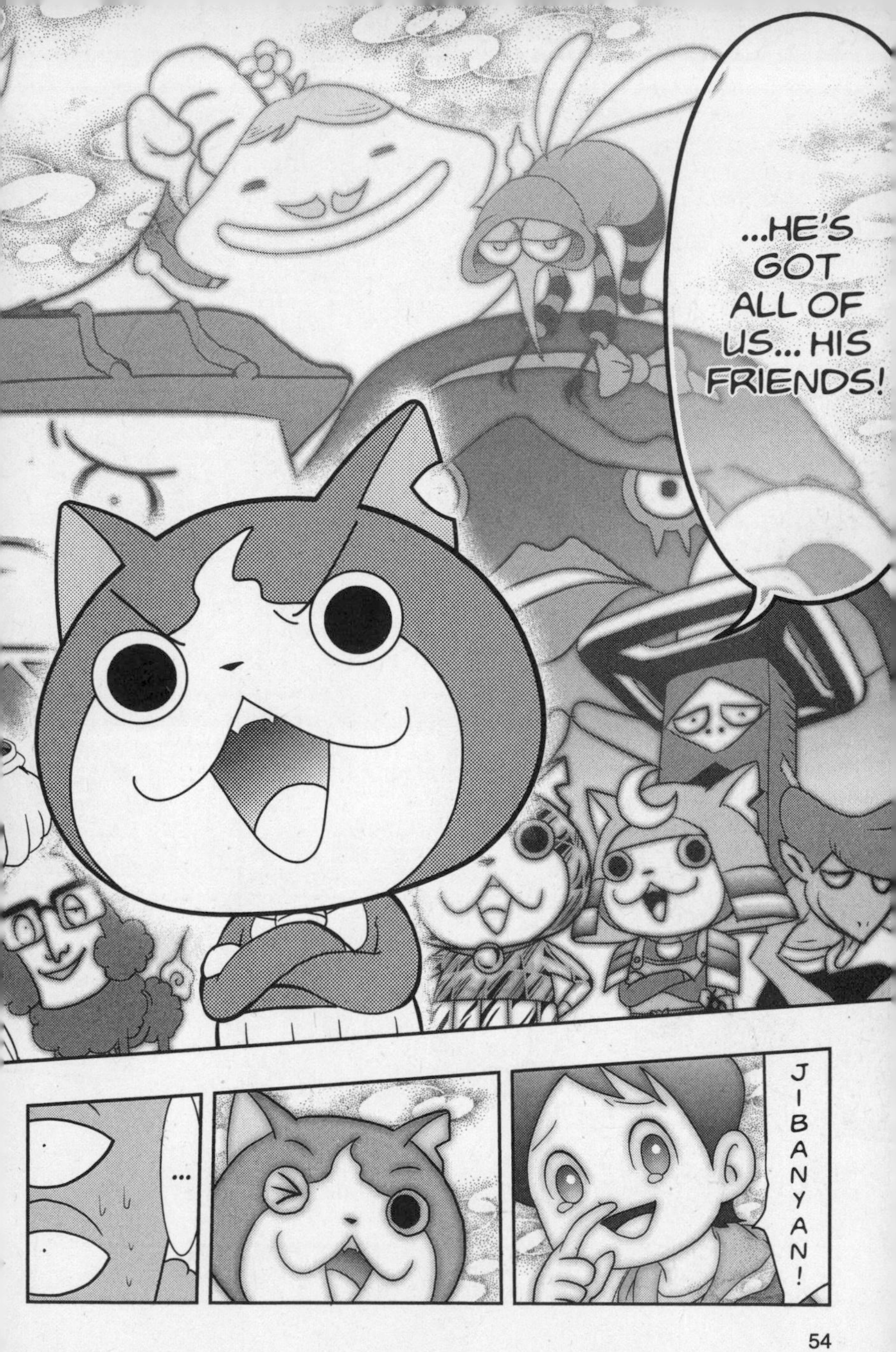
...HE'S GOT ALL OF US... HIS FRIENDS!
JIBANYAN!
...

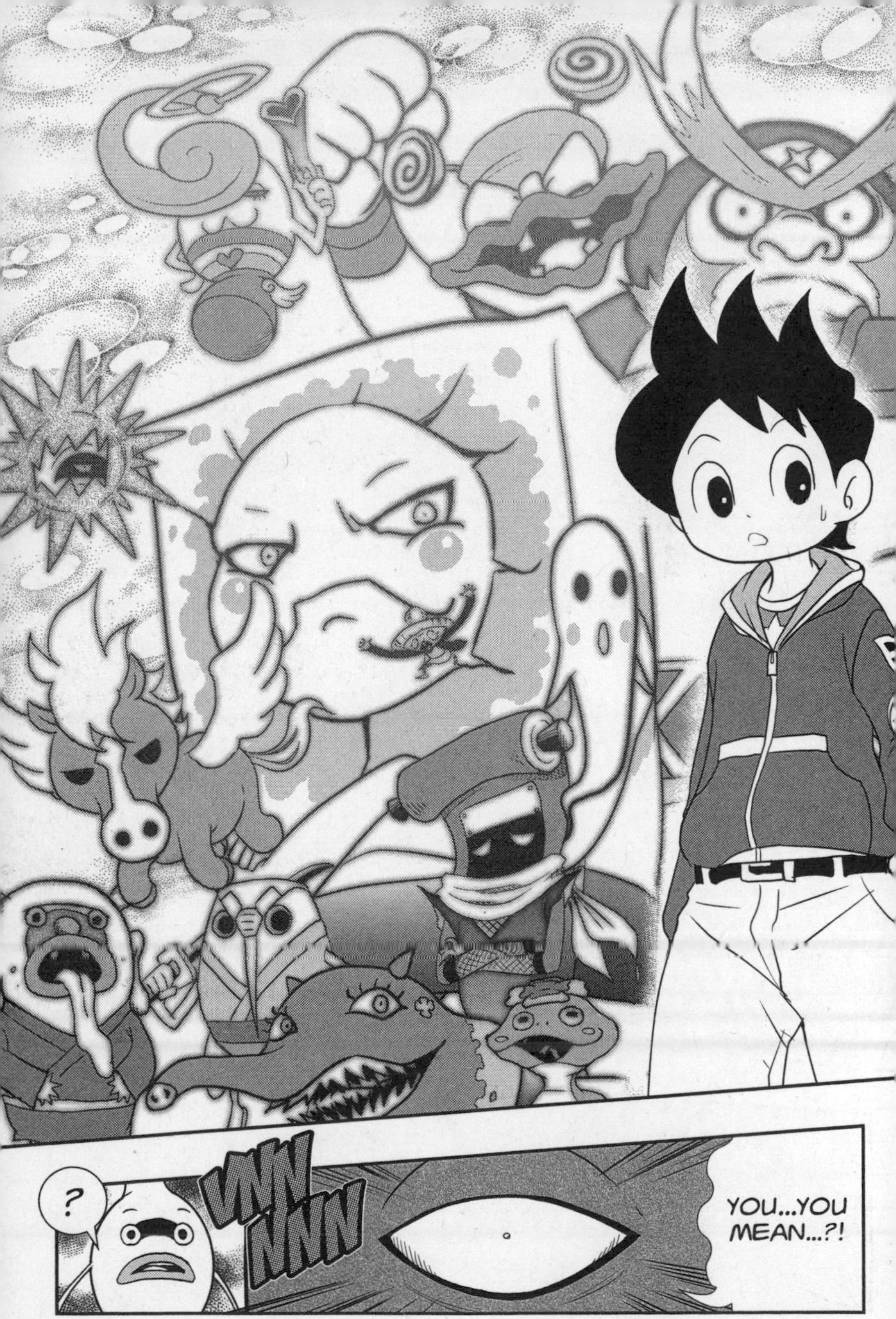
YOU...YOU MEAN...?!
VNN NNN
?

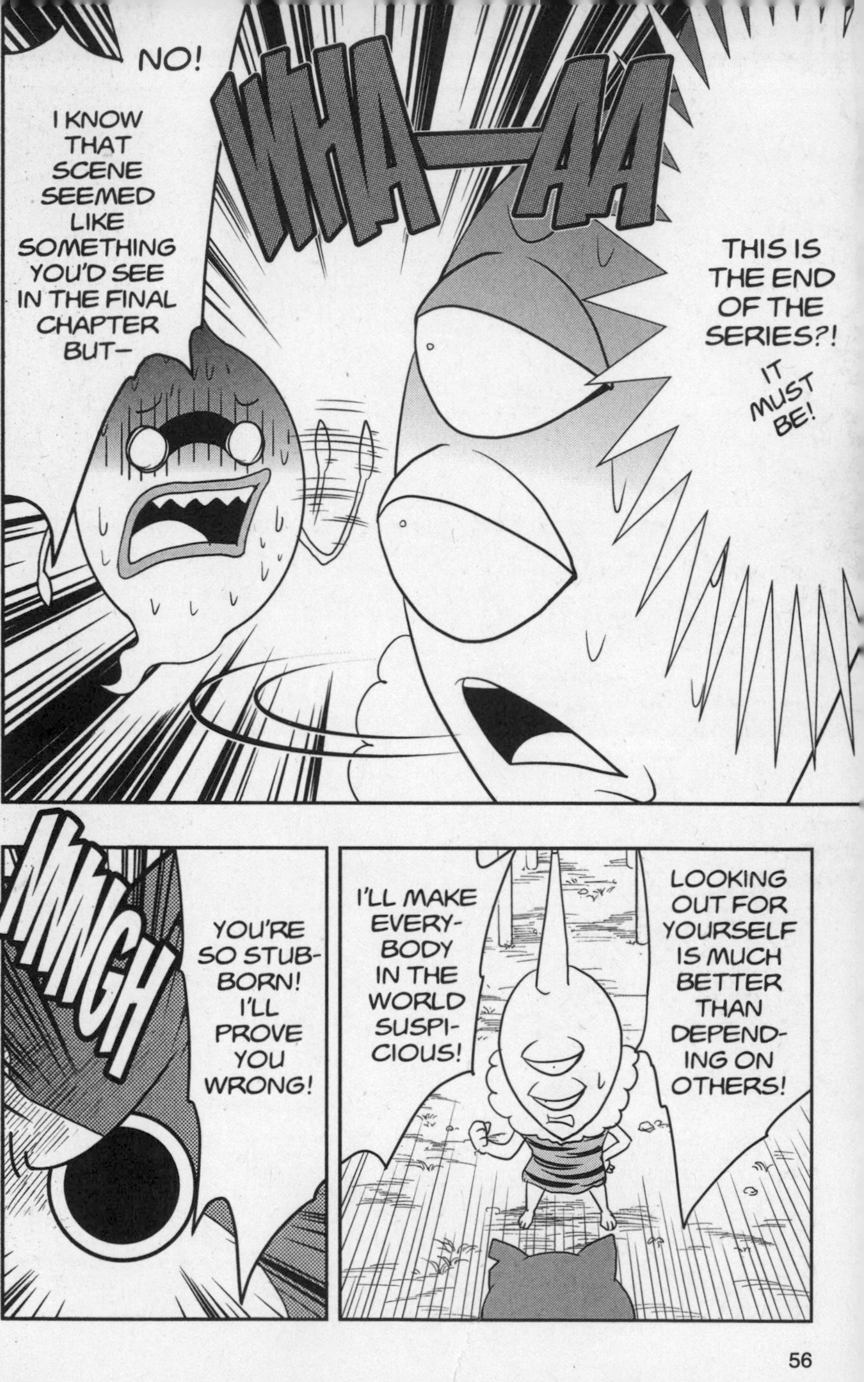
THIS IS THE END OF THE SERIES?!
IT MUST BE!
WHHA—AA
NO!
I KNOW THAT SCENE SEEMED LIKE SOMETHING YOU'D SEE IN THE FINAL CHAPTER BUT—
LOOKING OUT FOR YOURSELF IS MUCH BETTER THAN DEPEND-ING ON OTHERS!
I'LL MAKE EVERY-BODY IN THE WORLD SUSPI-CIOUS!
YOU'RE SO STUB-BORN! I'LL PROVE YOU WRONG!
MMGH

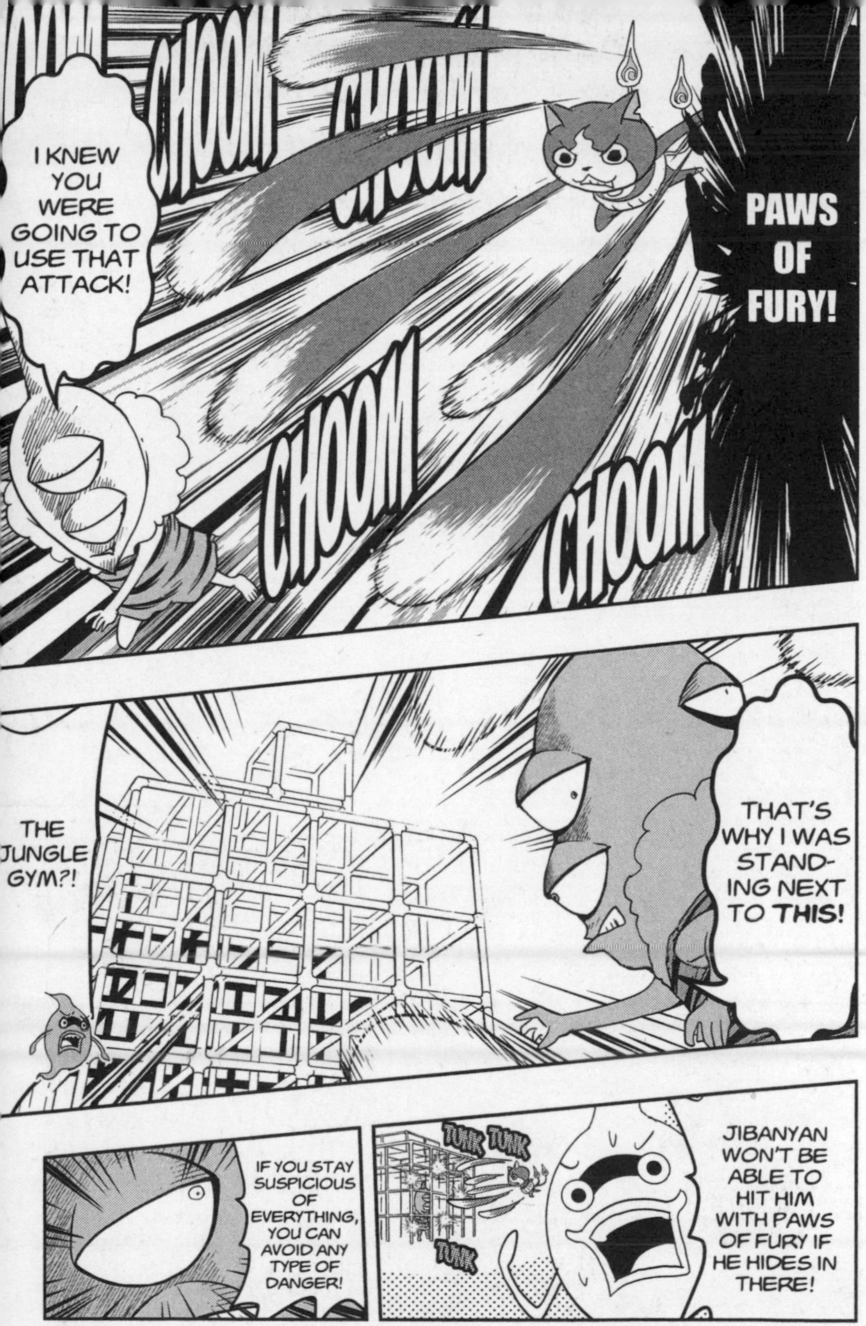
PAWS OF FURY!
CHOOM CHOOM CHOOM CHOOM CHOOM
I KNEW YOU WERE GOING TO USE THAT ATTACK!
THAT'S WHY I WAS STAND-ING NEXT TO THIS!
THE JUNGLE GYM?!
JIBANYAN WON'T BE ABLE TO HIT HIM WITH PAWS OF FURY IF HE HIDES IN THERE!
TUNK TUNK
TUNK
IF YOU STAY SUSPICIOUS OF EVERYTHING, YOU CAN AVOID ANY TYPE OF DANGER!

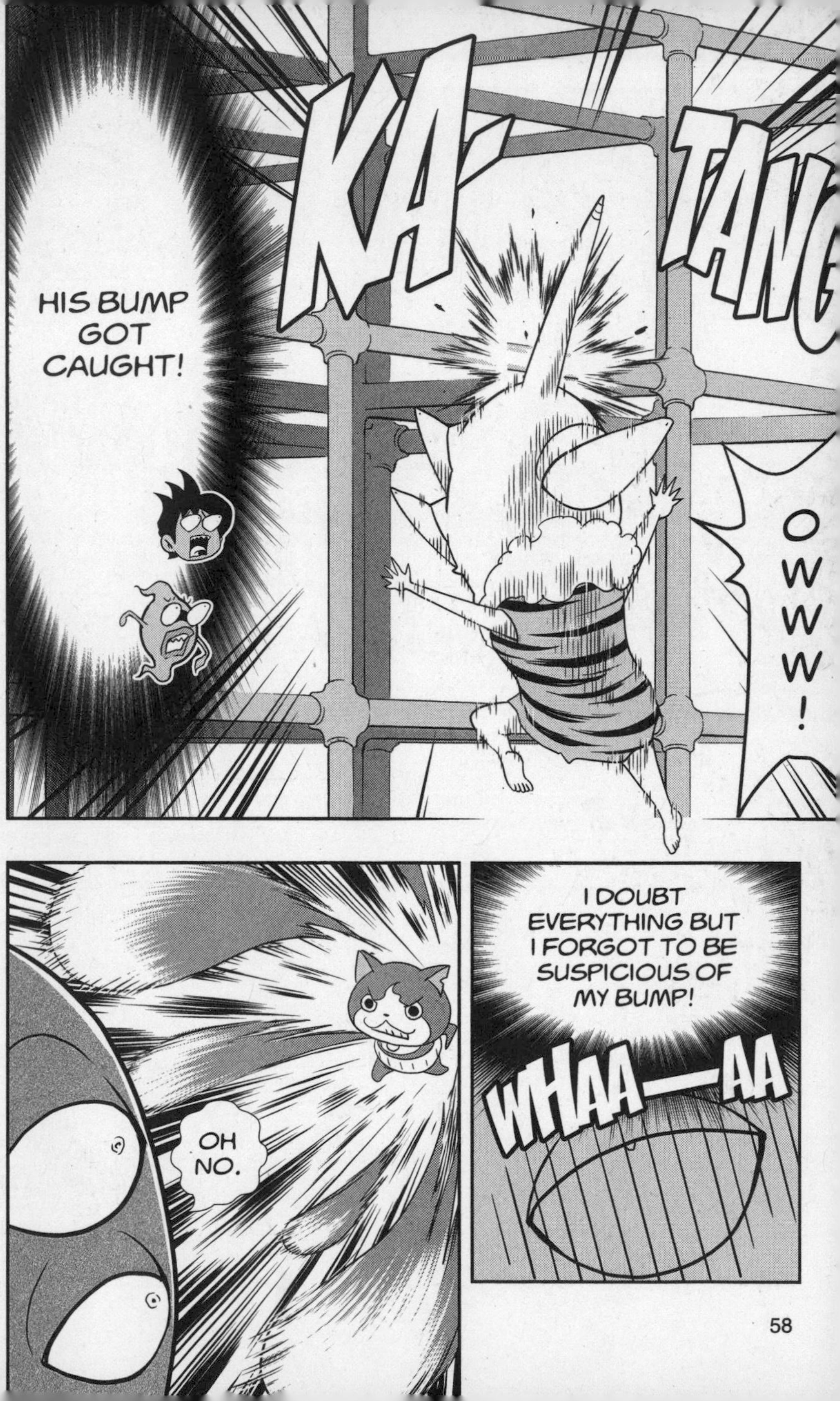
KA-TANG
OWWW!
HIS BUMP GOT CAUGHT!
I DOUBT EVERYTHING BUT I FORGOT TO BE SUSPICIOUS OF MY BUMP!
WHAA—AA
OH NO.

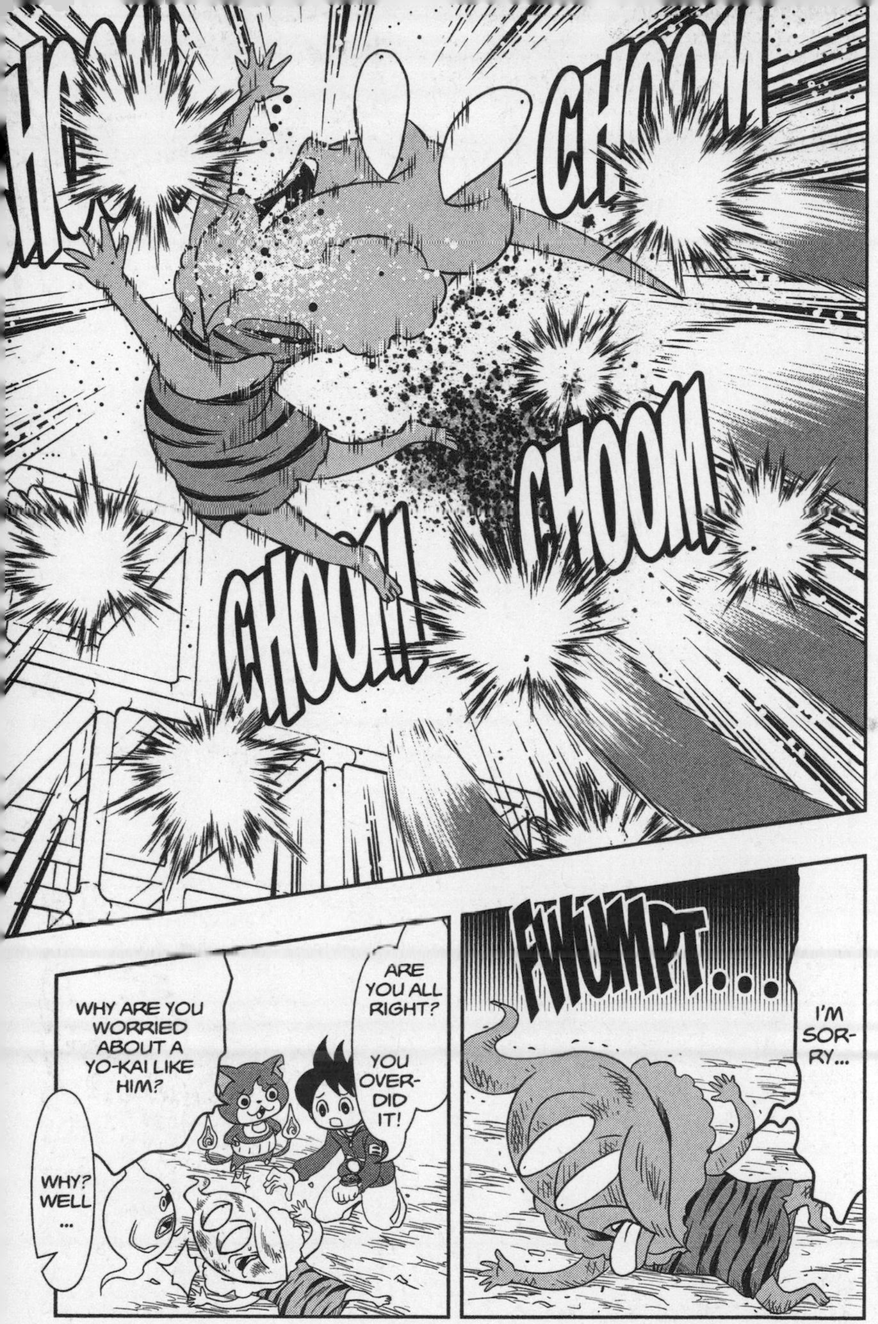
CHOOM
CHOOM
CHOOM
FWUMPT...
I'M SOR-RY...
ARE YOU ALL RIGHT?
YOU OVER-DID IT!
WHY ARE YOU WORRIED ABOUT A YO-KAI LIKE HIM?
WHY? WELL ...

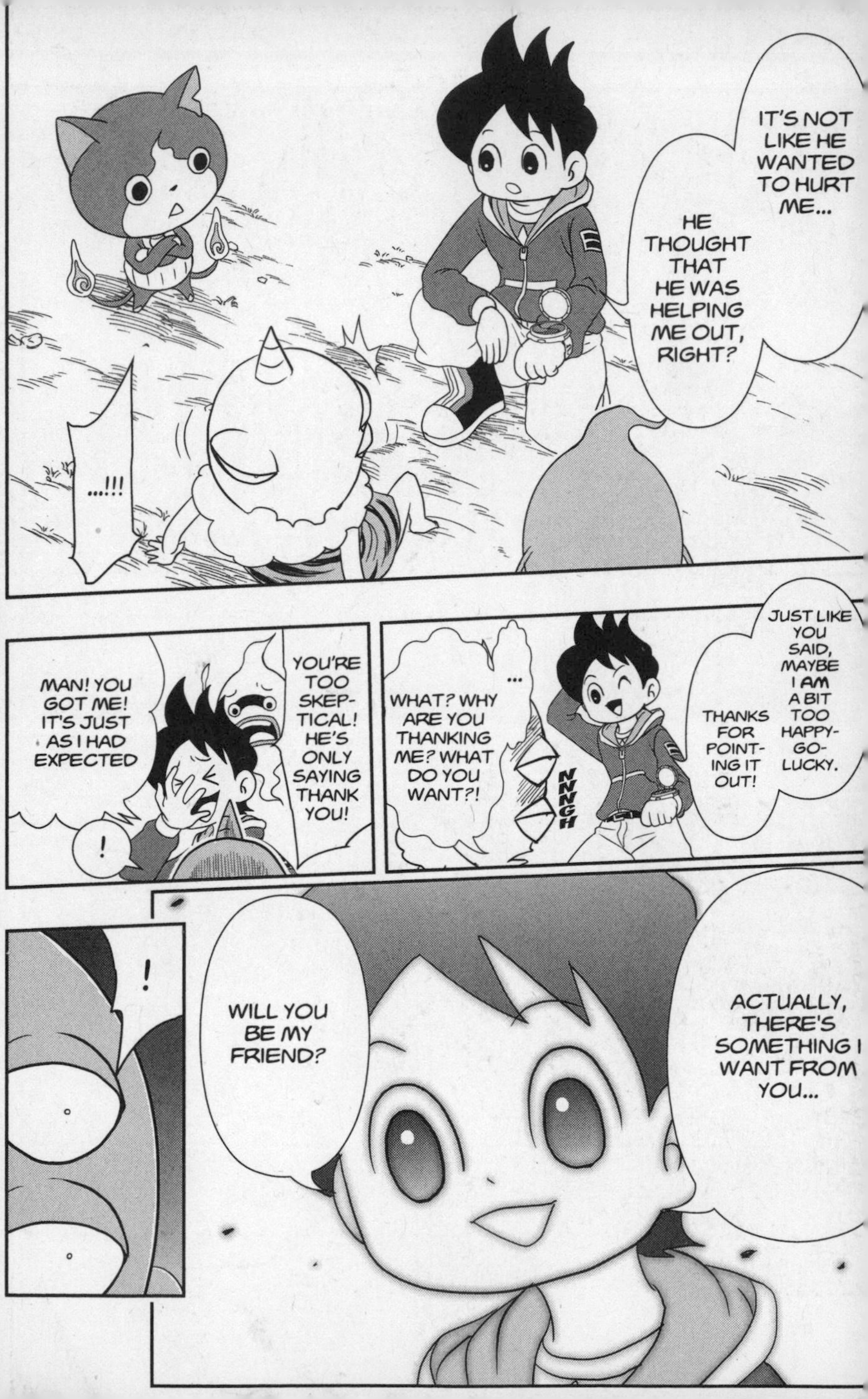
IT'S NOT LIKE HE WANTED TO HURT ME...
HE THOUGHT THAT HE WAS HELPING ME OUT, RIGHT?
...!!!
JUST LIKE YOU SAID, MAYBE I AM A BIT TOO HAPPY-GO-LUCKY.
THANKS FOR POINTING IT OUT!
...
NNNGH
WHAT? WHY ARE YOU THANKING ME? WHAT DO YOU WANT?!
YOU'RE TOO SKEPTICAL! HE'S ONLY SAYING THANK YOU!
MAN! YOU GOT ME! IT'S JUST AS I HAD EXPECTED
!
ACTUALLY, THERE'S SOMETHING I WANT FROM YOU...
WILL YOU BE MY FRIEND?
!

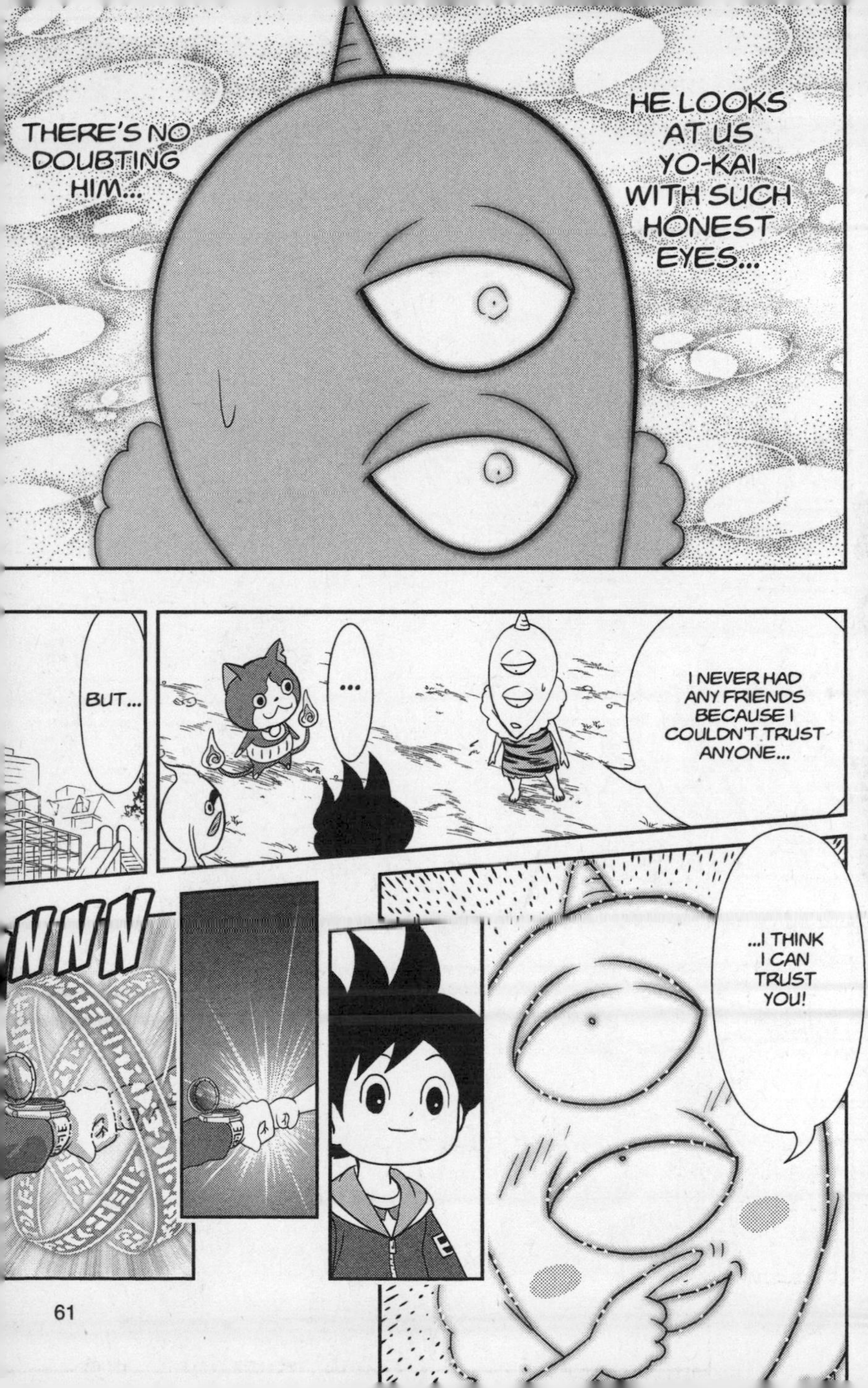
HE LOOKS AT US YO-KAI WITH SUCH HONEST EYES...
THERE'S NO DOUBTING HIM...
I NEVER HAD ANY FRIENDS BECAUSE I COULDN'T TRUST ANYONE...
...
BUT...
...I THINK I CAN TRUST YOU!
NNN

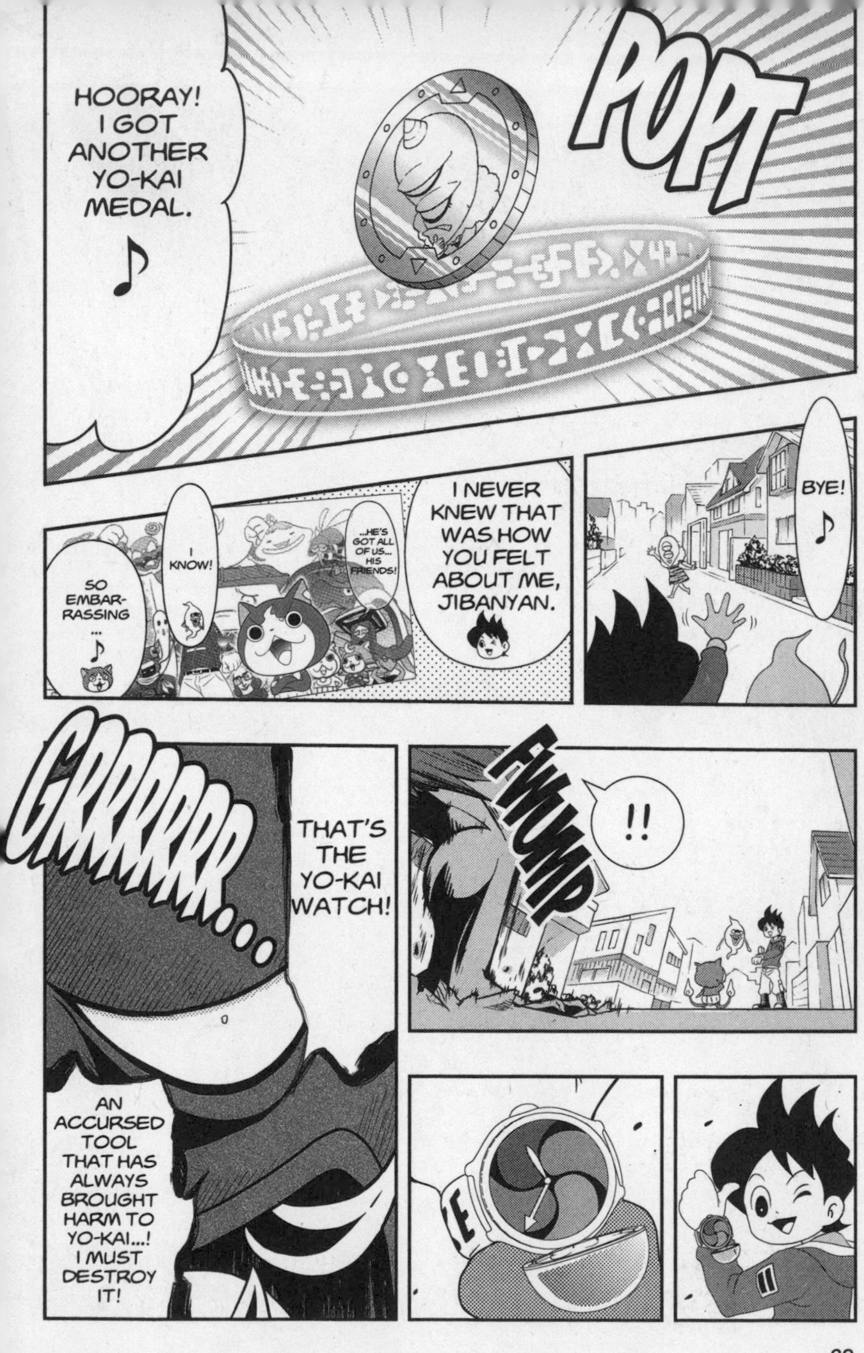
POP!
HOORAY! I GOT ANOTHER YO-KAI MEDAL. ♪
BYE! ♪
I NEVER KNEW THAT WAS HOW YOU FELT ABOUT ME, JIBANYAN.
...HE'S GOT ALL OF US... HIS FRIENDS!
I KNOW!
SO EMBAR-RASSING... ♪
FWUMP
!!
GRRRRRR...
THAT'S THE YO-KAI WATCH!
AN ACCURSED TOOL THAT HAS ALWAYS BROUGHT HARM TO YO-KAI...! I MUST DESTROY IT!

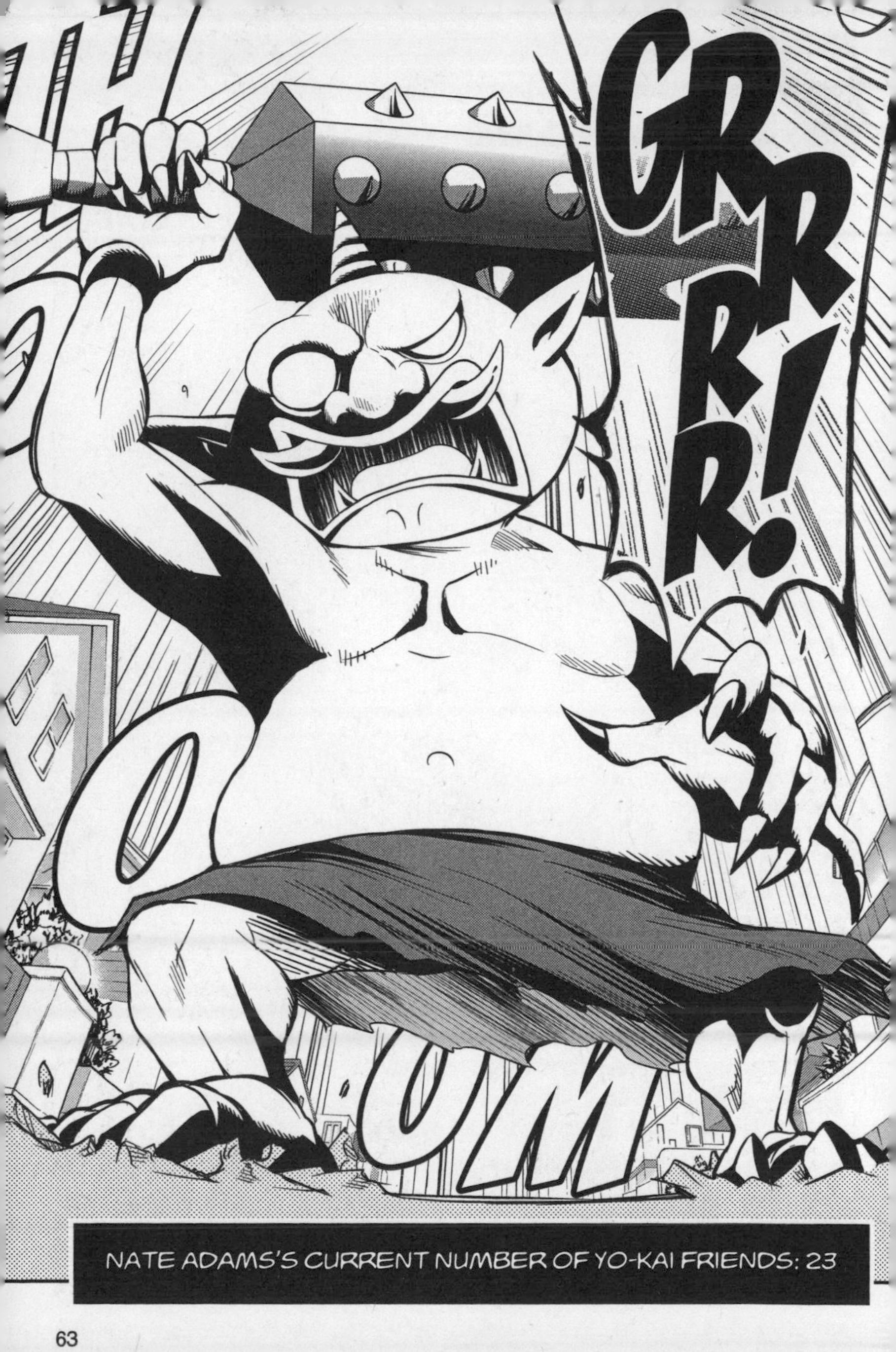
GRRRR!
NATE ADAMS'S CURRENT NUMBER OF YO-KAI FRIENDS: 23

CHAPTER 28:
PROTECT THE YO-KAI WATCH!
FEATURING YO-KAI GARGAROS

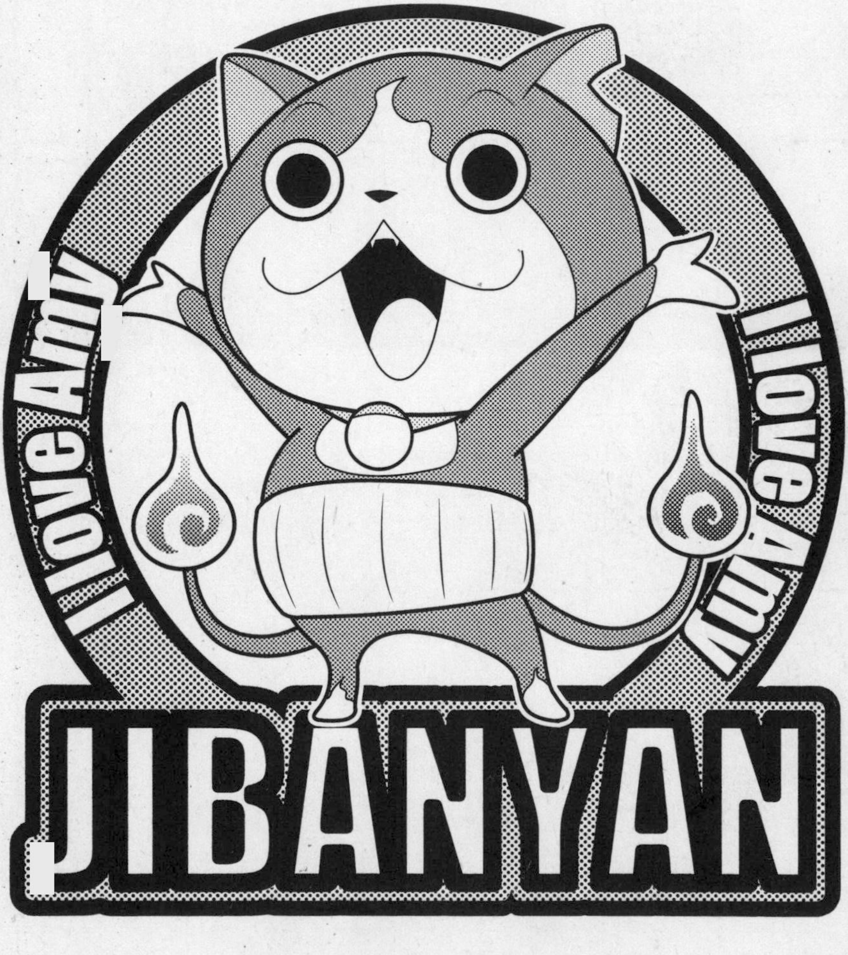
I love Amy
I love Amy
JIBANYAN

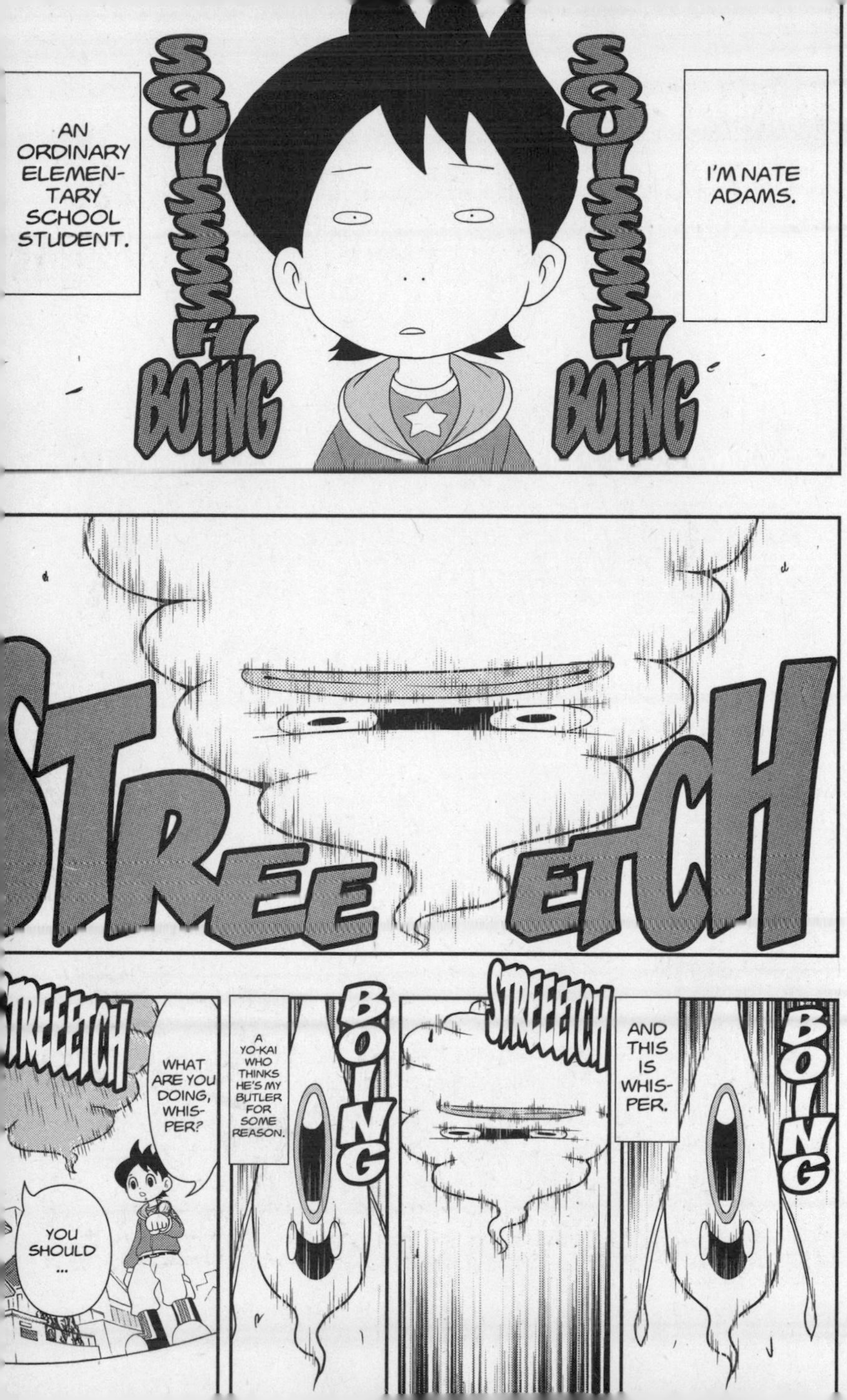
I'M NATE ADAMS.
SQUISSH BOING
AN ORDINARY ELEMENTARY SCHOOL STUDENT.
SQUISSH BOING
STREE ETCH
BOING
AND THIS IS WHISPER.
STREEETCH
BOING
A YO-KAI WHO THINKS HE'S MY BUTLER FOR SOME REASON.
STREEETCH
WHAT ARE YOU DOING, WHISPER?
YOU SHOULD ...

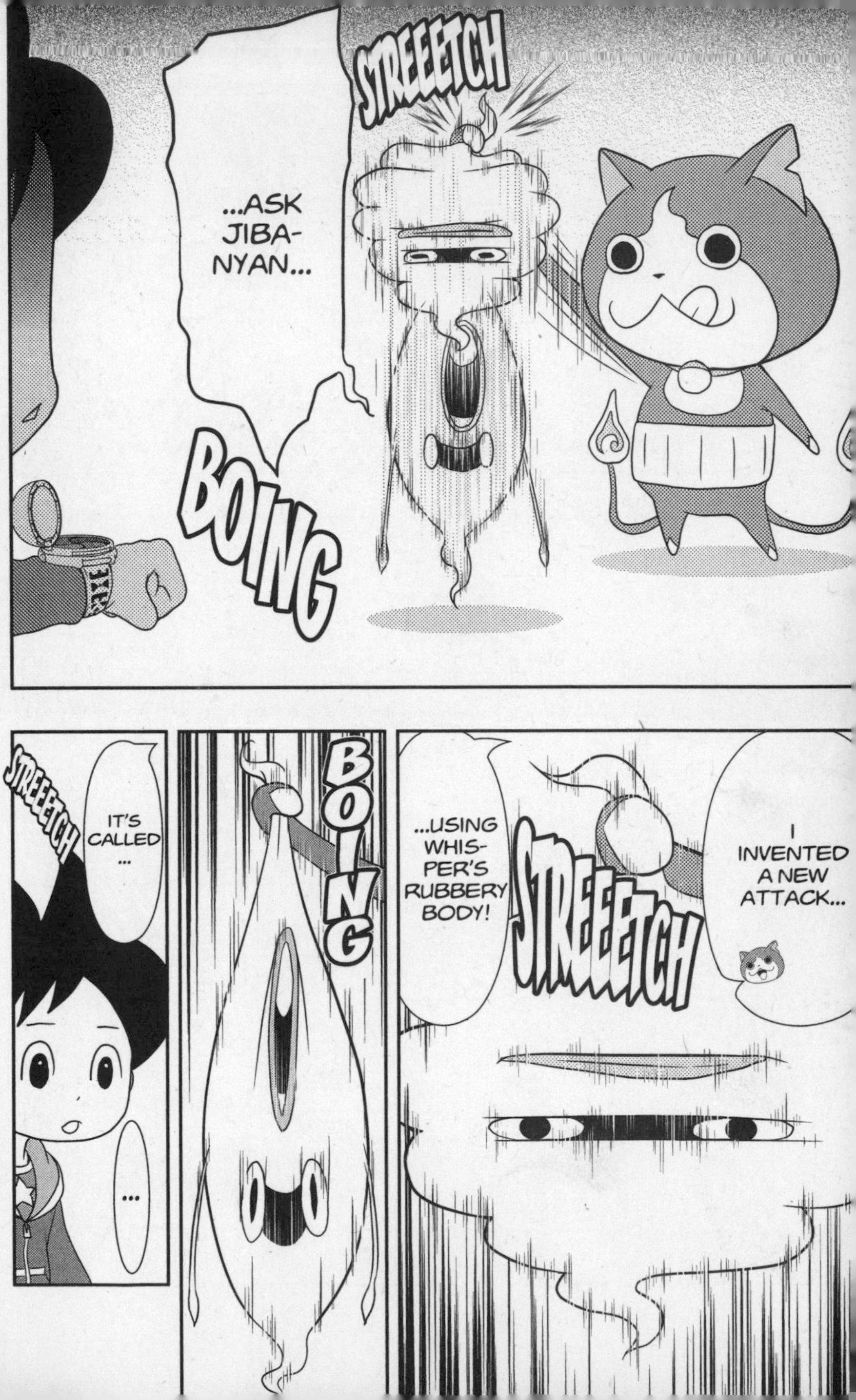
STREEETCH
...ASK JIBA-NYAN...
BOING
I INVENTED A NEW ATTACK...
STREEETCH
...USING WHISPER'S RUBBERY BODY!
BOING
STREEETCH
IT'S CALLED ...
...

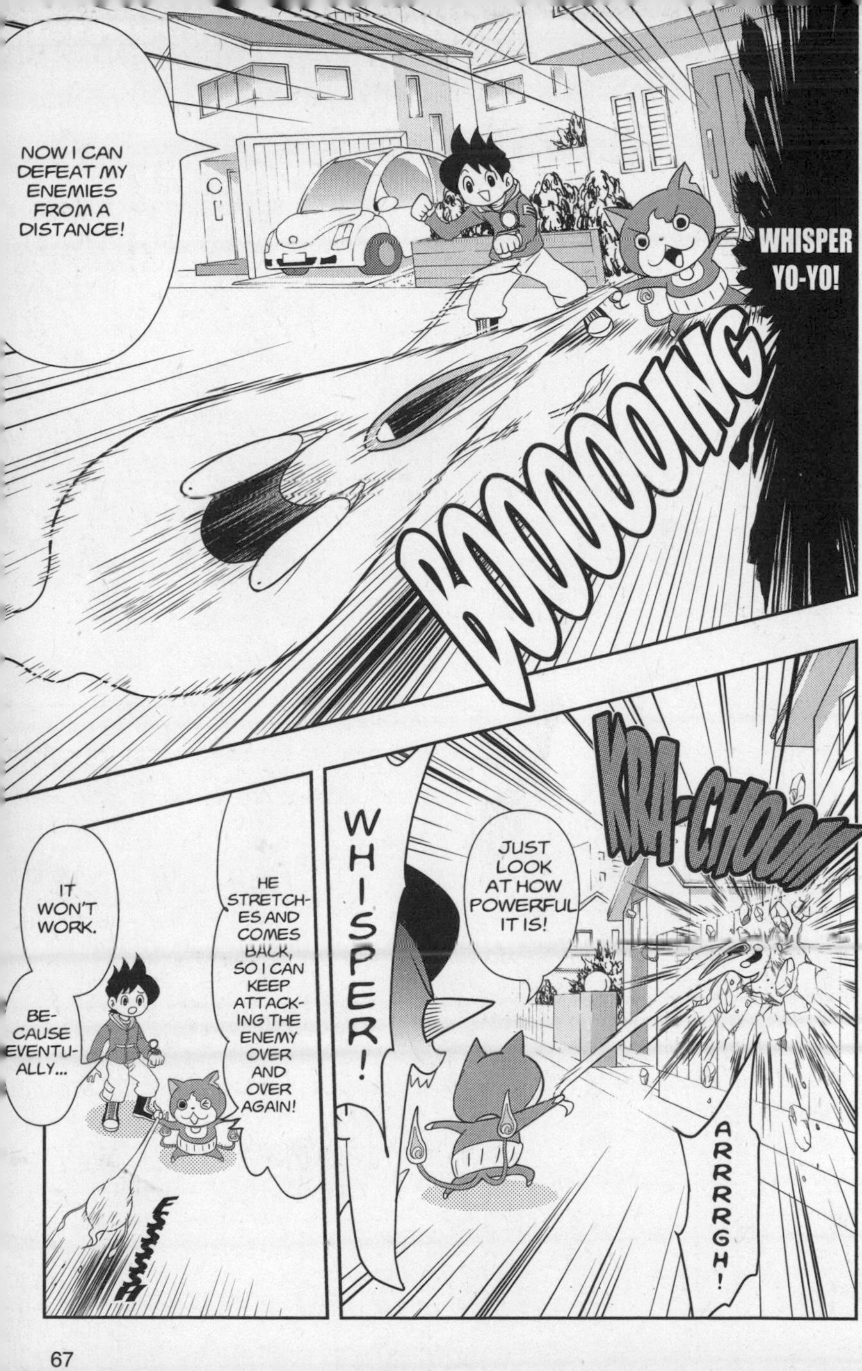
WHISPER YO-YO!
BOOOOOING
NOW I CAN DEFEAT MY ENEMIES FROM A DISTANCE!
KRA-CHOOM
ARRRRGH!
JUST LOOK AT HOW POWERFUL IT IS!
WHISPER!
HE STRETCH-ES AND COMES BACK, SO I CAN KEEP ATTACK-ING THE ENEMY OVER AND OVER AGAIN!
IT WON'T WORK.
BE-CAUSE EVENTU-ALLY...

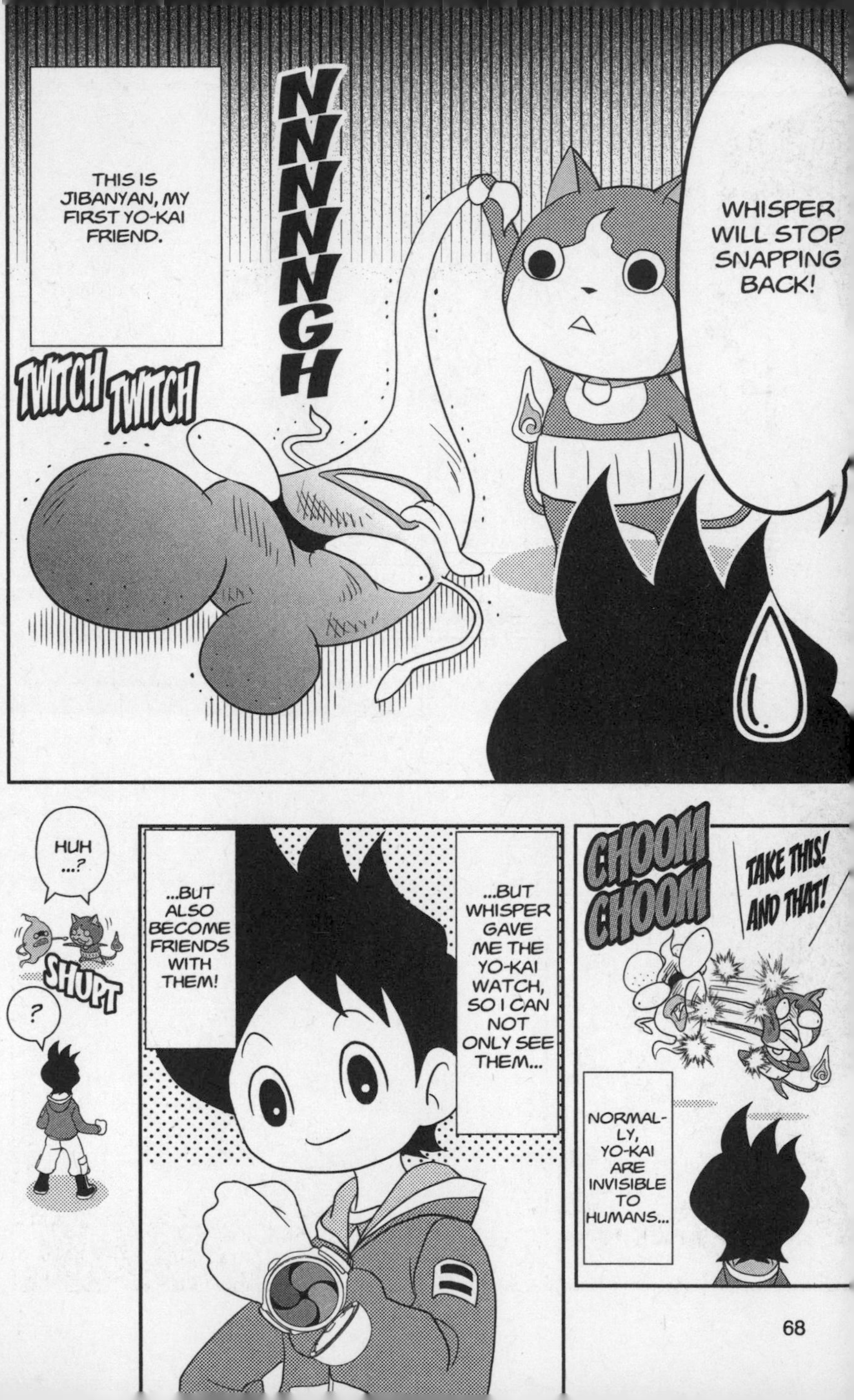
WHISPER WILL STOP SNAPPING BACK!
NNNNNGH
THIS IS JIBANYAN, MY FIRST YO-KAI FRIEND.
TWITCH TWITCH
CHOOM CHOOM
TAKE THIS! AND THAT!
NORMALLY, YO-KAI ARE INVISIBLE TO HUMANS...
...BUT WHISPER GAVE ME THE YO-KAI WATCH, SO I CAN NOT ONLY SEE THEM...
...BUT ALSO BECOME FRIENDS WITH THEM!
HUH ...?
SHUPT
?

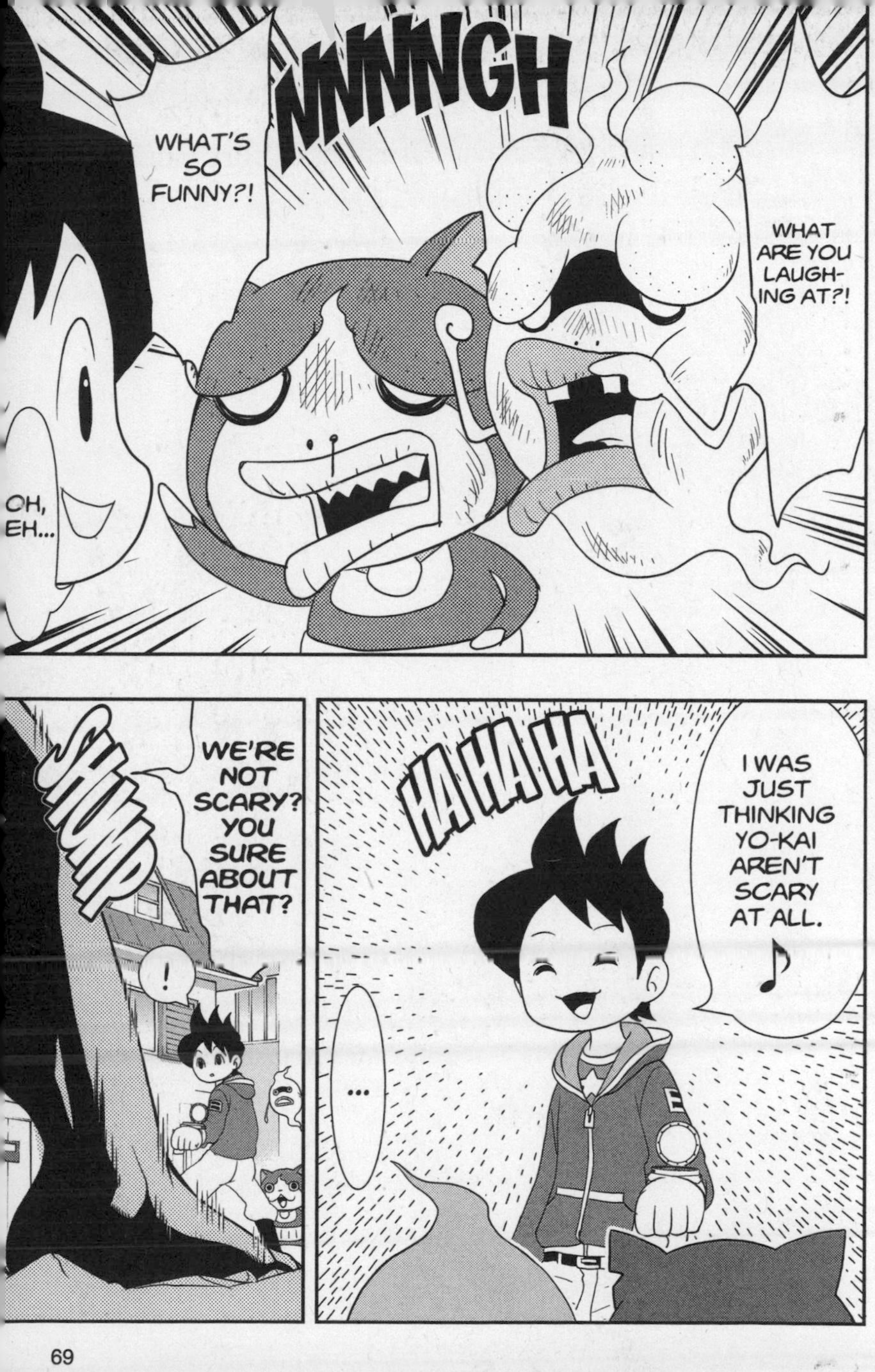
NNNNGH
WHAT ARE YOU LAUGH-ING AT?!
WHAT'S SO FUNNY?!
OH, EH...
HA HA HA HA
I WAS JUST THINKING YO-KAI AREN'T SCARY AT ALL. ♪
...
SHUMP
WE'RE NOT SCARY? YOU SURE ABOUT THAT?
!

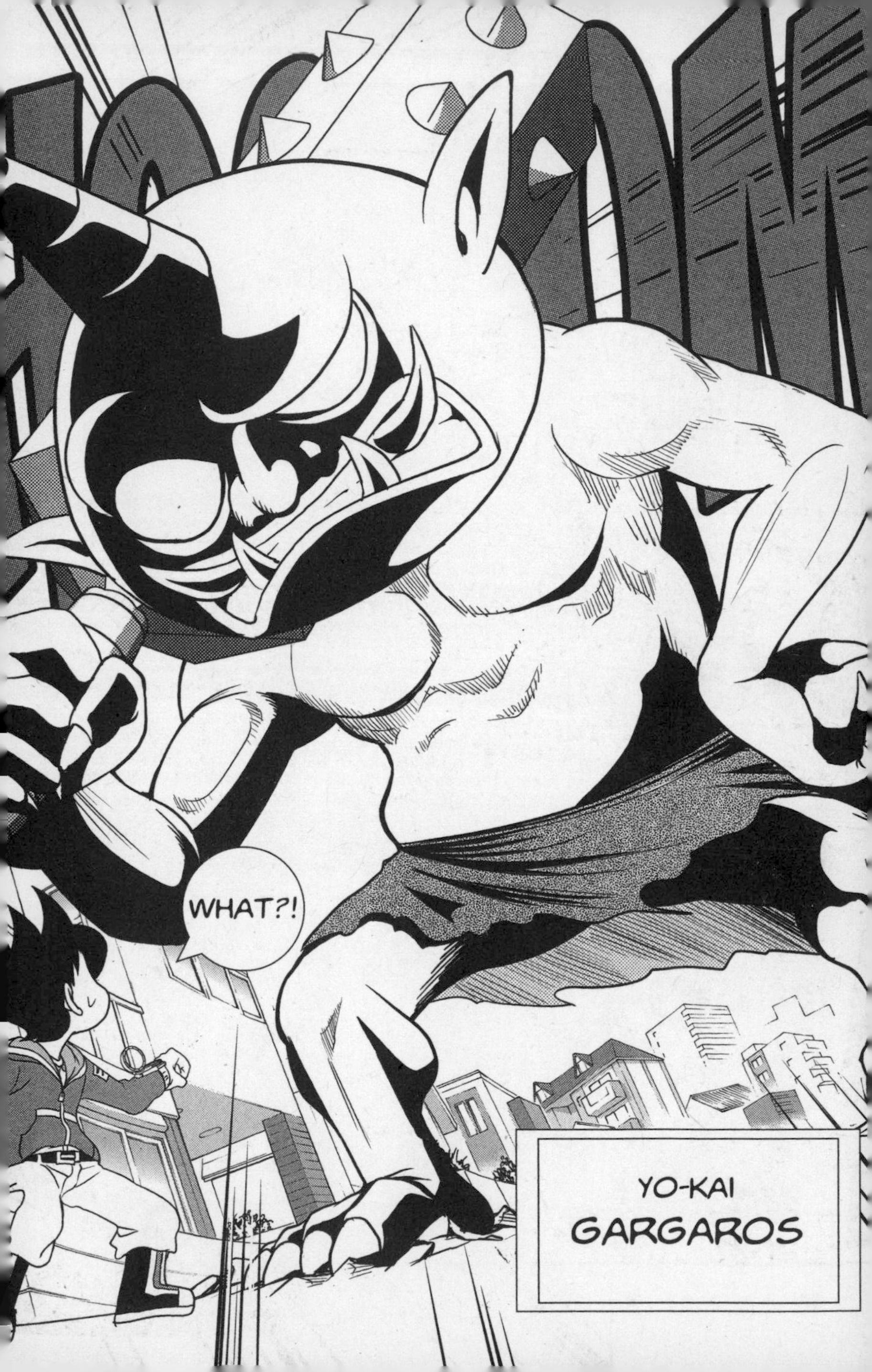
WHAT?!
YO-KAI GARGAROS

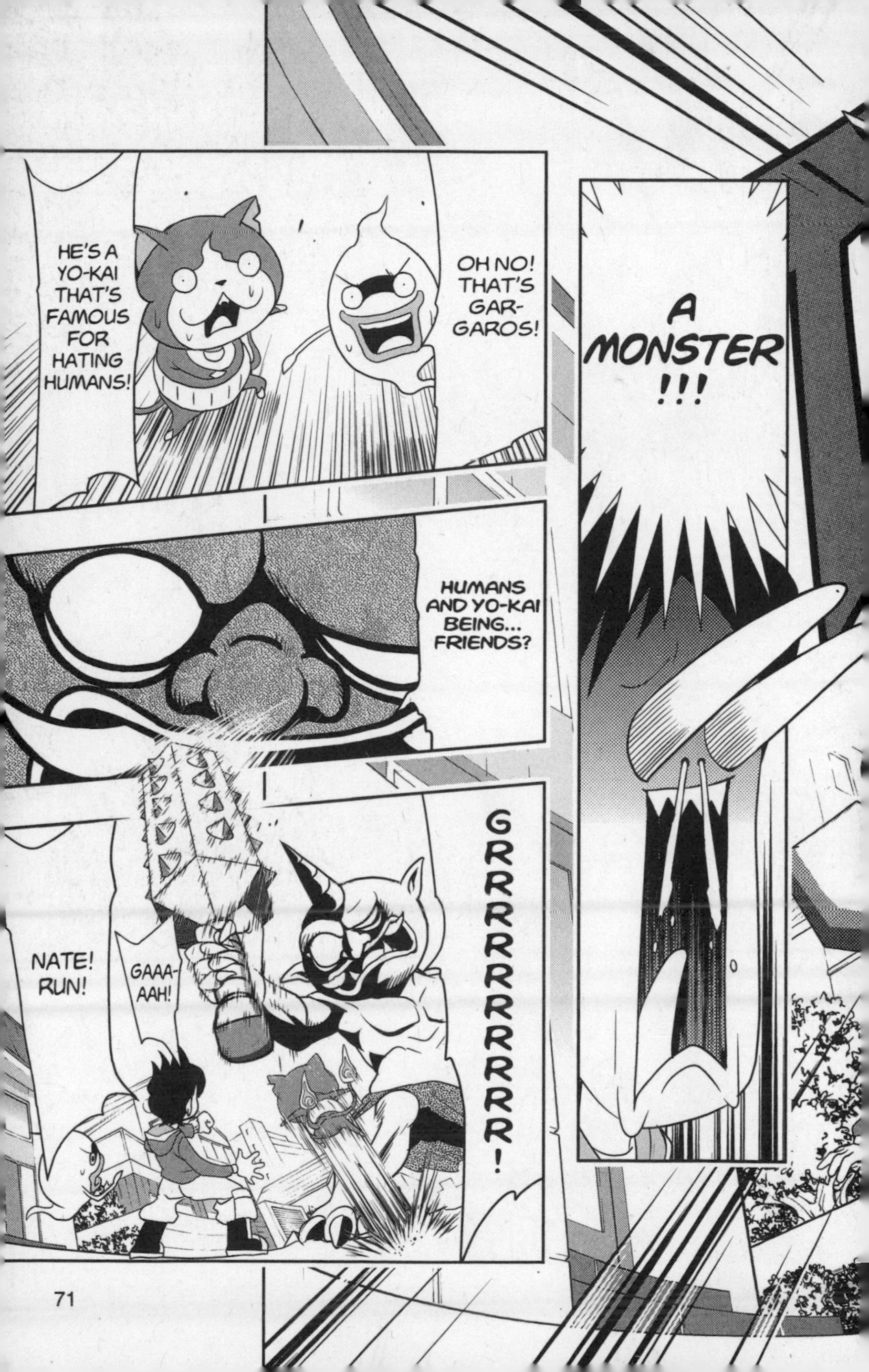
A MONSTER !!!
OH NO! THAT'S GAR-GAROS!
HE'S A YO-KAI THAT'S FAMOUS FOR HATING HUMANS!
HUMANS AND YO-KAI BEING... FRIENDS?
GRRRRRRRRRR!
GAAA-AAH!
NATE! RUN!

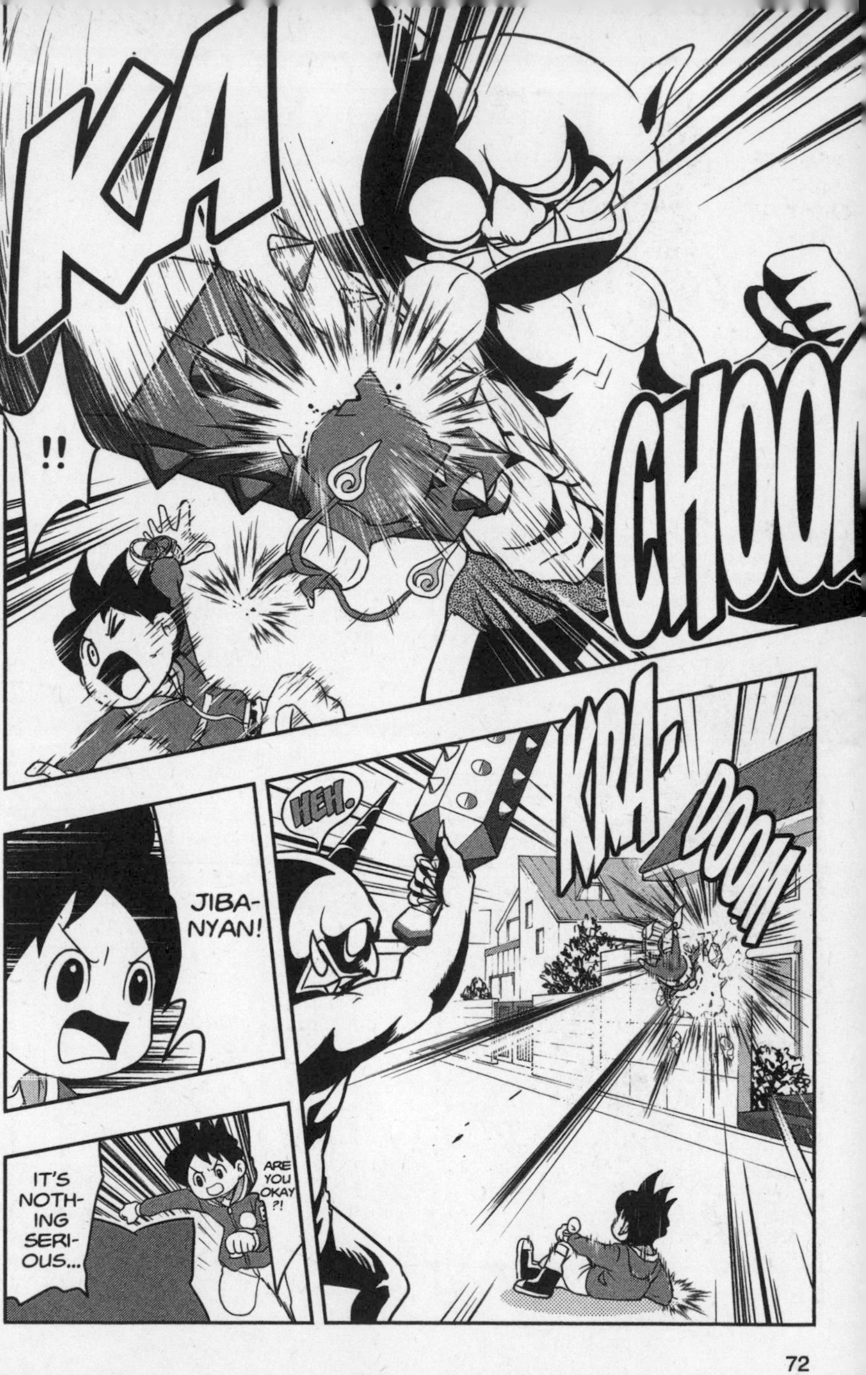
KA-
CHOOO
!!
HEH.
KRA-DOOM
JIBA-NYAN!
ARE YOU OKAY?!
IT'S NOTHING SERIOUS...

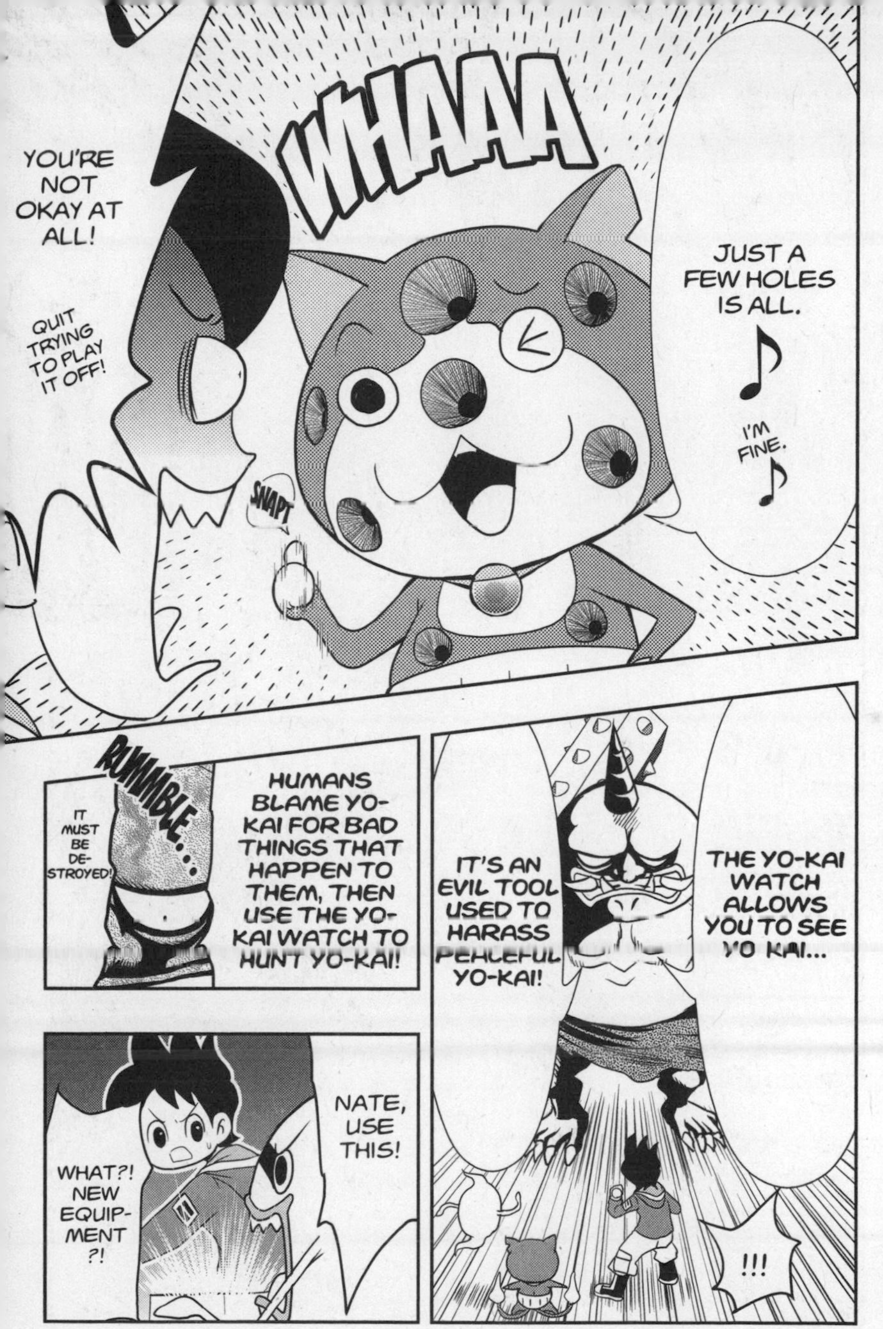
JUST A FEW HOLES IS ALL. ♪
I'M FINE. ♪
WHAAA
YOU'RE NOT OKAY AT ALL!
QUIT TRYING TO PLAY IT OFF!
SNAPT
THE YO-KAI WATCH ALLOWS YOU TO SEE YO-KAI...
IT'S AN EVIL TOOL USED TO HARASS PEACEFUL YO-KAI!
!!!
HUMANS BLAME YO-KAI FOR BAD THINGS THAT HAPPEN TO THEM, THEN USE THE YO-KAI WATCH TO HUNT YO-KAI!
IT MUST BE DE-STROYED!
RUMMMBLE...
NATE, USE THIS!
WHAT?! NEW EQUIP-MENT?!

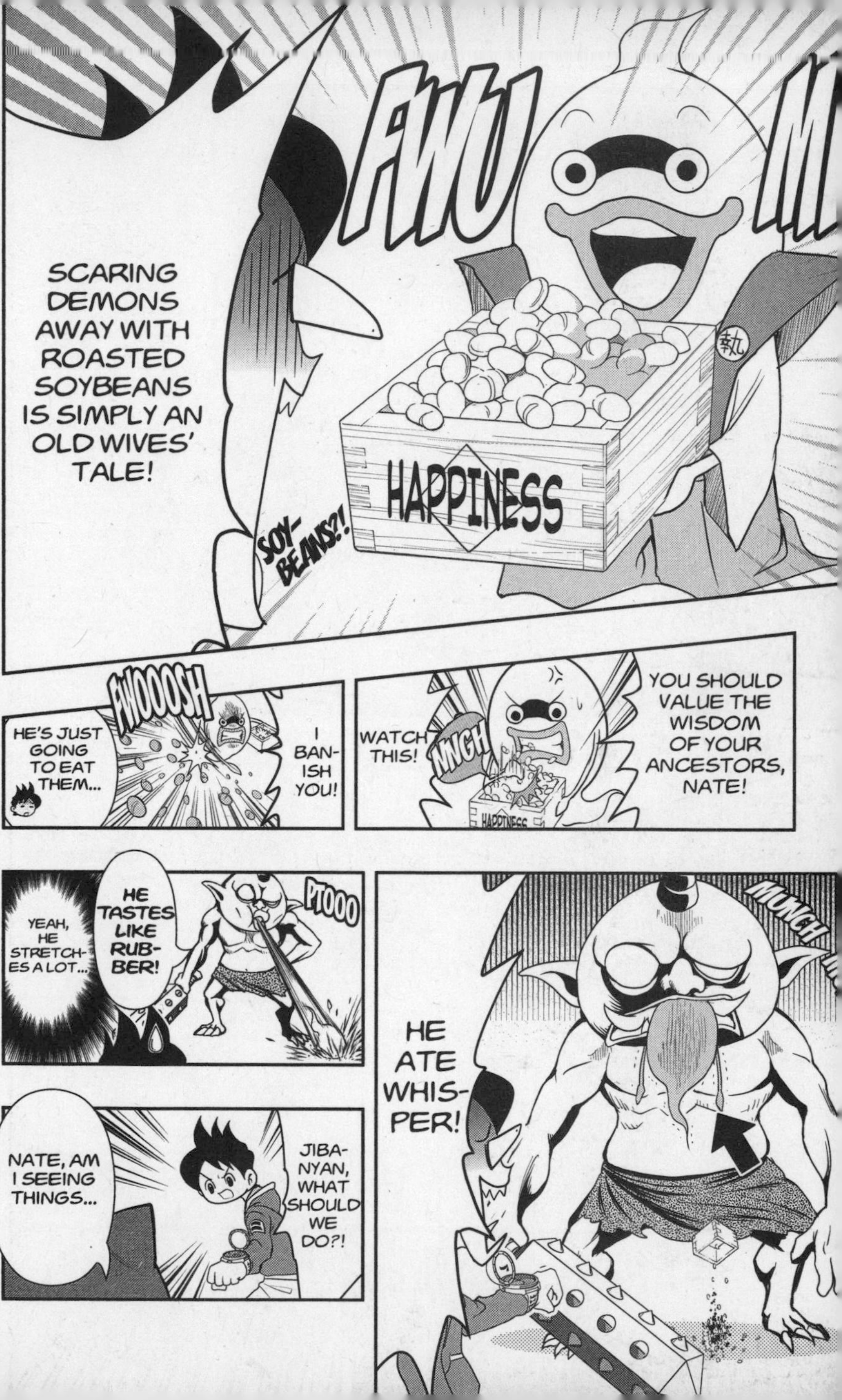
FWUMM
SCARING DEMONS AWAY WITH ROASTED SOYBEANS IS SIMPLY AN OLD WIVES' TALE!
HAPPINESS
SOY-BEANS?!
YOU SHOULD VALUE THE WISDOM OF YOUR ANCESTORS, NATE!
MNGH
WATCH THIS!
HAPPINESS
I BAN-ISH YOU!
FWOOOSH
HE'S JUST GOING TO EAT THEM...
MUNCH
HE ATE WHIS-PER!
PTOOO
HE TASTES LIKE RUB-BER!
YEAH, HE STRETCH-ES A LOT...
JIBA-NYAN, WHAT SHOULD WE DO?!
NATE, AM I SEEING THINGS...

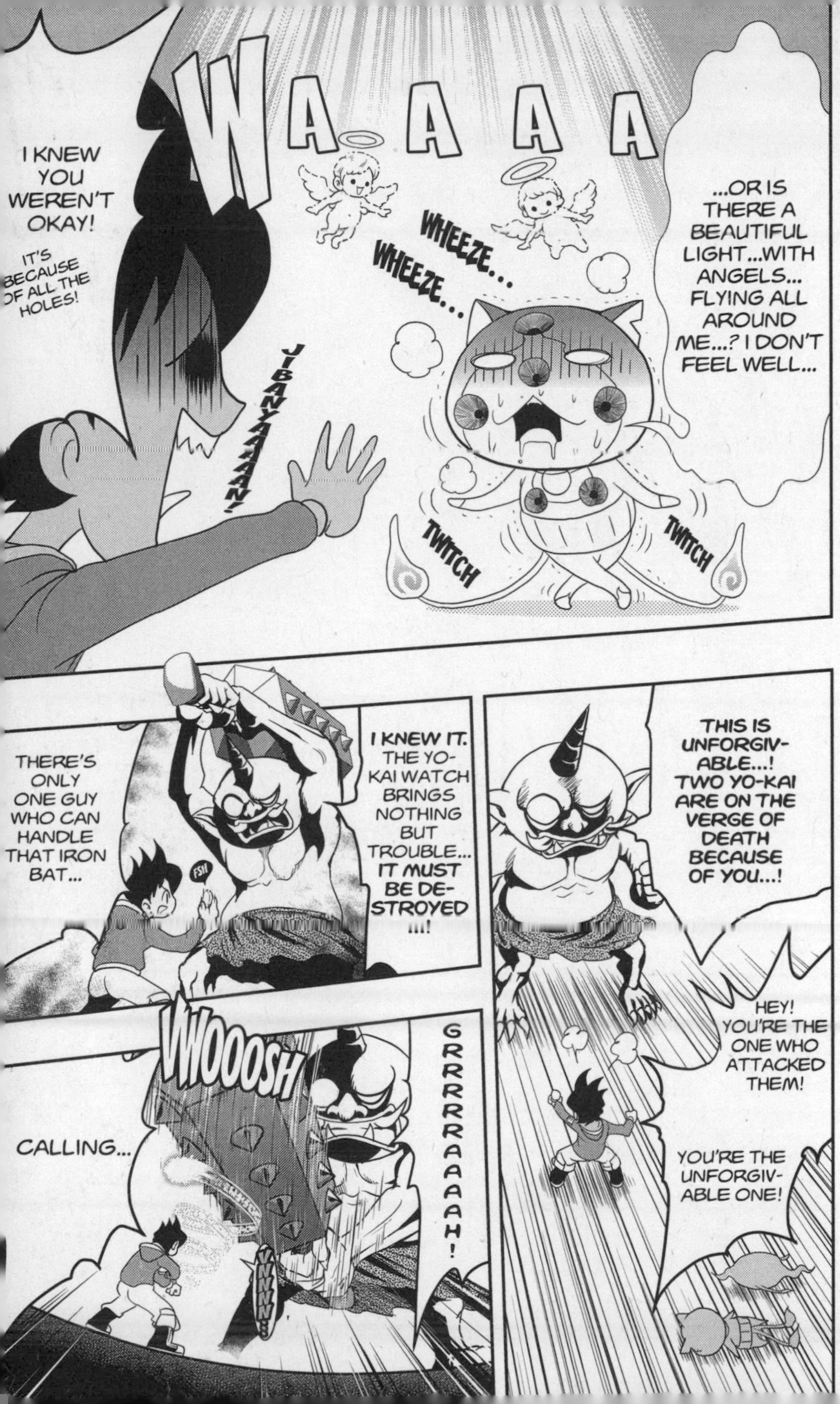
...OR IS THERE A BEAUTIFUL LIGHT...WITH ANGELS... FLYING ALL AROUND ME...? I DON'T FEEL WELL...
WAAAAA
WHEEZE... WHEEZE...
I KNEW YOU WEREN'T OKAY!
IT'S BECAUSE OF ALL THE HOLES!
JIBANYAAAAAAN!
TWITCH
TWITCH
THIS IS UNFORGIV-ABLE...! TWO YO-KAI ARE ON THE VERGE OF DEATH BECAUSE OF YOU...!
HEY! YOU'RE THE ONE WHO ATTACKED THEM!
YOU'RE THE UNFORGIV-ABLE ONE!
I KNEW IT. THE YO-KAI WATCH BRINGS NOTHING BUT TROUBLE... IT MUST BE DE-STROYED!!!
THERE'S ONLY ONE GUY WHO CAN HANDLE THAT IRON BAT...
GRRRRAAAAAH!
VWOOOSH
CALLING...
VNNNN

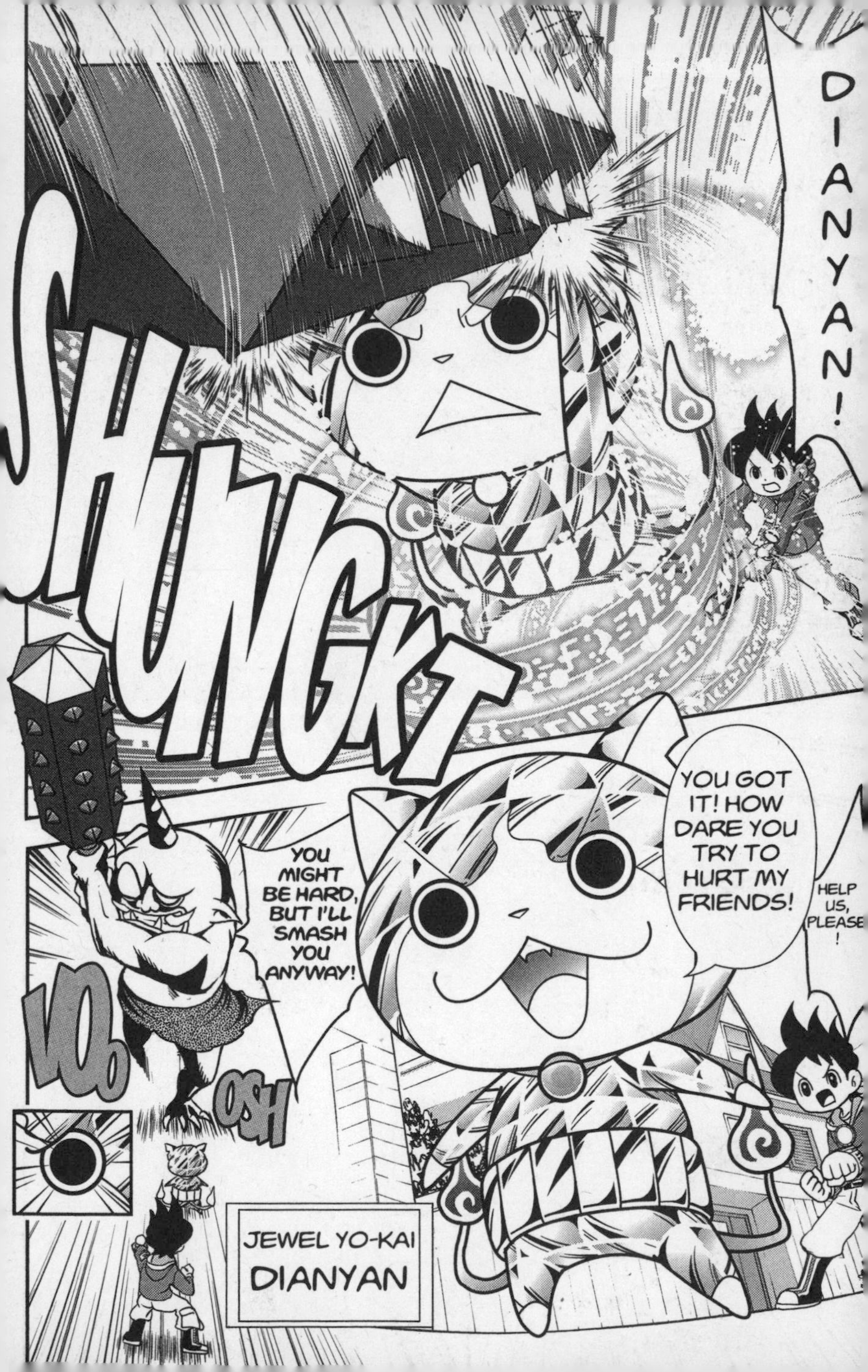
DIANYAN!
SHUNGKT
HELP US, PLEASE!
YOU GOT IT! HOW DARE YOU TRY TO HURT MY FRIENDS!
JEWEL YO-KAI DIANYAN
YOU MIGHT BE HARD, BUT I'LL SMASH YOU ANYWAY!
VOOOSH

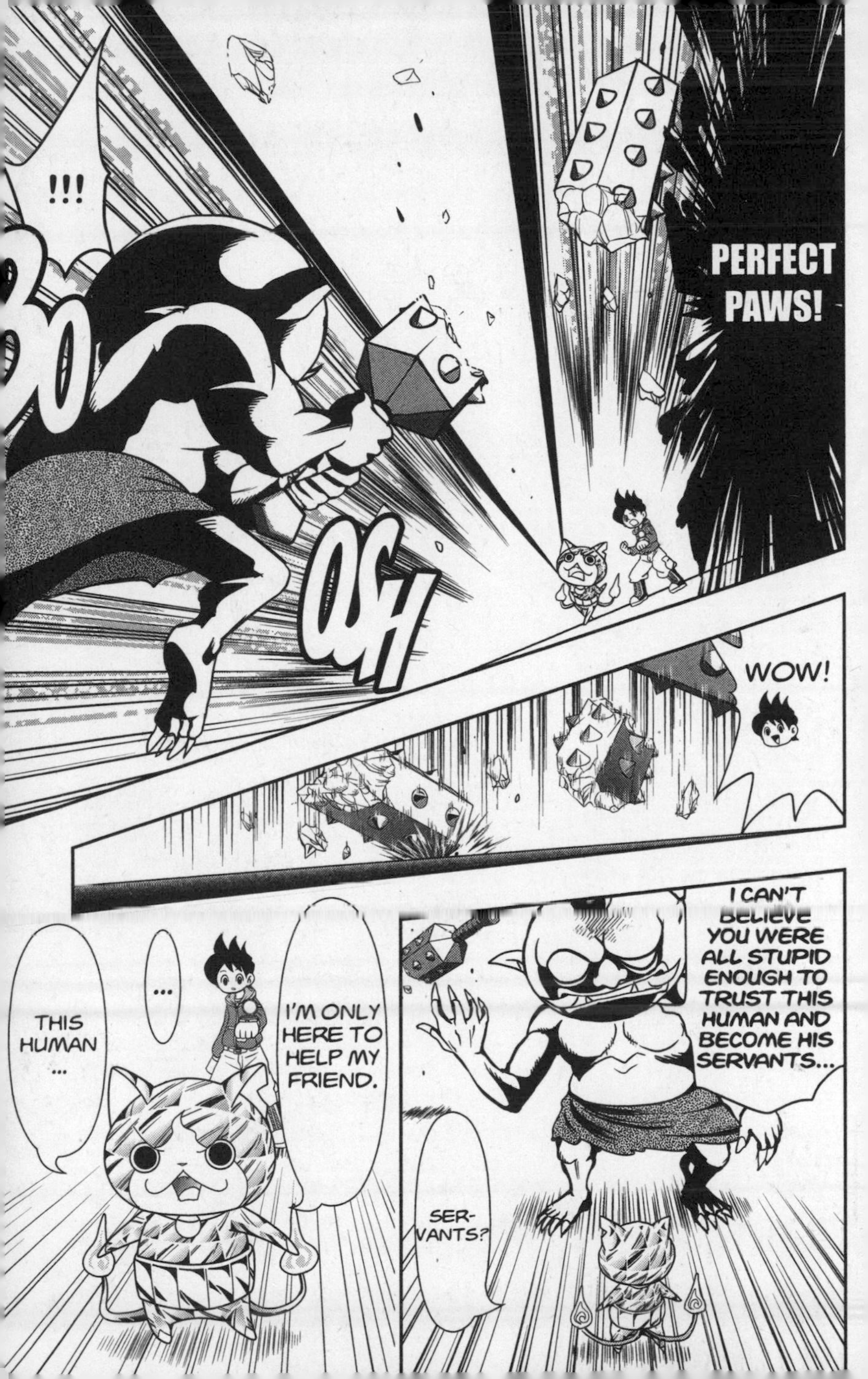
PERFECT PAWS!
!!!
BOOSH
WOW!
I CAN'T BELIEVE YOU WERE ALL STUPID ENOUGH TO TRUST THIS HUMAN AND BECOME HIS SERVANTS...
SER-VANTS?
I'M ONLY HERE TO HELP MY FRIEND.
...
THIS HUMAN ...

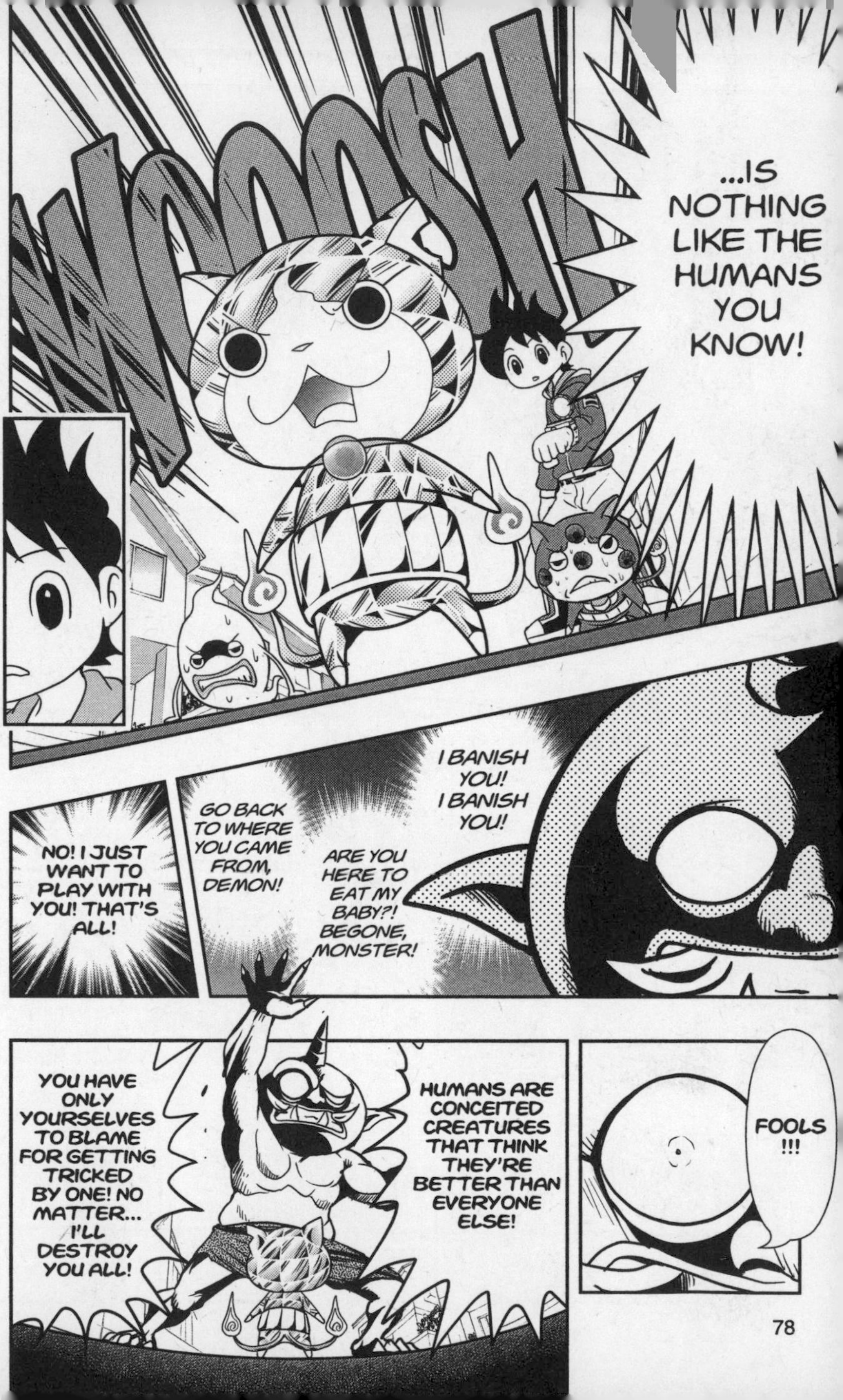
...IS NOTHING LIKE THE HUMANS YOU KNOW!
WHOOOSH
I BANISH YOU! I BANISH YOU!
ARE YOU HERE TO EAT MY BABY?! BEGONE, MONSTER!
GO BACK TO WHERE YOU CAME FROM, DEMON!
NO! I JUST WANT TO PLAY WITH YOU! THAT'S ALL!
FOOLS !!!
HUMANS ARE CONCEITED CREATURES THAT THINK THEY'RE BETTER THAN EVERYONE ELSE!
YOU HAVE ONLY YOURSELVES TO BLAME FOR GETTING TRICKED BY ONE! NO MATTER... I'LL DESTROY YOU ALL!

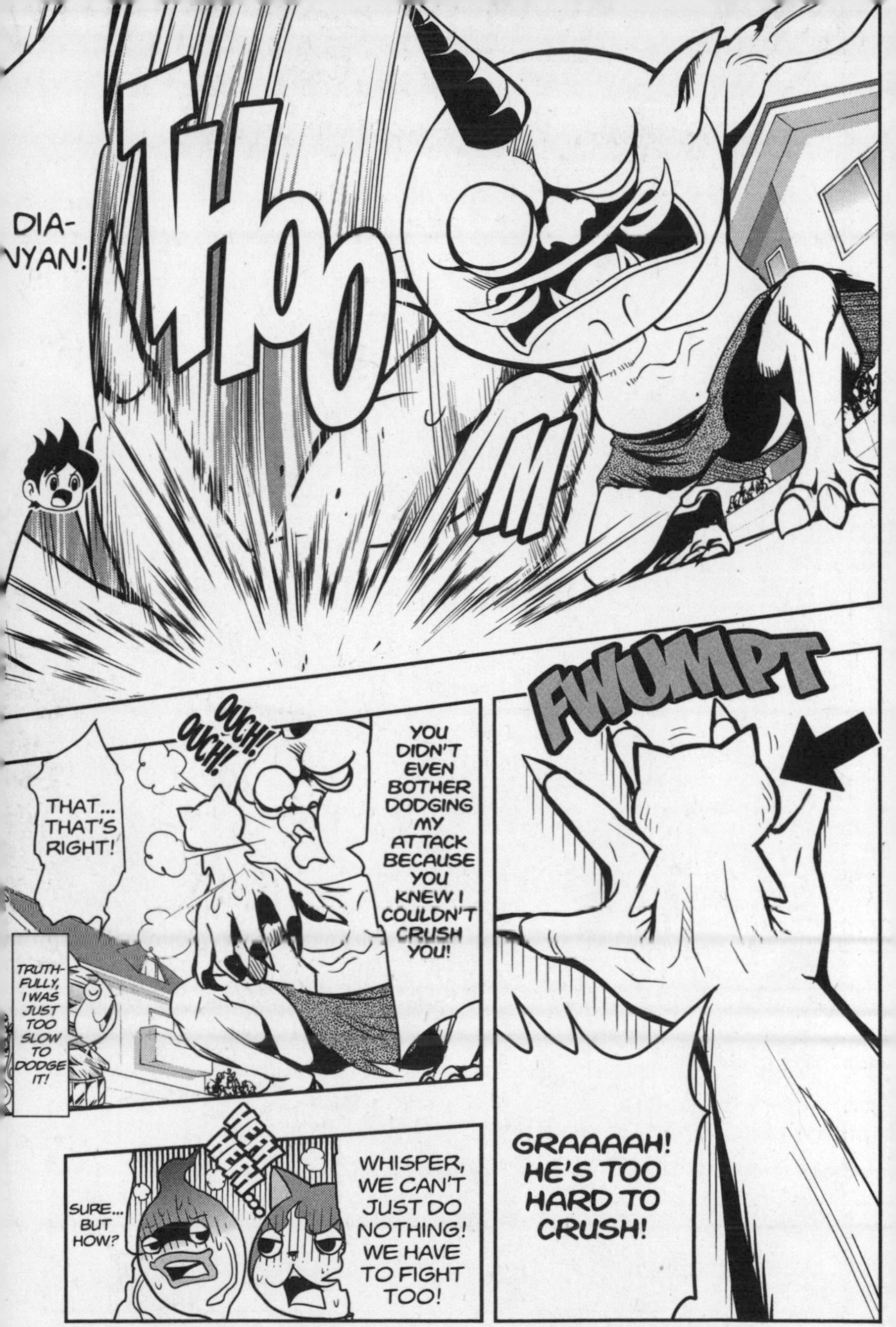
THOOM
DIA-NYAN!
FWUMPT
GRAAAAH! HE'S TOO HARD TO CRUSH!
OUCH! OUCH!
YOU DIDN'T EVEN BOTHER DODGING MY ATTACK BECAUSE YOU KNEW I COULDN'T CRUSH YOU!
THAT... THAT'S RIGHT!
TRUTH-FULLY, I WAS JUST TOO SLOW TO DODGE IT!
HEH HEH...
WHISPER, WE CAN'T JUST DO NOTHING! WE HAVE TO FIGHT TOO!
SURE... BUT HOW?

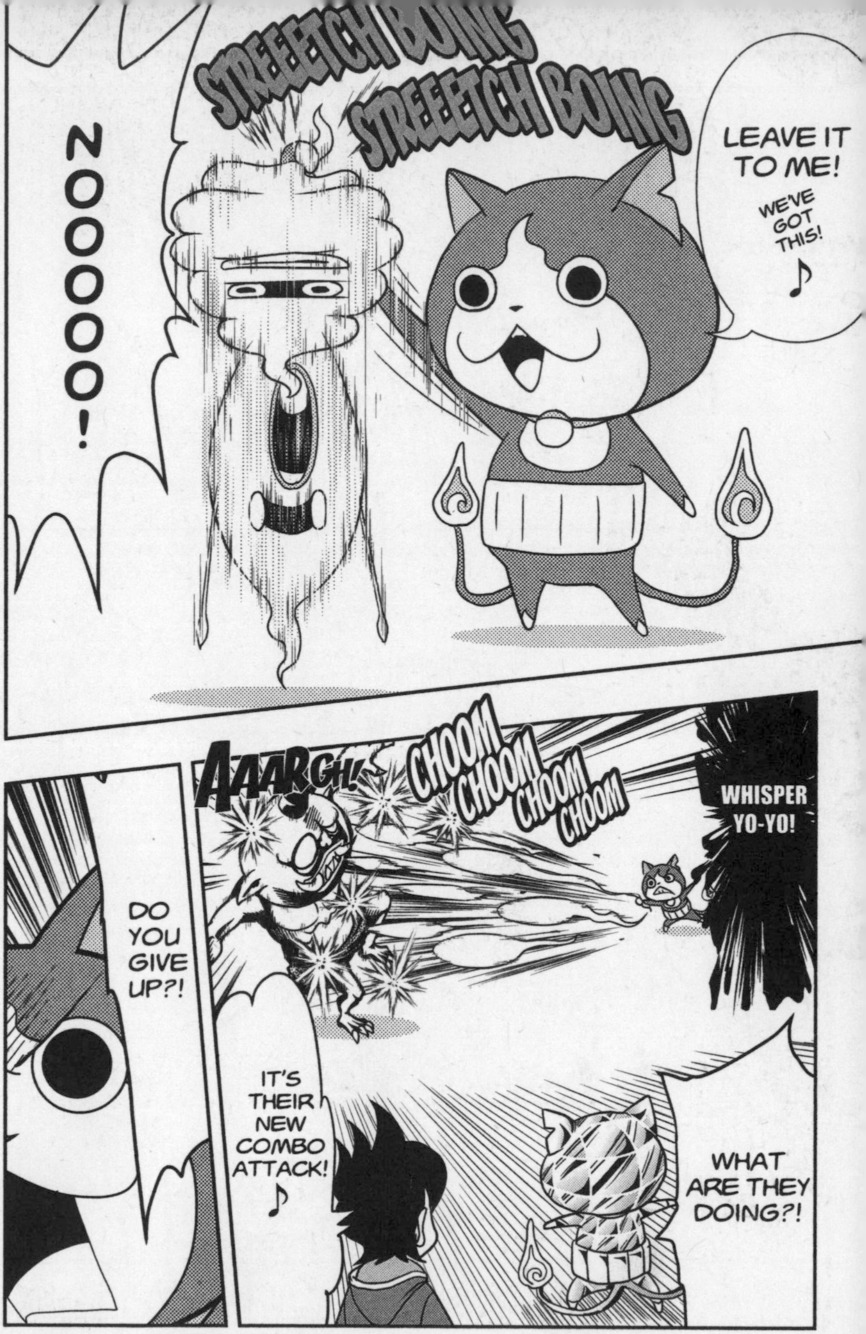
LEAVE IT TO ME!
WE'VE GOT THIS! ♪
STREEETCH BOING STREEETCH BOING
NOOOOOO!
WHISPER YO-YO!
CHOOM CHOOM CHOOM CHOOM
AAARGH!
WHAT ARE THEY DOING?!
IT'S THEIR NEW COMBO ATTACK! ♪
DO YOU GIVE UP?!

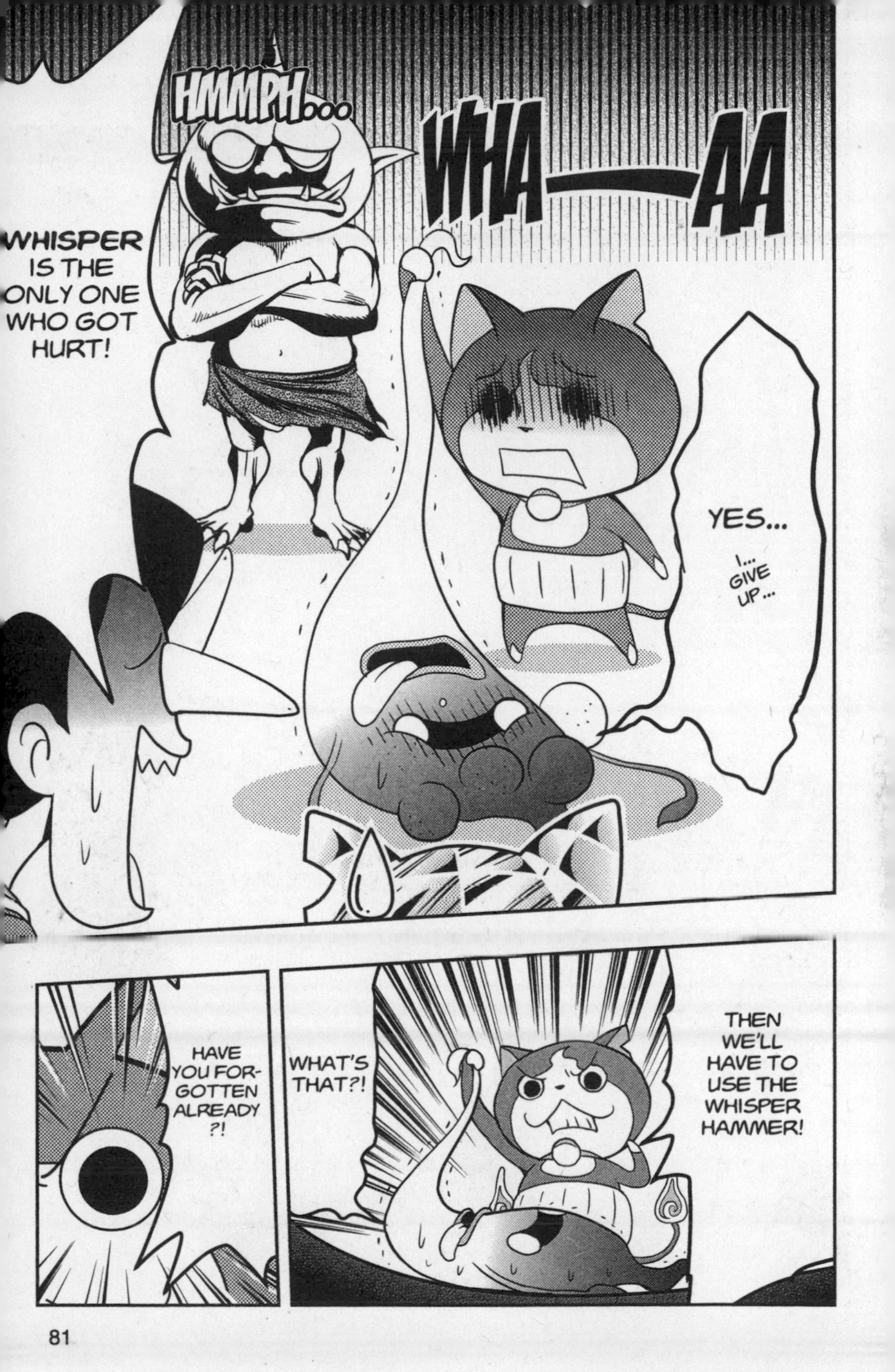
WHA—AA
YES...
I... GIVE UP...
HMMPH...
WHISPER IS THE ONLY ONE WHO GOT HURT!
THEN WE'LL HAVE TO USE THE WHISPER HAMMER!
WHAT'S THAT?!
HAVE YOU FOR-GOTTEN ALREADY ?!

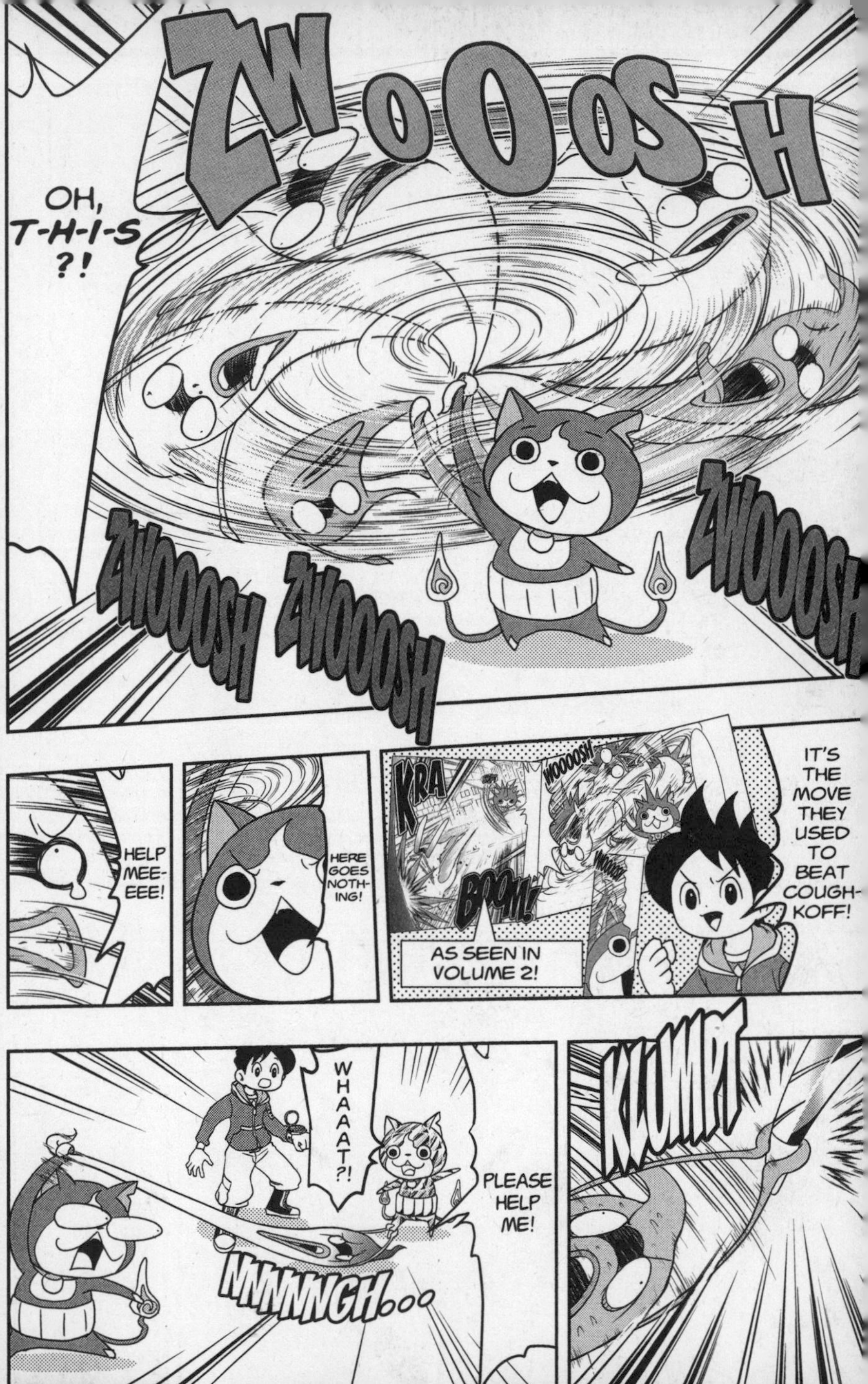
ZWOOOSH
OH, T-H-I-S?!
ZWOOOSH
ZWOOOSH
ZWOOOSH
IT'S THE MOVE THEY USED TO BEAT COUGH-KOFF!
KRA
WOOOOSH
BOOM!
AS SEEN IN VOLUME 2!
HERE GOES NOTHING!
HELP MEEE-EEE!
KLUMPT
WHAAAAT?!
PLEASE HELP ME!
NNNNNGH...

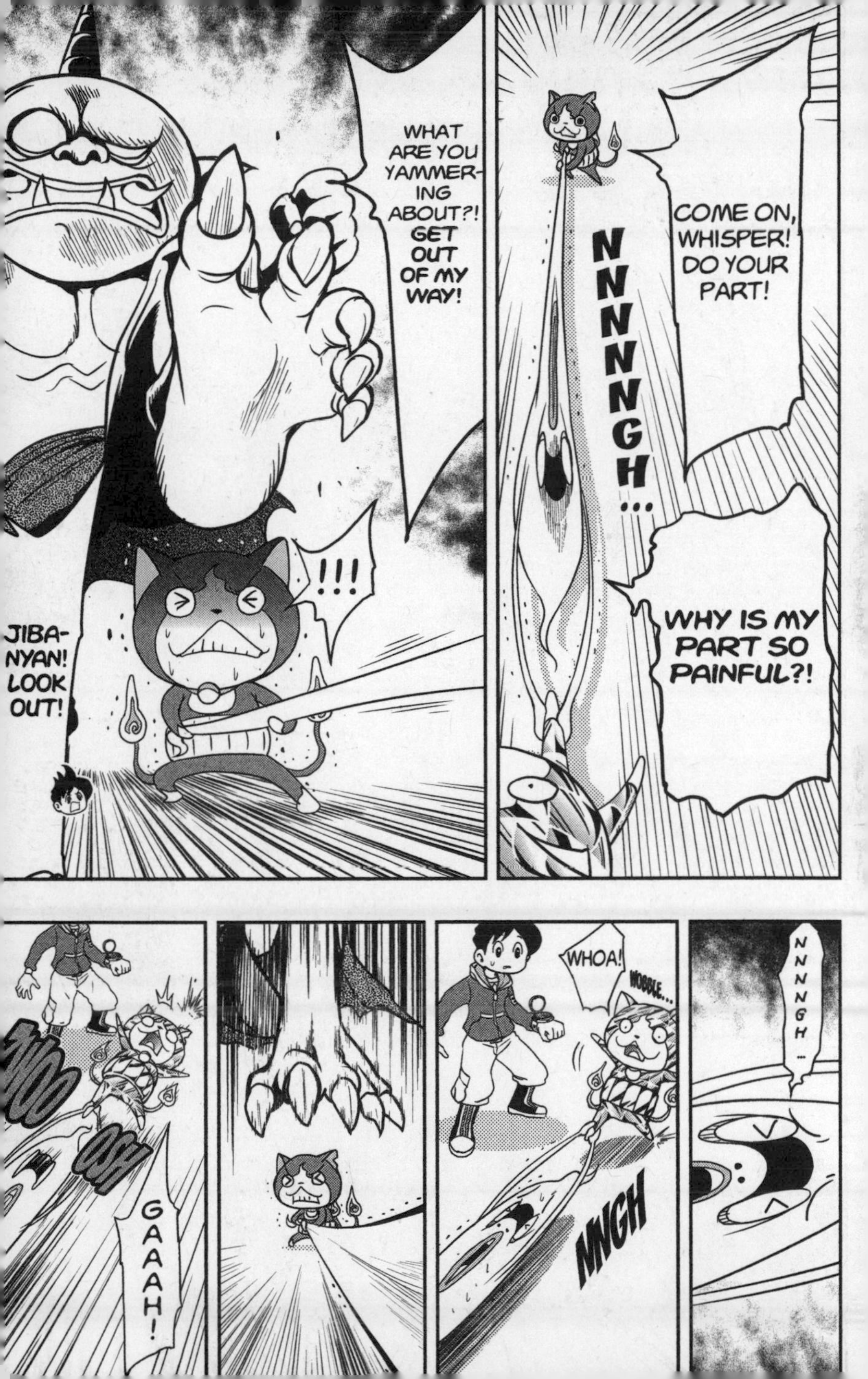
COME ON, WHISPER! DO YOUR PART!
NNNNNGH...
WHY IS MY PART SO PAINFUL?!
WHAT ARE YOU YAMMERING ABOUT?! GET OUT OF MY WAY!
!!!
JIBA-NYAN! LOOK OUT!
NNNNGH...
WHOA!
WOBBLE...
NNGH
WHOOSH
GAAAAH!

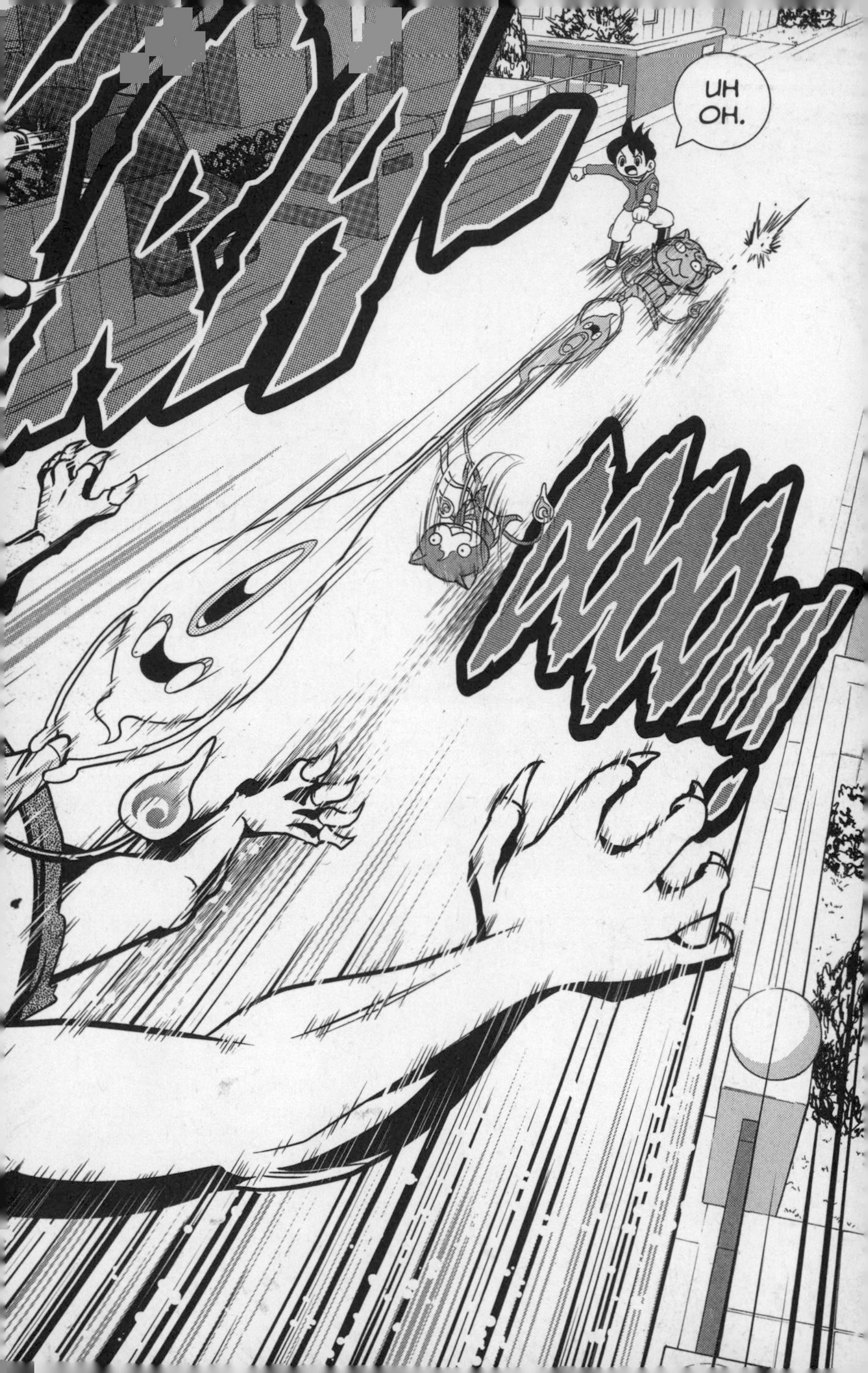
UH OH.

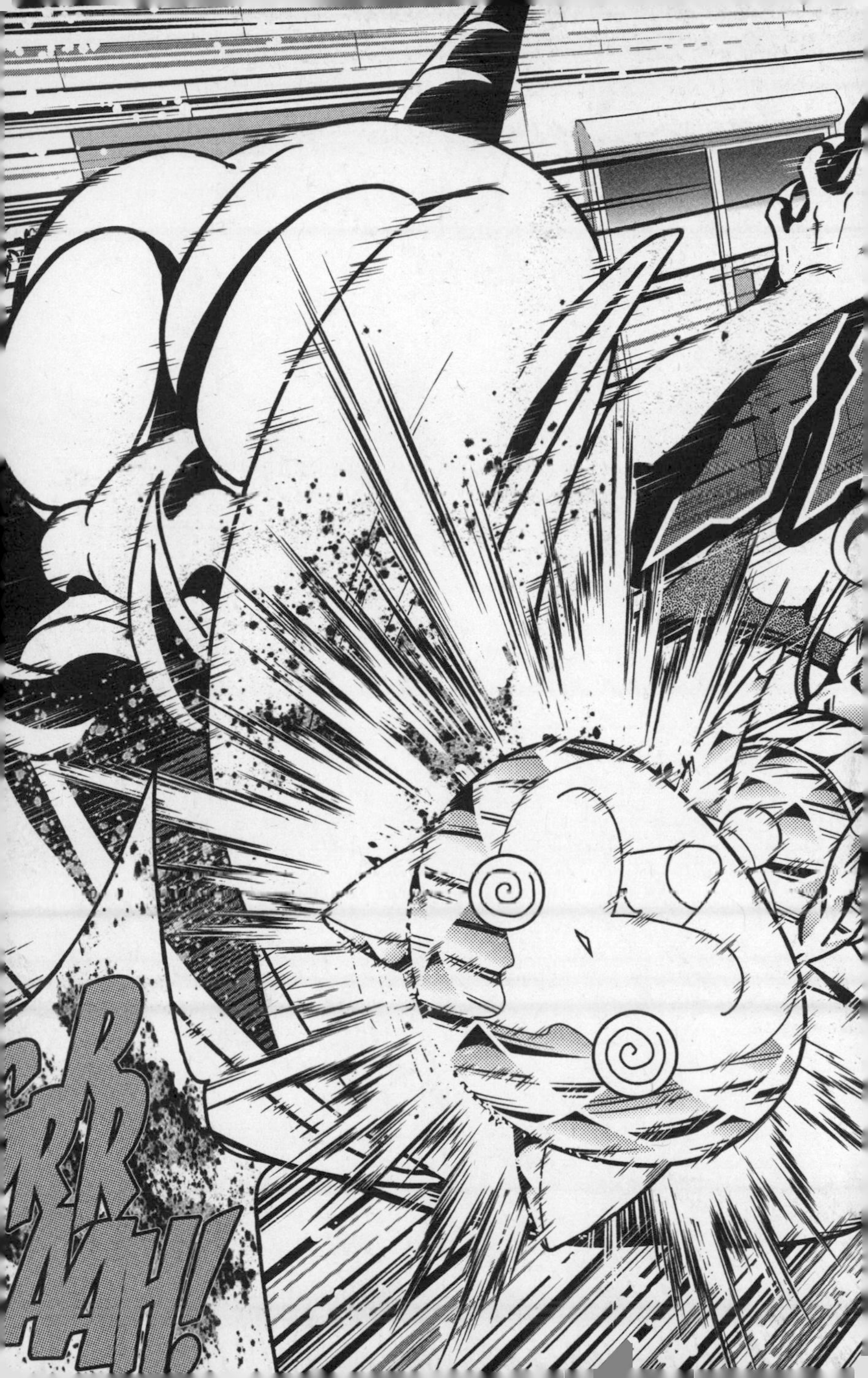
RR AAH!

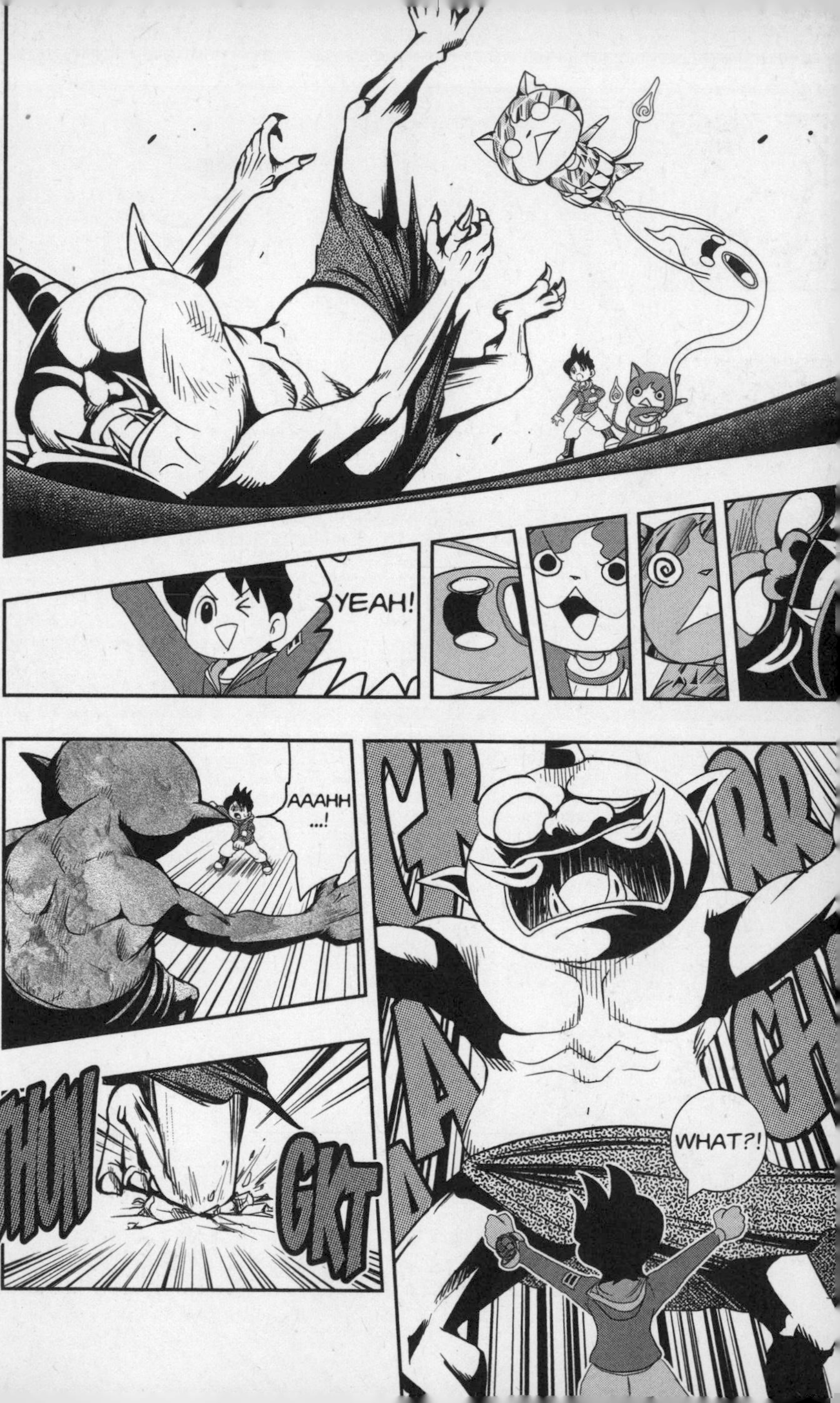
YEAH!
WHAT?!
AAAHH ...!

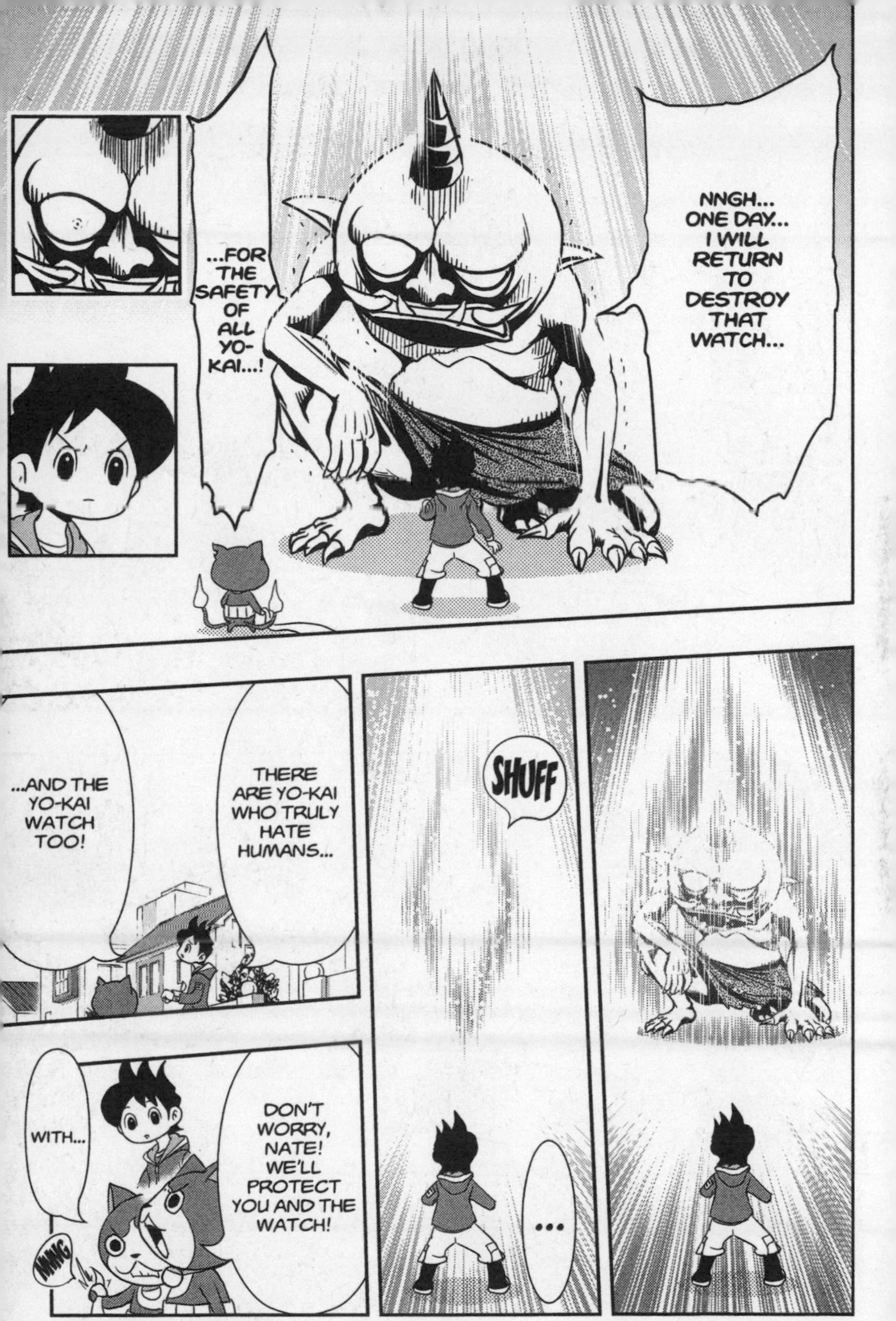
NNGH... ONE DAY... I WILL RETURN TO DESTROY THAT WATCH...
...FOR THE SAFETY OF ALL YO-KAI...!
SHUFF
...
THERE ARE YO-KAI WHO TRULY HATE HUMANS...
...AND THE YO-KAI WATCH TOO!
DON'T WORRY, NATE! WE'LL PROTECT YOU AND THE WATCH!
WITH...

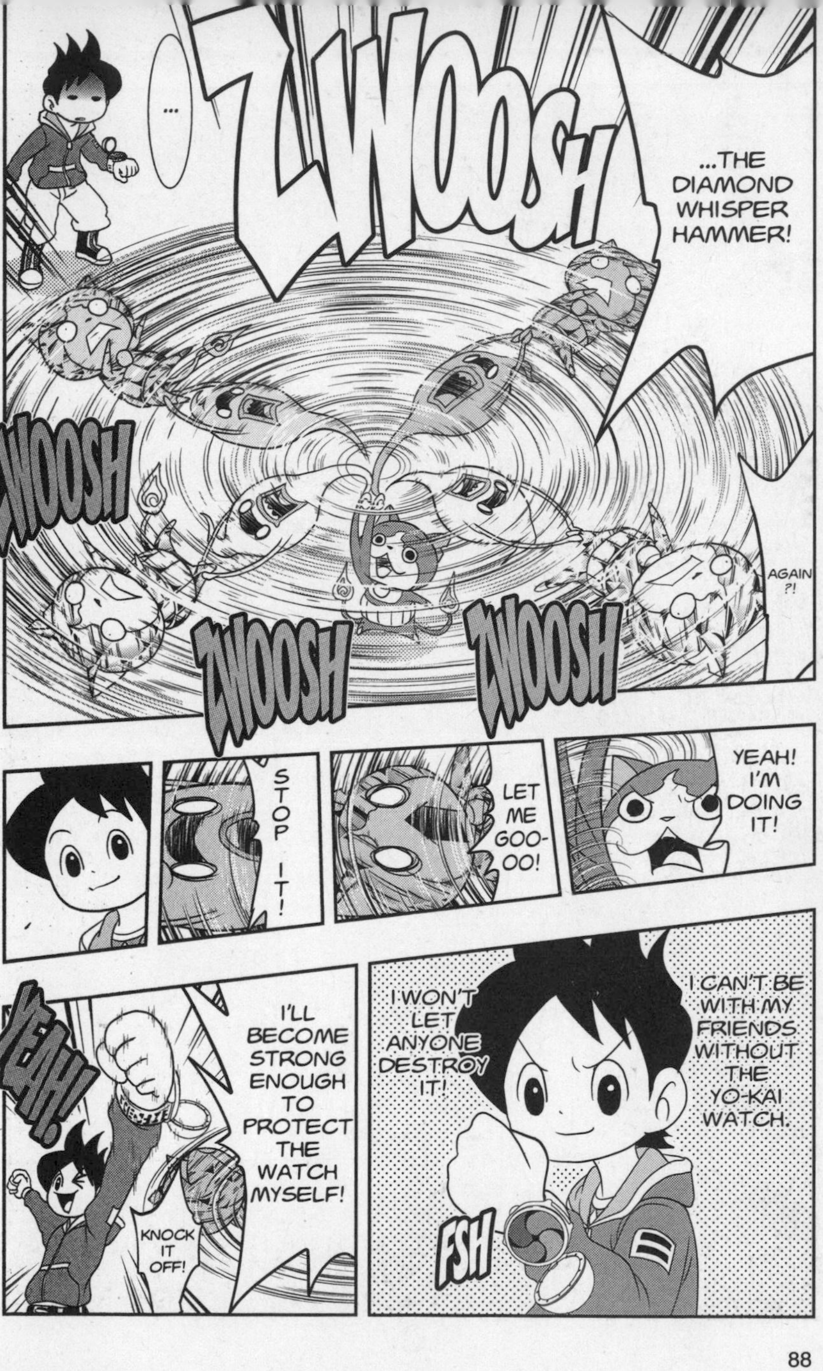

...THE DIAMOND WHISPER HAMMER!
ZWOOSH
...
AGAIN?!
ZWOOSH
ZWOOSH
ZWOOSH
YEAH! I'M DOING IT!
LET ME GOO-OO!
STOP IT!
I CAN'T BE WITH MY FRIENDS WITHOUT THE YO-KAI WATCH.
I WON'T LET ANYONE DESTROY IT!
FSH
I'LL BECOME STRONG ENOUGH TO PROTECT THE WATCH MYSELF!
YEAH!
KNOCK IT OFF!

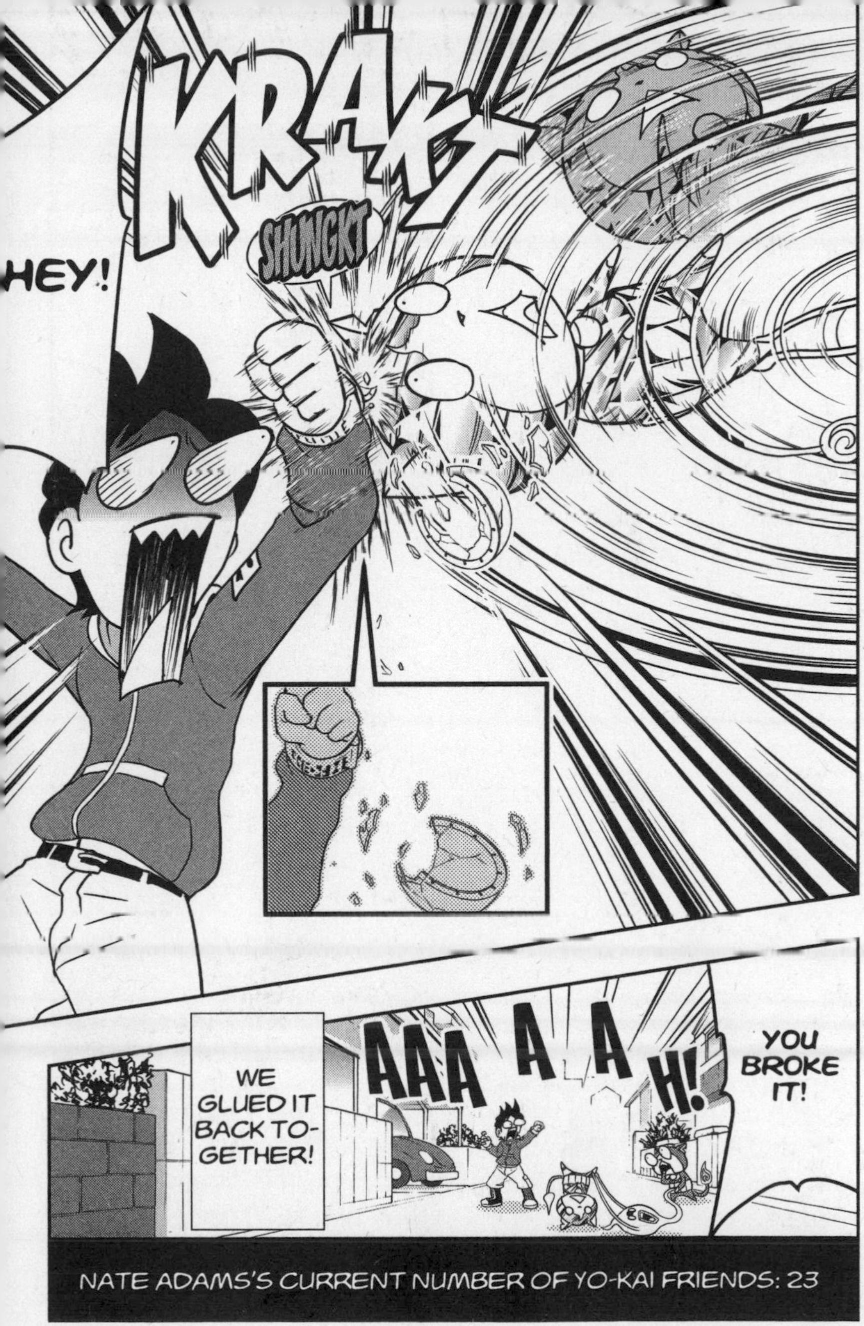
KRAKT
SHUNGKT
HEY!
YOU BROKE IT!
AAAAAH!
WE GLUED IT BACK TO-GETHER!
NATE ADAMS'S CURRENT NUMBER OF YO-KAI FRIENDS: 23

REPAIR #1

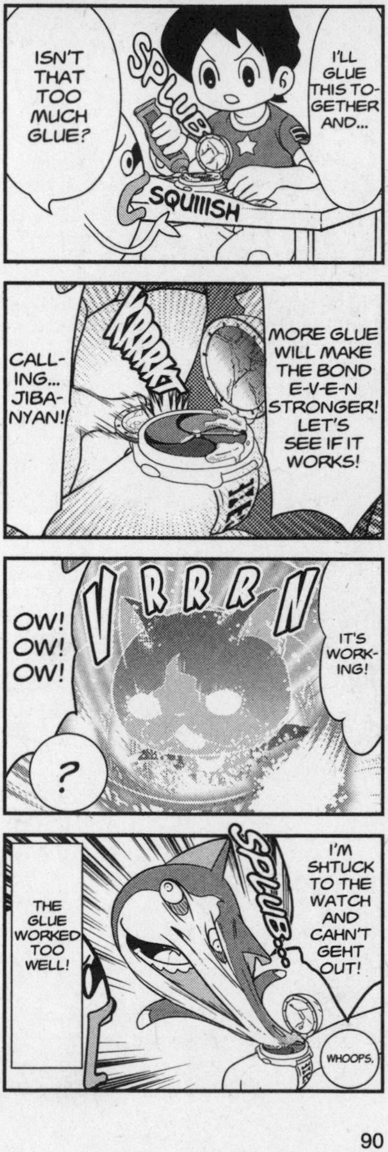
I'LL GLUE THIS TO-GETHER AND...
SPLUB
ISN'T THAT TOO MUCH GLUE?
SQUIIISH
MORE GLUE WILL MAKE THE BOND E-V-E-N STRONGER! LET'S SEE IF IT WORKS!
KRRRKT
CALL-ING... JIBA-NYAN!
VRRRN
IT'S WORK-ING!
OW! OW! OW!
?
I'M SHTUCK TO THE WATCH AND CAHN'T GEHT OUT!
SPLUB...
THE GLUE WORKED TOO WELL!
WHOOPS.

CHAPTER 29: DANCE FIGHT! ♪

FEATURING DANCE LOVER YO-KAI STEPPA

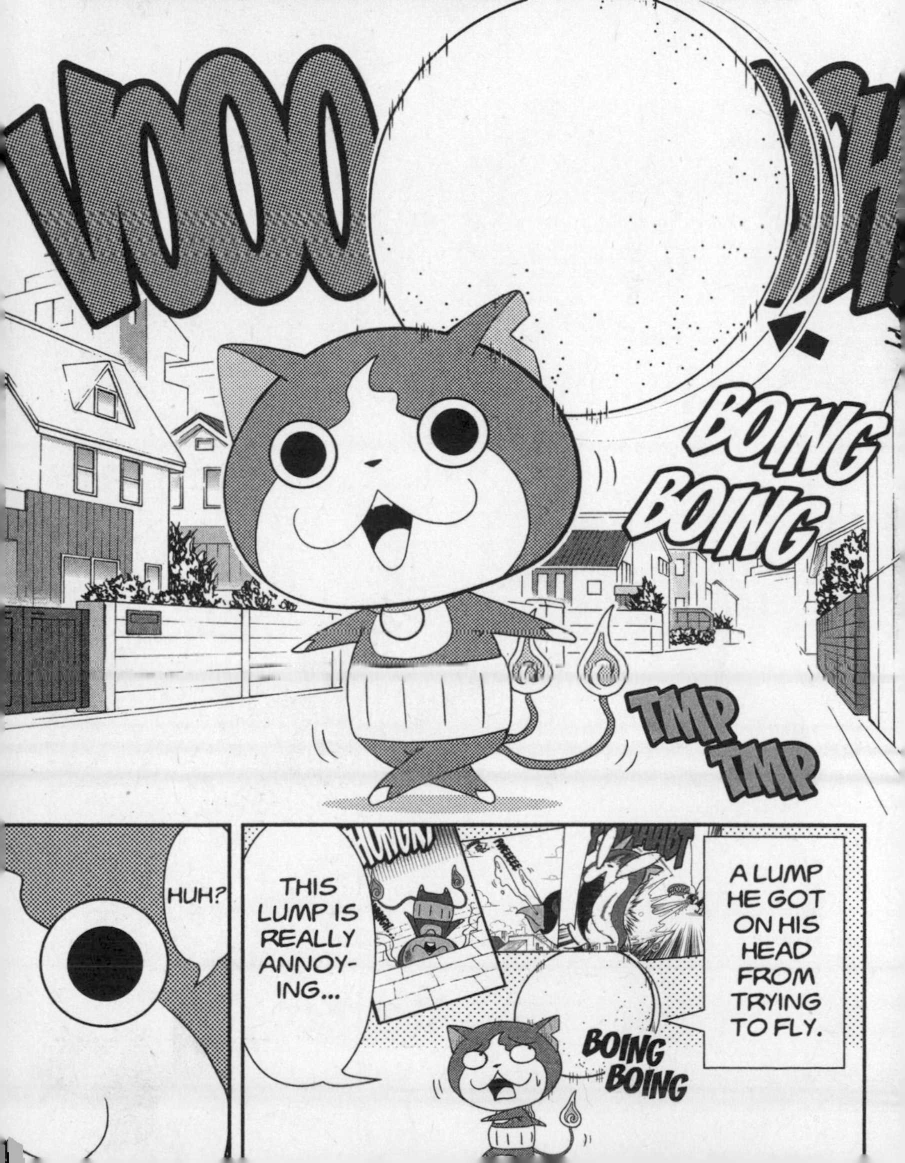
BOING
BOING
TMP
TMP
A LUMP HE GOT ON HIS HEAD FROM TRYING TO FLY.
THIS LUMP IS REALLY ANNOY-ING...
BOING
BOING
HUH?

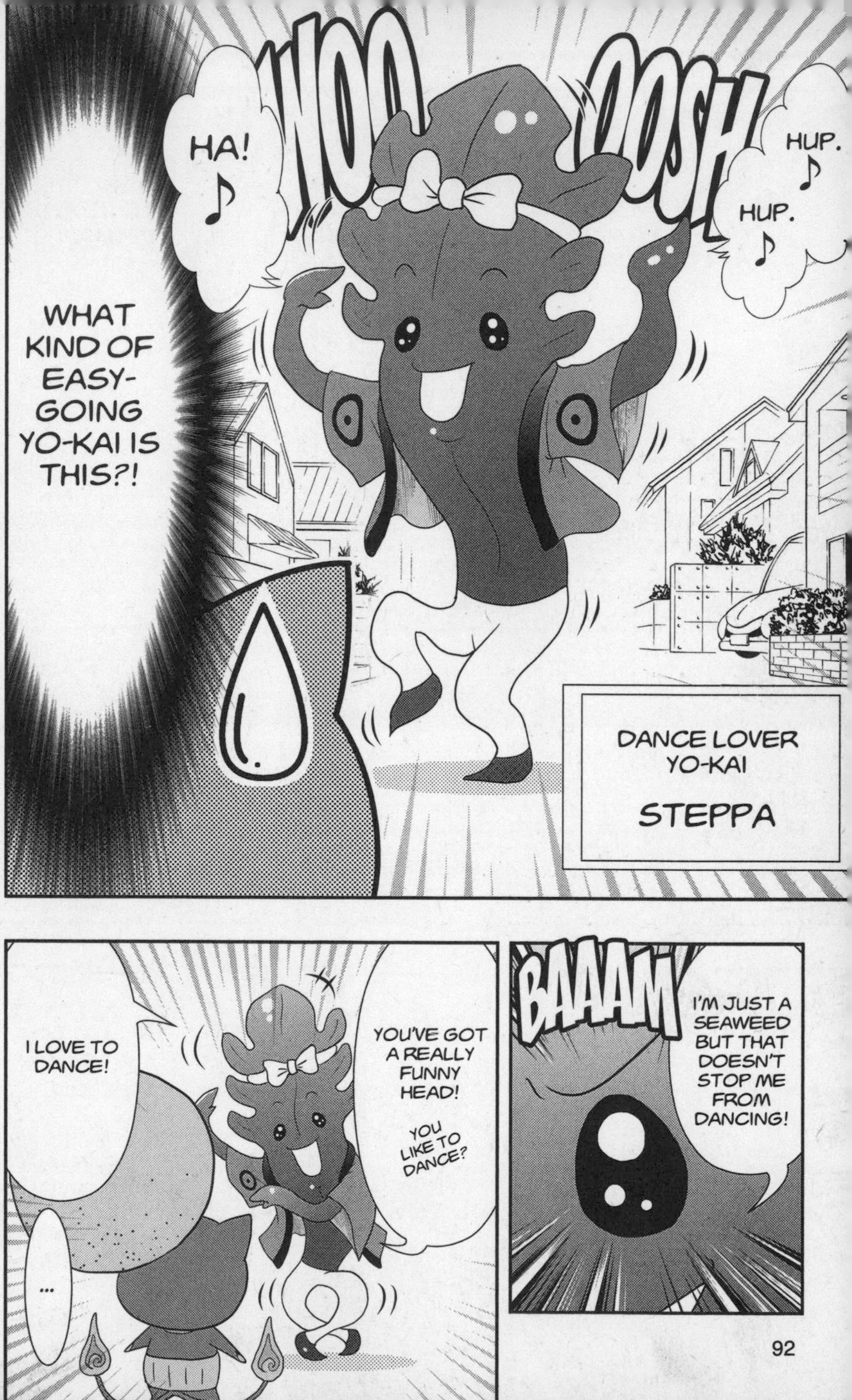
HUP. ♪
HUP. ♪
WOOOOSH
HA! ♪
WHAT KIND OF EASY-GOING YO-KAI IS THIS?!
DANCE LOVER YO-KAI
STEPPA
BAAAM
I'M JUST A SEAWEED BUT THAT DOESN'T STOP ME FROM DANCING!
YOU'VE GOT A REALLY FUNNY HEAD!
YOU LIKE TO DANCE?
I LOVE TO DANCE!
...

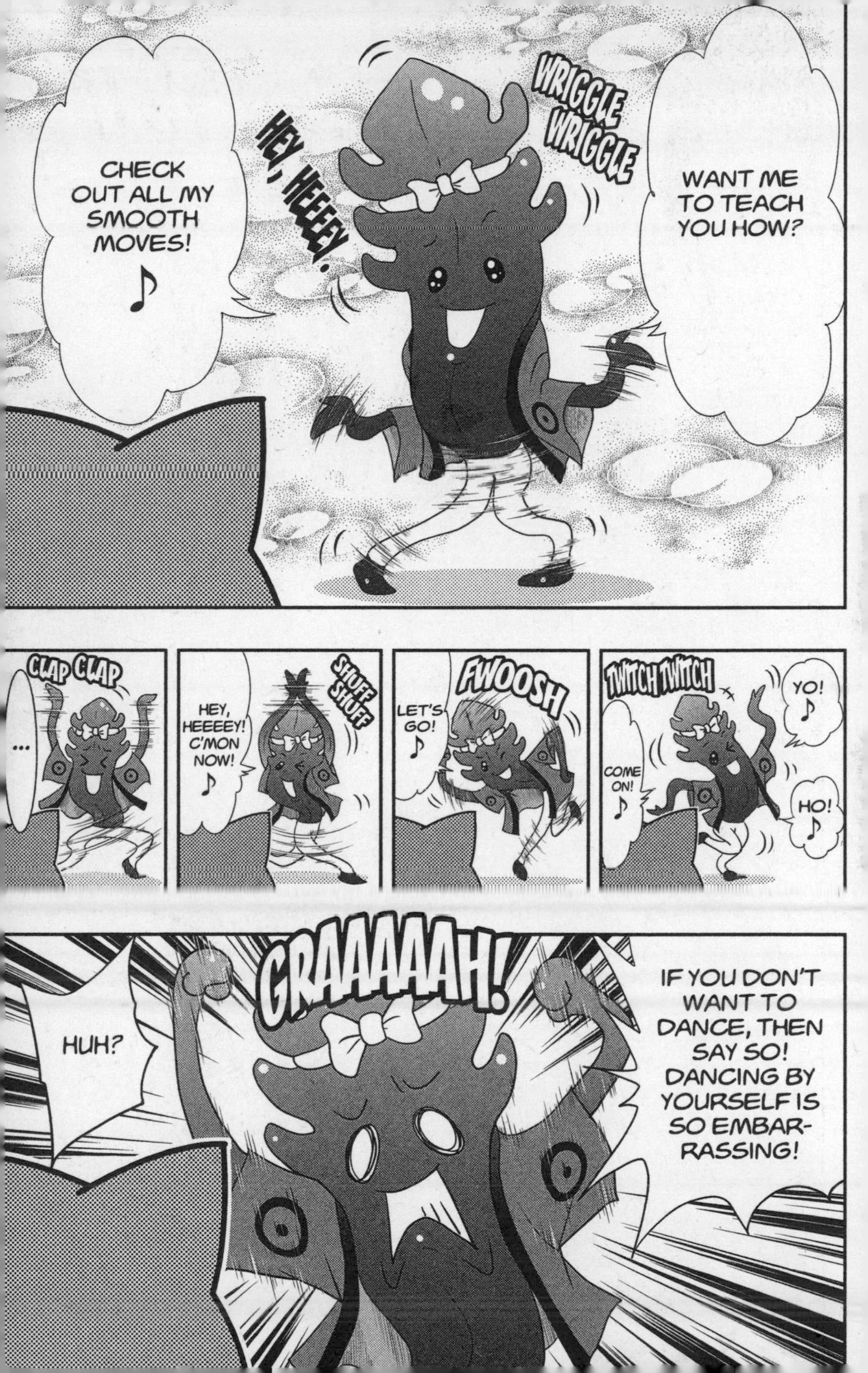
WANT ME TO TEACH YOU HOW?
WRIGGLE WRIGGLE
HEY, HEEEEY
CHECK OUT ALL MY SMOOTH MOVES! ♪
TWITCH TWITCH
YO! ♪
HO! ♪
COME ON! ♪
FWOOSH
LET'S GO! ♪
SHUFF SHUFF
HEY, HEEEEY! C'MON NOW! ♪
CLAP CLAP
...
IF YOU DON'T WANT TO DANCE, THEN SAY SO! DANCING BY YOURSELF IS SO EMBAR-RASSING!
GRAAAAAH!
HUH?

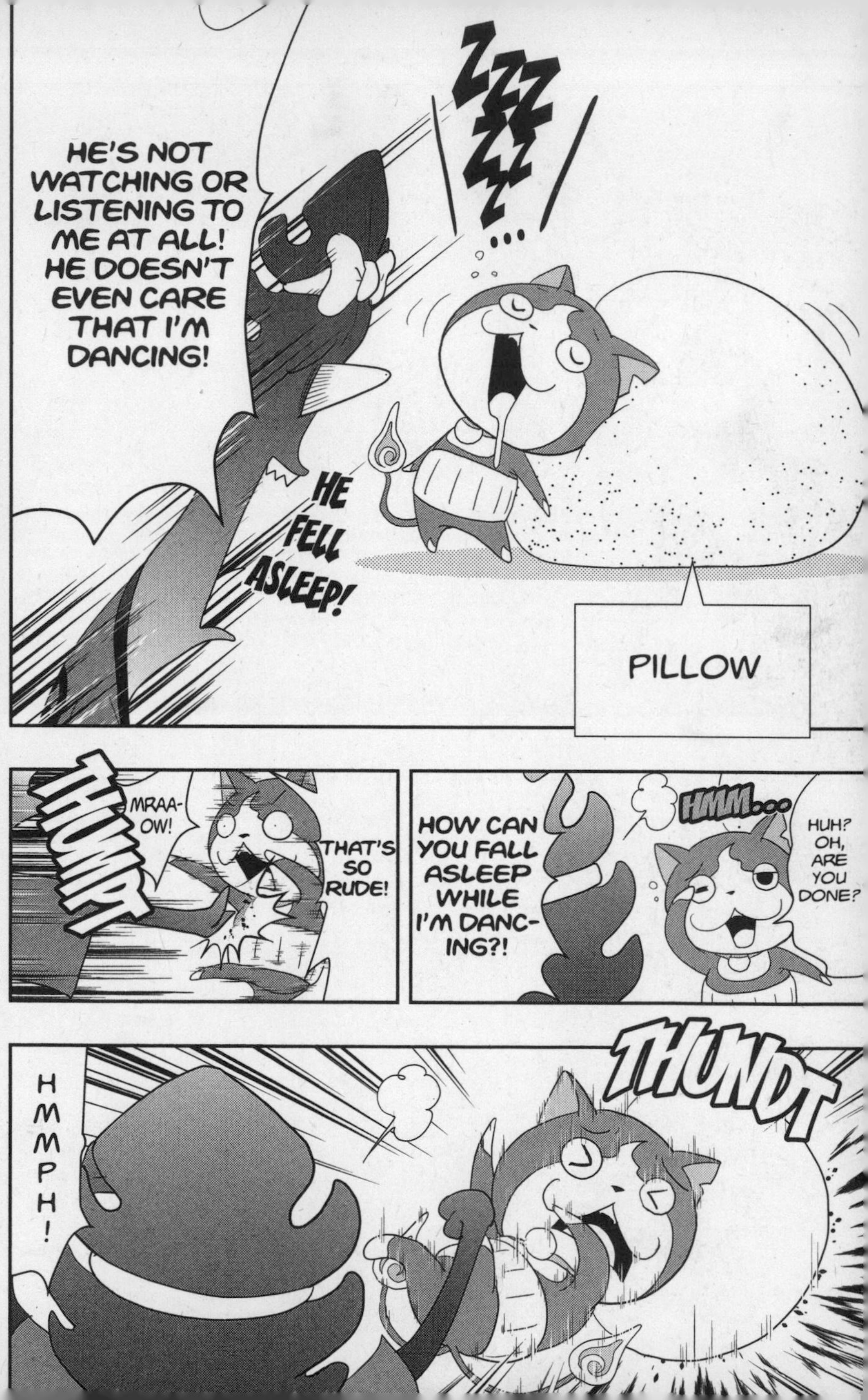
ZZZZZ...
HE'S NOT WATCHING OR LISTENING TO ME AT ALL! HE DOESN'T EVEN CARE THAT I'M DANCING!
HE FELL ASLEEP!
PILLOW
HMM...
HUH? OH, ARE YOU DONE?
HOW CAN YOU FALL ASLEEP WHILE I'M DANC-ING?!
THAT'S SO RUDE!
MRAA-OW!
THUMP!
THUNDT
HMMPH!

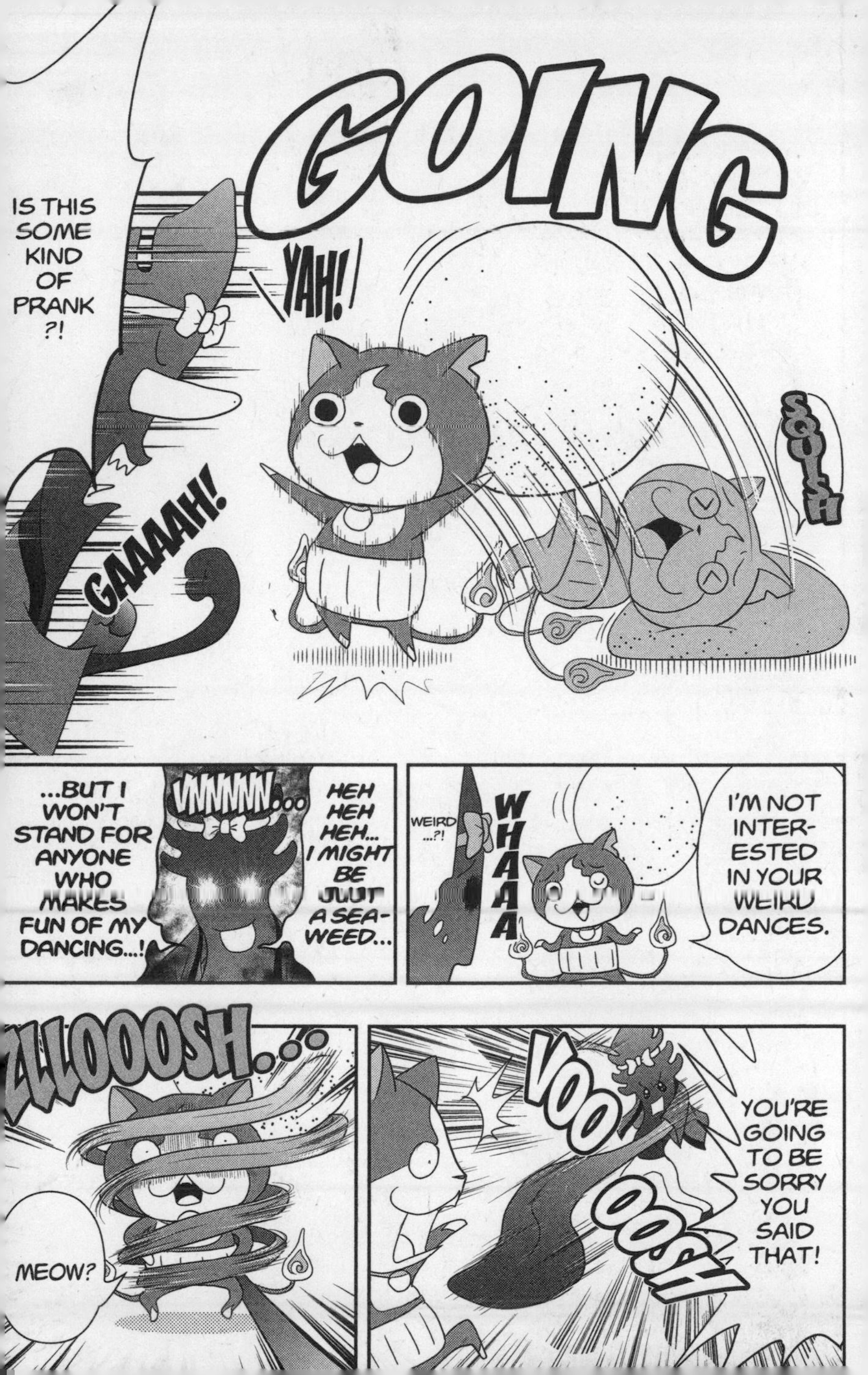
GOING
SQUISH
YAH!
IS THIS SOME KIND OF PRANK?!
GAAAAH!
I'M NOT INTER-ESTED IN YOUR WEIRD DANCES.
WHAAAA
WEIRD ...?!
HEH HEH HEH... I MIGHT BE JUST A SEA-WEED...
VNNNNN...
...BUT I WON'T STAND FOR ANYONE WHO MAKES FUN OF MY DANCING...!
VOOOOSH!
YOU'RE GOING TO BE SORRY YOU SAID THAT!
ZLLOOOSH...
MEOW?

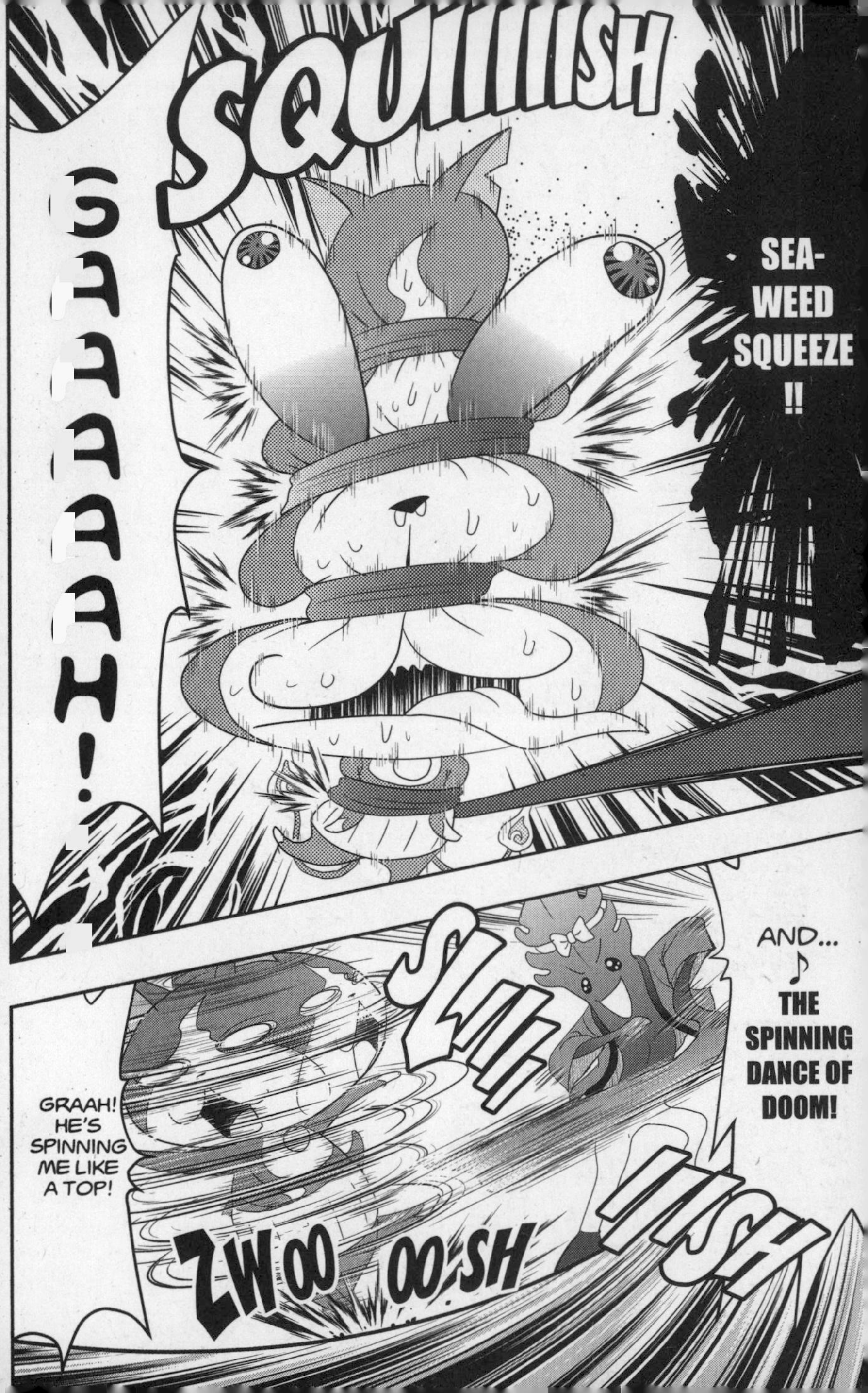
SEA-WEED SQUEEZE!!
SQUIIIIISH
GAAAAAH!
AND... ♪ THE SPINNING DANCE OF DOOM!
SWIIIIIISH
GRAAH! HE'S SPINNING ME LIKE A TOP!
ZWOOOOSH

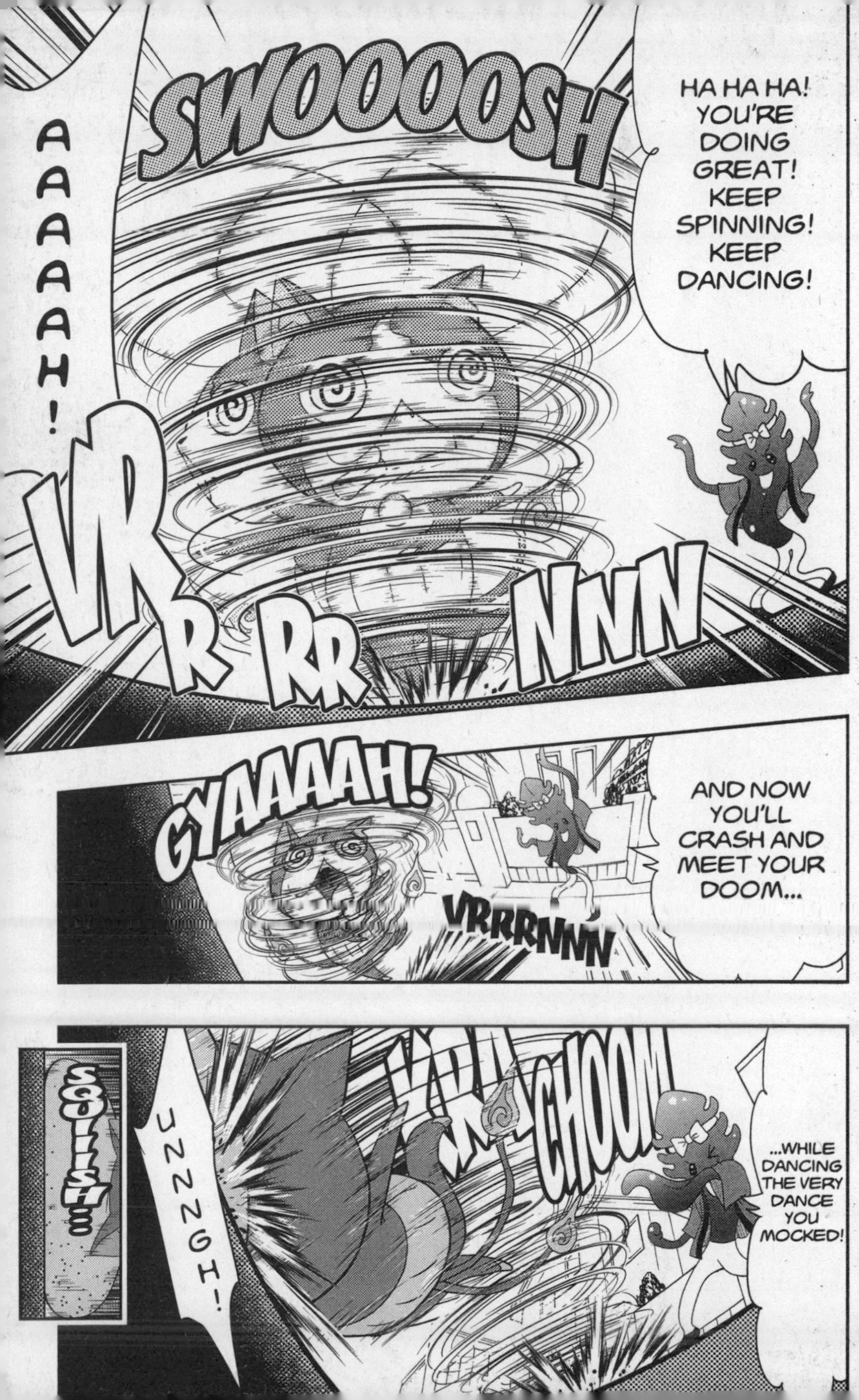
HA HA HA! YOU'RE DOING GREAT! KEEP SPINNING! KEEP DANCING!
SWOOOOOSH
AAAAAAH!
VRRRRNNN
AND NOW YOU'LL CRASH AND MEET YOUR DOOM...
GYAAAAAH!
VRRRRNNNN
...WHILE DANCING THE VERY DANCE YOU MOCKED!
CHOOM
UNNNGH!
SQUISH!...

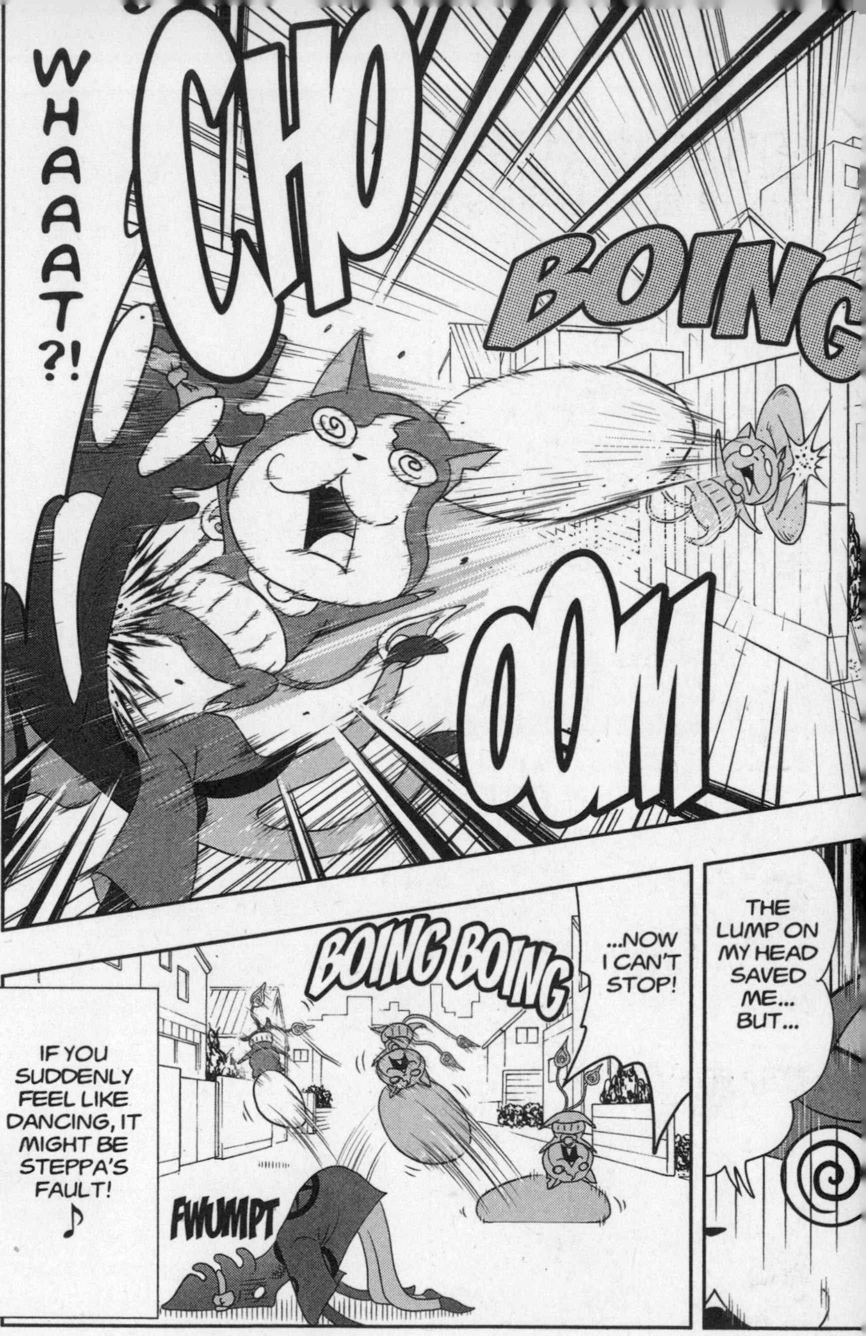
BOING
CHO
OOM
WHAAAAT?!
THE LUMP ON MY HEAD SAVED ME... BUT...
...NOW I CAN'T STOP!
BOING BOING
FWUMPT
IF YOU SUDDENLY FEEL LIKE DANCING, IT MIGHT BE STEPPA'S FAULT! ♪

REPAIR #2

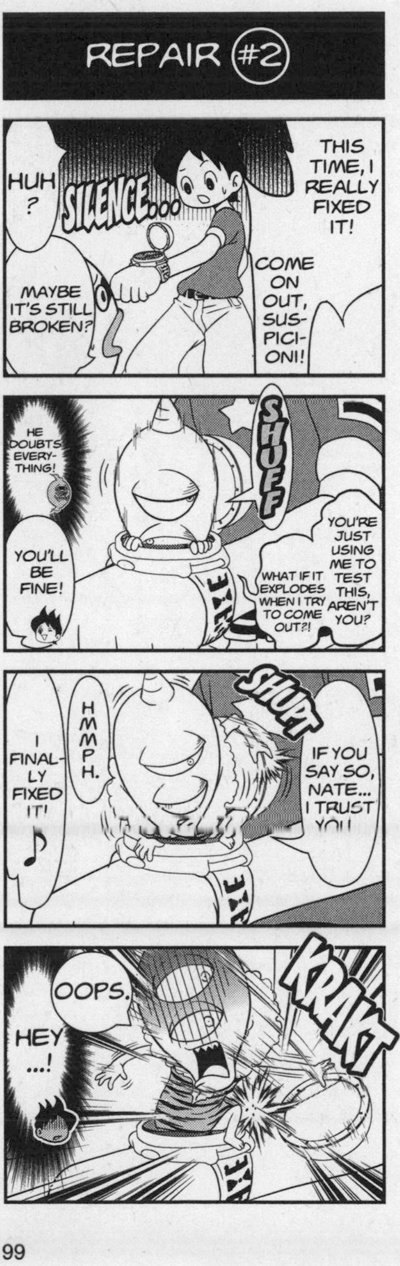
THIS TIME, I REALLY FIXED IT!
COME ON OUT, SUSPICIONI!
SILENCE...
HUH?
MAYBE IT'S STILL BROKEN?
SHUFF
YOU'RE JUST USING ME TO TEST THIS, AREN'T YOU?
WHAT IF IT EXPLODES WHEN I TRY TO COME OUT?!
HE DOUBTS EVERYTHING!
YOU'LL BE FINE!
SHUPT
IF YOU SAY SO, NATE... I TRUST YOU!
HMMPH.
I FINALLY FIXED IT! ♪
KRAKT
OOPS.
HEY...!

CHAPTER 30: TOO LAZY TO FIGHT?!

FEATURING LAZY YO-KAI CUTTA-NAH

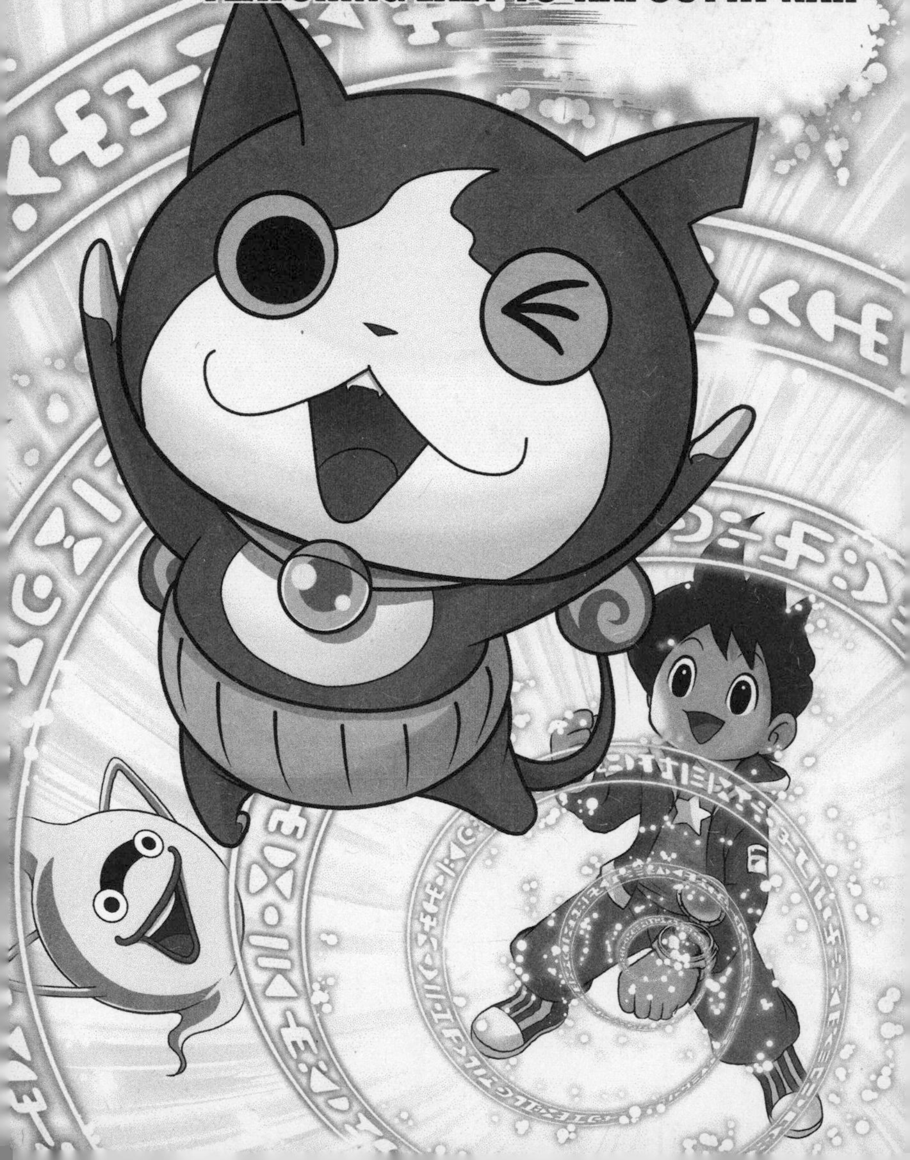

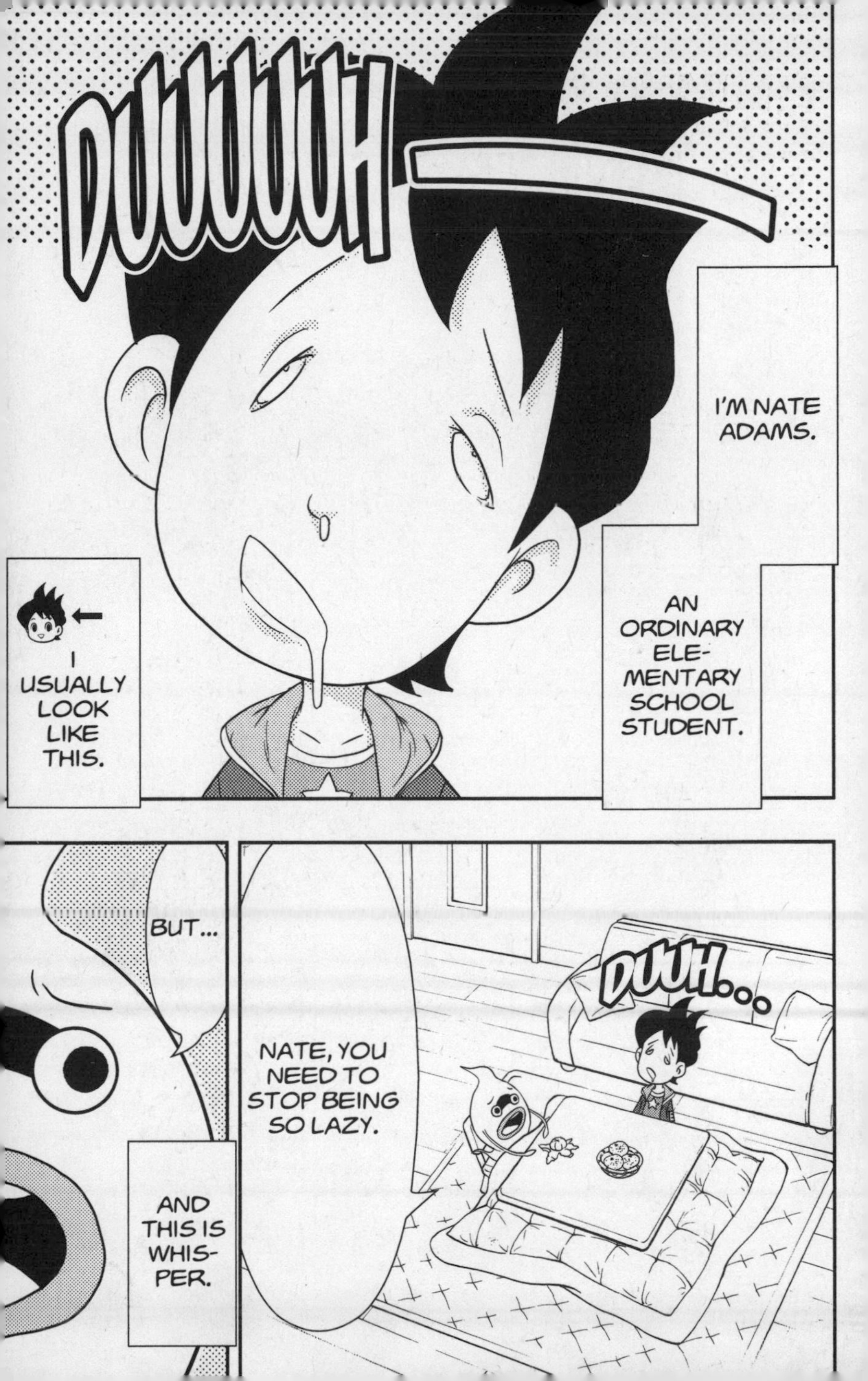
DUUUUUH!
I'M NATE ADAMS.
AN ORDINARY ELEMENTARY SCHOOL STUDENT.
I USUALLY LOOK LIKE THIS.
DUUH...
NATE, YOU NEED TO STOP BEING SO LAZY.
BUT...
AND THIS IS WHISPER.

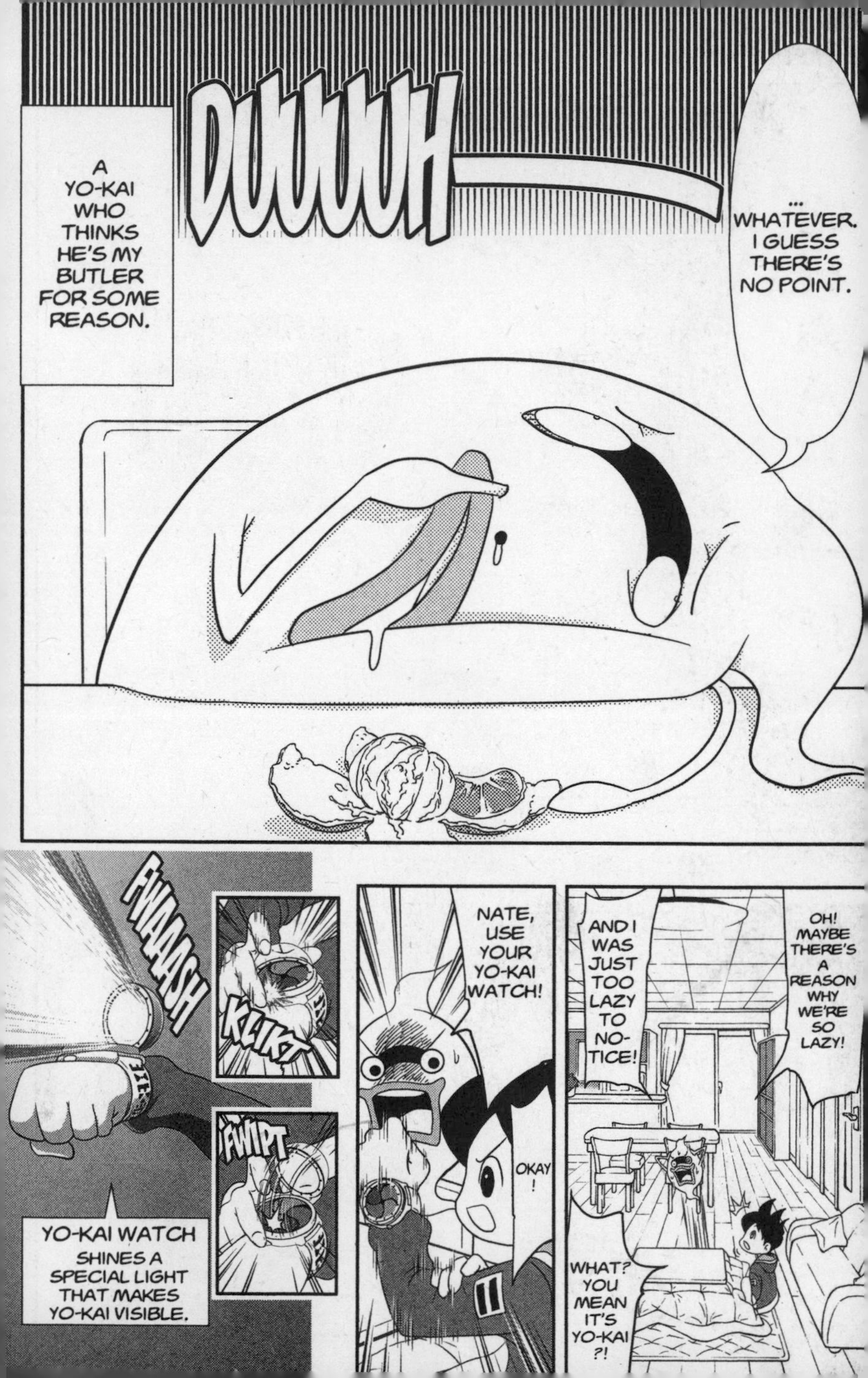
... WHATEVER. I GUESS THERE'S NO POINT.
DUUUUH
A YO-KAI WHO THINKS HE'S MY BUTLER FOR SOME REASON.
OH! MAYBE THERE'S A REASON WHY WE'RE SO LAZY!
AND I WAS JUST TOO LAZY TO NO-TICE!
WHAT? YOU MEAN IT'S YO-KAI?!
NATE, USE YOUR YO-KAI WATCH!
OKAY!
KLIKT
FWIPT
FWAAASH
YO-KAI WATCH SHINES A SPECIAL LIGHT THAT MAKES YO-KAI VISIBLE.

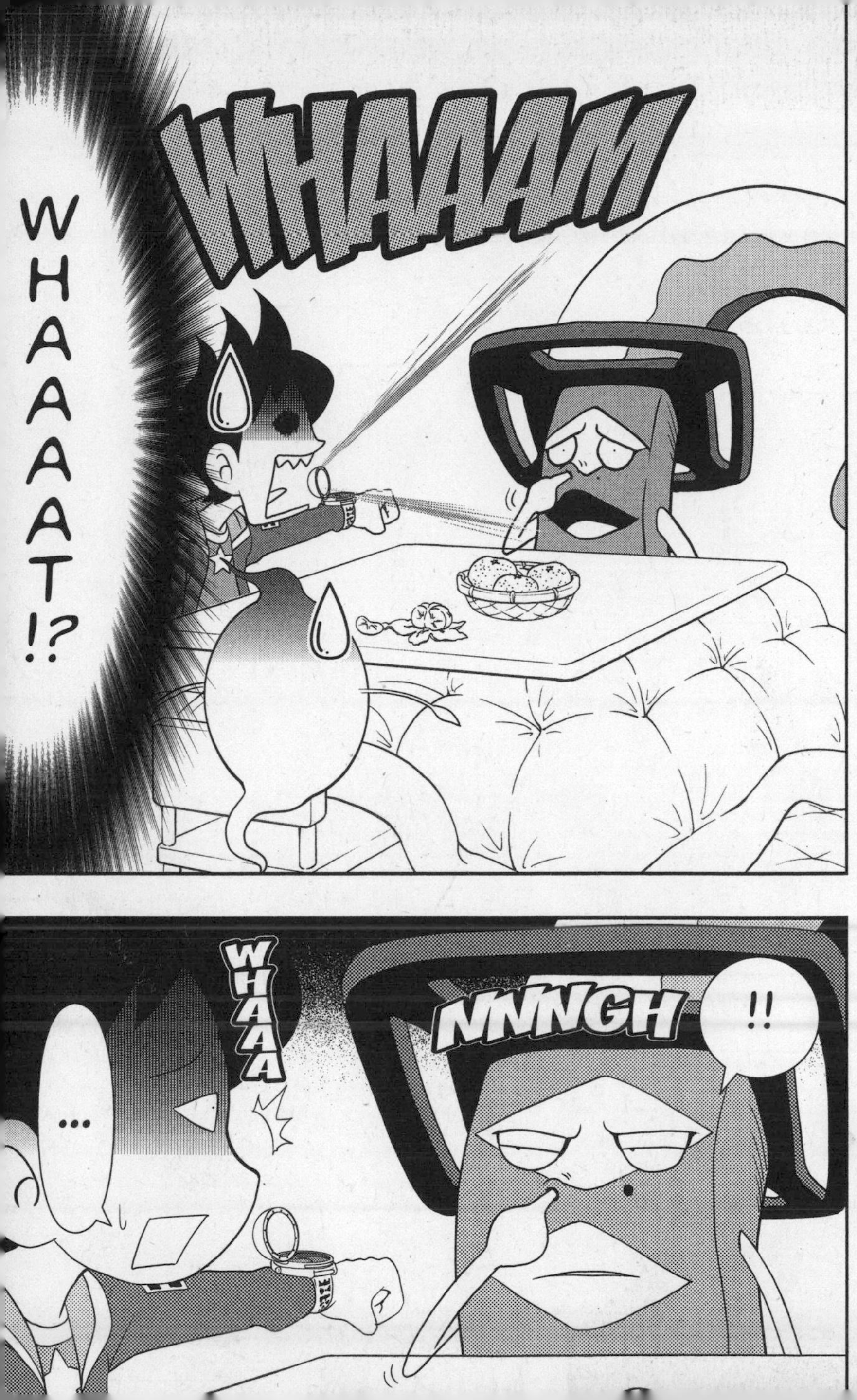
WHAAAM
WHAAAAT!?
!!
NNNGH
WHAAA
...

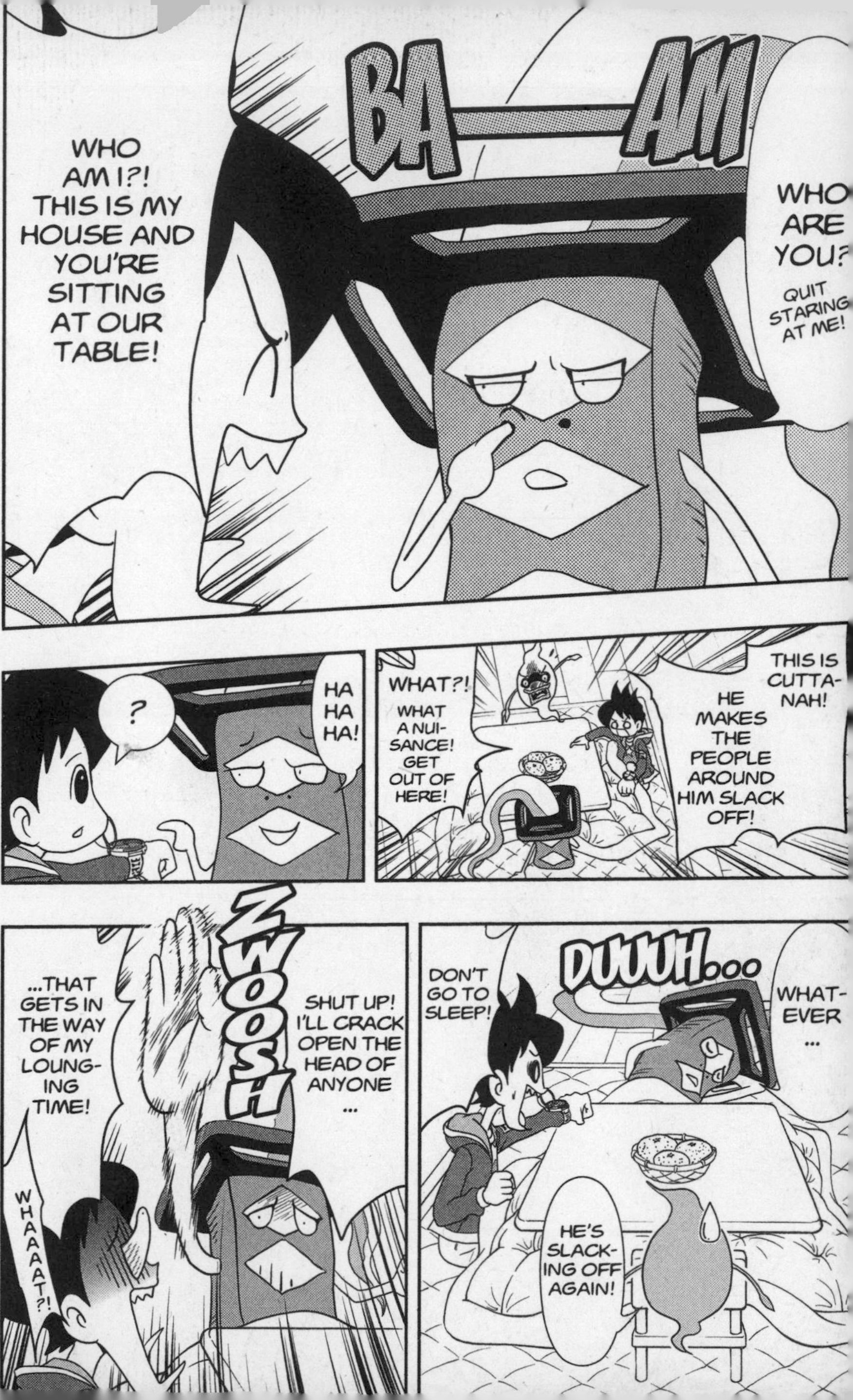
BA—AM
WHO ARE YOU?
QUIT STARING AT ME!
WHO AM I?! THIS IS MY HOUSE AND YOU'RE SITTING AT OUR TABLE!
THIS IS CUTTA-NAH!
HE MAKES THE PEOPLE AROUND HIM SLACK OFF!
WHAT?!
WHAT A NUI-SANCE! GET OUT OF HERE!
HA HA HA!
?
WHAT-EVER ...
DUUUH...
DON'T GO TO SLEEP!
HE'S SLACK-ING OFF AGAIN!
SHUT UP! I'LL CRACK OPEN THE HEAD OF ANYONE ...
ZWOOSH
...THAT GETS IN THE WAY OF MY LOUNG-ING TIME!
WHAAAAAT?!

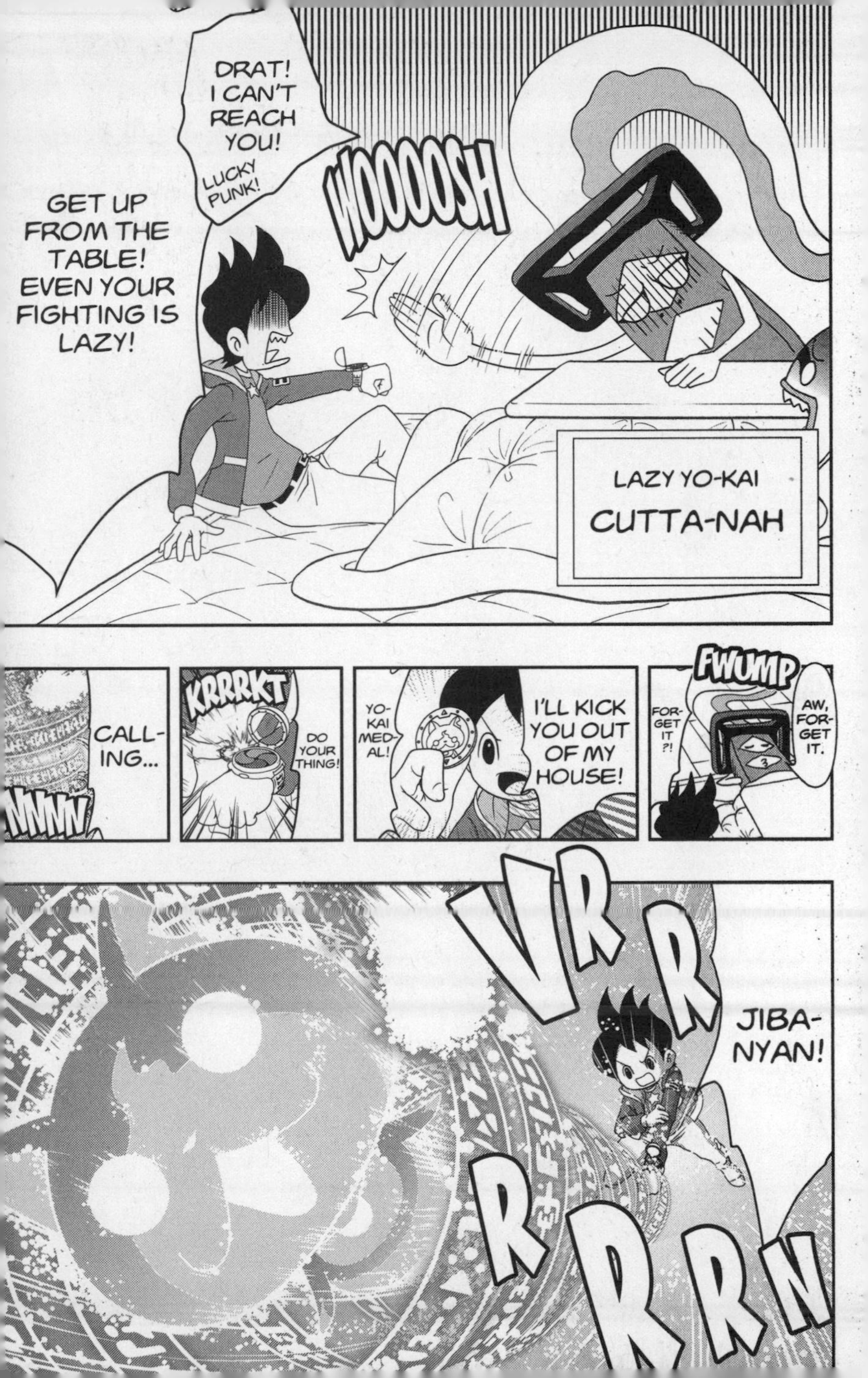
DRAT! I CAN'T REACH YOU!
LUCKY PUNK!
WOOOOSH
GET UP FROM THE TABLE! EVEN YOUR FIGHTING IS LAZY!
LAZY YO-KAI
CUTTA-NAH
FWUMP
AW, FOR-GET IT.
FOR-GET IT?!
I'LL KICK YOU OUT OF MY HOUSE!
YO-KAI MED-AL!
KRRRKT
DO YOUR THING!
CALL-ING...
NNNNN
VRRRRRRN
JIBA-NYAN!

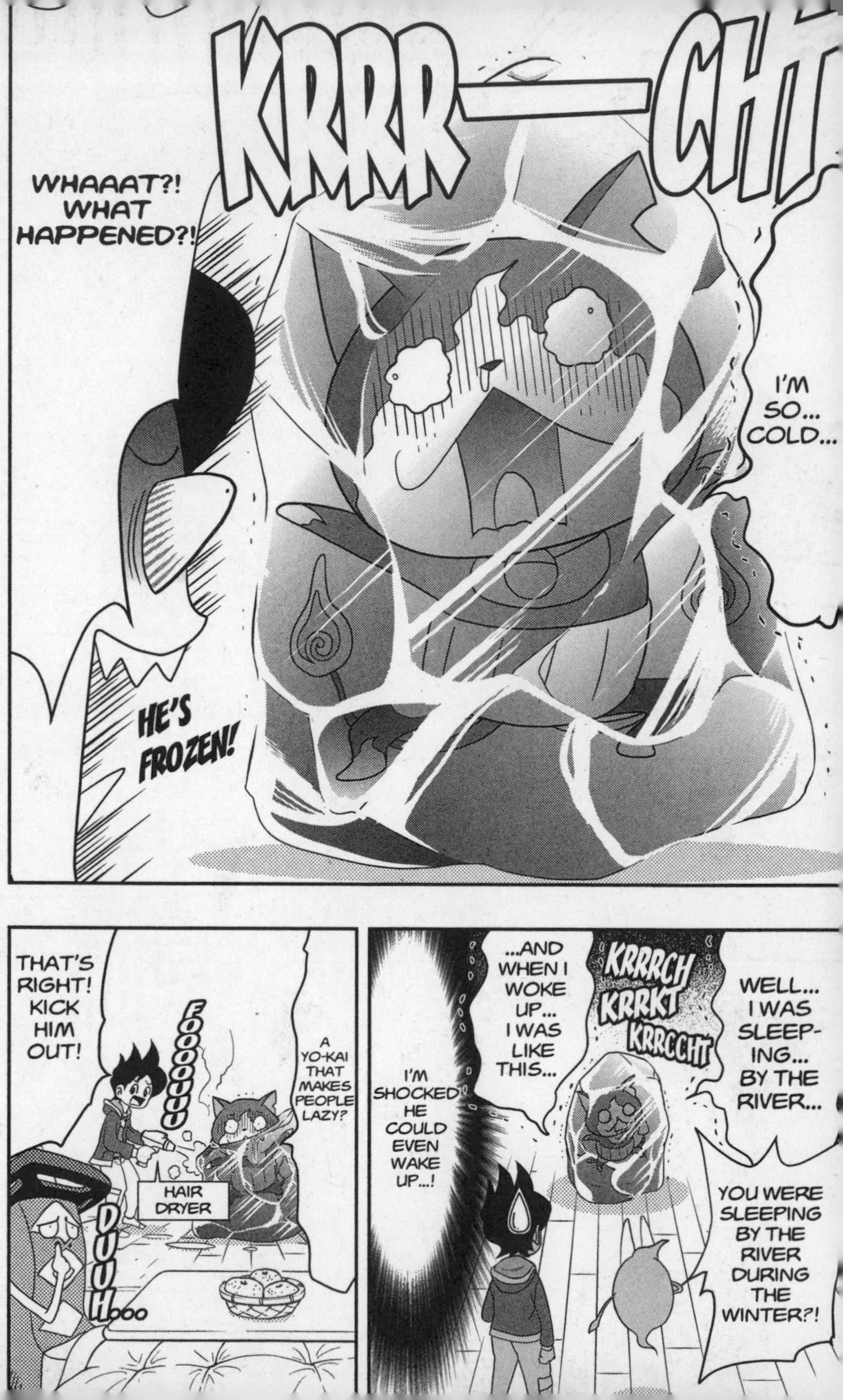
KRRR—CHT
WHAAAT?! WHAT HAPPENED?!
I'M SO... COLD...
HE'S FROZEN!
WELL... I WAS SLEEP-ING... BY THE RIVER...
KRRRCH KRRKT KRRCCHT
...AND WHEN I WOKE UP... I WAS LIKE THIS...
YOU WERE SLEEPING BY THE RIVER DURING THE WINTER?!
I'M SHOCKED HE COULD EVEN WAKE UP...!
A YO-KAI THAT MAKES PEOPLE LAZY?
THAT'S RIGHT! KICK HIM OUT!
FOOOOUUU
HAIR DRYER
DUUHooo

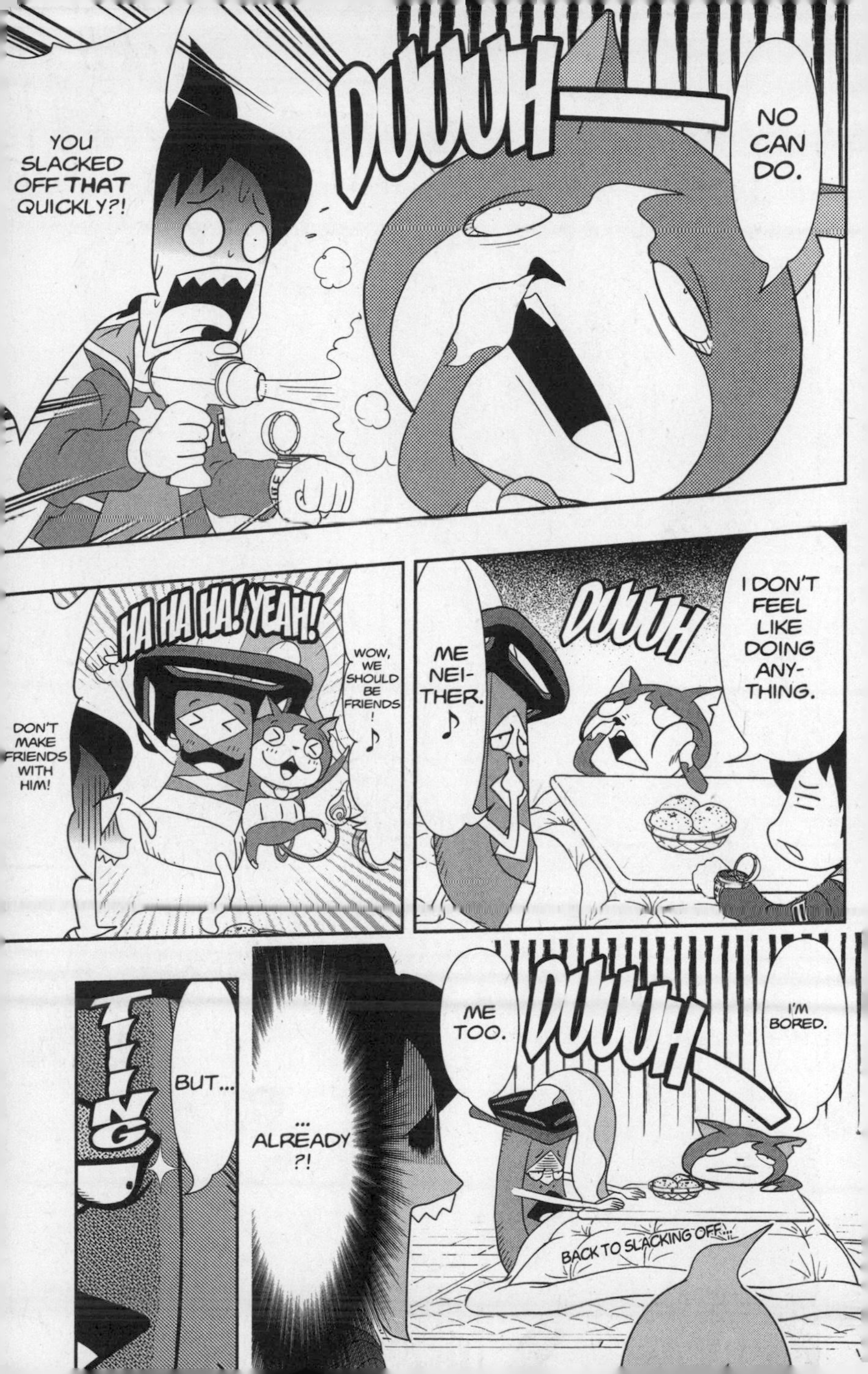
NO CAN DO.
DUUUH—
YOU SLACKED OFF THAT QUICKLY?!
I DON'T FEEL LIKE DOING ANY-THING.
DUUUH
ME NEI-THER. ♪
WOW, WE SHOULD BE FRIENDS! ♪
HA HA HA! YEAH!
DON'T MAKE FRIENDS WITH HIM!
I'M BORED.
DUUUH—
ME TOO.
BACK TO SLACKING OFF...
...ALREADY?!
BUT...
TIING!

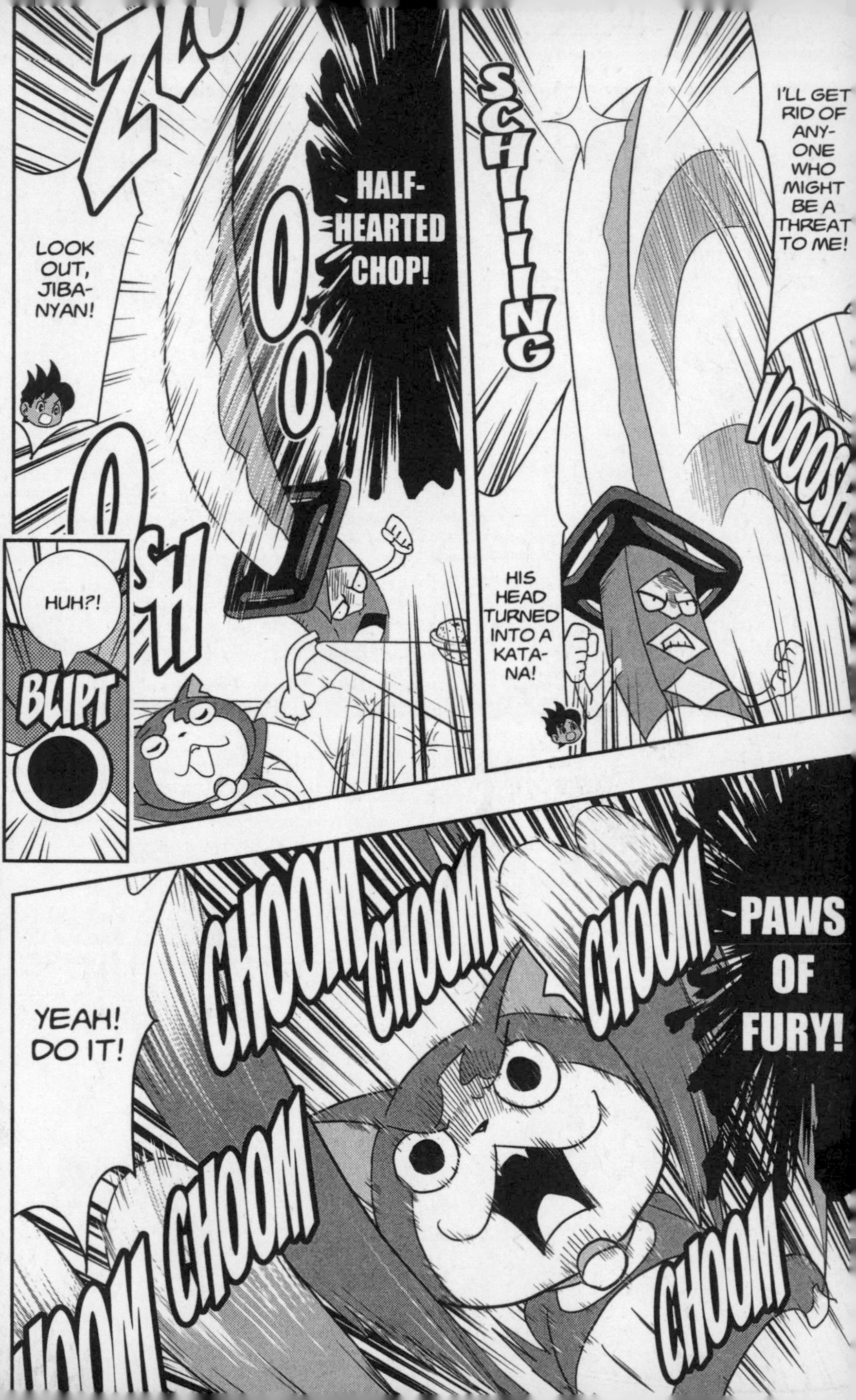
SCHIIIING
I'LL GET RID OF ANY-ONE WHO MIGHT BE A THREAT TO ME!
HIS HEAD TURNED INTO A KATA-NA!
VOOOOSH
HALF-HEARTED CHOP!
LOOK OUT, JIBA-NYAN!
HUH?!
BLIPT
PAWS OF FURY!
CHOOM
CHOOM
CHOOM
YEAH! DO IT!
CHOOM
CHOOM

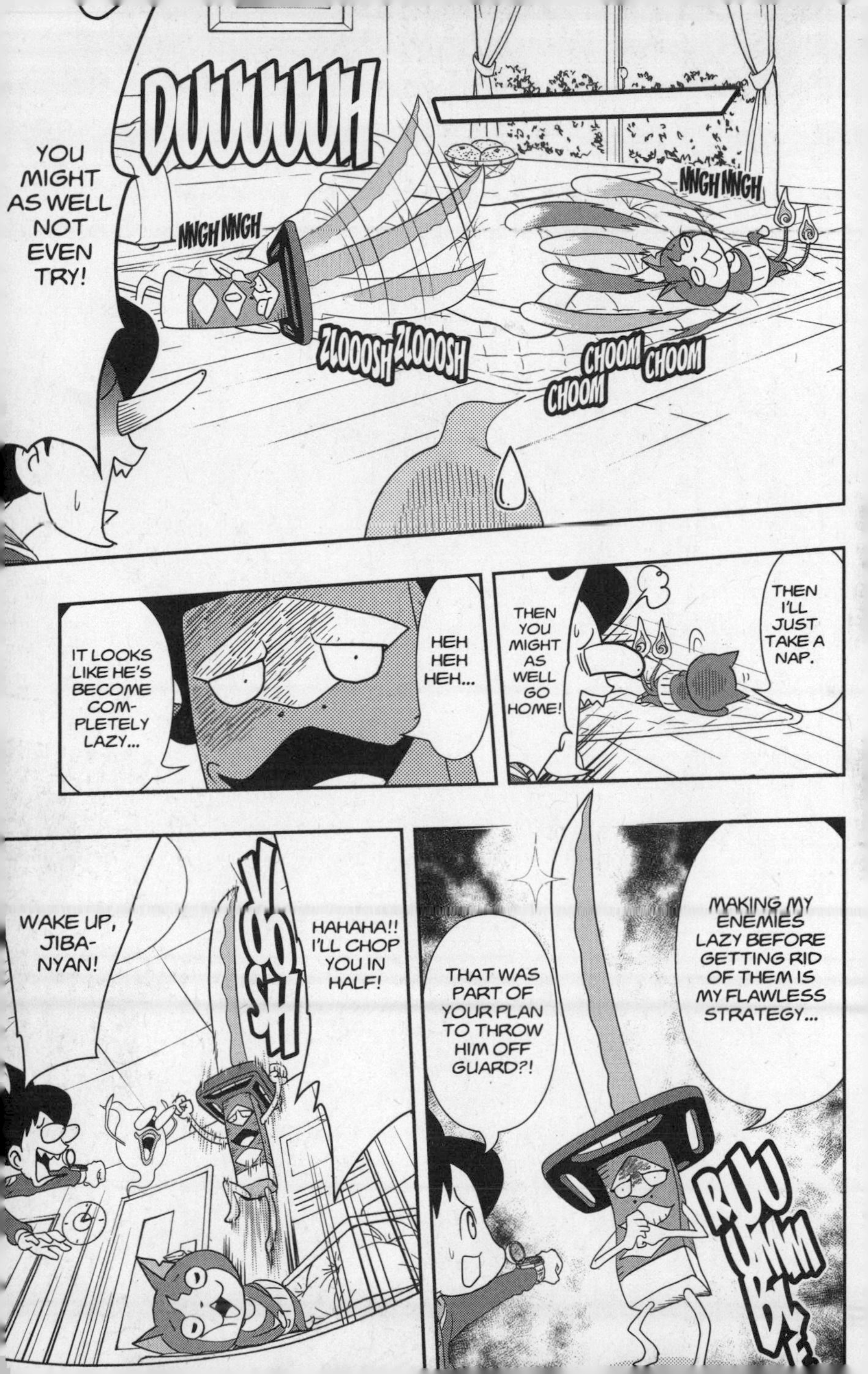
DUUUUUH
NNGH NNGH
NNGH NNGH
CHOOM CHOOM CHOOM
ZLOOOSH ZLOOOSH
YOU MIGHT AS WELL NOT EVEN TRY!
THEN I'LL JUST TAKE A NAP.
THEN YOU MIGHT AS WELL GO HOME!
HEH HEH HEH...
IT LOOKS LIKE HE'S BECOME COM-PLETELY LAZY...
MAKING MY ENEMIES LAZY BEFORE GETTING RID OF THEM IS MY FLAWLESS STRATEGY...
THAT WAS PART OF YOUR PLAN TO THROW HIM OFF GUARD?!
RUUUMMBLE
HAHAHA!! I'LL CHOP YOU IN HALF!
VOOSH
WAKE UP, JIBA-NYAN!

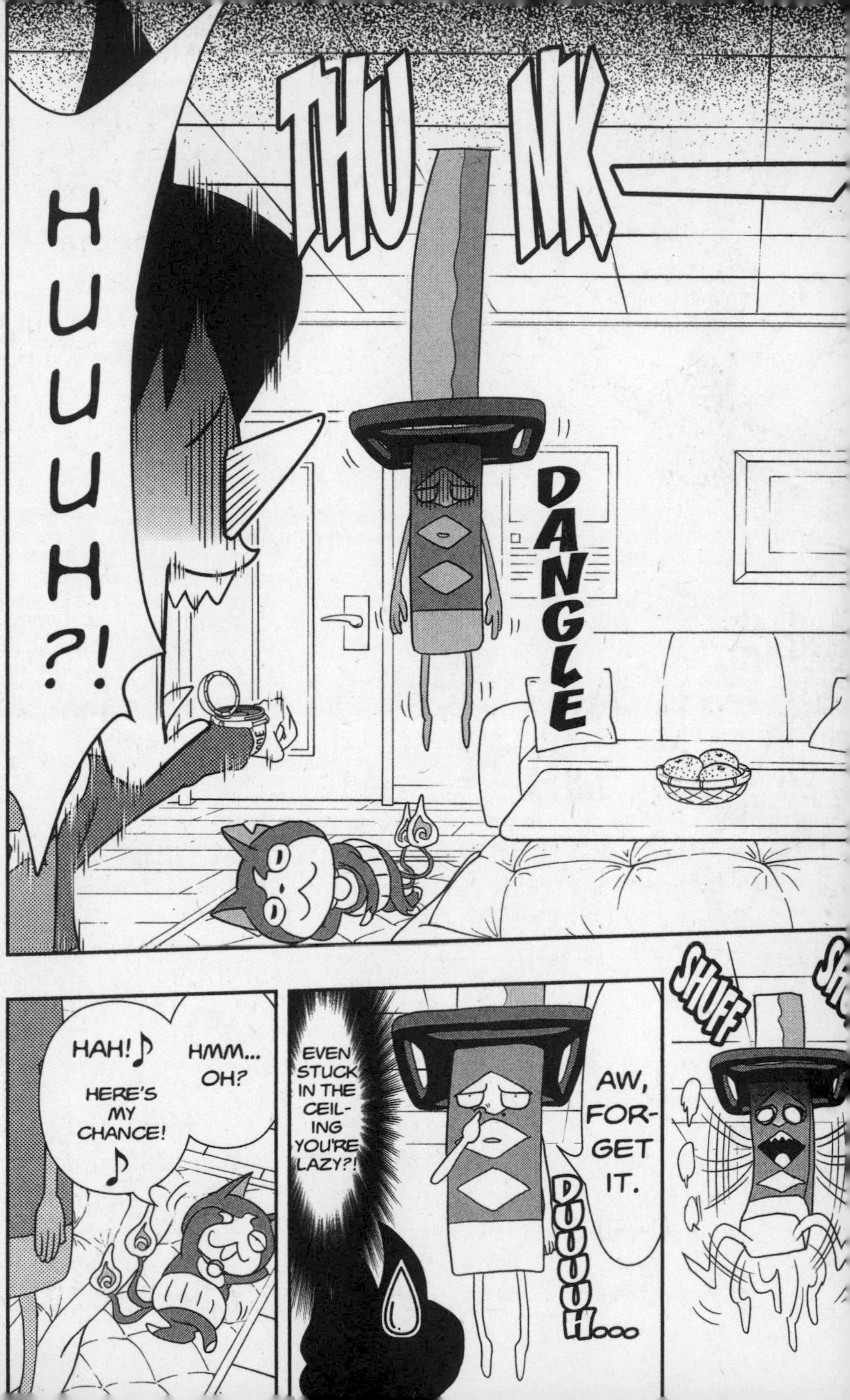
THUNK
DANGLE
HUUUH?!
SHUFF
AW, FOR-GET IT.
DUUUUUH...
EVEN STUCK IN THE CEIL-ING YOU'RE LAZY?!
HMM... OH?
HAH! ♪ HERE'S MY CHANCE! ♪

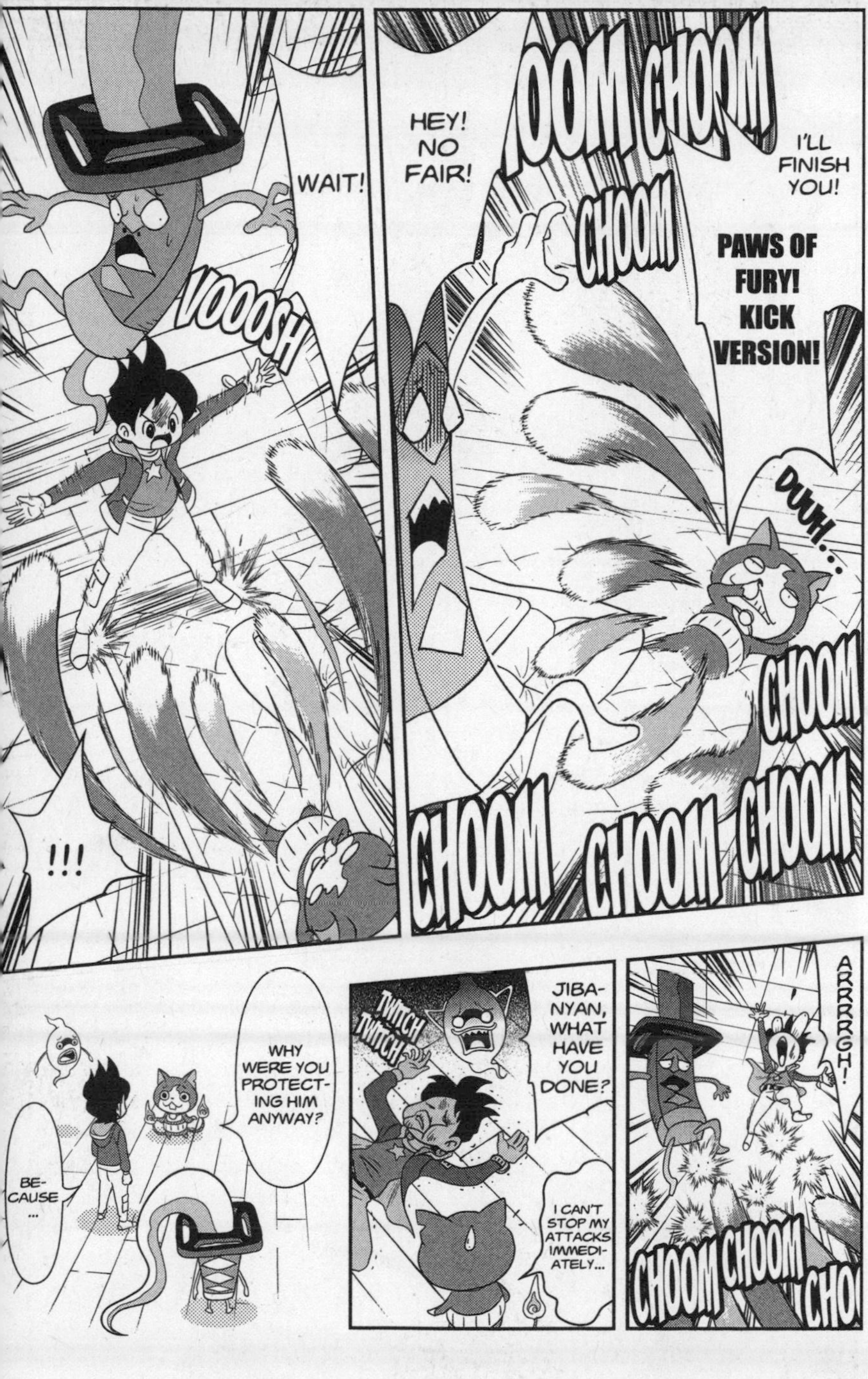
I'LL FINISH YOU!
PAWS OF FURY! KICK VERSION!
OOM CHOOM
CHOOM
HEY! NO FAIR!
DUUH...
CHOOM
CHOOM
CHOOM
CHOOM
WAIT!
VOOOSH
!!!
ARRRRGH!
CHOOM CHOOM CHO
JIBA-NYAN, WHAT HAVE YOU DONE?
TWITCH TWITCH
I CAN'T STOP MY ATTACKS IMMEDI-ATELY...
WHY WERE YOU PROTECT-ING HIM ANYWAY?
BE-CAUSE ...

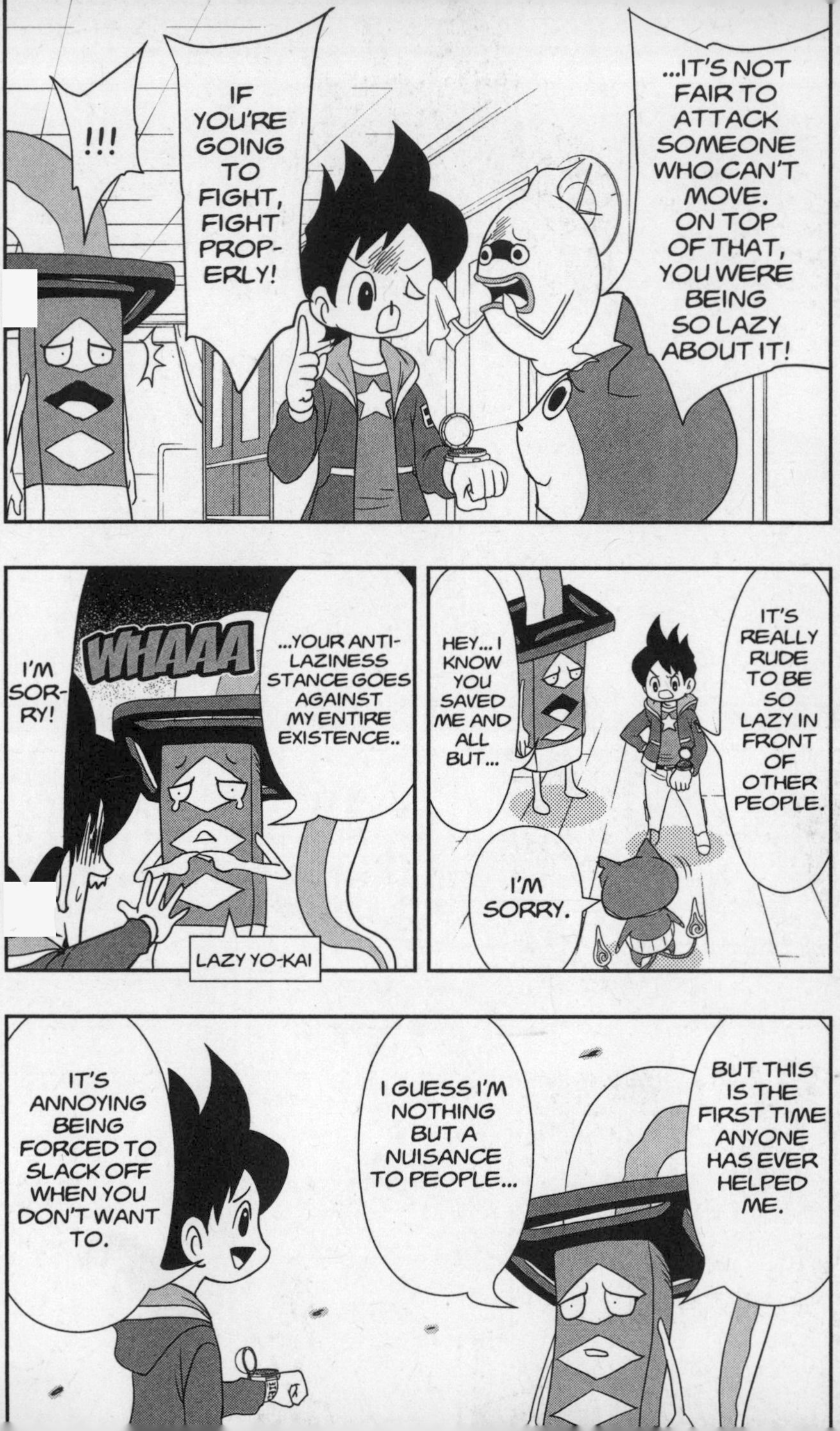
...IT'S NOT FAIR TO ATTACK SOMEONE WHO CAN'T MOVE. ON TOP OF THAT, YOU WERE BEING SO LAZY ABOUT IT!
IF YOU'RE GOING TO FIGHT, FIGHT PROPERLY!
!!!
IT'S REALLY RUDE TO BE SO LAZY IN FRONT OF OTHER PEOPLE.
I'M SORRY.
HEY... I KNOW YOU SAVED ME AND ALL BUT...
...YOUR ANTI-LAZINESS STANCE GOES AGAINST MY ENTIRE EXISTENCE..
WHAAA
I'M SORRY!
LAZY YO-KAI
BUT THIS IS THE FIRST TIME ANYONE HAS EVER HELPED ME.
I GUESS I'M NOTHING BUT A NUISANCE TO PEOPLE...
IT'S ANNOYING BEING FORCED TO SLACK OFF WHEN YOU DON'T WANT TO.

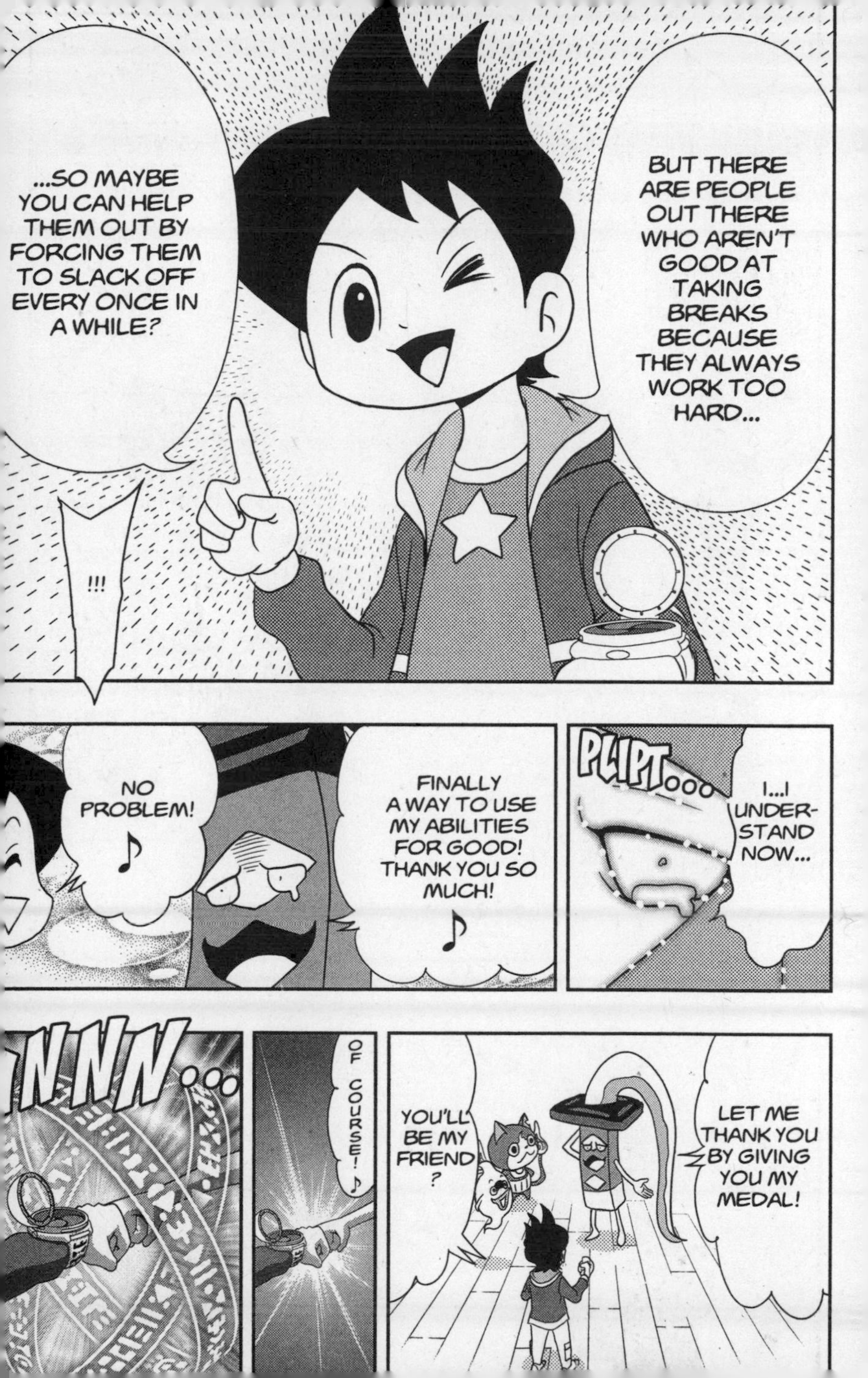
BUT THERE ARE PEOPLE OUT THERE WHO AREN'T GOOD AT TAKING BREAKS BECAUSE THEY ALWAYS WORK TOO HARD...
...SO MAYBE YOU CAN HELP THEM OUT BY FORCING THEM TO SLACK OFF EVERY ONCE IN A WHILE?
!!!
PLIPT...
I...I UNDER-STAND NOW...
FINALLY A WAY TO USE MY ABILITIES FOR GOOD! THANK YOU SO MUCH! ♪
NO PROBLEM! ♪
LET ME THANK YOU BY GIVING YOU MY MEDAL!
YOU'LL BE MY FRIEND?
OF COURSE! ♪
NNNN...

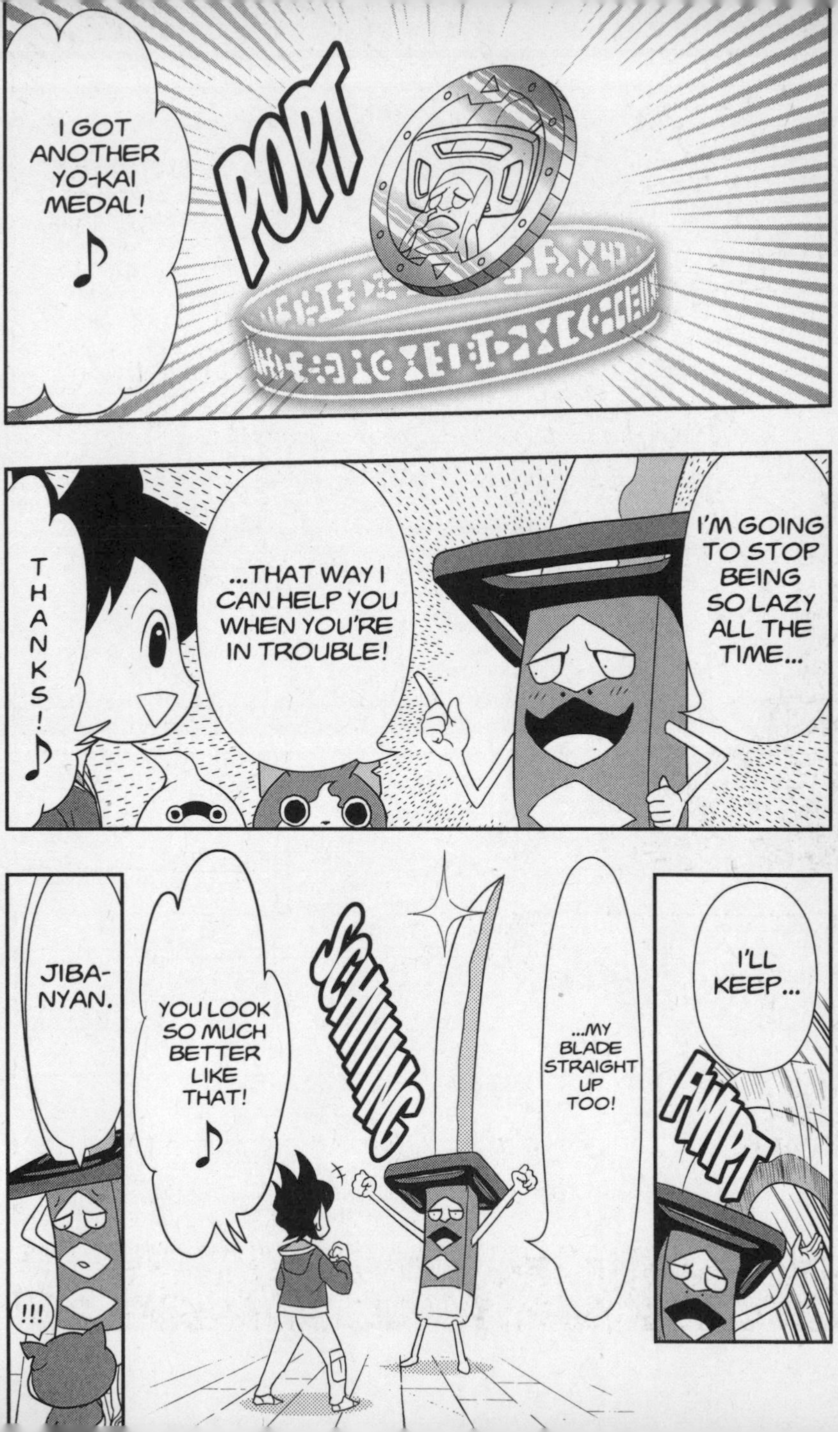
I GOT ANOTHER YO-KAI MEDAL! ♪
POPT
I'M GOING TO STOP BEING SO LAZY ALL THE TIME...
...THAT WAY I CAN HELP YOU WHEN YOU'RE IN TROUBLE!
THANKS! ♪
I'LL KEEP...
FWIPT
...MY BLADE STRAIGHT UP TOO!
SCHING
YOU LOOK SO MUCH BETTER LIKE THAT! ♪
JIBA-NYAN.
!!!

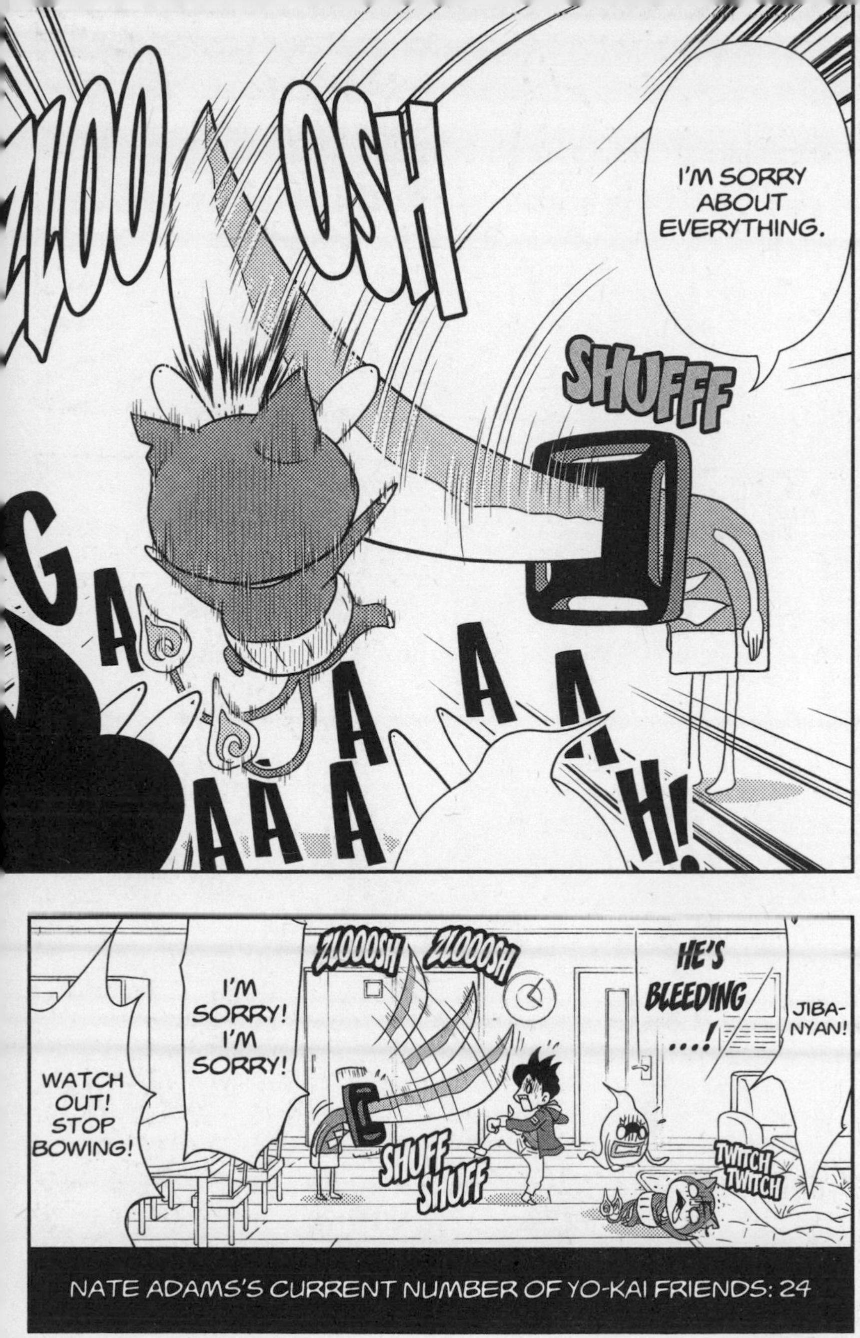
I'M SORRY ABOUT EVERYTHING.
SHUFFF
ZLOOOSH
GAAAAAAAAH!
JIBA-NYAN!
HE'S BLEEDING ...!
ZLOOOSH
ZLOOOSH
I'M SORRY! I'M SORRY!
SHUFF SHUFF
TWITCH TWITCH
WATCH OUT! STOP BOWING!
NATE ADAMS'S CURRENT NUMBER OF YO-KAI FRIENDS: 24

LATER...
I THINK I'M BETTER OFF BEING LAZY.
DUUH
YEAH, IT'S NOT AS DAN-GER-OUS...
THANKS FOR EVERY-THING.
SHUFF
NOW YOU CAN BOW WITHOUT HURTING ANYONE!
I'LL SEE YOU LA-TER!
ZWOOSH
VOOOSH
ARRRGH!
GAAAAAH!!
ZZ
OOOSH

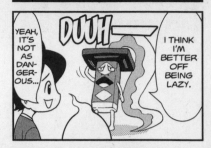

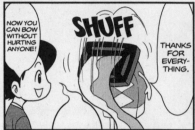

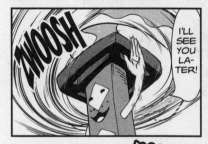

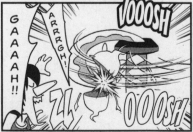

CHAPTER 31: STAY OUT OF THE WAY!

FEATURING BLOCKING YO-KAI BLOWKADE

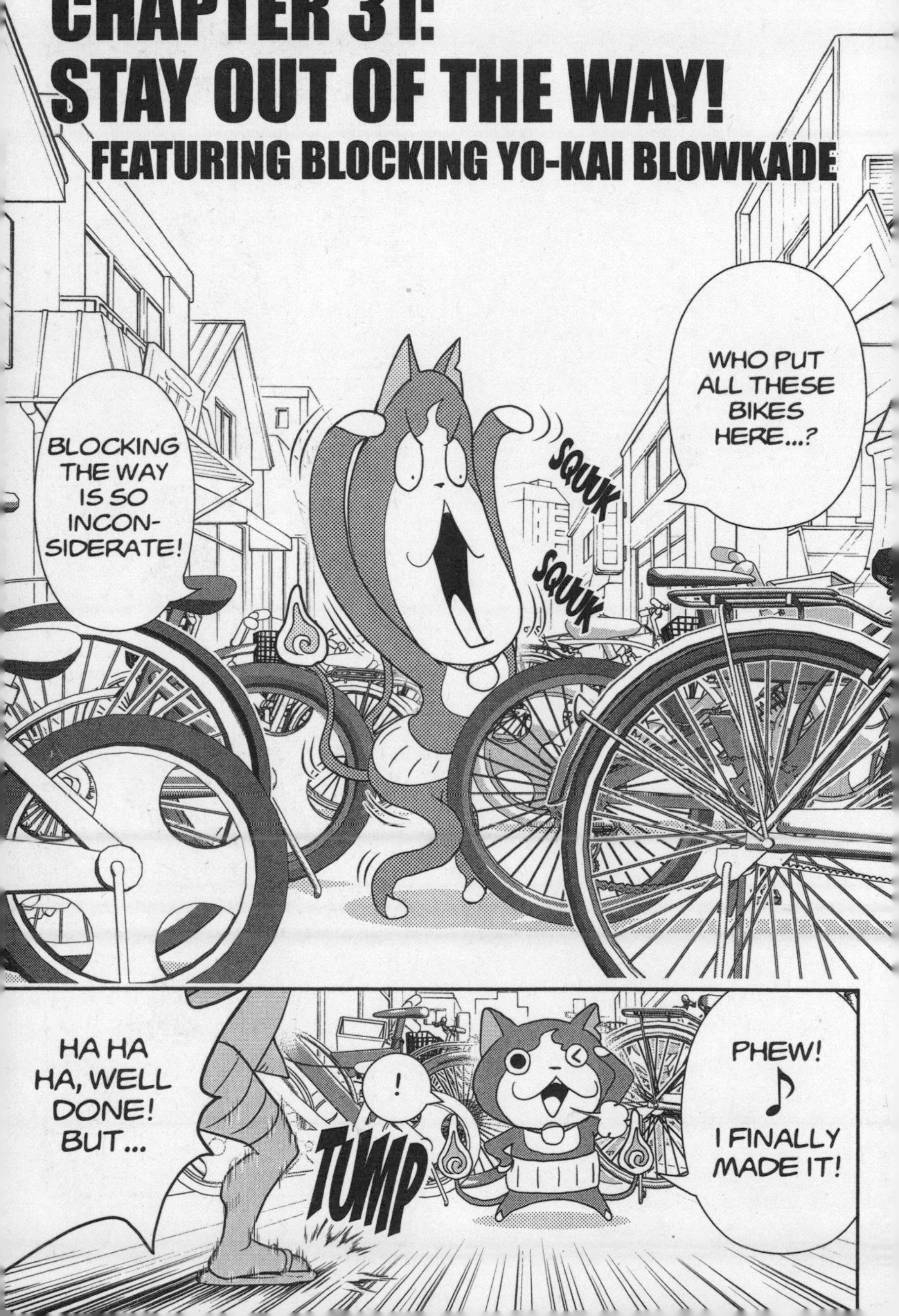
WHO PUT ALL THESE BIKES HERE...?
SQUUK
SQUUK
BLOCKING THE WAY IS SO INCON-SIDERATE!
PHEW! ♪ I FINALLY MADE IT!
!
TUMP
HA HA HA, WELL DONE! BUT...

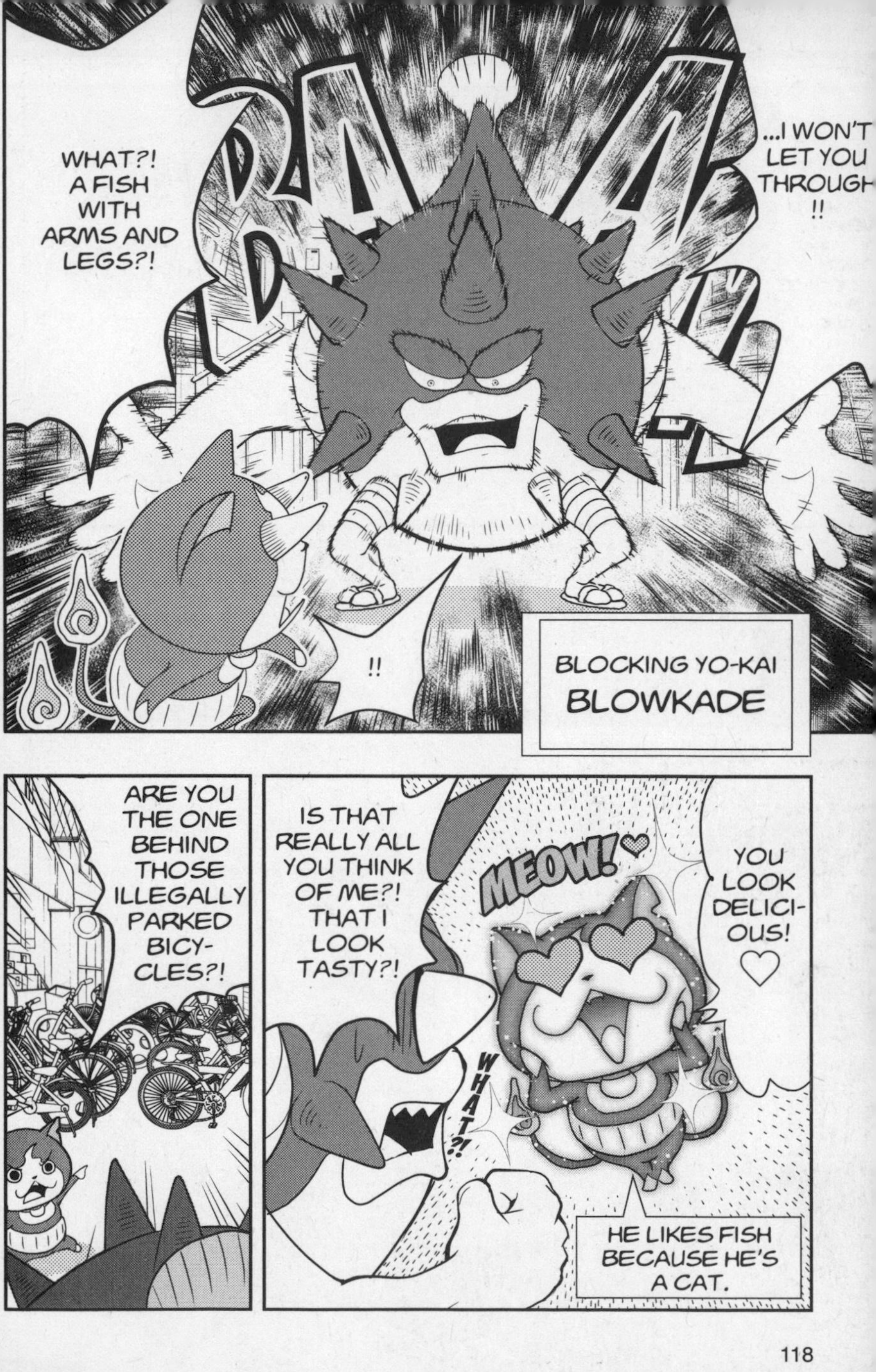
...I WON'T LET YOU THROUGH !!
WHAT?! A FISH WITH ARMS AND LEGS?!
!!
BLOCKING YO-KAI
BLOWKADE
YOU LOOK DELICI-OUS! ♡
MEOW! ♥
IS THAT REALLY ALL YOU THINK OF ME?! THAT I LOOK TASTY?!
WHAT?!
HE LIKES FISH BECAUSE HE'S A CAT.
ARE YOU THE ONE BEHIND THOSE ILLEGALLY PARKED BICY-CLES?!

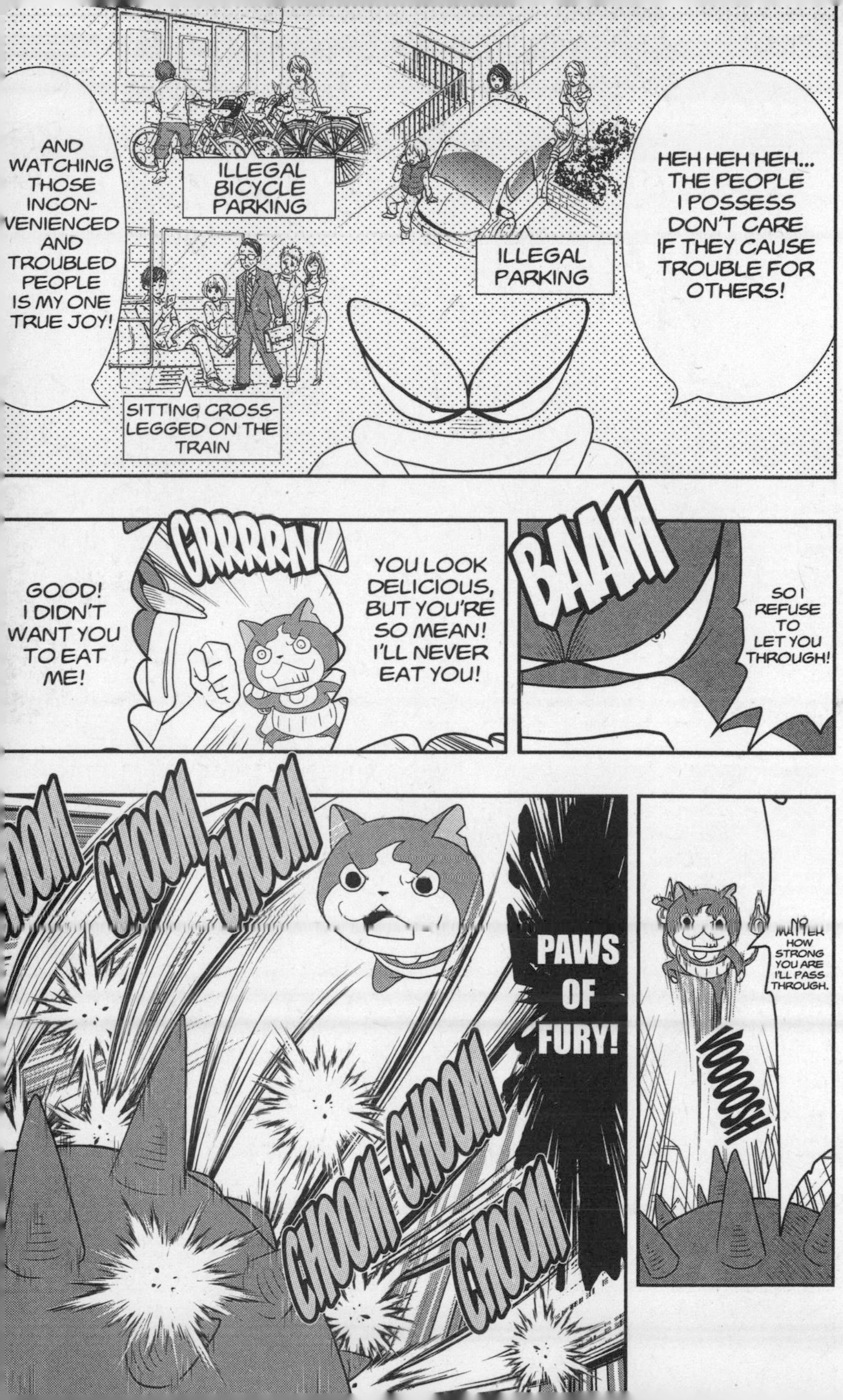
HEH HEH HEH... THE PEOPLE I POSSESS DON'T CARE IF THEY CAUSE TROUBLE FOR OTHERS!
ILLEGAL PARKING
ILLEGAL BICYCLE PARKING
AND WATCHING THOSE INCON-VENIENCED AND TROUBLED PEOPLE IS MY ONE TRUE JOY!
SITTING CROSS-LEGGED ON THE TRAIN
BAAM
SO I REFUSE TO LET YOU THROUGH!
GRRRRN
YOU LOOK DELICIOUS, BUT YOU'RE SO MEAN! I'LL NEVER EAT YOU!
GOOD! I DIDN'T WANT YOU TO EAT ME!
NO MATTER HOW STRONG YOU ARE I'LL PASS THROUGH.
VOOOOSH
PAWS OF FURY!
CHOOM
CHOOM
CHOOM
CHOOM
CHOOM
CHOOM

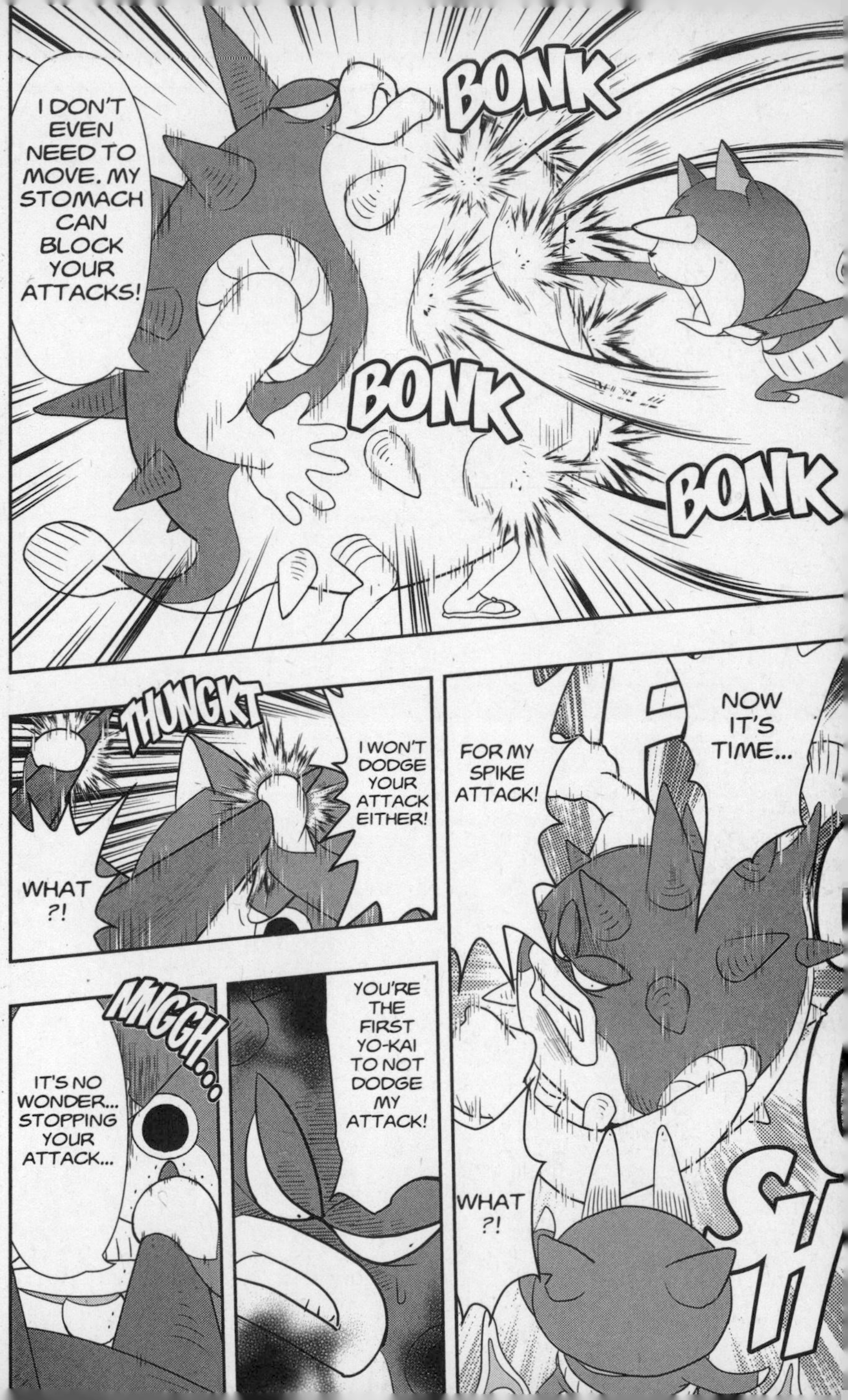
BONK
BONK
BONK
I DON'T EVEN NEED TO MOVE. MY STOMACH CAN BLOCK YOUR ATTACKS!
NOW IT'S TIME...
FOR MY SPIKE ATTACK!
WHAT ?!
I WON'T DODGE YOUR ATTACK EITHER!
THUNGKT
WHAT ?!
YOU'RE THE FIRST YO-KAI TO NOT DODGE MY ATTACK!
MNGGH...
IT'S NO WONDER... STOPPING YOUR ATTACK...

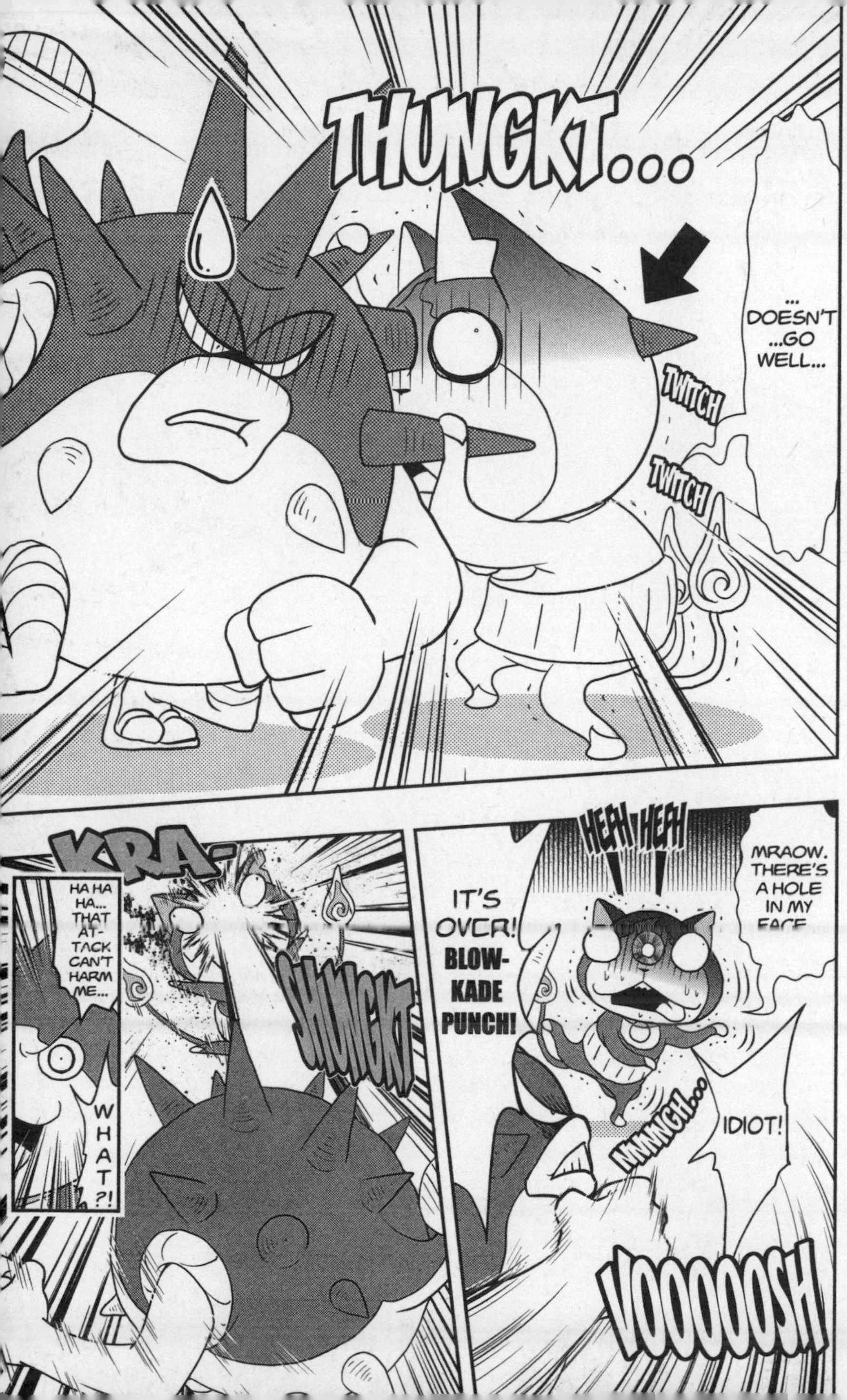
THUNGKT...
... DOESN'T ...GO WELL...
TWITCH
TWITCH
HEFH HEFH
MRAOW. THERE'S A HOLE IN MY FACE
IT'S OVER! BLOW-KADE PUNCH!
IDIOT!
NNNNGH...
VOOOOOSH
KRA-
HA HA HA... THAT AT-TACK CAN'T HARM ME...
SHUNGKT
WHAT?!

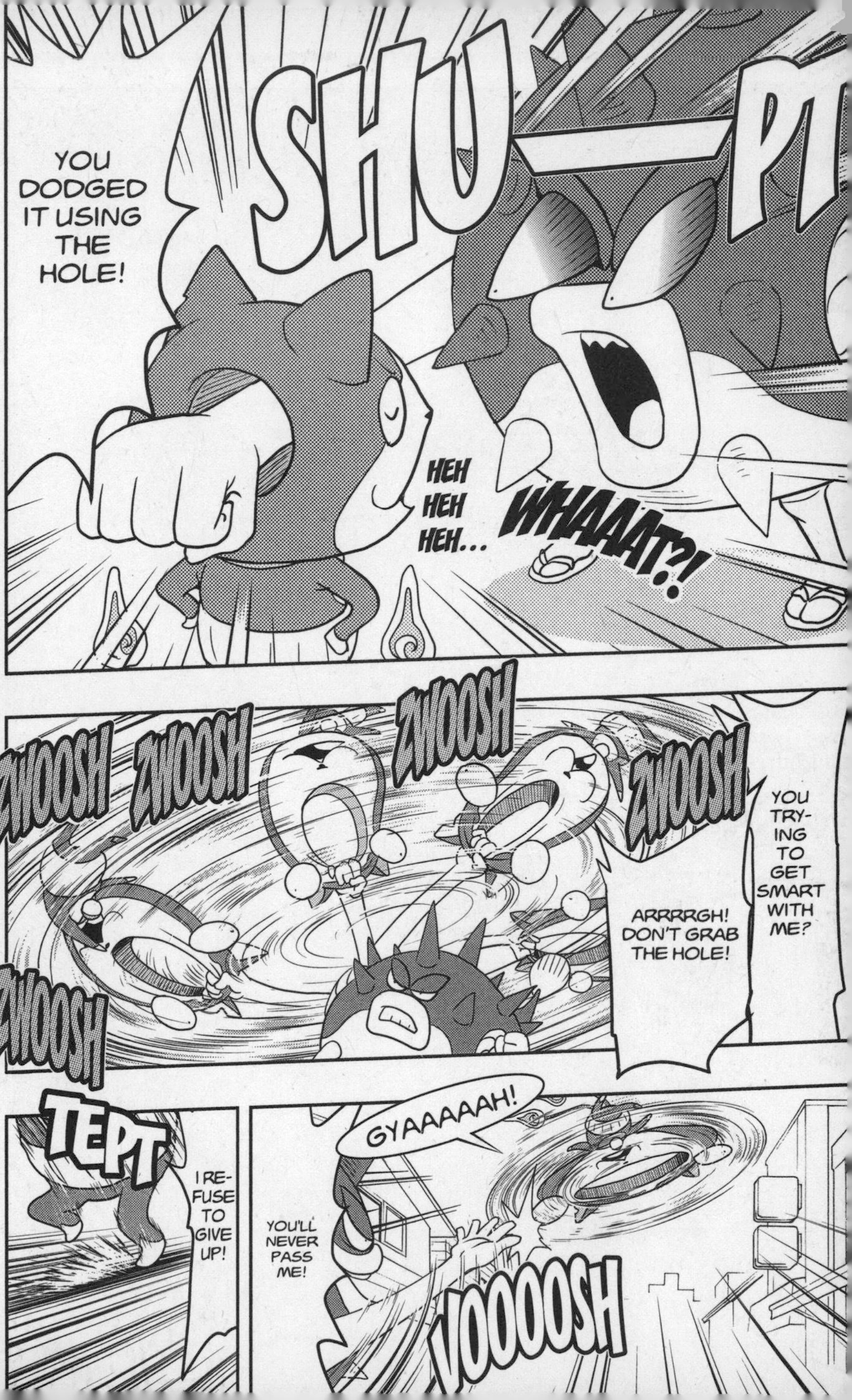

SHU—PT
YOU DODGED IT USING THE HOLE!
WHAAAT?!
HEH HEH HEH...
YOU TRYING TO GET SMART WITH ME?
ZWOOSH
ZWOOSH
ARRRRGH! DON'T GRAB THE HOLE!
ZWOOSH
ZWOOSH
ZWOOSH
GYAAAAAH!
YOU'LL NEVER PASS ME!
VOOOOSH
TEPT
I RE-FUSE TO GIVE UP!

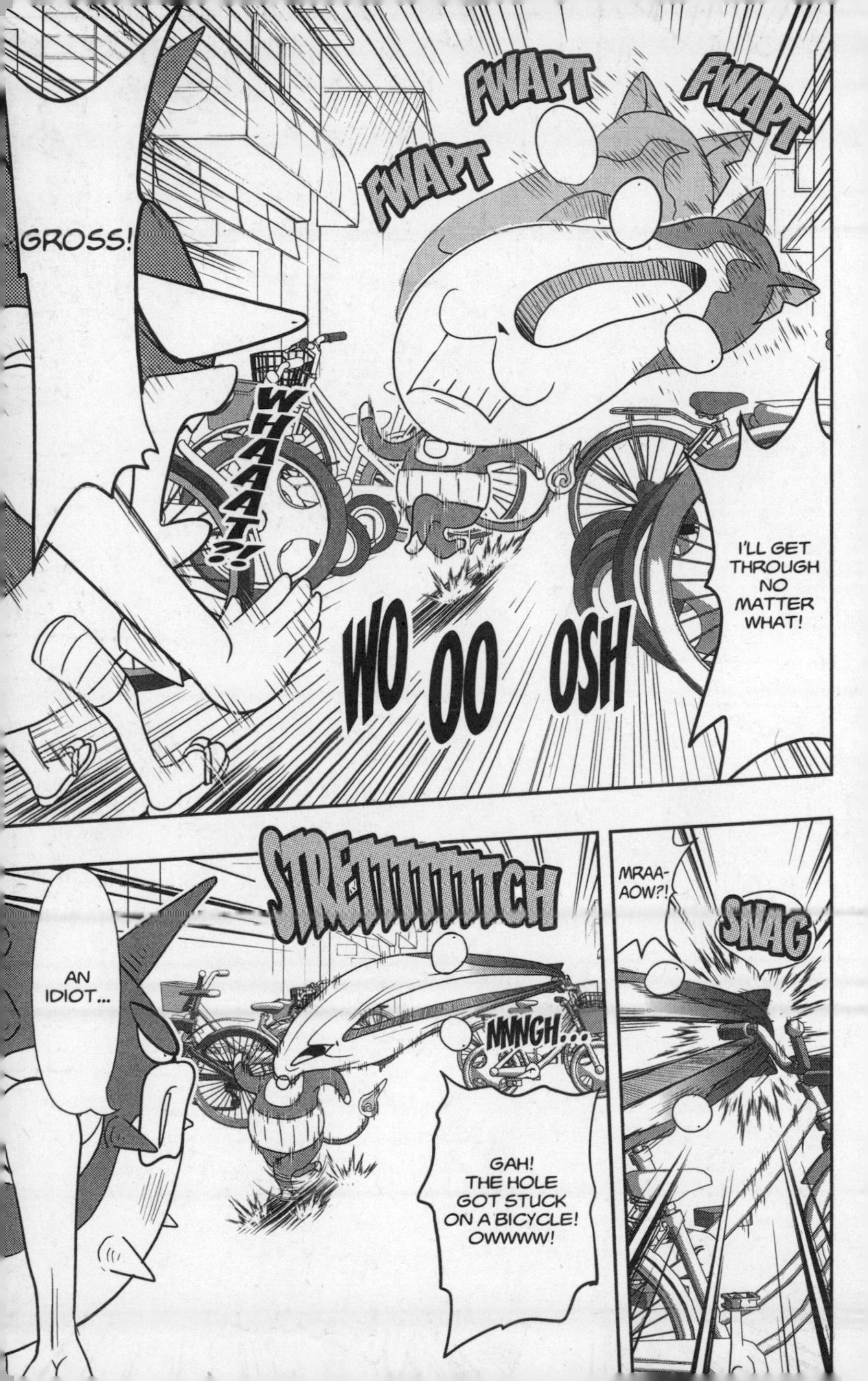
FWAPT
FWAPT
FWAPT
I'LL GET THROUGH NO MATTER WHAT!
GROSS!
WHAAAAT?!
WO OO OSH
MRAA-AOW?!
SNAG
STRETTTTTTTCH
MNNGH...
GAH! THE HOLE GOT STUCK ON A BICYCLE! OWWWW!
AN IDIOT...

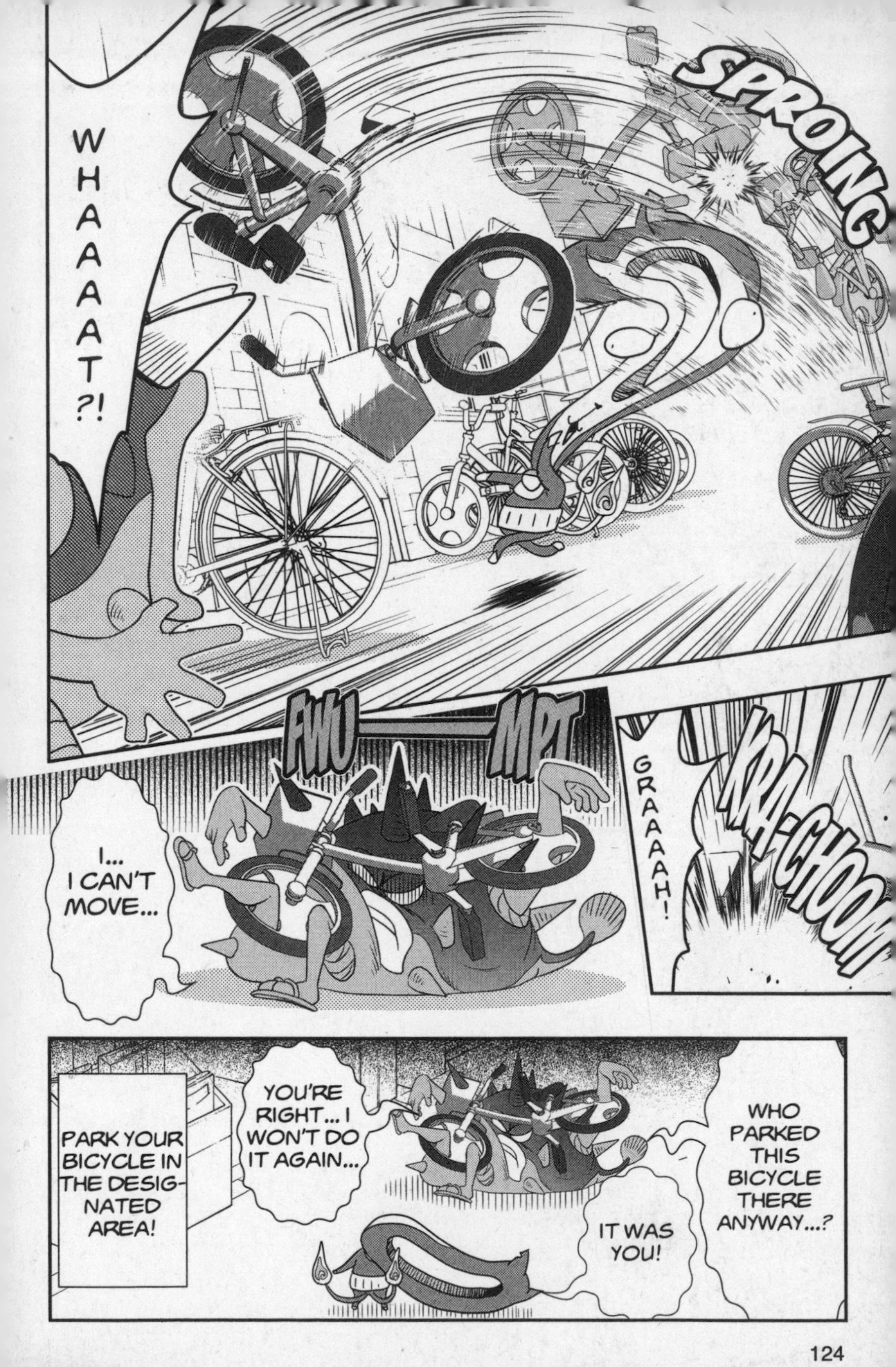
SPROING
WHAAAAAT?!
KRA-CHOOM
GRAAAAAH!
FWUMPT
I... I CAN'T MOVE...
WHO PARKED THIS BICYCLE THERE ANYWAY...?
IT WAS YOU!
YOU'RE RIGHT... I WON'T DO IT AGAIN...
PARK YOUR BICYCLE IN THE DESIG-NATED AREA!

CHAPTER 32: BEHOLD: THE JIBANYAN OF THE FUTURE?!

FEATURING ROBOT YO-KAI ROBONYAN

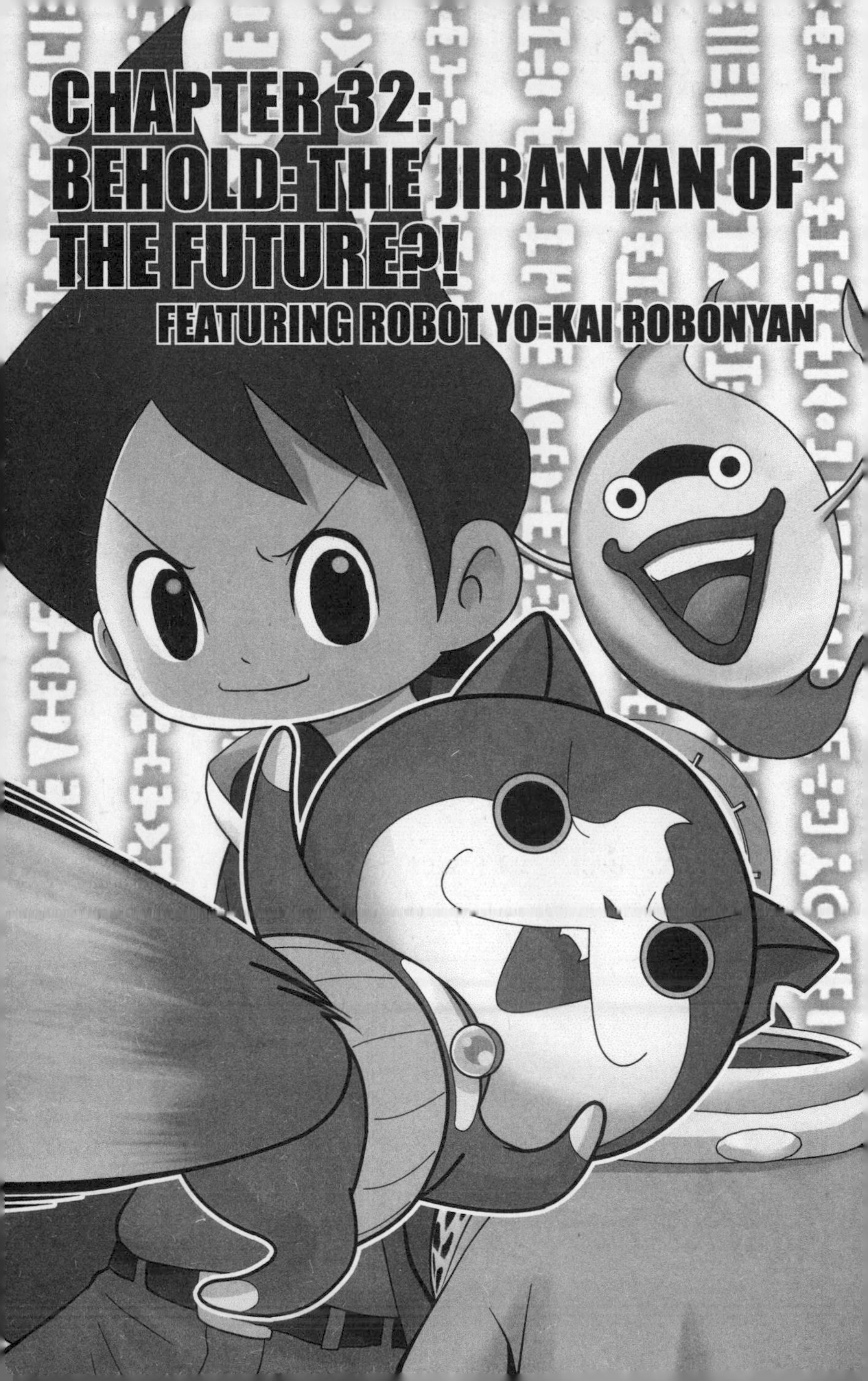

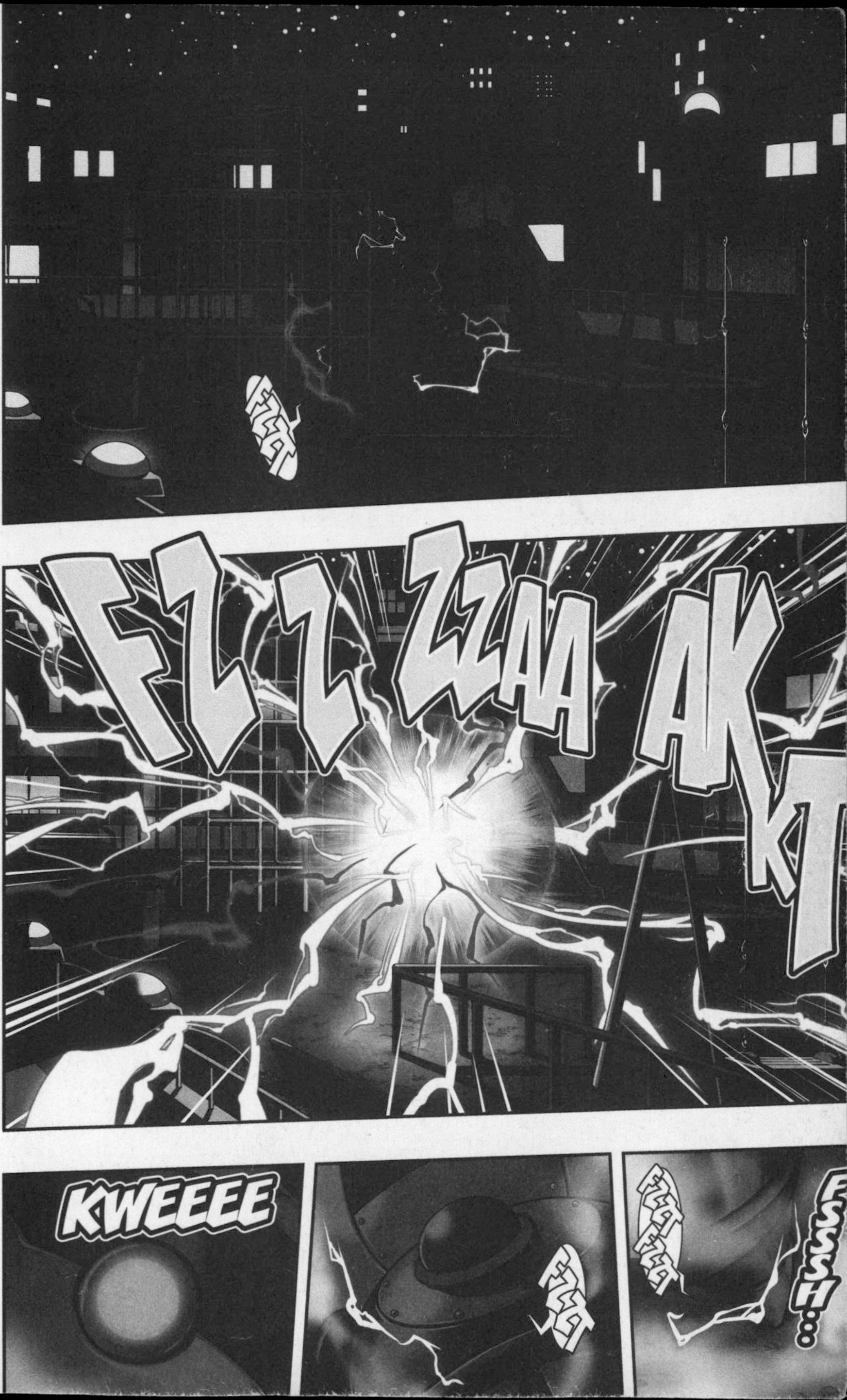
FZZT
FZZZZAAAK
KT
FSSSH...
FZZT FZZT
FZZT
KWEEEE

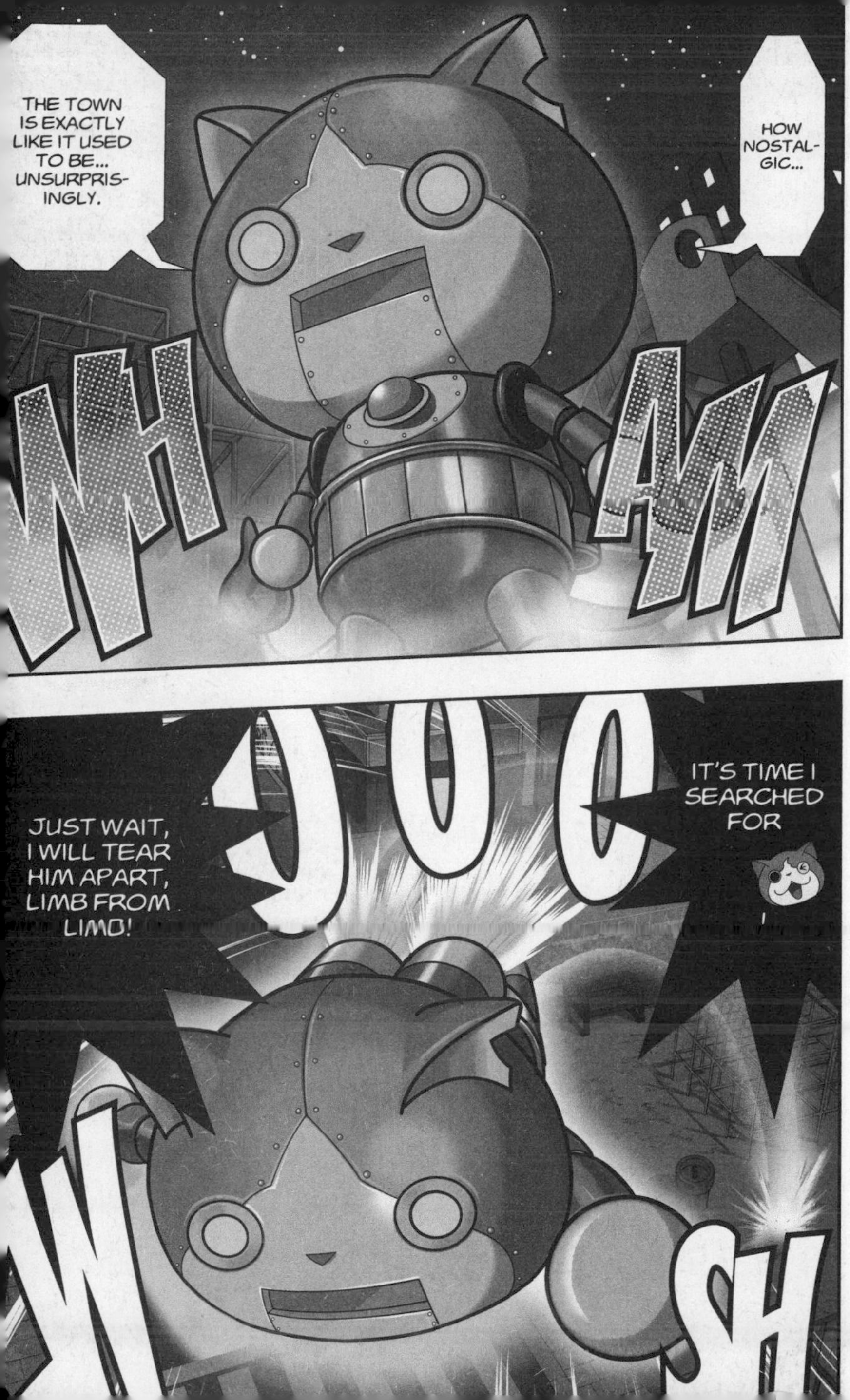
HOW NOSTAL-GIC...
THE TOWN IS EXACTLY LIKE IT USED TO BE... UNSURPRIS-INGLY.
WHAM
IT'S TIME I SEARCHED FOR
JUST WAIT, I WILL TEAR HIM APART, LIMB FROM LIMB!

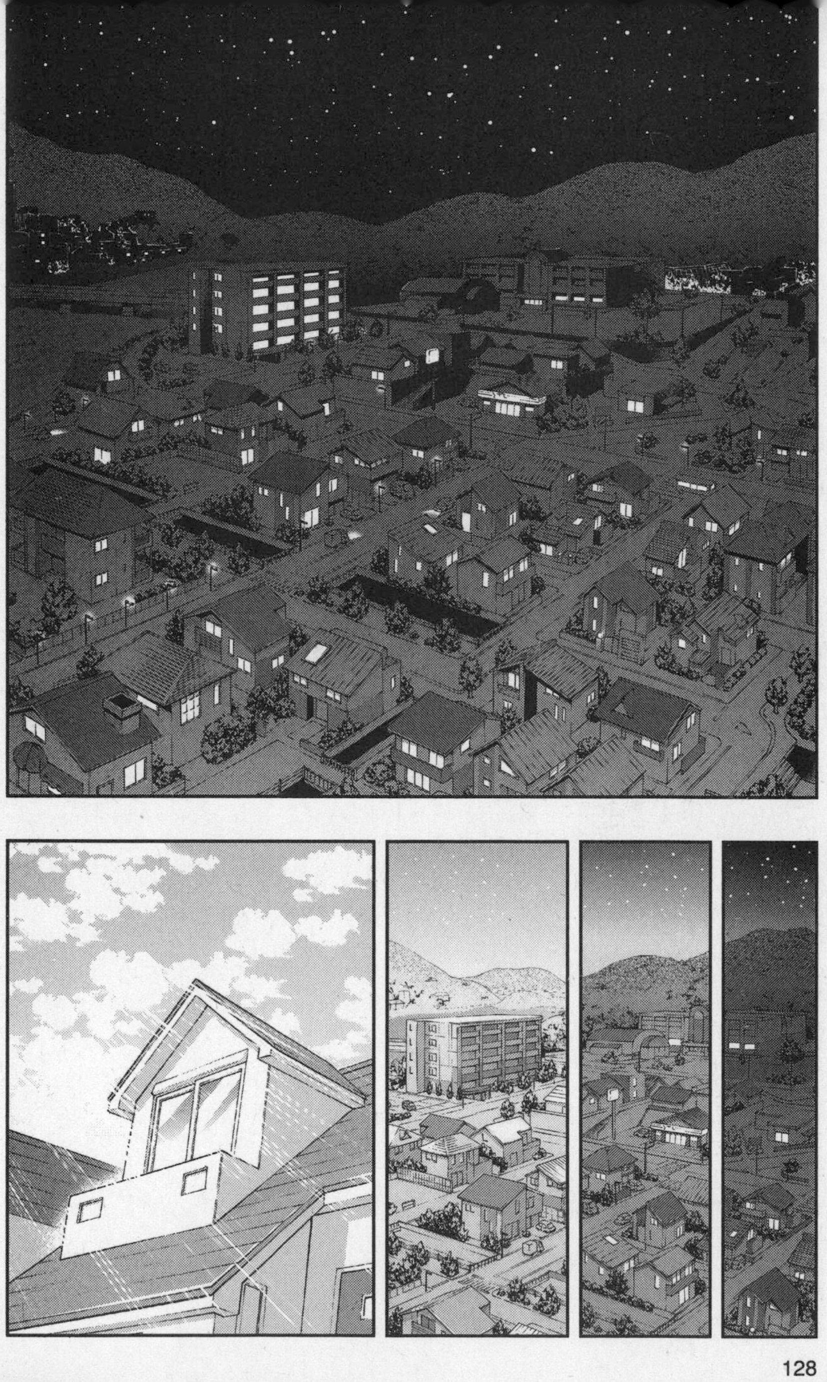

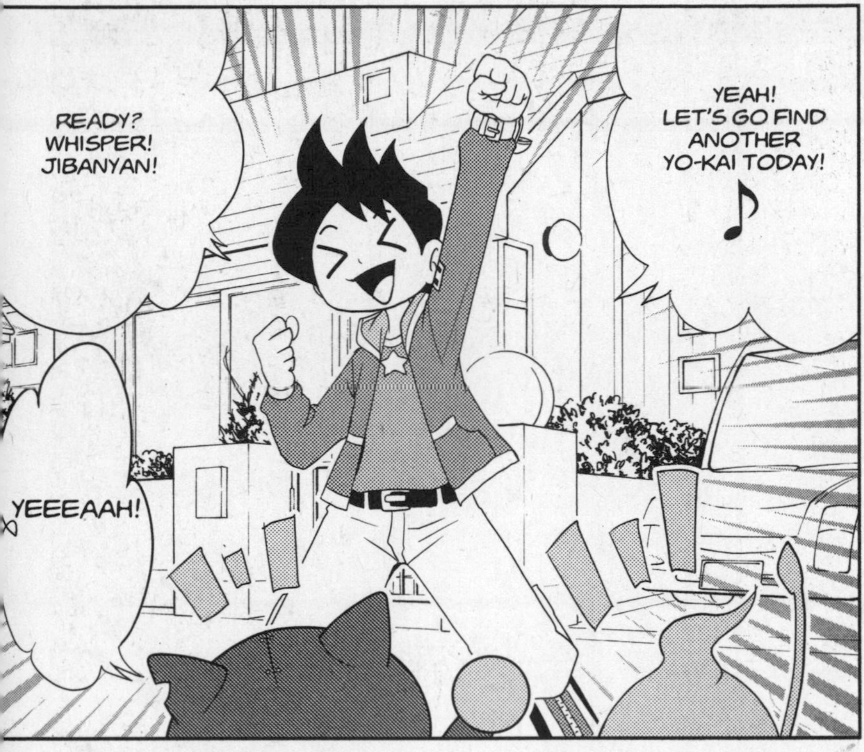
YEAH! LET'S GO FIND ANOTHER YO-KAI TODAY! ♪
READY? WHISPER! JIBANYAN!
YEEEAAH!

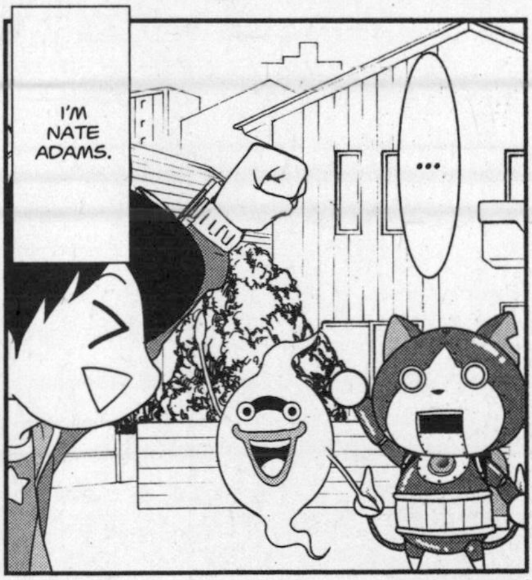
I'M NATE ADAMS.
...

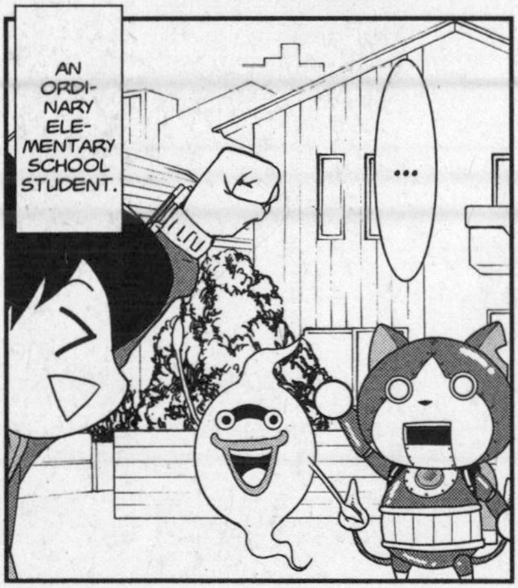
AN ORDINARY ELEMENTARY SCHOOL STUDENT.
...

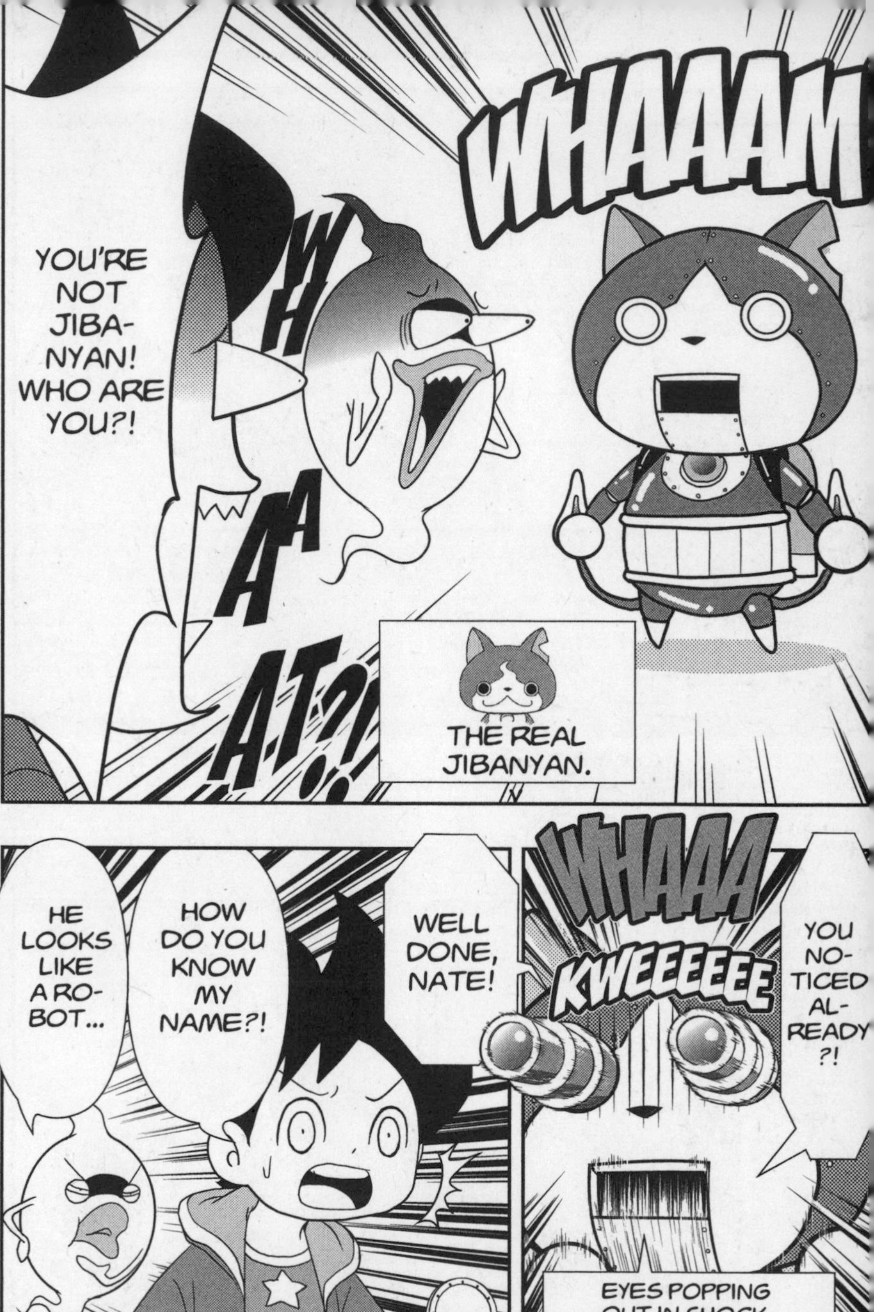

WHAAAAM
YOU'RE NOT JIBA-NYAN! WHO ARE YOU?!
WHAAA.T?!
THE REAL JIBANYAN.
WHAAAA
KWEEEEEE
YOU NO-TICED AL-READY?!
EYES POPPING OUT IN SHOCK.
WELL DONE, NATE!
HOW DO YOU KNOW MY NAME?!
HE LOOKS LIKE A RO-BOT...

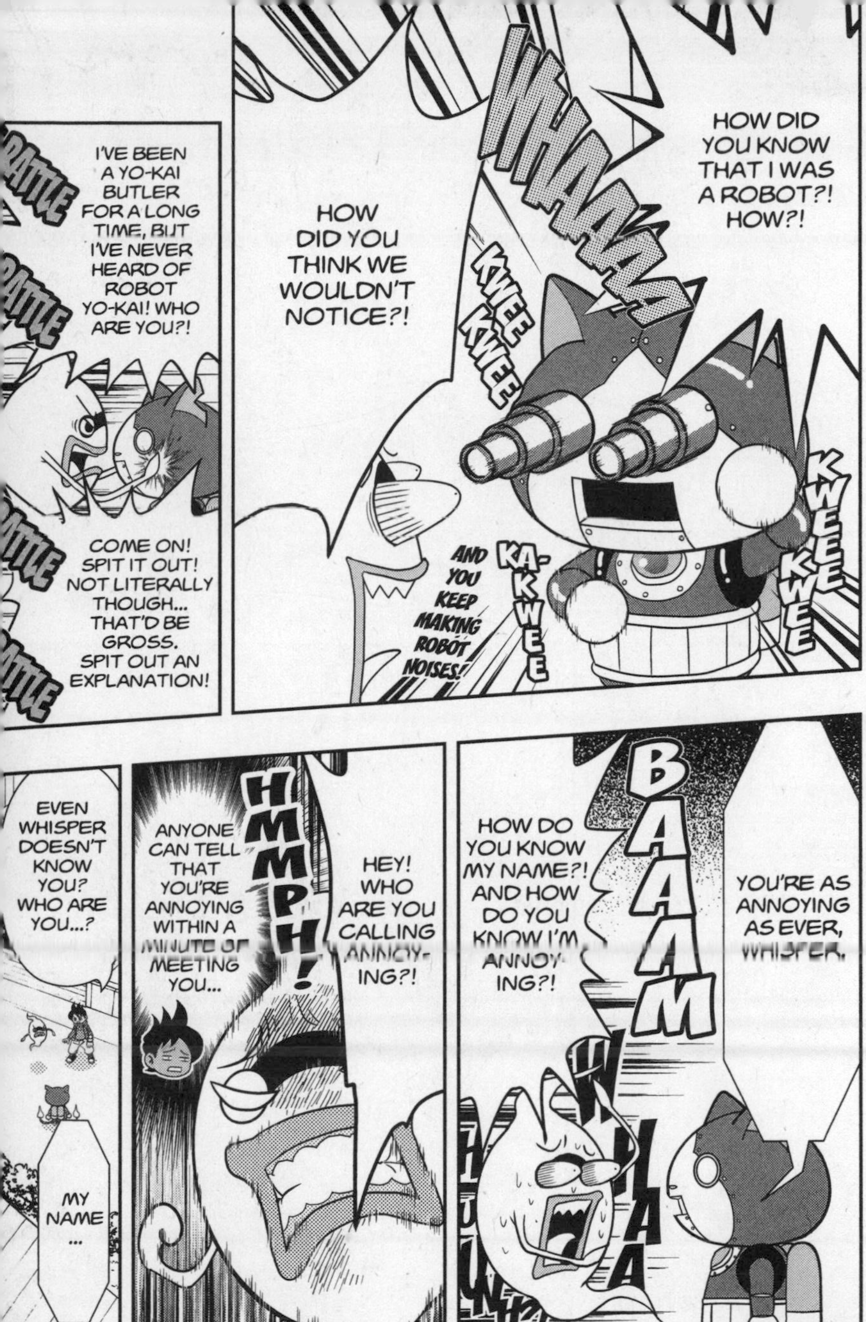
HOW DID YOU KNOW THAT I WAS A ROBOT?! HOW?!
HOW DID YOU THINK WE WOULDN'T NOTICE?!
KWEE KWEE
KWEEKWEE
KA-KWEE
AND YOU KEEP MAKING ROBOT NOISES!
I'VE BEEN A YO-KAI BUTLER FOR A LONG TIME, BUT I'VE NEVER HEARD OF ROBOT YO-KAI! WHO ARE YOU?!
RATTLE
RATTLE
RATTLE
RATTLE
COME ON! SPIT IT OUT! NOT LITERALLY THOUGH... THAT'D BE GROSS. SPIT OUT AN EXPLANATION!
YOU'RE AS ANNOYING AS EVER, WHISPER.
HOW DO YOU KNOW MY NAME?! AND HOW DO YOU KNOW I'M ANNOYING?!
HEY! WHO ARE YOU CALLING ANNOYING?!
HMMPH!
ANYONE CAN TELL THAT YOU'RE ANNOYING WITHIN A MINUTE OF MEETING YOU...
EVEN WHISPER DOESN'T KNOW YOU? WHO ARE YOU...?
MY NAME ...

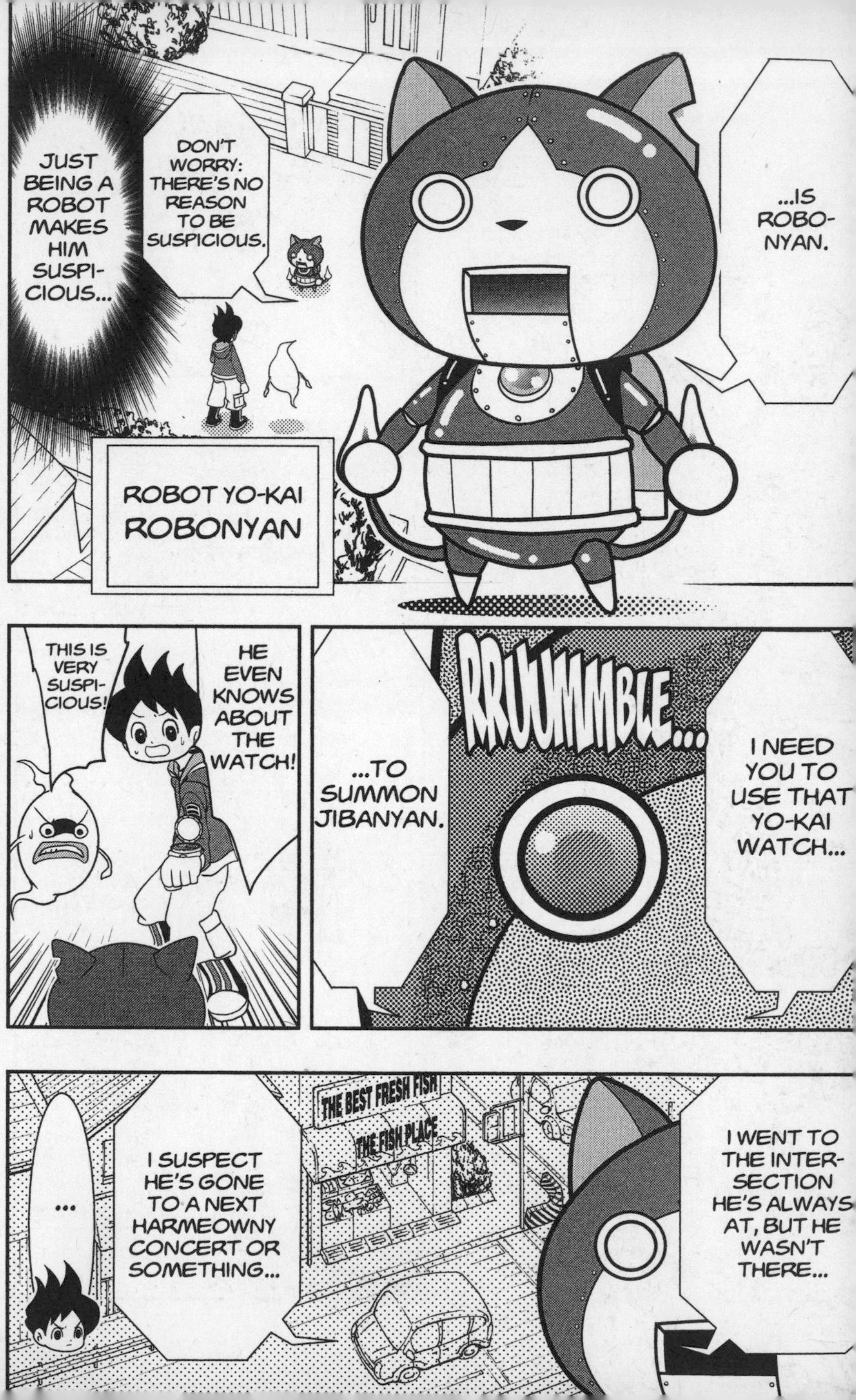
...IS ROBO-NYAN.
ROBOT YO-KAI ROBONYAN
DON'T WORRY: THERE'S NO REASON TO BE SUSPICIOUS.
JUST BEING A ROBOT MAKES HIM SUSPICIOUS...
I NEED YOU TO USE THAT YO-KAI WATCH...
RRUUMMBLE...
...TO SUMMON JIBANYAN.
HE EVEN KNOWS ABOUT THE WATCH!
THIS IS VERY SUSPICIOUS!
I WENT TO THE INTERSECTION HE'S ALWAYS AT, BUT HE WASN'T THERE...
THE BEST FRESH FISH
THE FISH PLACE
I SUSPECT HE'S GONE TO A NEXT HARMEOWNY CONCERT OR SOMETHING...
...

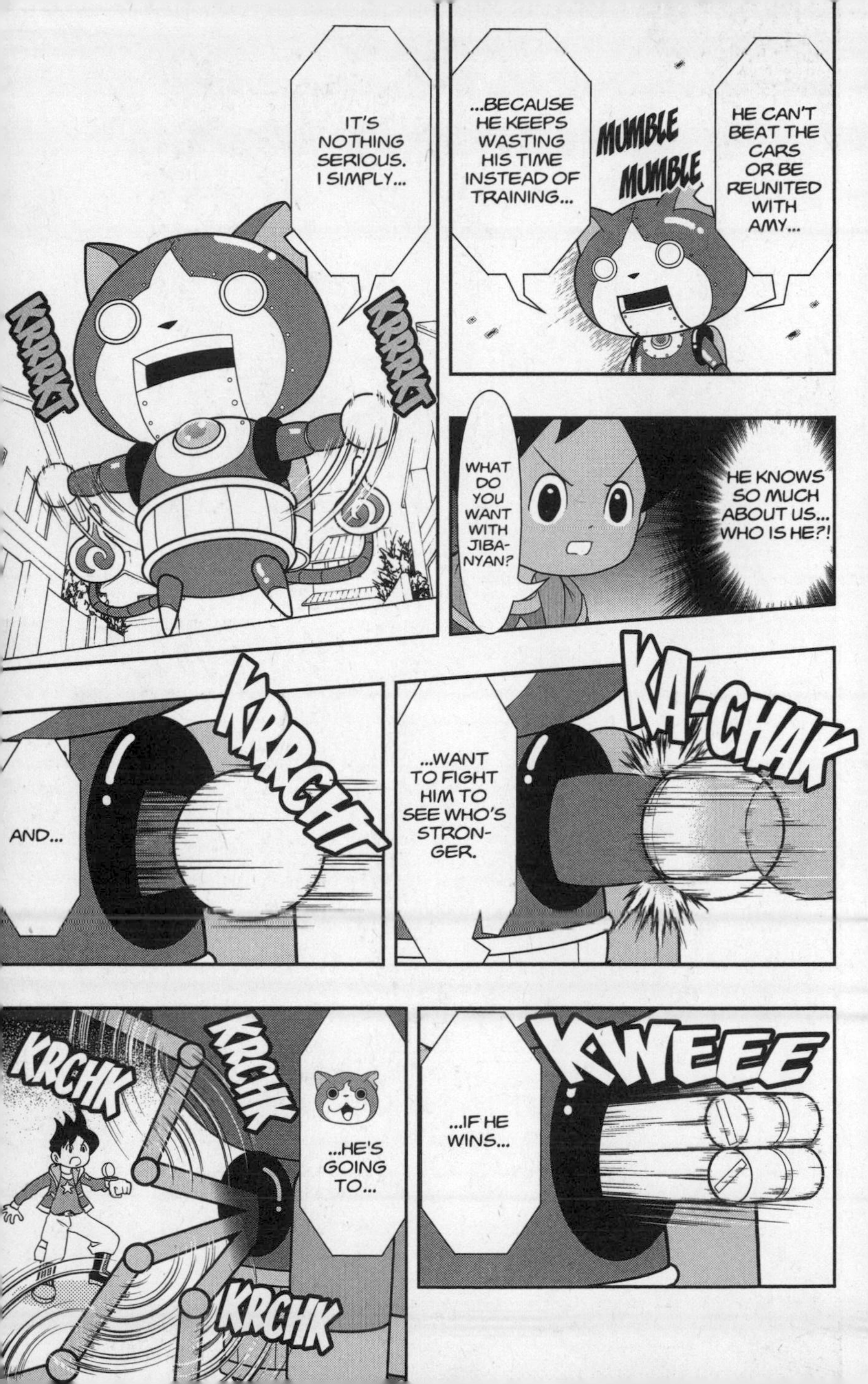
HE CAN'T BEAT THE CARS OR BE REUNITED WITH AMY...
MUMBLE MUMBLE
...BECAUSE HE KEEPS WASTING HIS TIME INSTEAD OF TRAINING...
HE KNOWS SO MUCH ABOUT US... WHO IS HE?!
WHAT DO YOU WANT WITH JIBA-NYAN?
KRRRKT
IT'S NOTHING SERIOUS. I SIMPLY...
KRRRKT
KA-CHAK
...WANT TO FIGHT HIM TO SEE WHO'S STRON-GER.
KRRCHT
AND...
K-WEEE
...IF HE WINS...
...HE'S GOING TO...
KRCHK
KRCHK
KRCHK

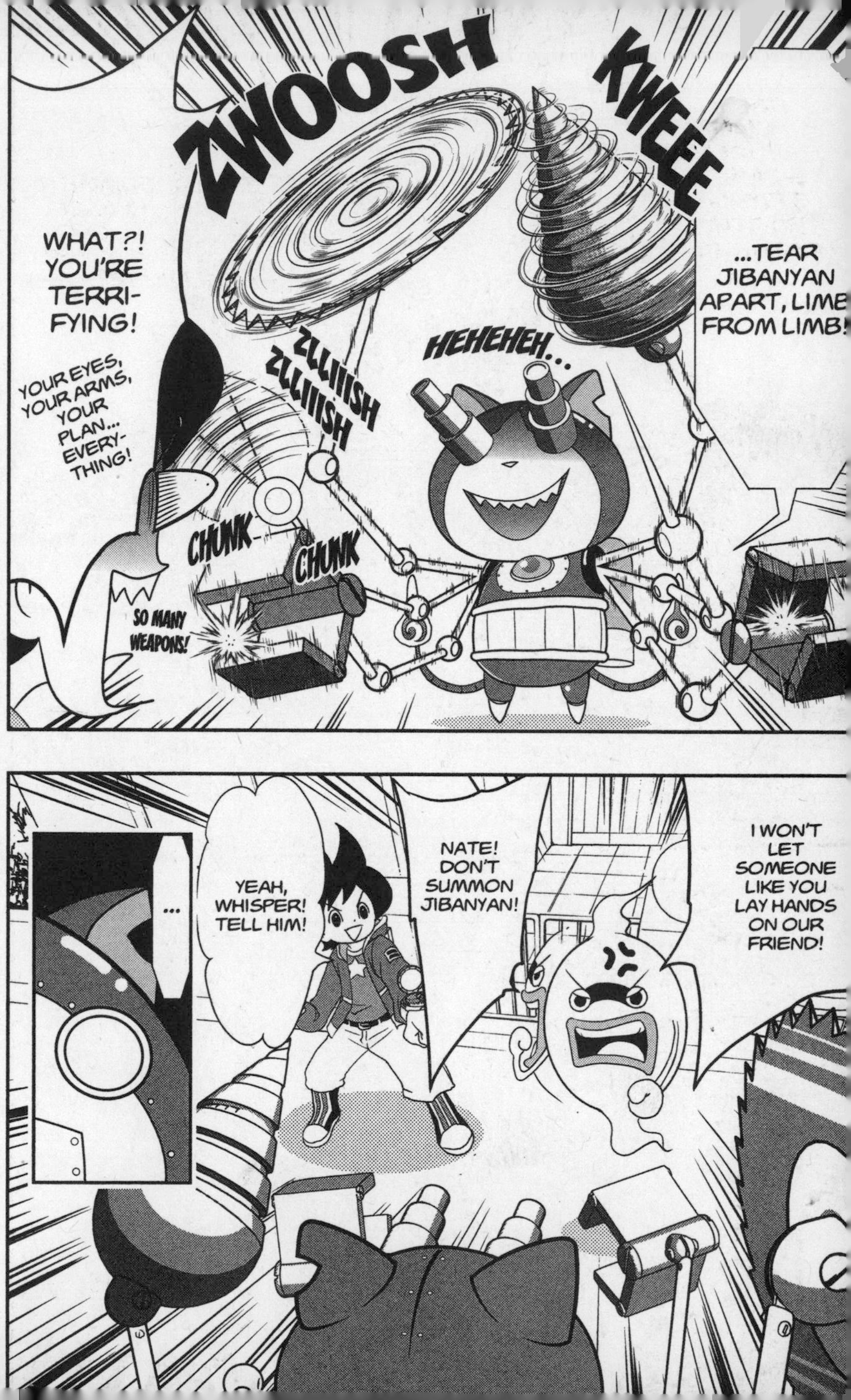
KWEEE
ZWOOSH
...TEAR JIBANYAN APART, LIMB FROM LIMB!
HEHEHEH...
ZLLIIISH
ZLLIIISH
WHAT?! YOU'RE TERRI-FYING!
YOUR EYES, YOUR ARMS, YOUR PLAN... EVERY-THING!
CHUNK
CHUNK
SO MANY WEAPONS!
I WON'T LET SOMEONE LIKE YOU LAY HANDS ON OUR FRIEND!
NATE! DON'T SUMMON JIBANYAN!
YEAH, WHISPER! TELL HIM!
...

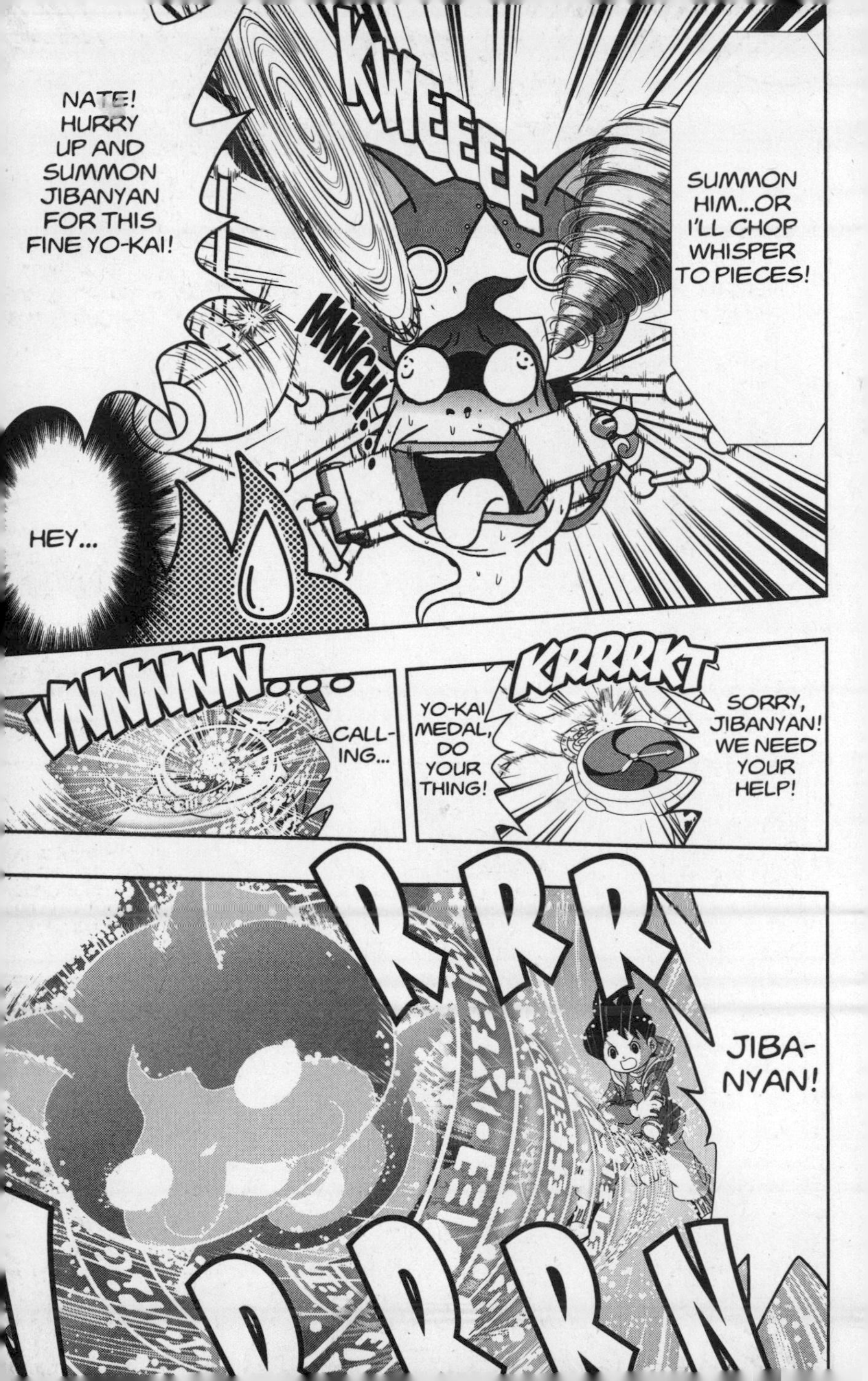
SUMMON HIM...OR I'LL CHOP WHISPER TO PIECES!
KWEEEEE
MMNGH
NATE! HURRY UP AND SUMMON JIBANYAN FOR THIS FINE YO-KAI!
HEY...
KRRRKT
SORRY, JIBANYAN! WE NEED YOUR HELP!
YO-KAI MEDAL, DO YOUR THING!
CALLING...
VNNNNNN...
RRR
JIBA-NYAN!
DRRN

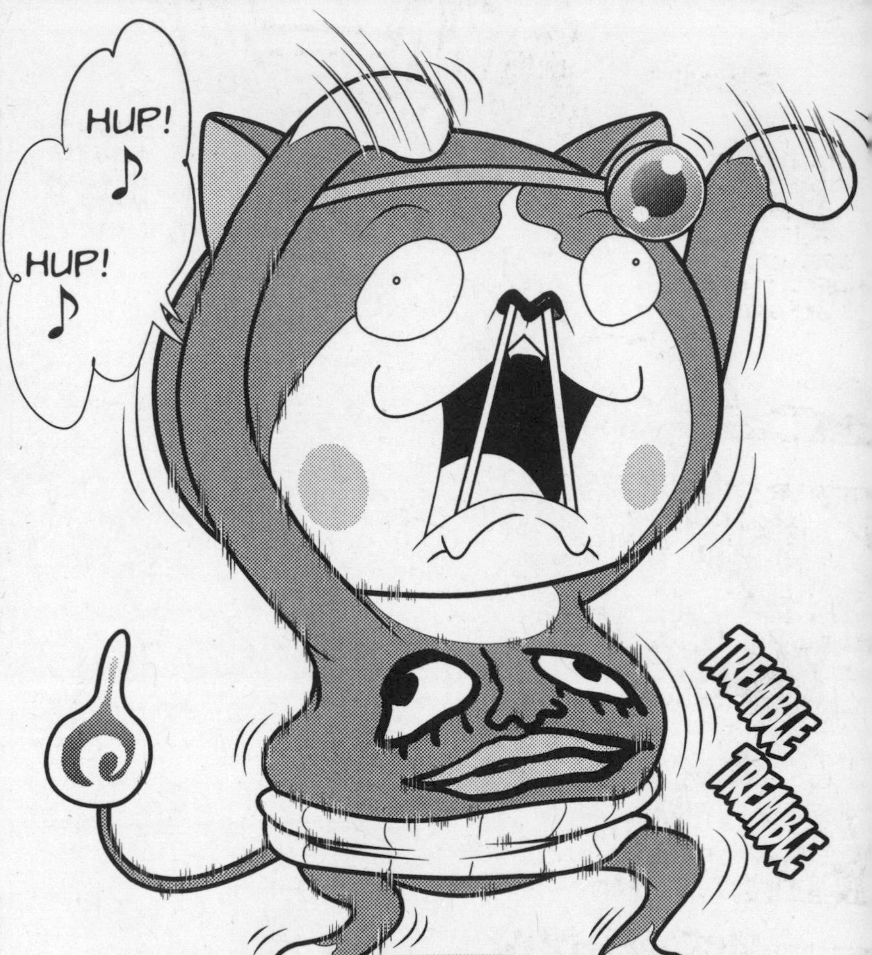
HUP! ♪
HUP! ♪
TREMBLE TREMBLE

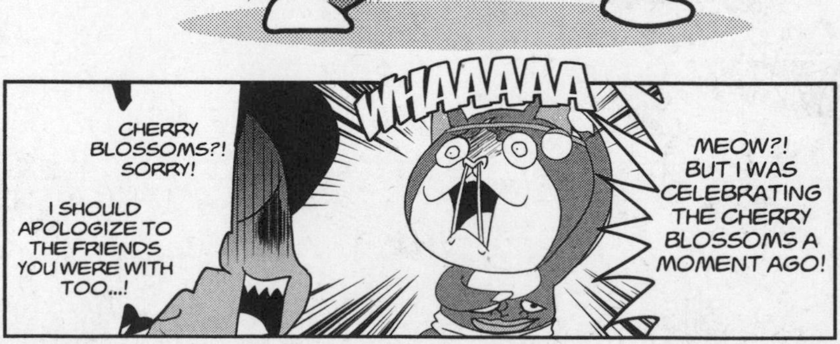
WHAAAAAA
MEOW?! BUT I WAS CELEBRATING THE CHERRY BLOSSOMS A MOMENT AGO!
CHERRY BLOSSOMS?! SORRY!
I SHOULD APOLOGIZE TO THE FRIENDS YOU WERE WITH TOO...!

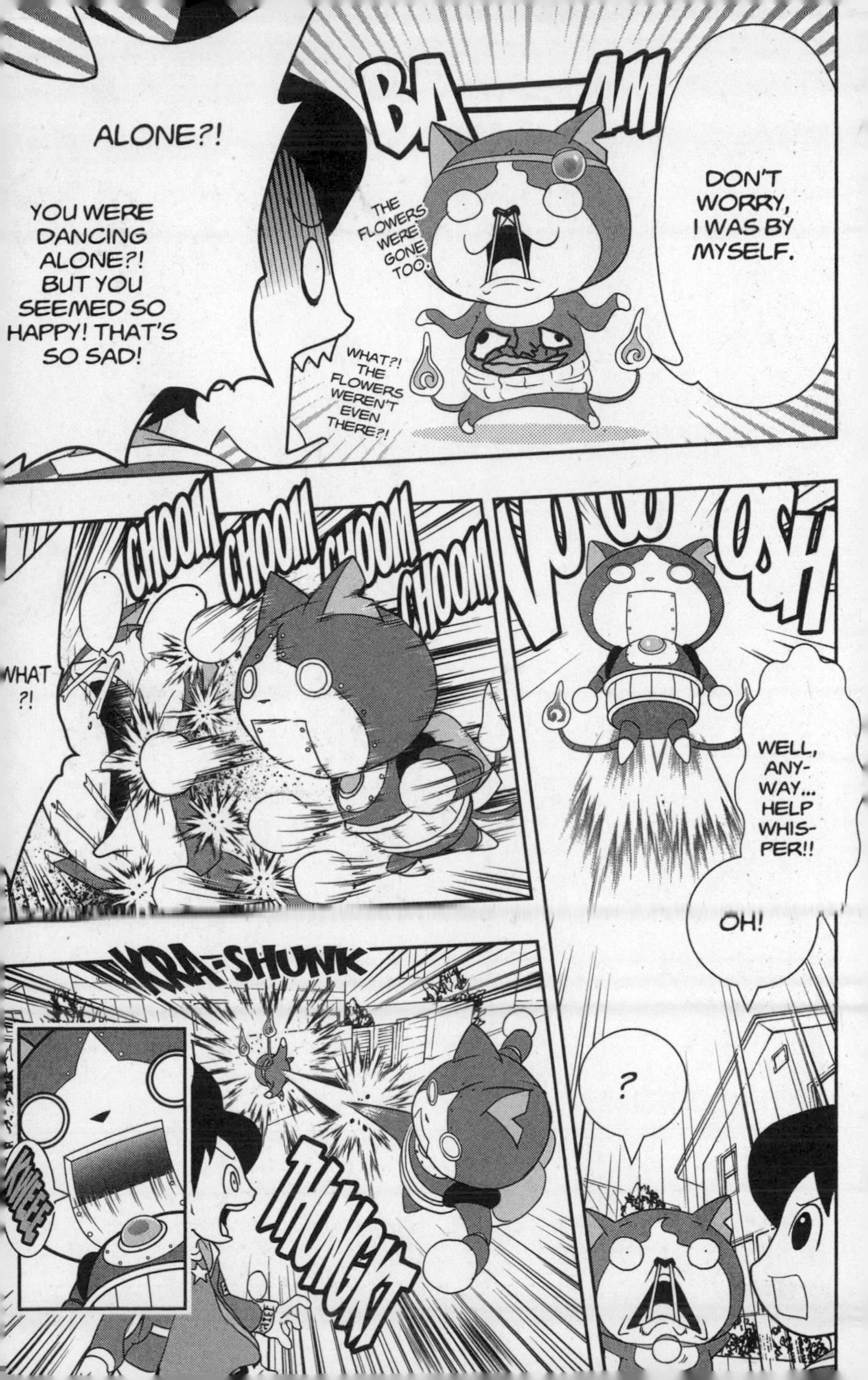
DON'T WORRY, I WAS BY MYSELF.
BAM
THE FLOWERS WERE GONE TOO.
WHAT?! THE FLOWERS WEREN'T EVEN THERE?!
ALONE?!
YOU WERE DANCING ALONE?! BUT YOU SEEMED SO HAPPY! THAT'S SO SAD!
VOOOSH
WELL, ANY-WAY... HELP WHIS-PER!!
OH!
?
CHOOM
CHOOM
CHOOM
CHOOM
WHAT ?!
KRA-SHUNK
THUNK!
KWEEE

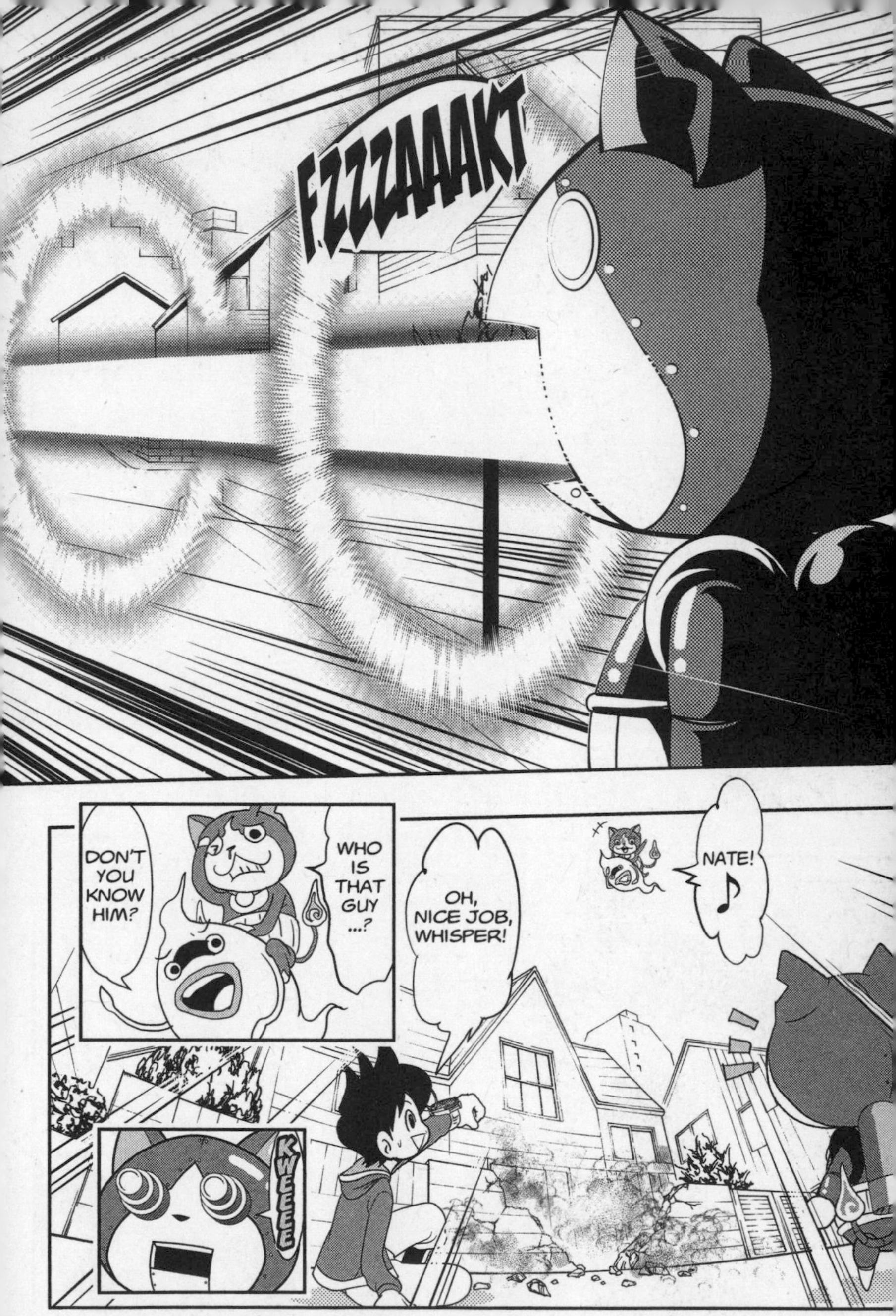
FZZZAAAKT
NATE! ♪
OH, NICE JOB, WHISPER!
WHO IS THAT GUY ...?
DON'T YOU KNOW HIM?
KWEEEE

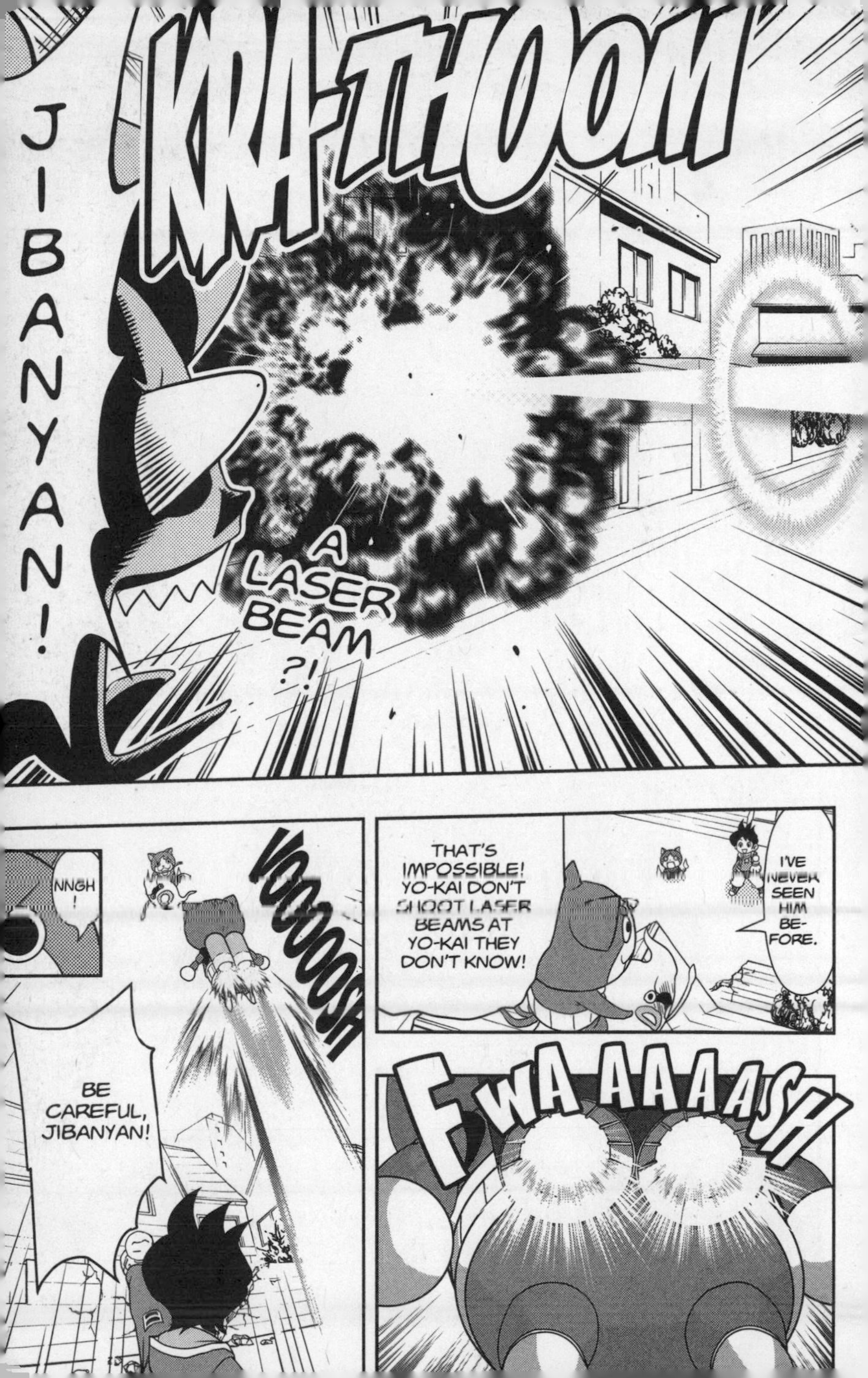
KRA-THOOM
A LASER BEAM?!
JIBANYAN!
I'VE NEVER SEEN HIM BEFORE.
THAT'S IMPOSSIBLE! YO-KAI DON'T SHOOT LASER BEAMS AT YO-KAI THEY DON'T KNOW!
FWAAAAASH
VOOOOOSH
NNGH!
BE CAREFUL, JIBANYAN!

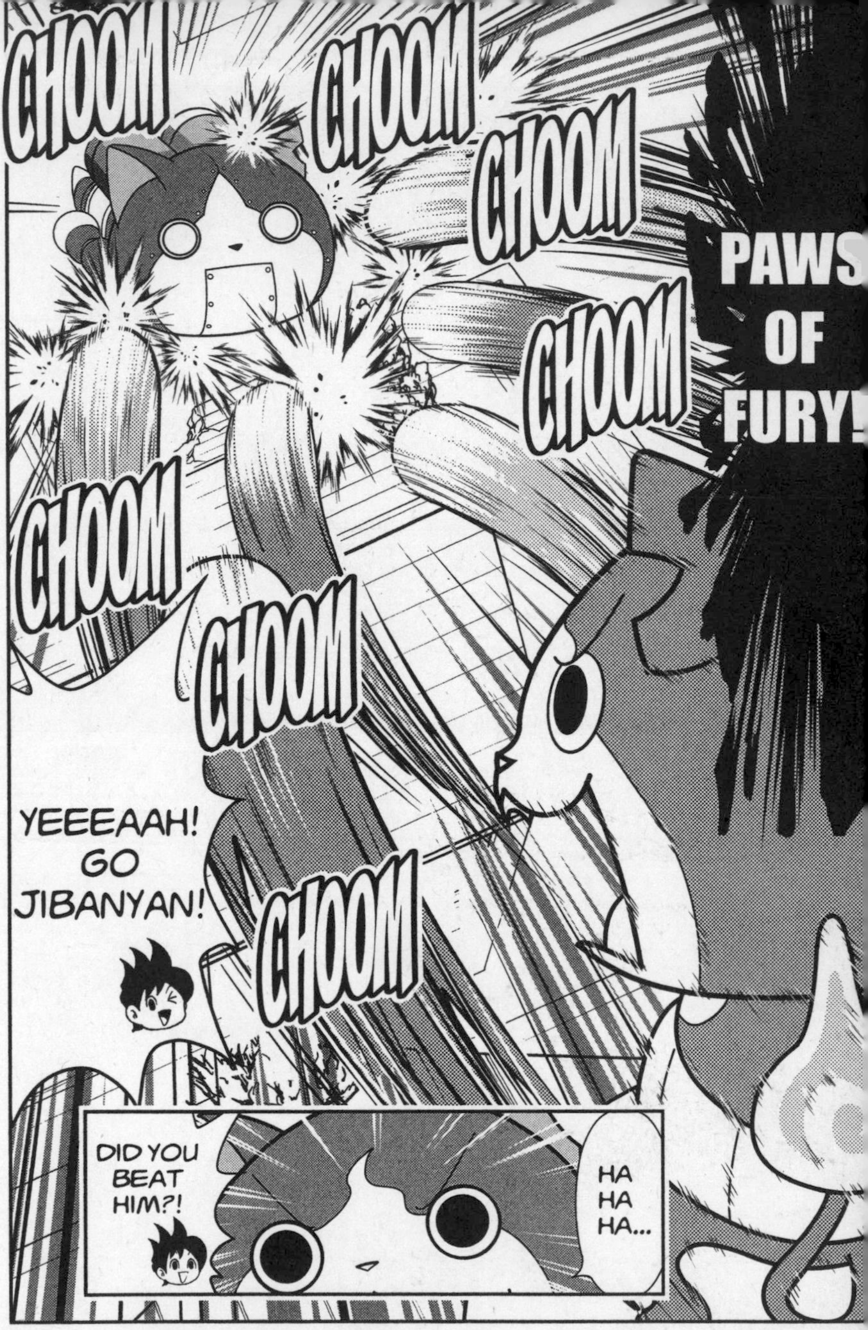
PAWS OF FURY!
CHOOM
CHOOM
CHOOM
CHOOM
CHOOM
CHOOM
CHOOM
YEEEAAH! GO JIBANYAN!
HA HA HA...
DID YOU BEAT HIM?!

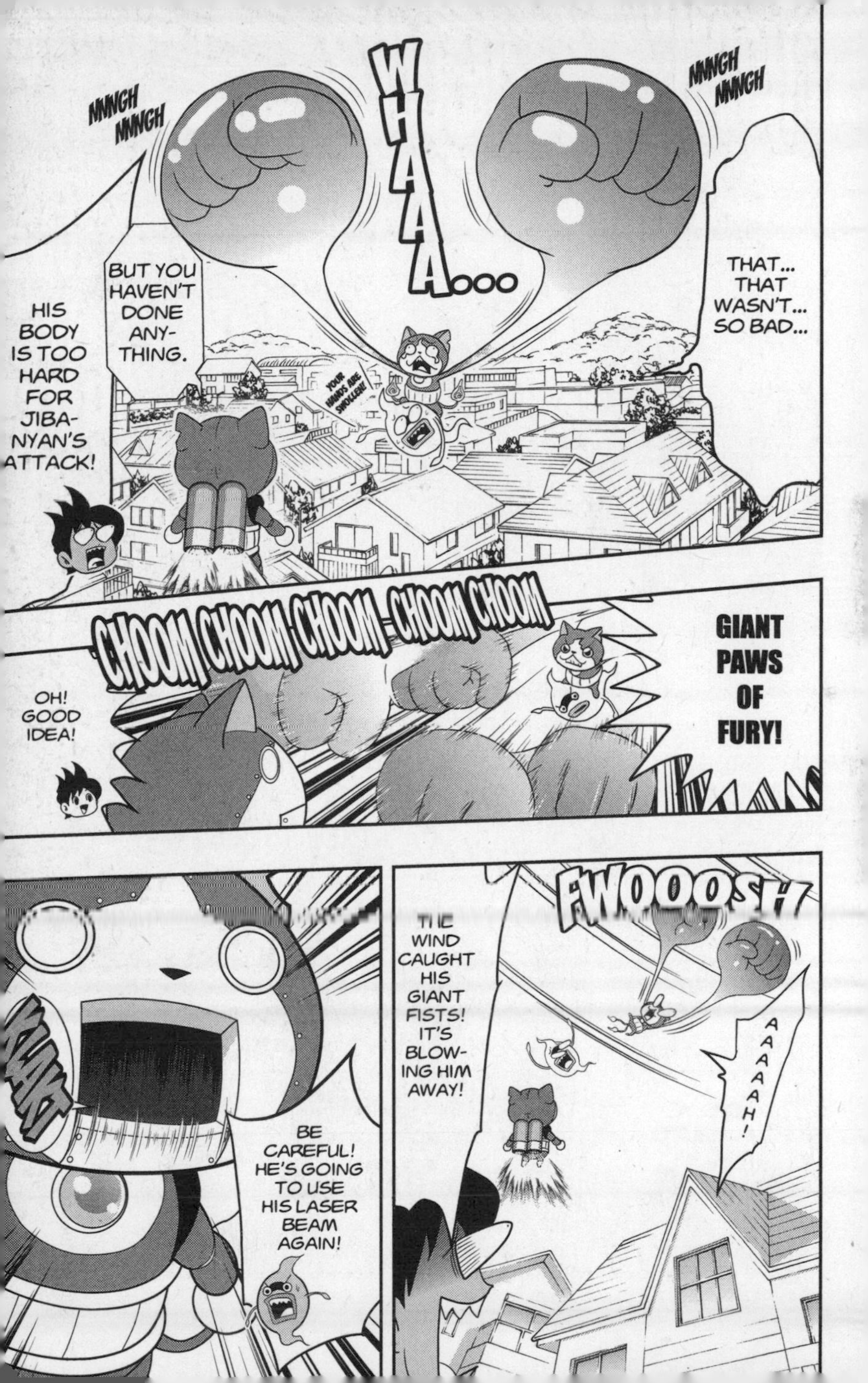
NNNGH NNNGH
THAT... THAT WASN'T... SO BAD...
WHAAAooo
NNNGH NNNGH
BUT YOU HAVEN'T DONE ANYTHING.
YOUR HANDS ARE SWOLLEN!
HIS BODY IS TOO HARD FOR JIBANYAN'S ATTACK!
GIANT PAWS OF FURY!
CHOOM CHOOM CHOOM CHOOM CHOOM
OH! GOOD IDEA!
FWOOOSH
AAAAAH!
THE WIND CAUGHT HIS GIANT FISTS! IT'S BLOWING HIM AWAY!
BE CAREFUL! HE'S GOING TO USE HIS LASER BEAM AGAIN!
KWAK!

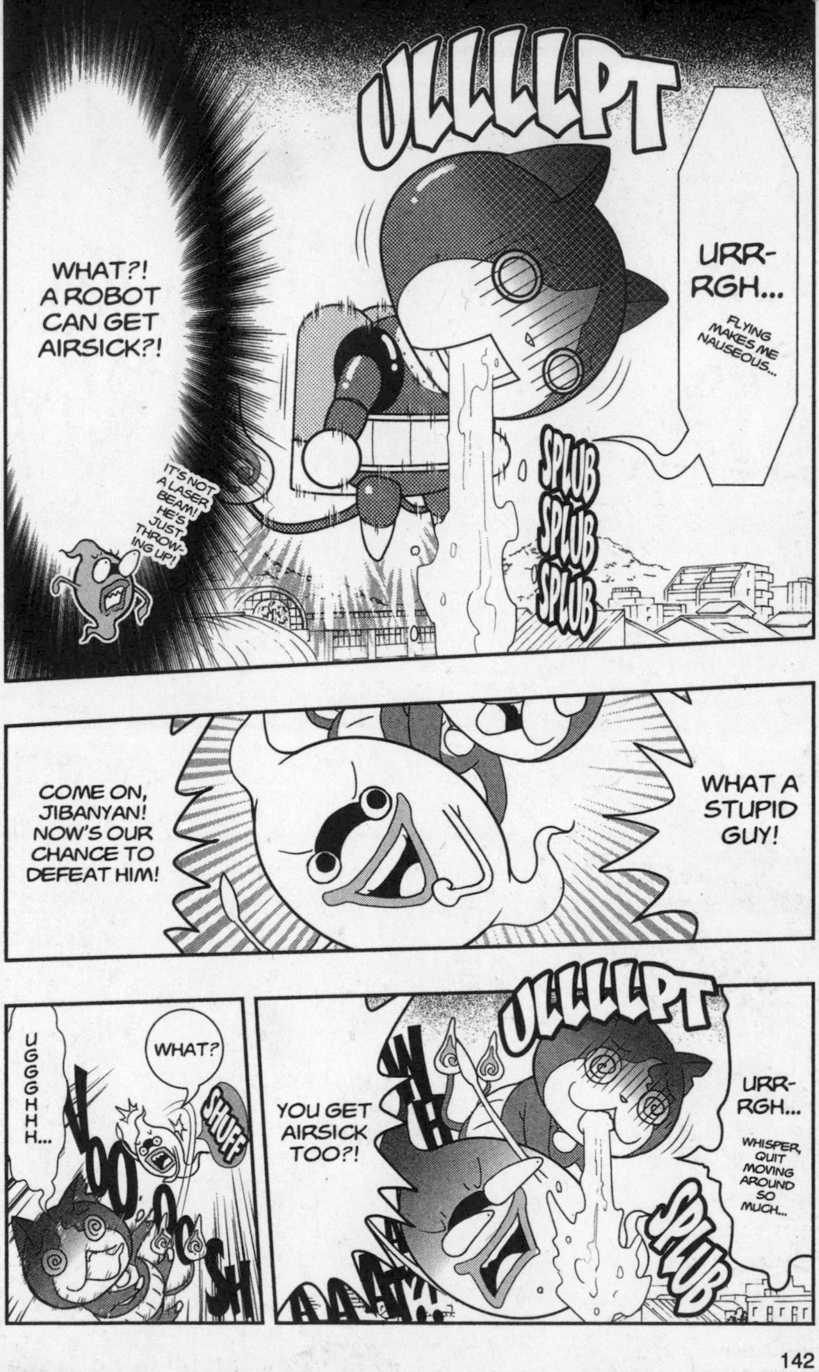
ULLLLPT
URR-RGH...
FLYING MAKES ME NAUSEOUS...
SPLUB SPLUB SPLUB
WHAT?! A ROBOT CAN GET AIRSICK?!
IT'S NOT A LASER BEAM! HE'S JUST THROWING UP!
WHAT A STUPID GUY!
COME ON, JIBANYAN! NOW'S OUR CHANCE TO DEFEAT HIM!
ULLLLPT
URR-RGH...
WHISPER, QUIT MOVING AROUND SO MUCH...
SPLUB
YOU GET AIRSICK TOO?!
WHAT?
SHUFF
UGGGHHH...

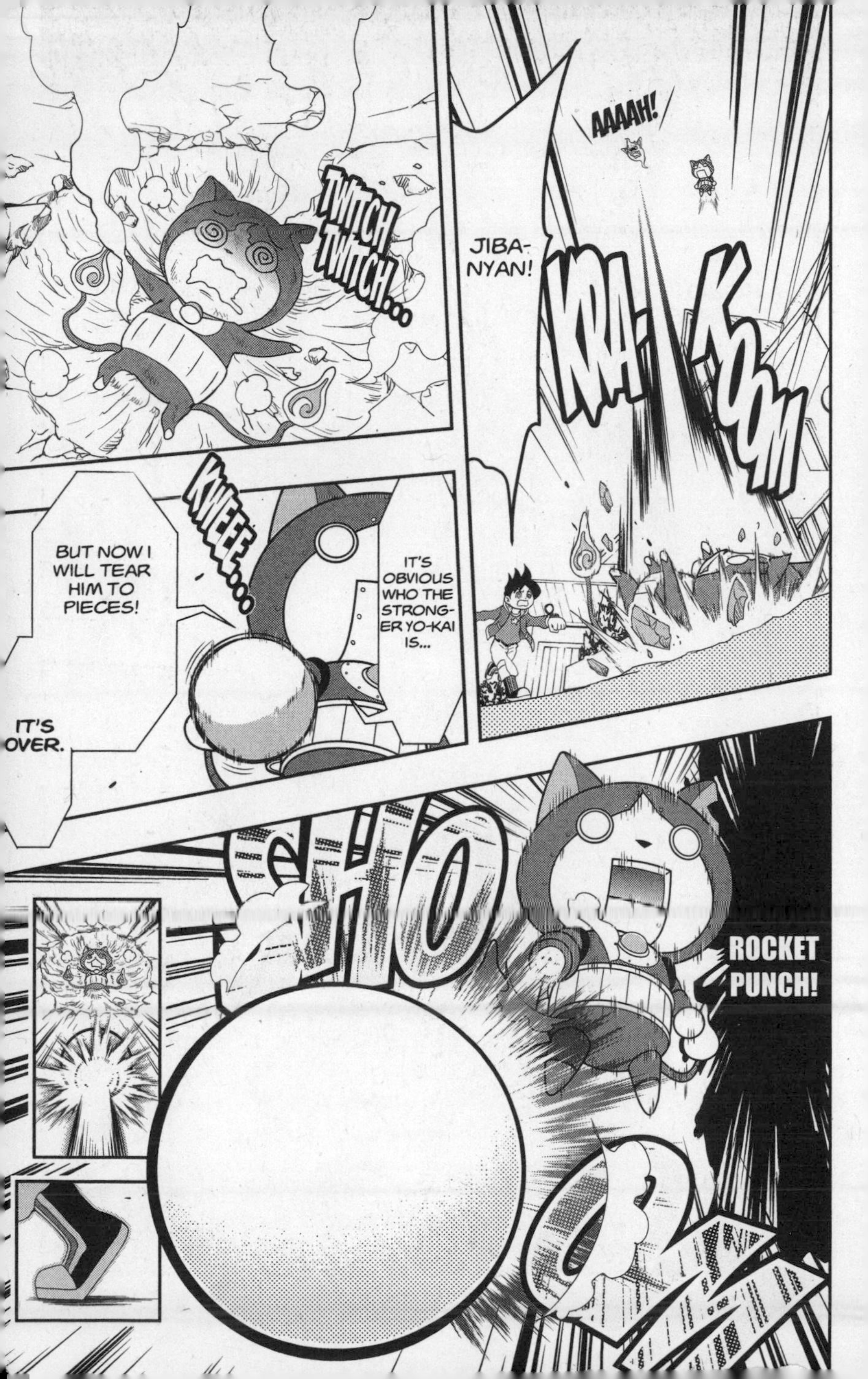
AAAAH!
JIBA-NYAN!
KRA-KOOM
TWITCH TWITCH...
KWEEE...
IT'S OBVIOUS WHO THE STRONGER YO-KAI IS...
BUT NOW I WILL TEAR HIM TO PIECES!
IT'S OVER.
ROCKET PUNCH!
SHOO

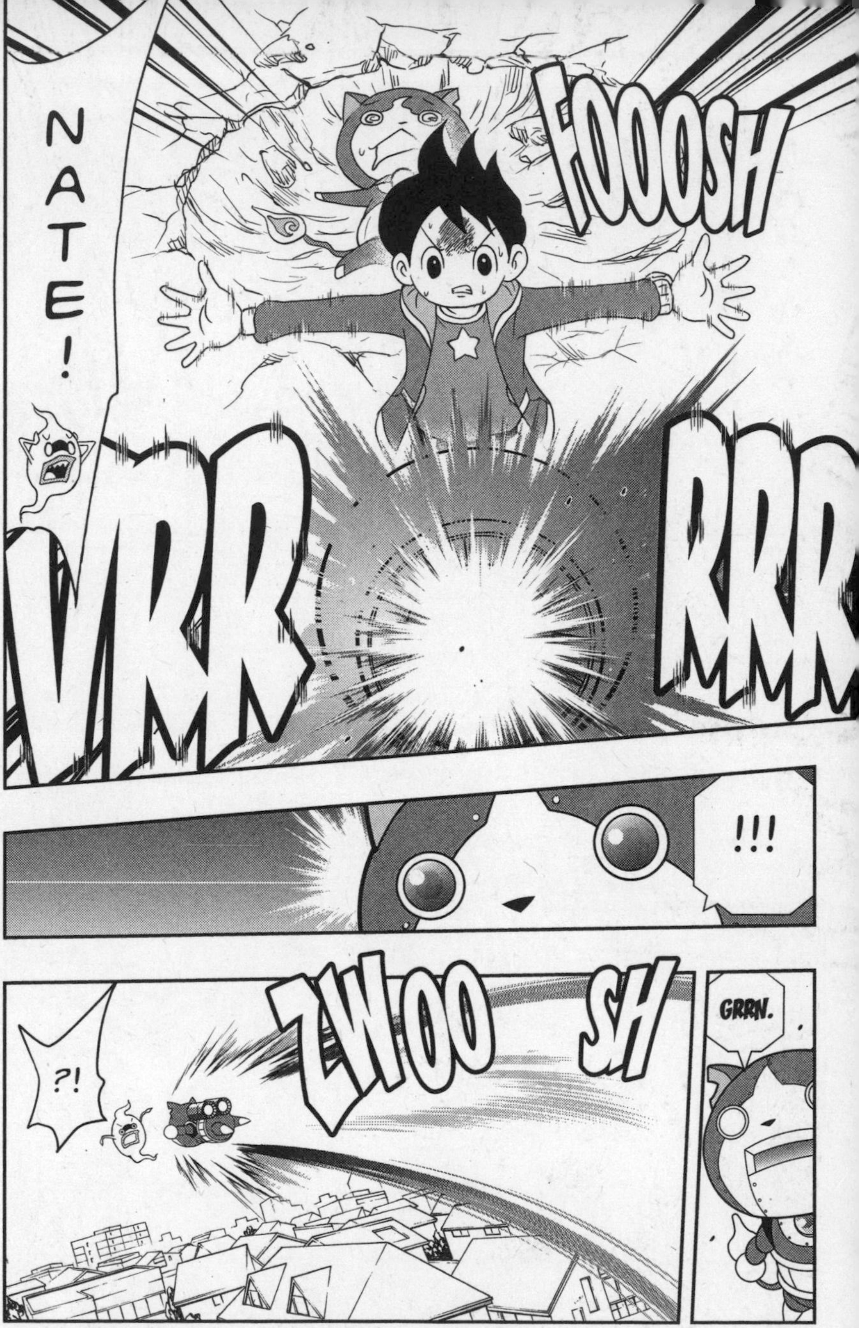
FOOOSH
NATE!
VRR RRR
!!!
GRRN.
ZWOO SH
?!

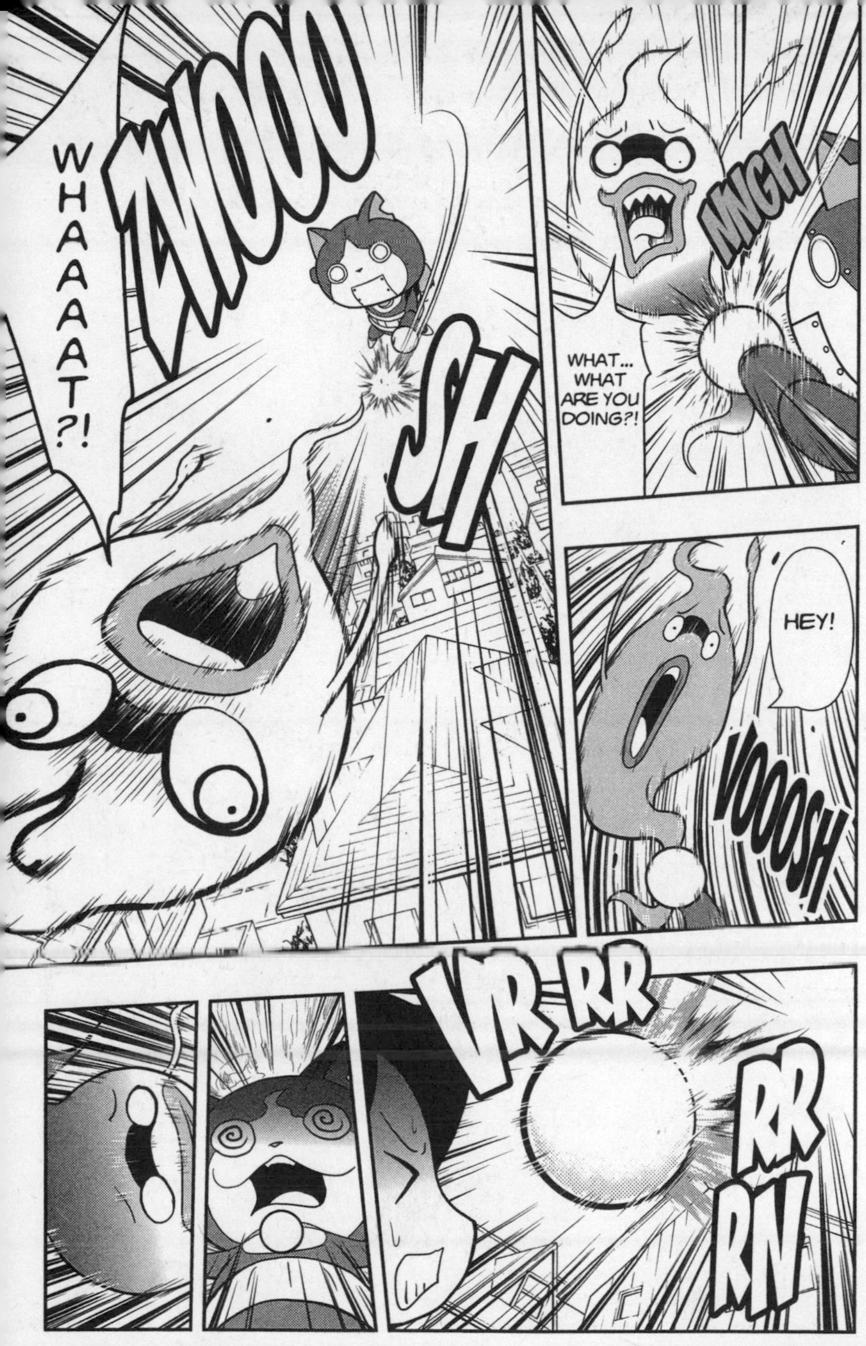
MNGH
WHAT... WHAT ARE YOU DOING?!
HEY!
VOOOSH
ZWOOO
SH
WHAAAAAT?!
VR-RR
RRRN

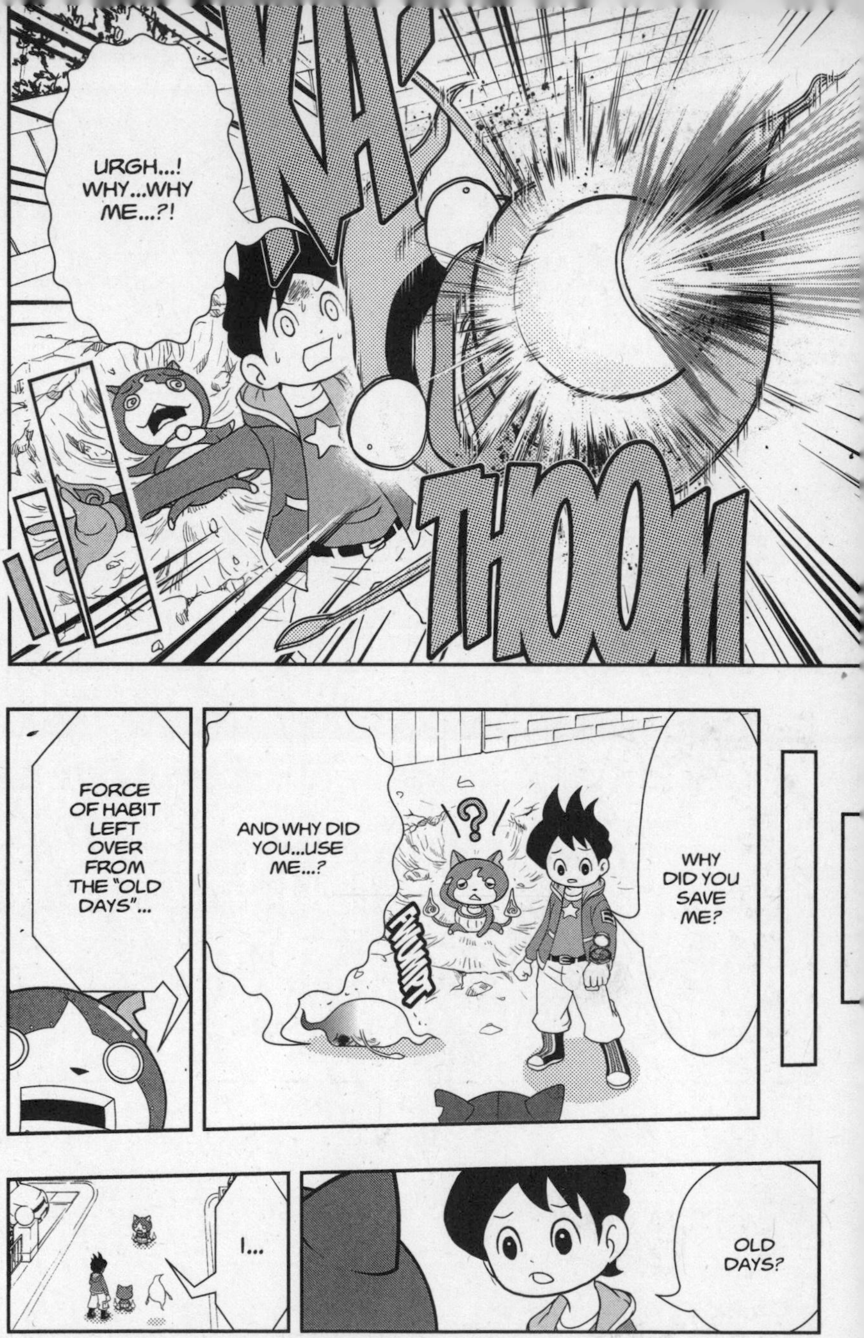
URGH...! WHY...WHY ME...?!
THOOM
WHY DID YOU SAVE ME?
AND WHY DID YOU...USE ME...?
FORCE OF HABIT LEFT OVER FROM THE "OLD DAYS"...
OLD DAYS?
I...

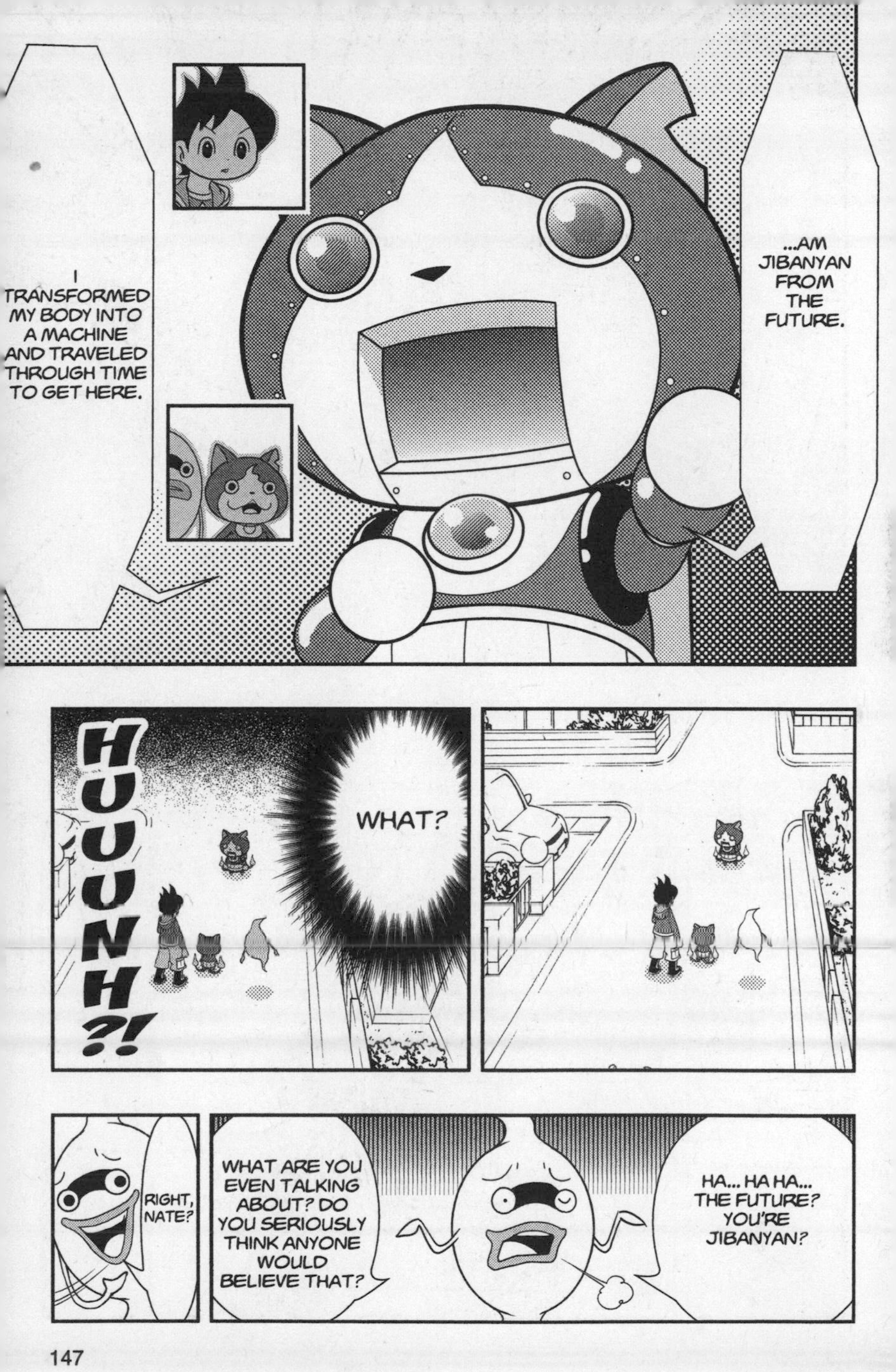
...AM JIBANYAN FROM THE FUTURE.
I TRANSFORMED MY BODY INTO A MACHINE AND TRAVELED THROUGH TIME TO GET HERE.
WHAT?
HUUUNH?!
HA... HA HA... THE FUTURE? YOU'RE JIBANYAN?
WHAT ARE YOU EVEN TALKING ABOUT? DO YOU SERIOUSLY THINK ANYONE WOULD BELIEVE THAT?
RIGHT, NATE?

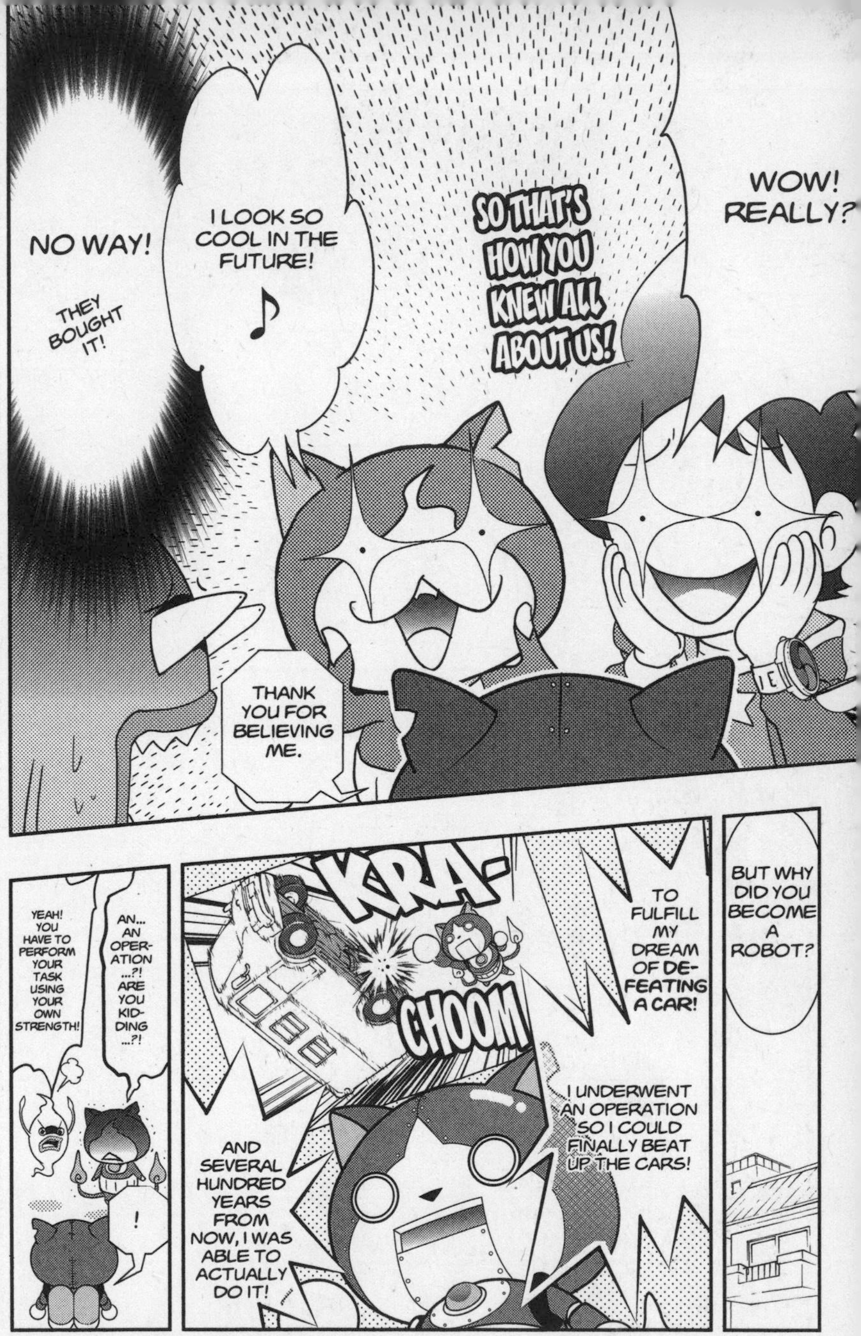
WOW! REALLY?
SO THAT'S HOW YOU KNEW ALL ABOUT US!
I LOOK SO COOL IN THE FUTURE! ♪
NO WAY!
THEY BOUGHT IT!
THANK YOU FOR BELIEVING ME.
BUT WHY DID YOU BECOME A ROBOT?
TO FULFILL MY DREAM OF DE-FEATING A CAR!
KRA-CHOOM
I UNDERWENT AN OPERATION SO I COULD FINALLY BEAT UP THE CARS!
AND SEVERAL HUNDRED YEARS FROM NOW, I WAS ABLE TO ACTUALLY DO IT!
AN... AN OPERATION ...?! ARE YOU KID-DING ...?!
YEAH! YOU HAVE TO PERFORM YOUR TASK USING YOUR OWN STRENGTH!
!

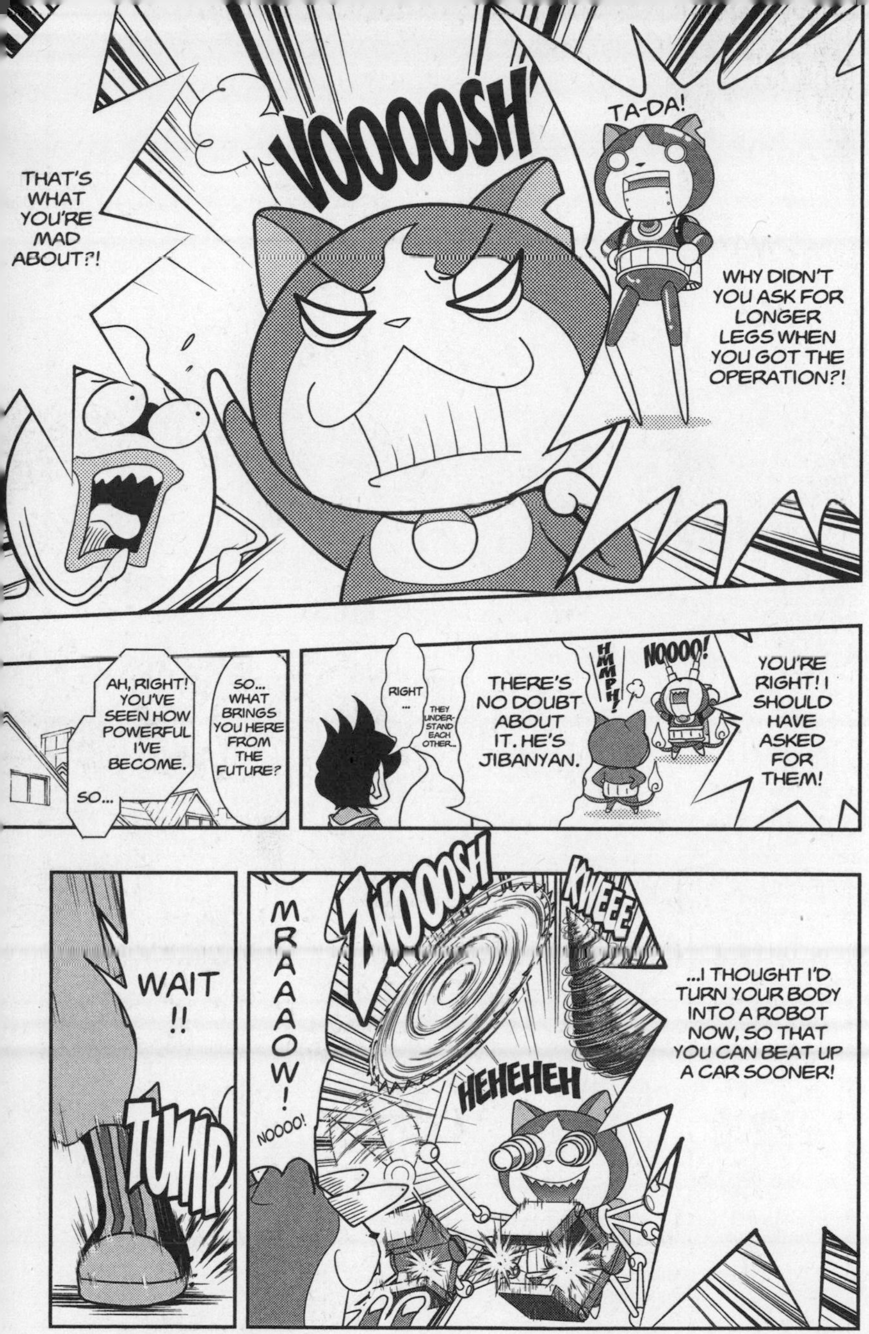
TA-DA!
VOOOOSH
WHY DIDN'T YOU ASK FOR LONGER LEGS WHEN YOU GOT THE OPERATION?!
THAT'S WHAT YOU'RE MAD ABOUT?!
NOOOO!
YOU'RE RIGHT! I SHOULD HAVE ASKED FOR THEM!
HMMPH!
THERE'S NO DOUBT ABOUT IT. HE'S JIBANYAN.
THEY UNDERSTAND EACH OTHER...
RIGHT...
SO... WHAT BRINGS YOU HERE FROM THE FUTURE?
AH, RIGHT! YOU'VE SEEN HOW POWERFUL I'VE BECOME.
SO...
KWEEE
ZWOOOSH
...I THOUGHT I'D TURN YOUR BODY INTO A ROBOT NOW, SO THAT YOU CAN BEAT UP A CAR SOONER!
MRAAAAOW!
HEHEHEH
NOOOO!
WAIT!!
TUMP

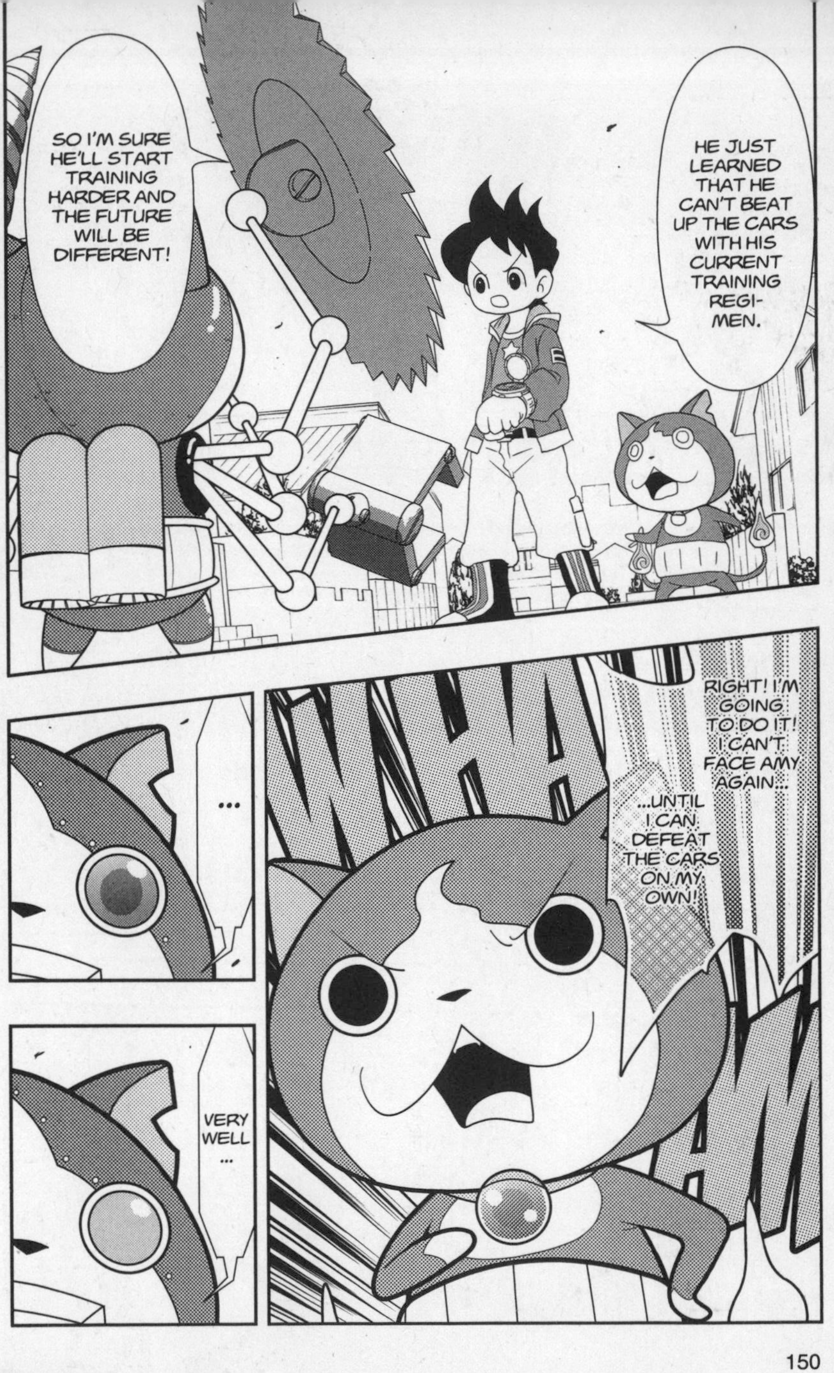
HE JUST LEARNED THAT HE CAN'T BEAT UP THE CARS WITH HIS CURRENT TRAINING REGI-MEN.
SO I'M SURE HE'LL START TRAINING HARDER AND THE FUTURE WILL BE DIFFERENT!
WHAM
RIGHT! I'M GOING TO DO IT! I CAN'T FACE AMY AGAIN...
...UNTIL I CAN DEFEAT THE CARS ON MY OWN!
...
VERY WELL...

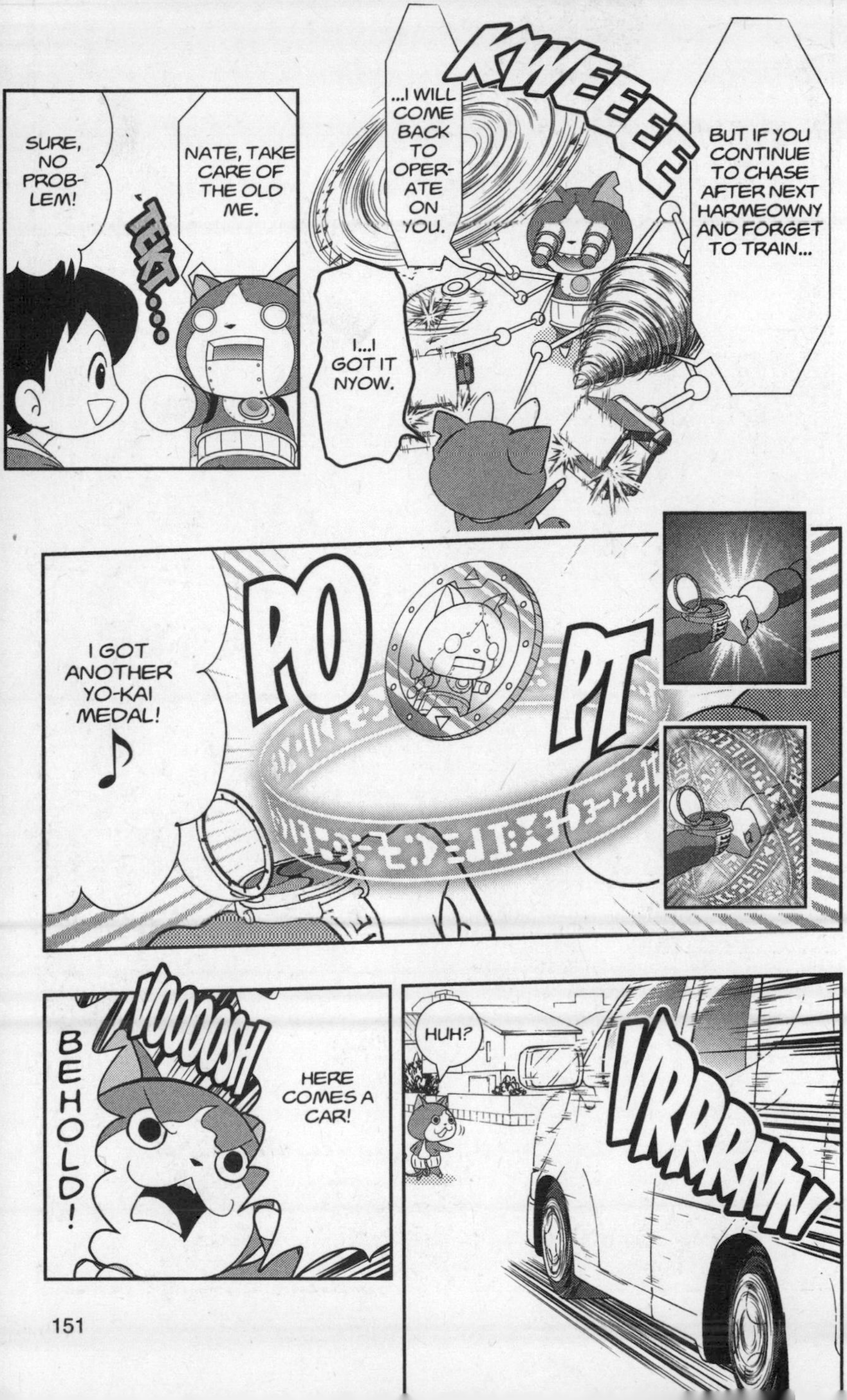
BUT IF YOU CONTINUE TO CHASE AFTER NEXT HARMEOWNY AND FORGET TO TRAIN...
KWEEEEE
...I WILL COME BACK TO OPER-ATE ON YOU.
I...I GOT IT NYOW.
NATE, TAKE CARE OF THE OLD ME.
TEKT...
SURE, NO PROB-LEM!
POPT
I GOT ANOTHER YO-KAI MEDAL! ♪
VRRRRNN
HUH?
VOOOOSH
HERE COMES A CAR!
BEHOLD!

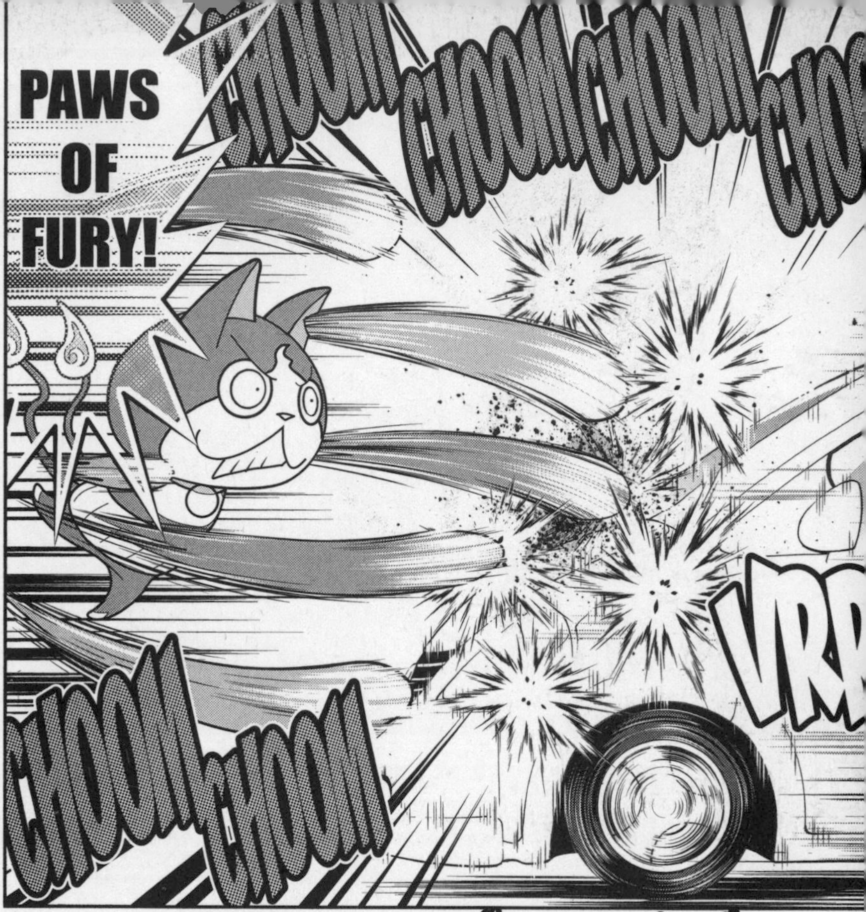
PAWS OF FURY!
CHOOM CHOOM CHOOM
CHOOM CHOOM

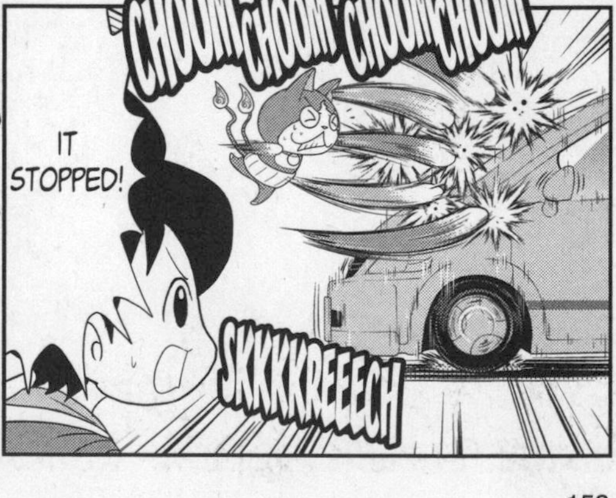
CHOOM CHOOM CHOOM CHOOM
IT STOPPED!
SKKKREEECH

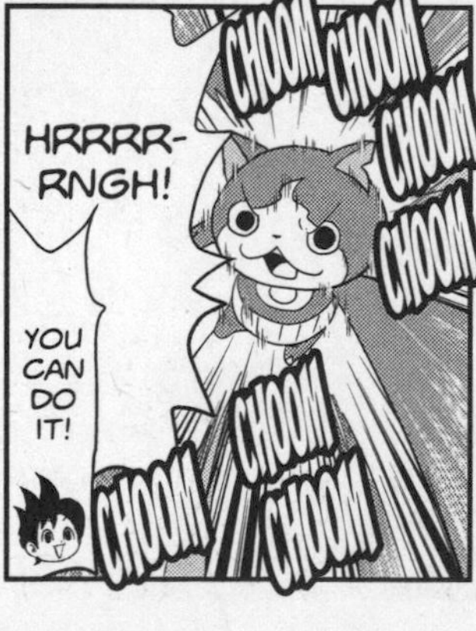
CHOOM CHOOM CHOOM CHOOM
HRRRR-RNGH!
YOU CAN DO IT!
CHOOM CHOOM CHOOM

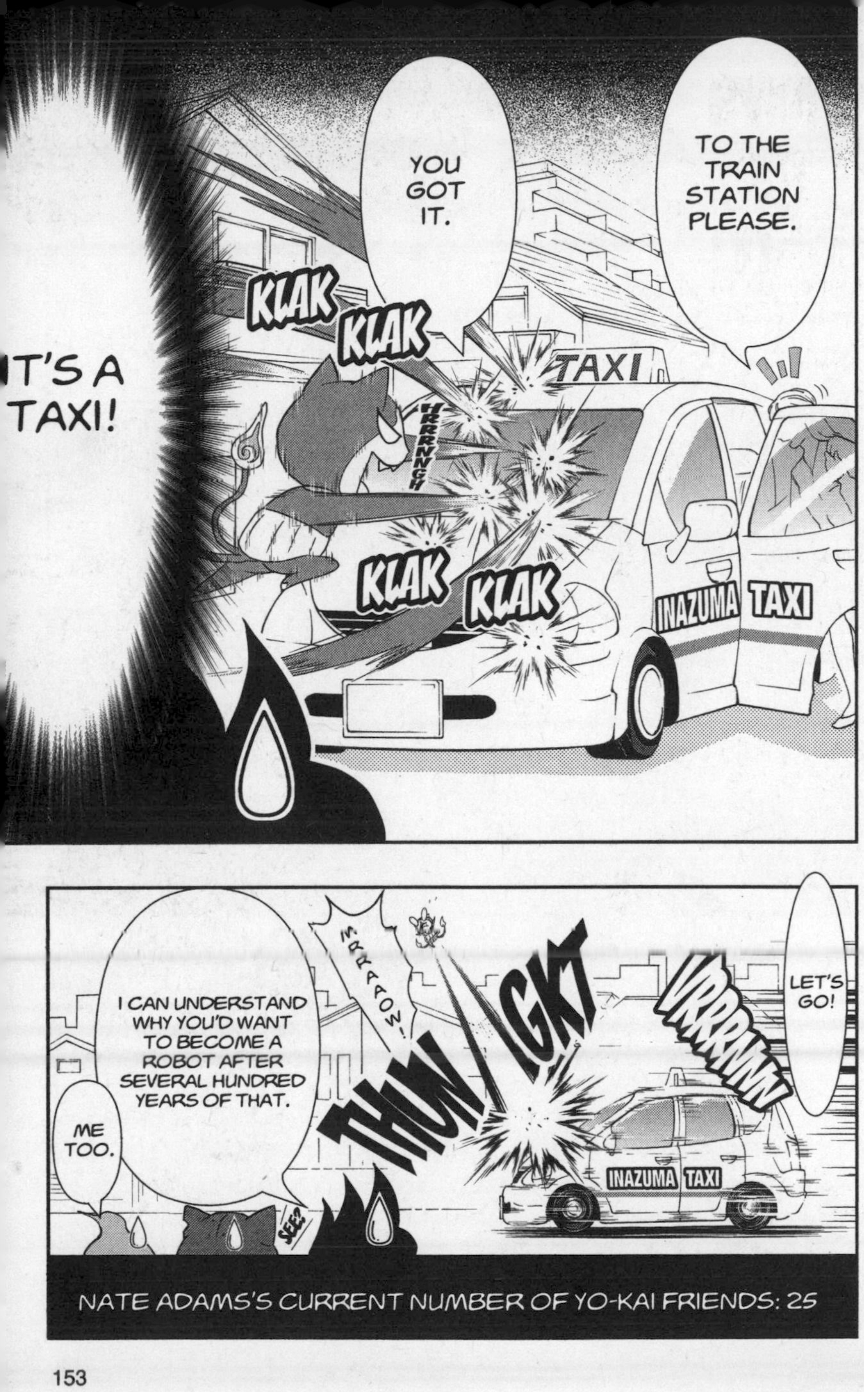
TO THE TRAIN STATION PLEASE.
YOU GOT IT.
KLAK
KLAK
HRRRNNGH
TAXI
KLAK
KLAK
INAZUMA TAXI
IT'S A TAXI!
LET'S GO!
GKT
THUN
MRRAAOW!
I CAN UNDERSTAND WHY YOU'D WANT TO BECOME A ROBOT AFTER SEVERAL HUNDRED YEARS OF THAT.
ME TOO.
SEE?
INAZUMA TAXI
NATE ADAMS'S CURRENT NUMBER OF YO-KAI FRIENDS: 25

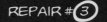

REPAIR #3

ROBO-NYAN... THE WATCH IS BROKEN... CAN YOU FIX IT?
PIECE OF CAKE!
KWEE KWEE
KWEE
WOW. ♪
SKRRRKT
I USED THE LATEST TECH-NOLOGY TO MAKE IT EVEN SMALL-ER.
WOW, IT'S THE SIZE OF A RING! I GOTTA SHOW JIBANYAN!
YO-KAI MEDAL, DO YOUR THING...
OH!
IT WON'T FIT...

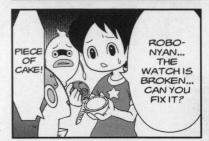

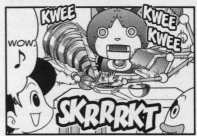

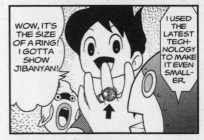

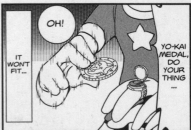

CHAPTER 33: DON'T PLAY WITH WEAPONS!

FEATURING LOW PROFILE YO-KAI BLANDON

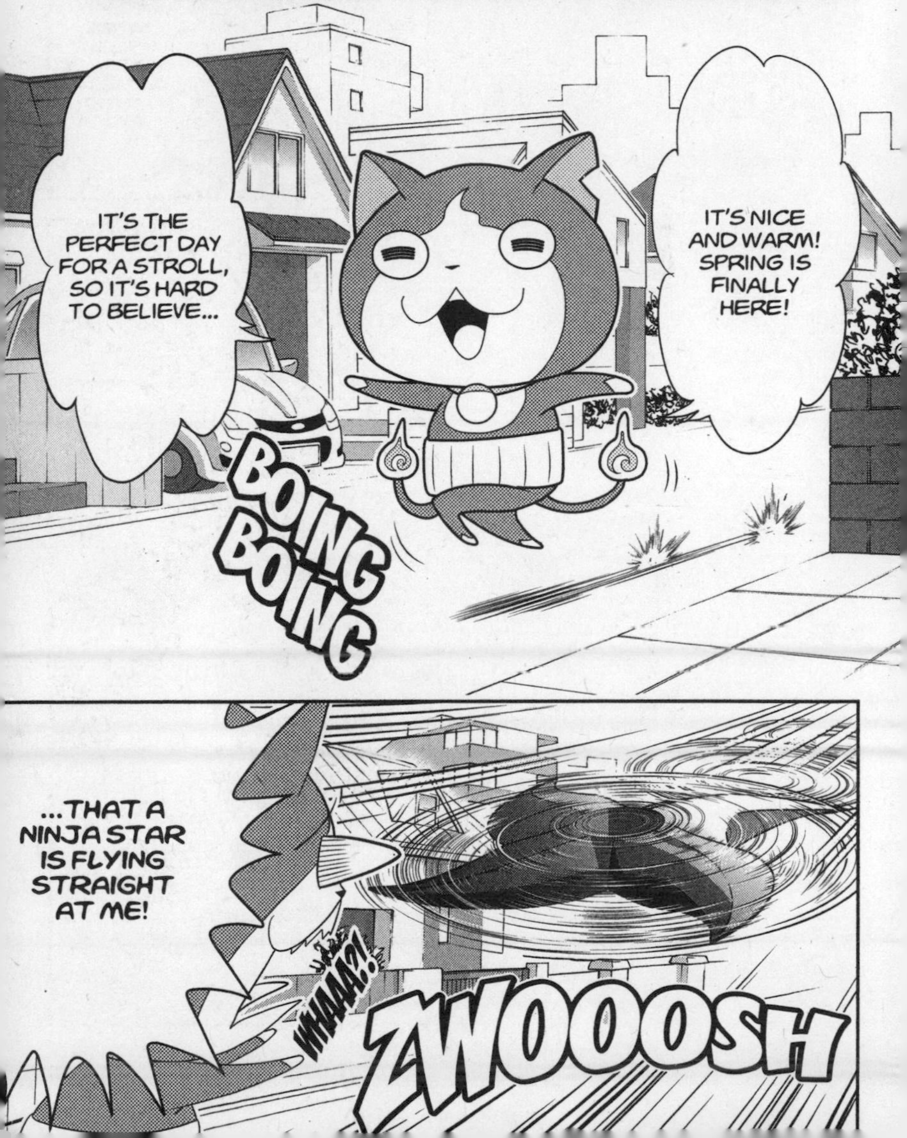
IT'S NICE AND WARM! SPRING IS FINALLY HERE!
IT'S THE PERFECT DAY FOR A STROLL, SO IT'S HARD TO BELIEVE...
BOING BOING
...THAT A NINJA STAR IS FLYING STRAIGHT AT ME!
WHAAA?!
ZWOOOOSH

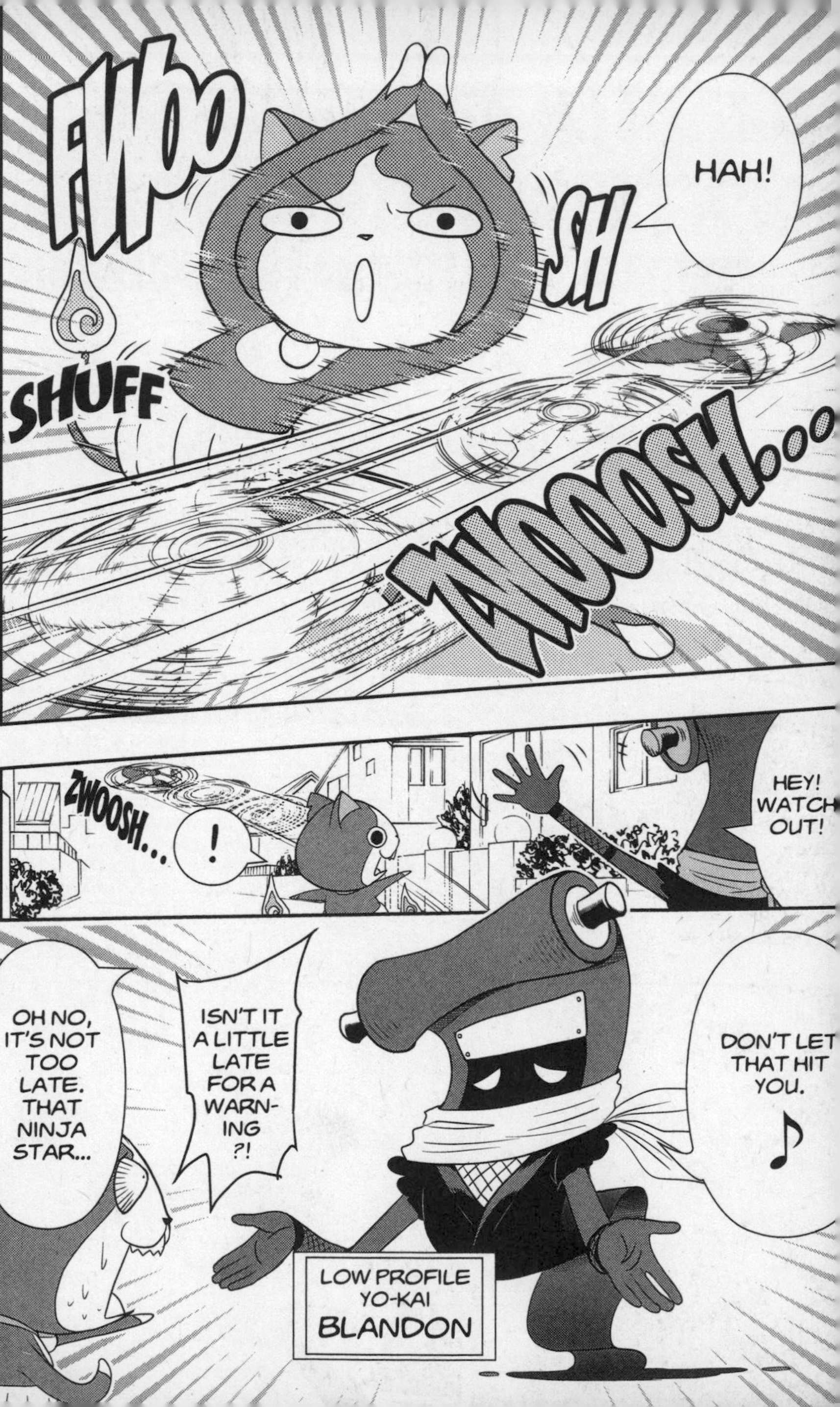
HAH!
FWOOSH
SHUFF
ZWOOOSH...
HEY! WATCH OUT!
!
ZWOOSH...
DON'T LET THAT HIT YOU. ♪
LOW PROFILE YO-KAI BLANDON
ISN'T IT A LITTLE LATE FOR A WARNING?!
OH NO, IT'S NOT TOO LATE. THAT NINJA STAR...

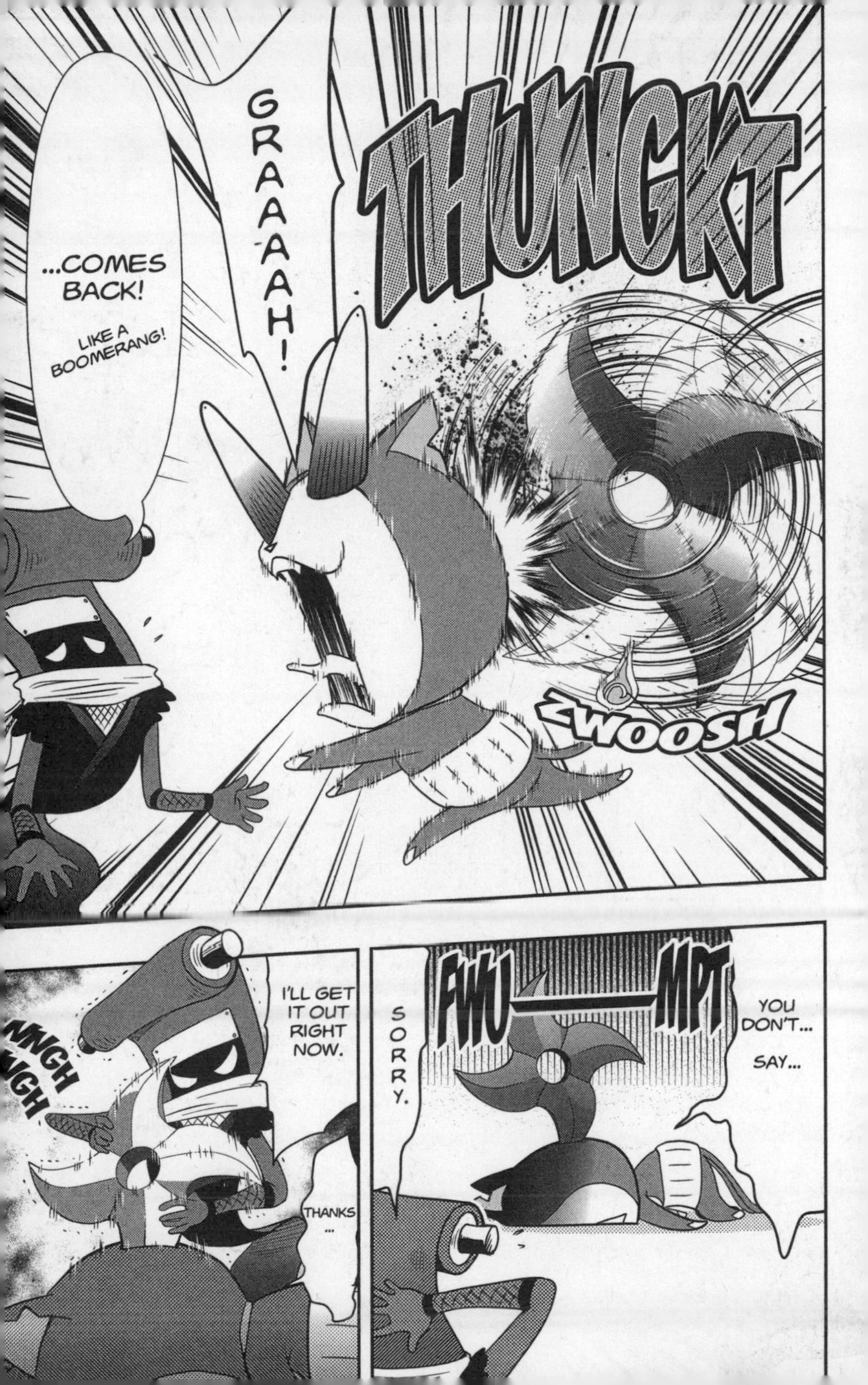
THUNCKT
GRAAAAAH!
...COMES BACK!
LIKE A BOOMERANG!
ZWOOSH
FWU——MPT
YOU DON'T...
SAY...
SORRY.
I'LL GET IT OUT RIGHT NOW.
NNGH
THANKS...

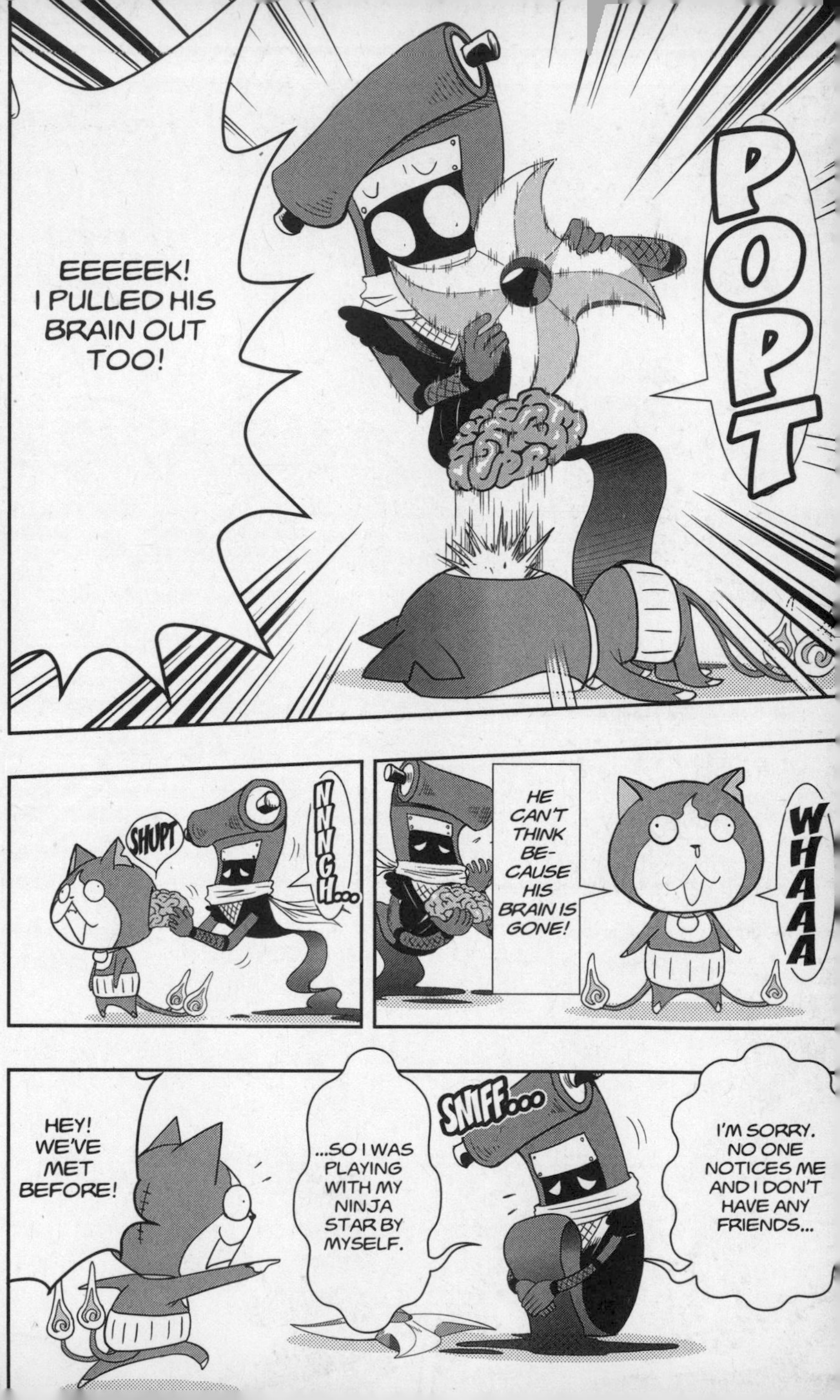
POPT
EEEEEK! I PULLED HIS BRAIN OUT TOO!
WHAAAA
HE CAN'T THINK BE-CAUSE HIS BRAIN IS GONE!
NNNGH...
SHUPT
I'M SORRY. NO ONE NOTICES ME AND I DON'T HAVE ANY FRIENDS...
SNIFF...
...SO I WAS PLAYING WITH MY NINJA STAR BY MYSELF.
HEY! WE'VE MET BEFORE!

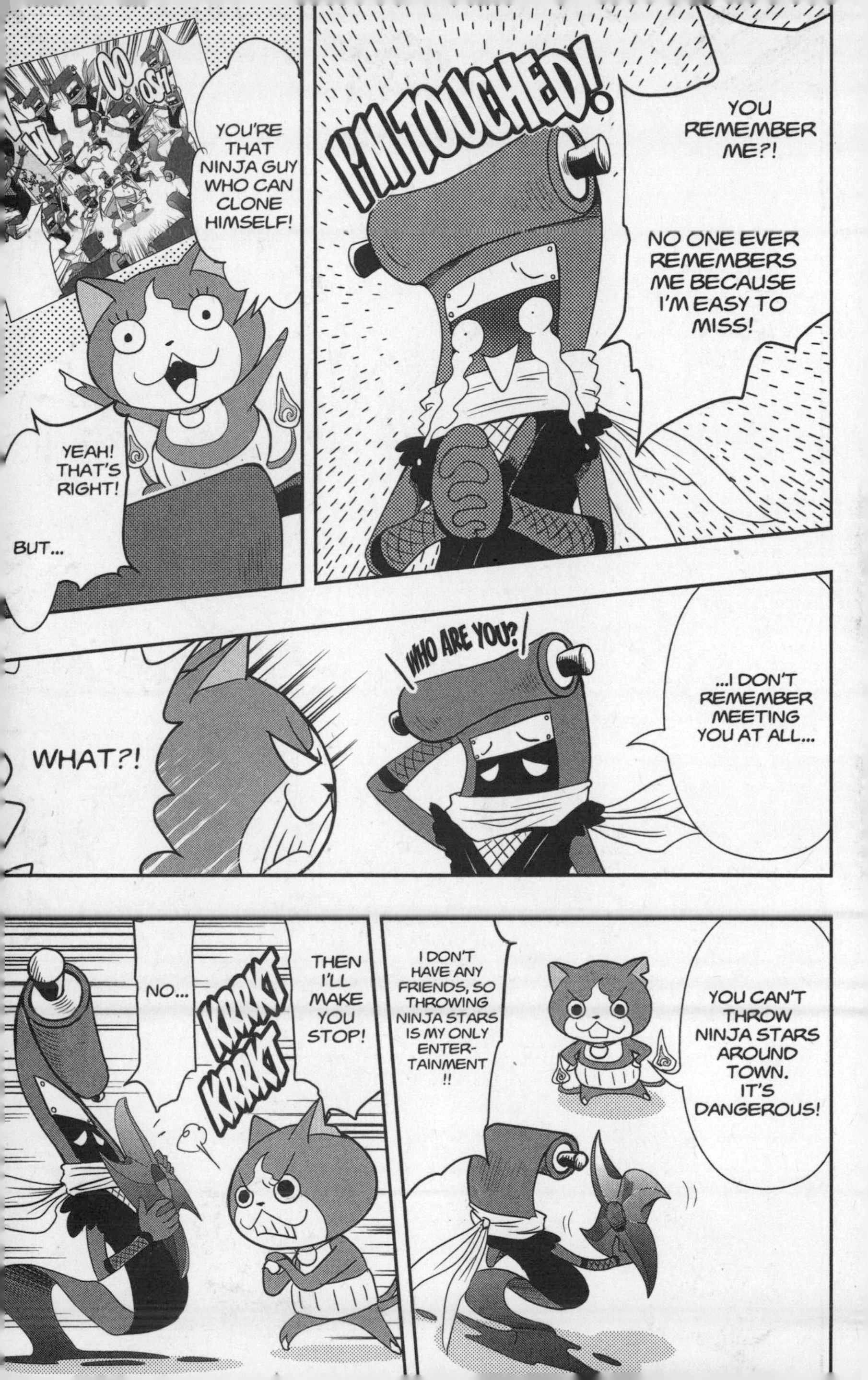
YOU REMEMBER ME?!
I'M TOUCHED!
NO ONE EVER REMEMBERS ME BECAUSE I'M EASY TO MISS!
YOU'RE THAT NINJA GUY WHO CAN CLONE HIMSELF!
YEAH! THAT'S RIGHT!
BUT...
...I DON'T REMEMBER MEETING YOU AT ALL...
WHO ARE YOU?!
WHAT?!
YOU CAN'T THROW NINJA STARS AROUND TOWN. IT'S DANGEROUS!
I DON'T HAVE ANY FRIENDS, SO THROWING NINJA STARS IS MY ONLY ENTERTAINMENT!!
THEN I'LL MAKE YOU STOP!
KRRKT KRRKT
NO...

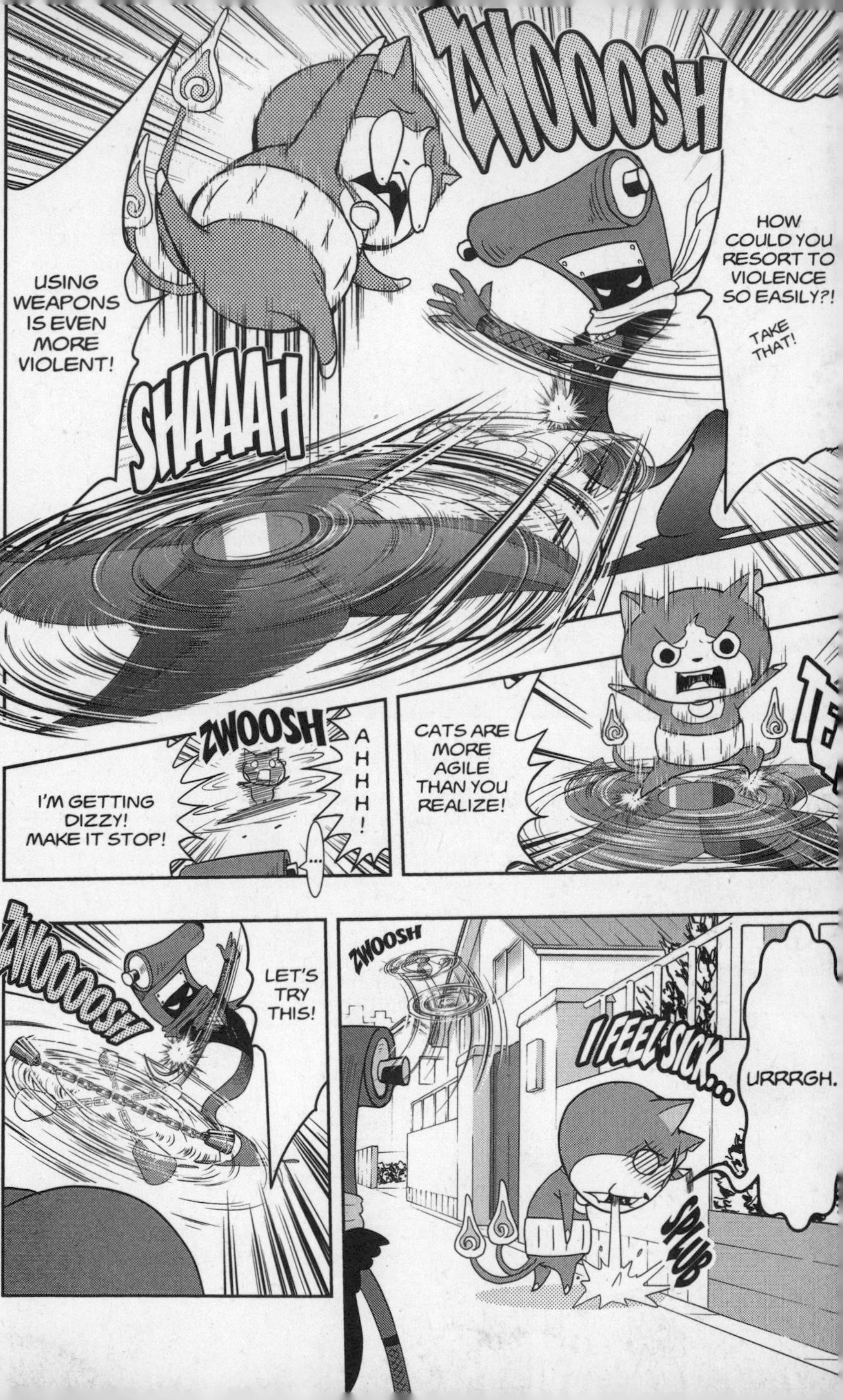
ZWOOOSH
HOW COULD YOU RESORT TO VIOLENCE SO EASILY?!
TAKE THAT!
USING WEAPONS IS EVEN MORE VIOLENT!
SHAAAH
CATS ARE MORE AGILE THAN YOU REALIZE!
ZWOOSH
AHHHH!
...
I'M GETTING DIZZY! MAKE IT STOP!
ZWOOSH
URRRGH.
I FEEL SICK...
SPLUB
LET'S TRY THIS!
ZWOOOOOSH

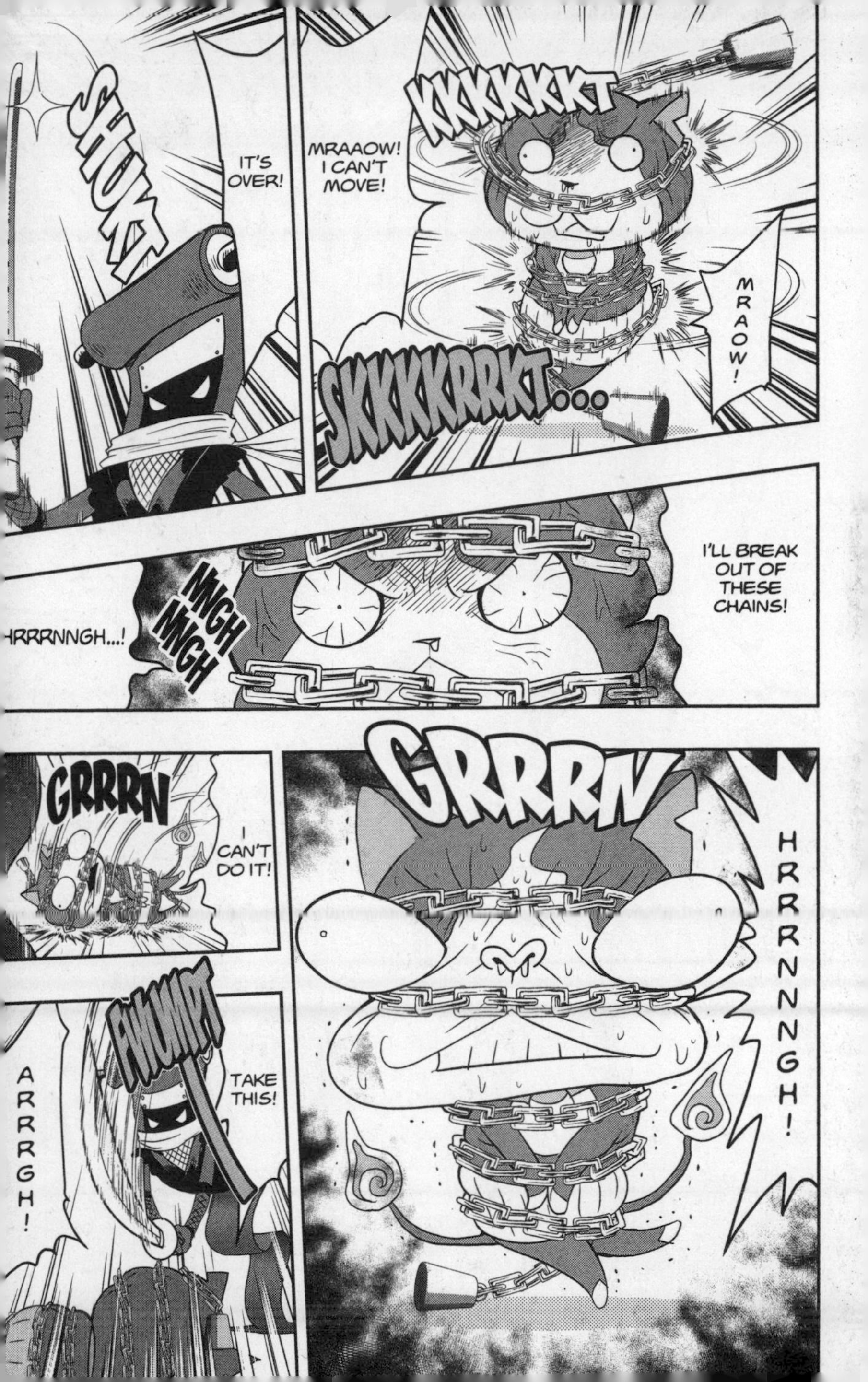
KKKKKKKT
MRAAOW! I CAN'T MOVE!
MRAOW!
SKKKKRRRKT...
SHUKT
IT'S OVER!
I'LL BREAK OUT OF THESE CHAINS!
MNGH MNGH
HRRRNNGH...!
GRRRN
HRRRNNNGH!
GRRRN
I CAN'T DO IT!
FWUMPT
TAKE THIS!
ARRRGH!

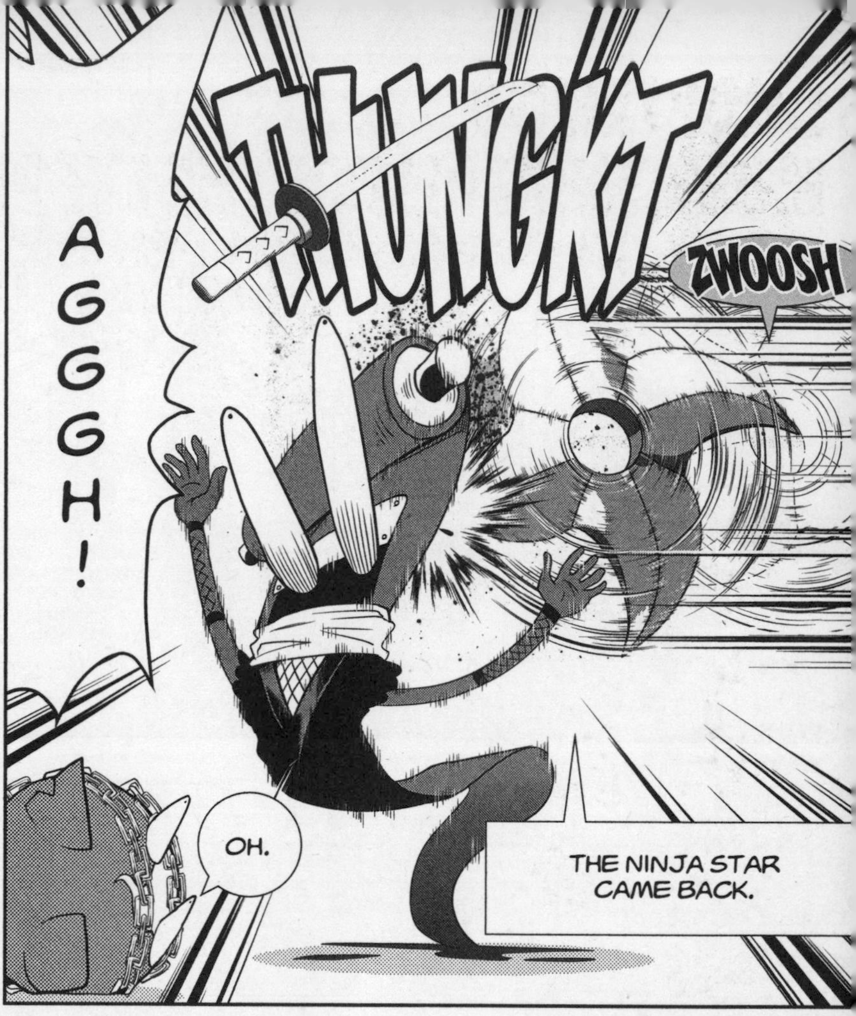
ZWOOSH
THUNCK
AGGGH!
THE NINJA STAR CAME BACK.
OH.

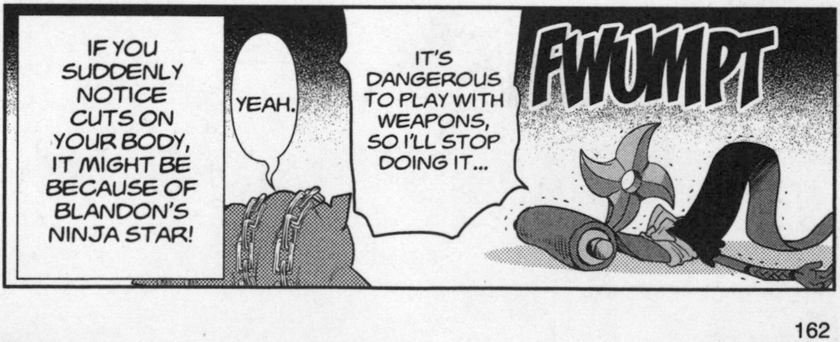
FWUMPT
IT'S DANGEROUS TO PLAY WITH WEAPONS, SO I'LL STOP DOING IT...
YEAH.
IF YOU SUDDENLY NOTICE CUTS ON YOUR BODY, IT MIGHT BE BECAUSE OF BLANDON'S NINJA STAR!

CHAPTER 34:
MORE THAN MEETS THE EYE?!
FEATURING ILLUSION YO-KAI ILLOO

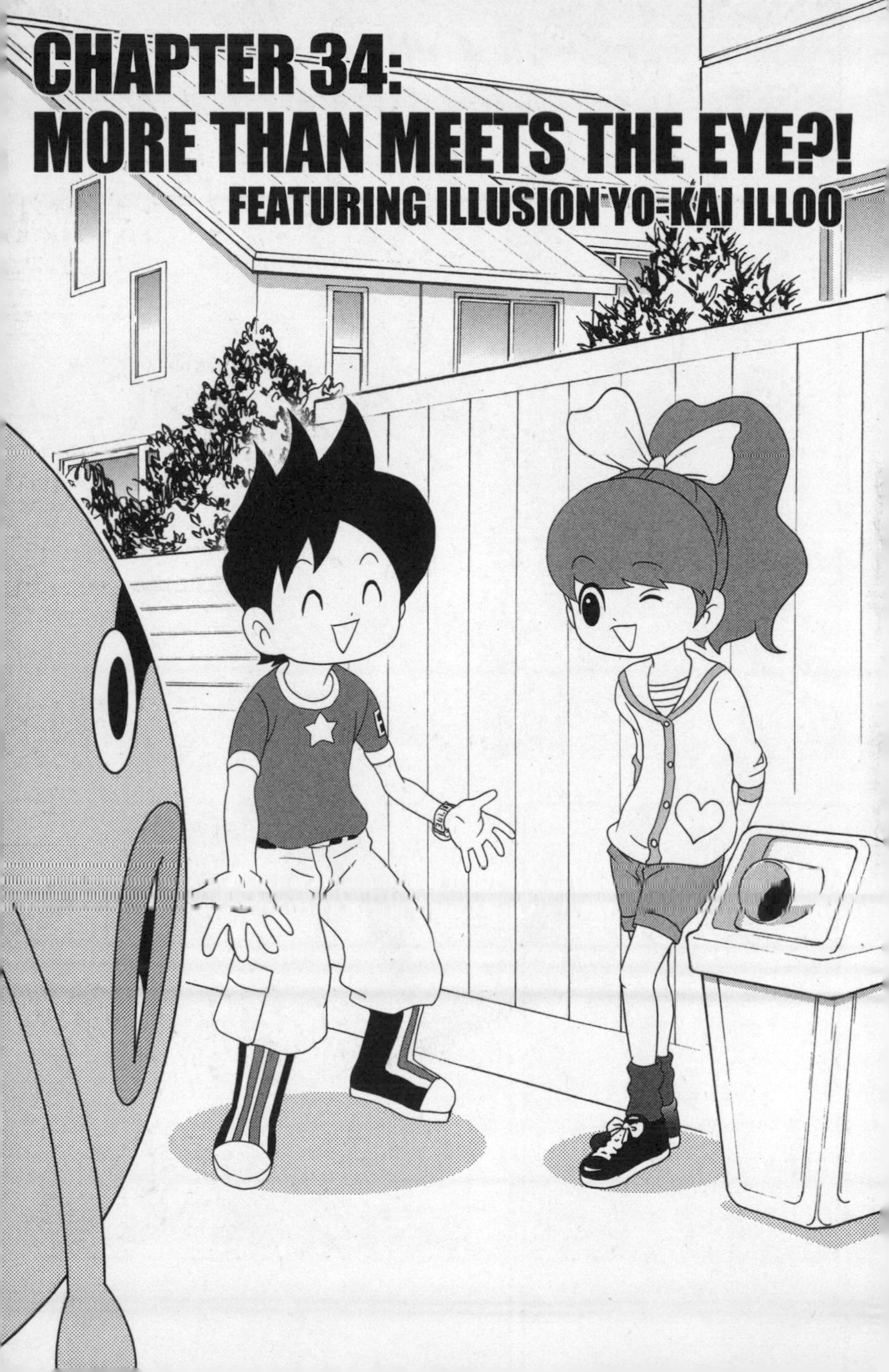

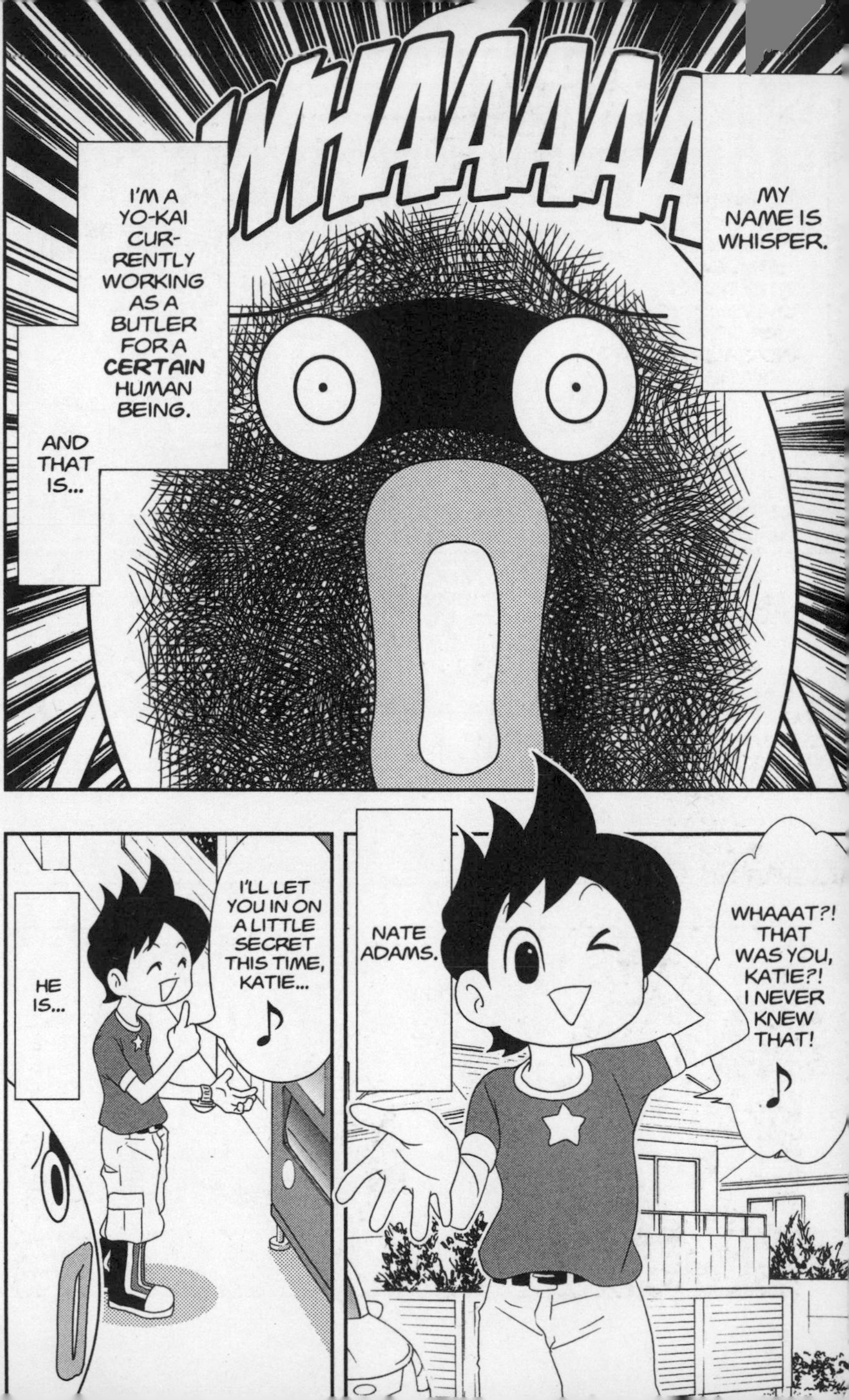
MY NAME IS WHISPER.
WHAAAAA
I'M A YO-KAI CURRENTLY WORKING AS A BUTLER FOR A CERTAIN HUMAN BEING.
AND THAT IS...
WHAAAT?! THAT WAS YOU, KATIE?! I NEVER KNEW THAT! ♪
NATE ADAMS.
I'LL LET YOU IN ON A LITTLE SECRET THIS TIME, KATIE... ♪
HE IS...

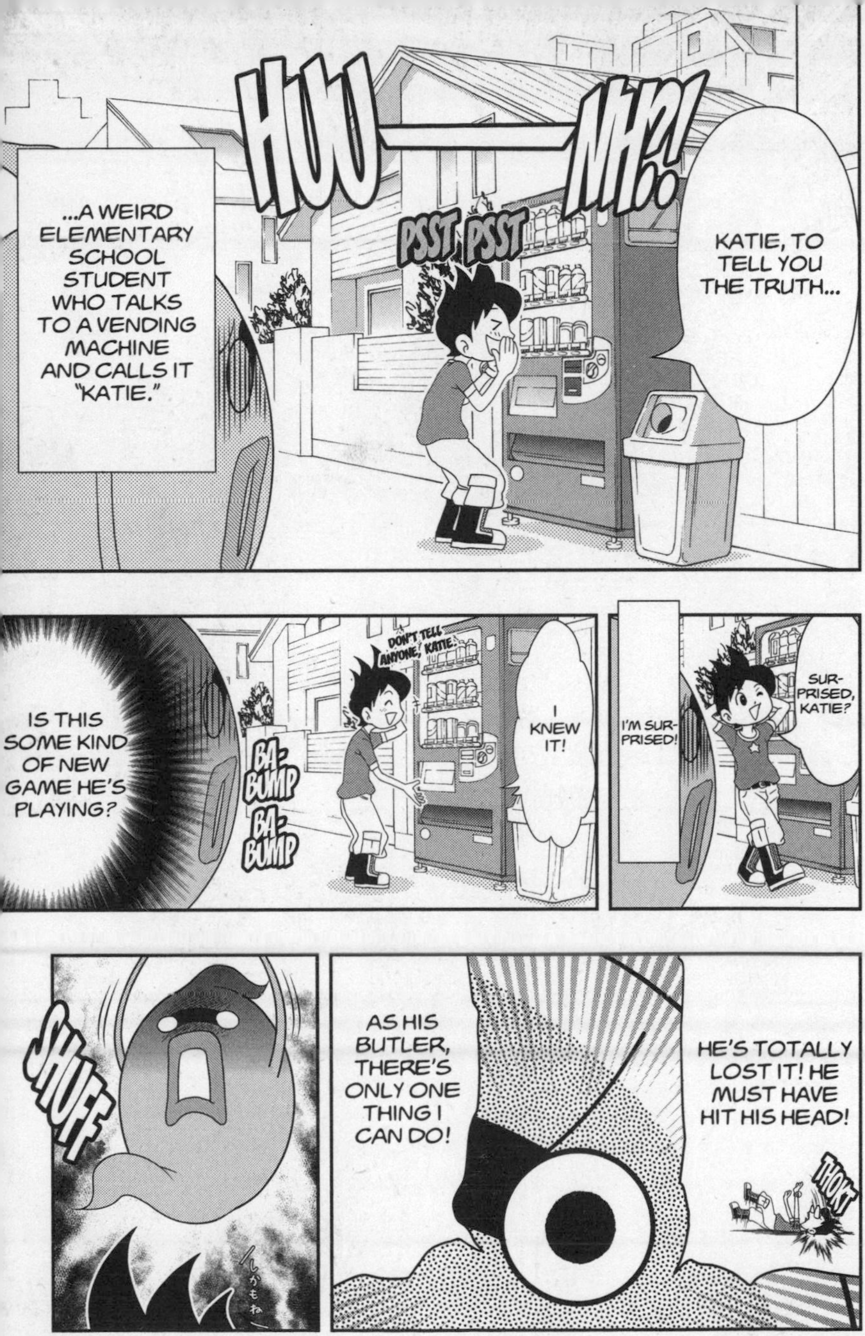

KATIE, TO TELL YOU THE TRUTH...
HUU—MH?!
PSST PSST
...A WEIRD ELEMENTARY SCHOOL STUDENT WHO TALKS TO A VENDING MACHINE AND CALLS IT "KATIE."
SUR-PRISED, KATIE?
I'M SUR-PRISED!
I KNEW IT!
DON'T TELL ANYONE, KATIE.
BA-BUMP BA-BUMP
IS THIS SOME KIND OF NEW GAME HE'S PLAYING?
HE'S TOTALLY LOST IT! HE MUST HAVE HIT HIS HEAD!
THOKT
AS HIS BUTLER, THERE'S ONLY ONE THING I CAN DO!
SHUFF
しかもね

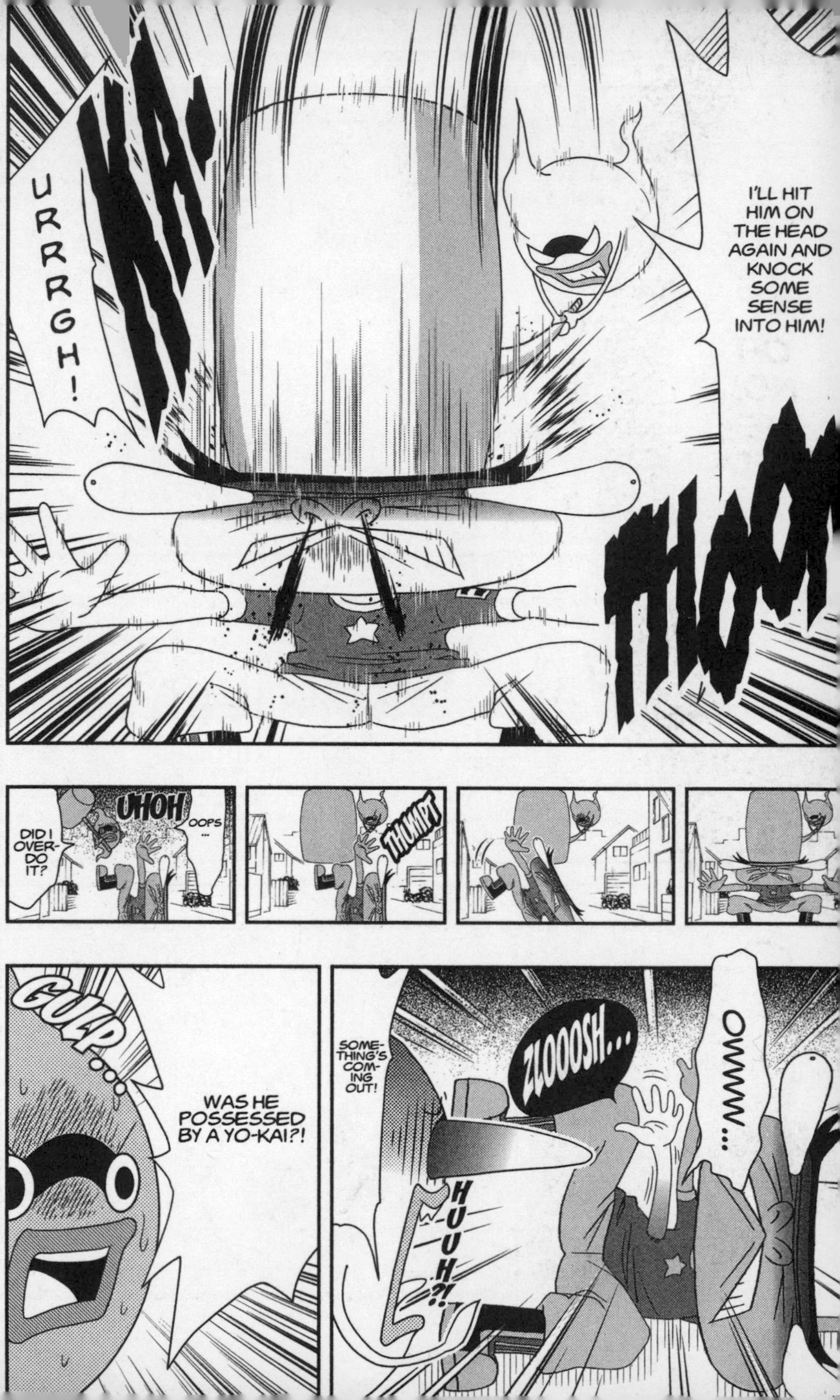
I'LL HIT HIM ON THE HEAD AGAIN AND KNOCK SOME SENSE INTO HIM!
URRRGH!
THUMPT
UHOH
OOPS ...
DID I OVER-DO IT?
OWWW...
ZLOOOSH...
SOME-THING'S COM-ING OUT!
HUUUH?!
WAS HE POSSESSED BY A YO-KAI?!
GULP...

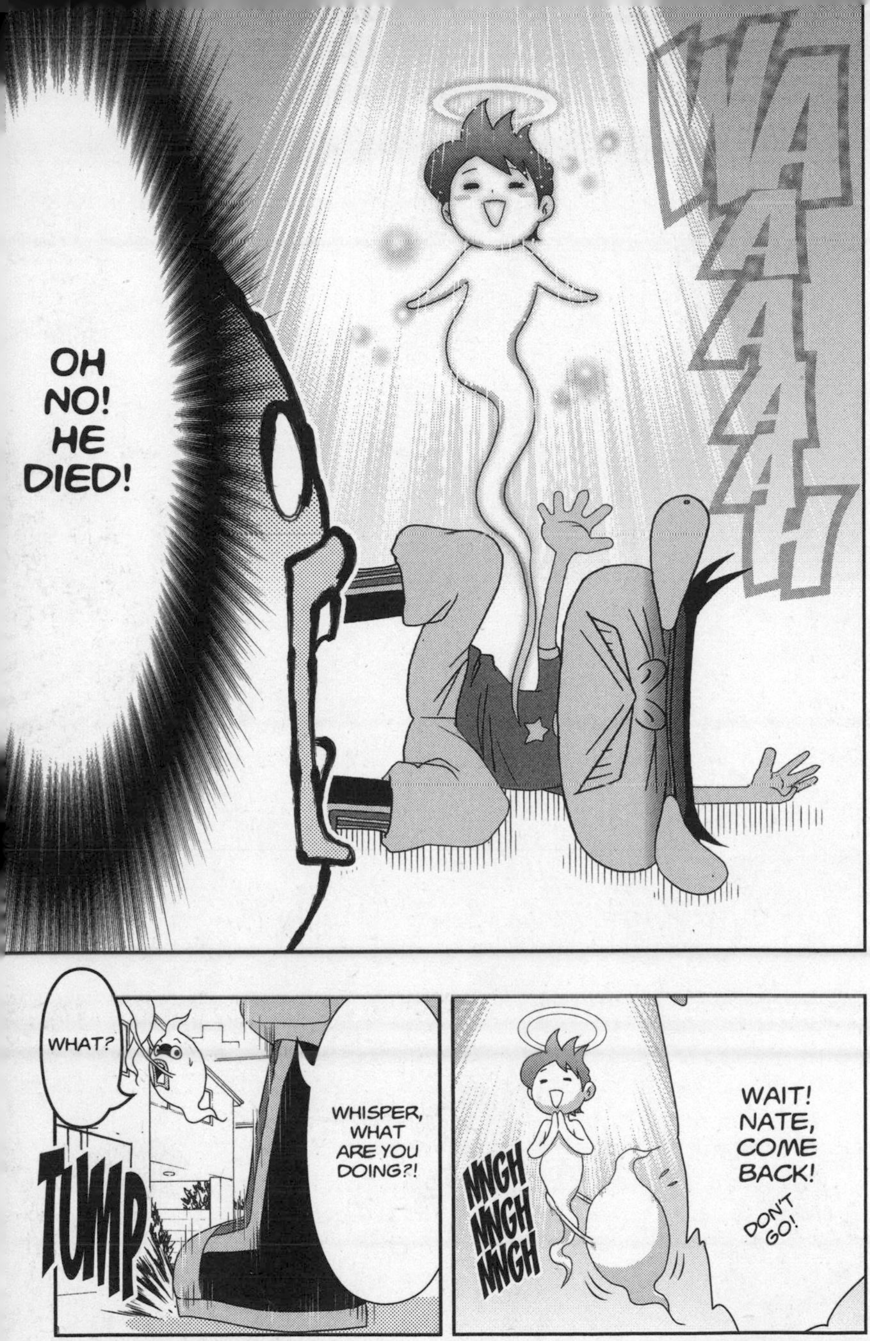
WAAAAH
OH NO! HE DIED!
WAIT! NATE, COME BACK!
DON'T GO!
MNGH MNGH MNGH
WHISPER, WHAT ARE YOU DOING?!
WHAT?
TUMP

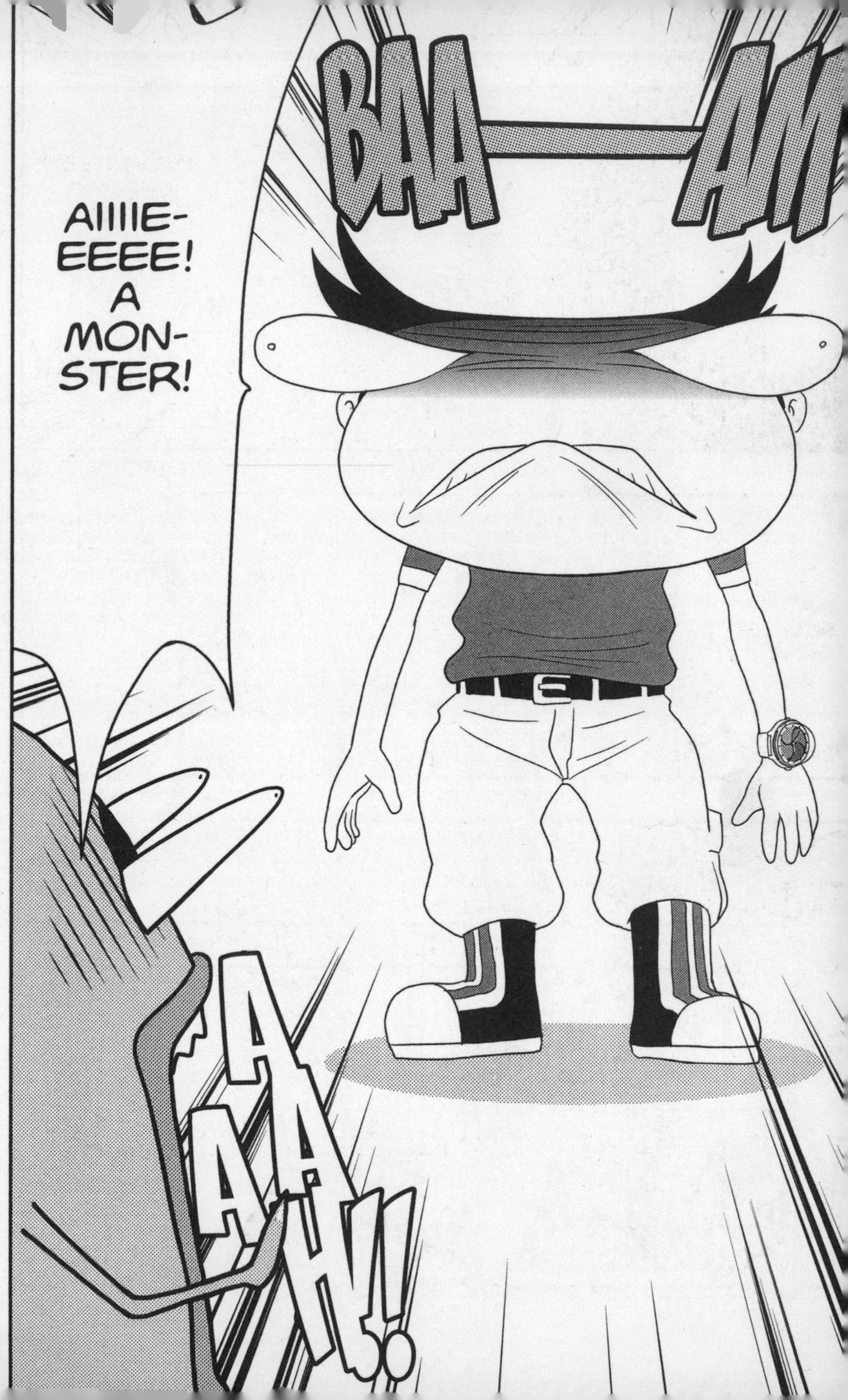
BAA—AM
AIIIIE-EEEEE! A MON-STER!
AAAH!!

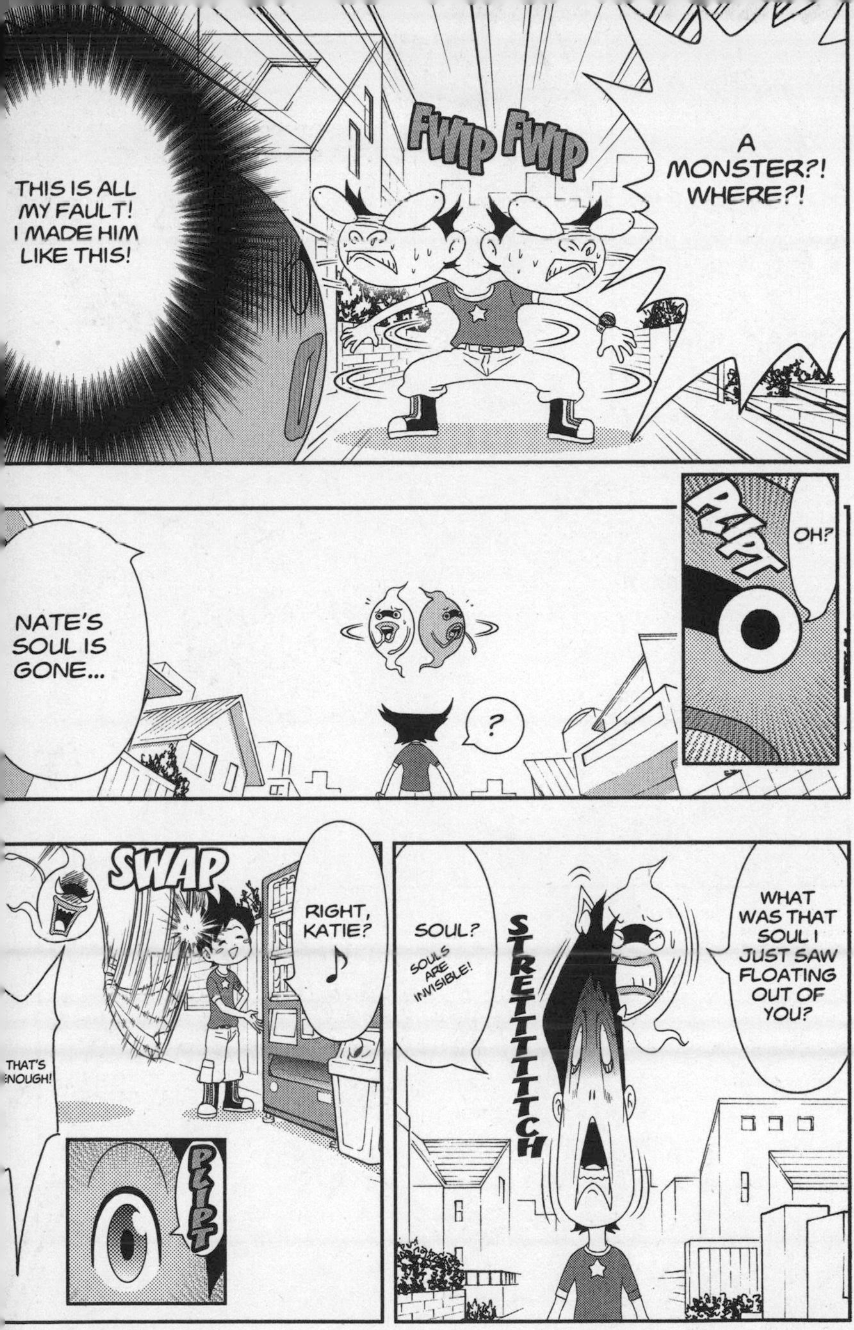
A MONSTER?! WHERE?!
FWIP FWIP
THIS IS ALL MY FAULT! I MADE HIM LIKE THIS!
PLIPT
OH?
?
NATE'S SOUL IS GONE...
WHAT WAS THAT SOUL I JUST SAW FLOATING OUT OF YOU?
STRETTTTTCH
SOUL?
SOULS ARE INVISIBLE!
RIGHT, KATIE? ♪
SWAP
THAT'S ENOUGH!
PLIPT

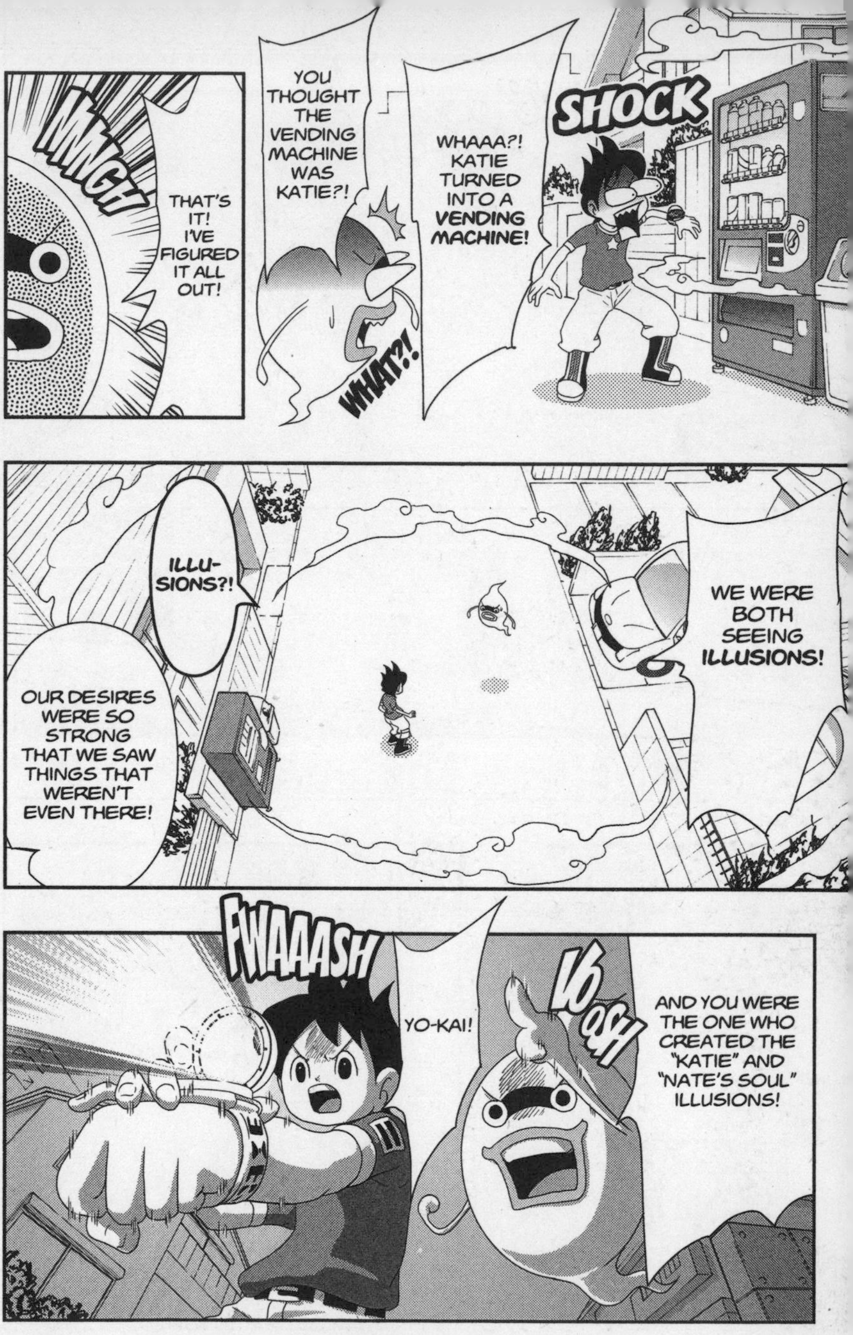
SHOCK
WHAAA?! KATIE TURNED INTO A VENDING MACHINE!
YOU THOUGHT THE VENDING MACHINE WAS KATIE?!
WHAT?!
MMGH
THAT'S IT! I'VE FIGURED IT ALL OUT!
WE WERE BOTH SEEING ILLUSIONS!
ILLU-SIONS?!
OUR DESIRES WERE SO STRONG THAT WE SAW THINGS THAT WEREN'T EVEN THERE!
AND YOU WERE THE ONE WHO CREATED THE "KATIE" AND "NATE'S SOUL" ILLUSIONS!
WOOSH
YO-KAI!
FWAAASH

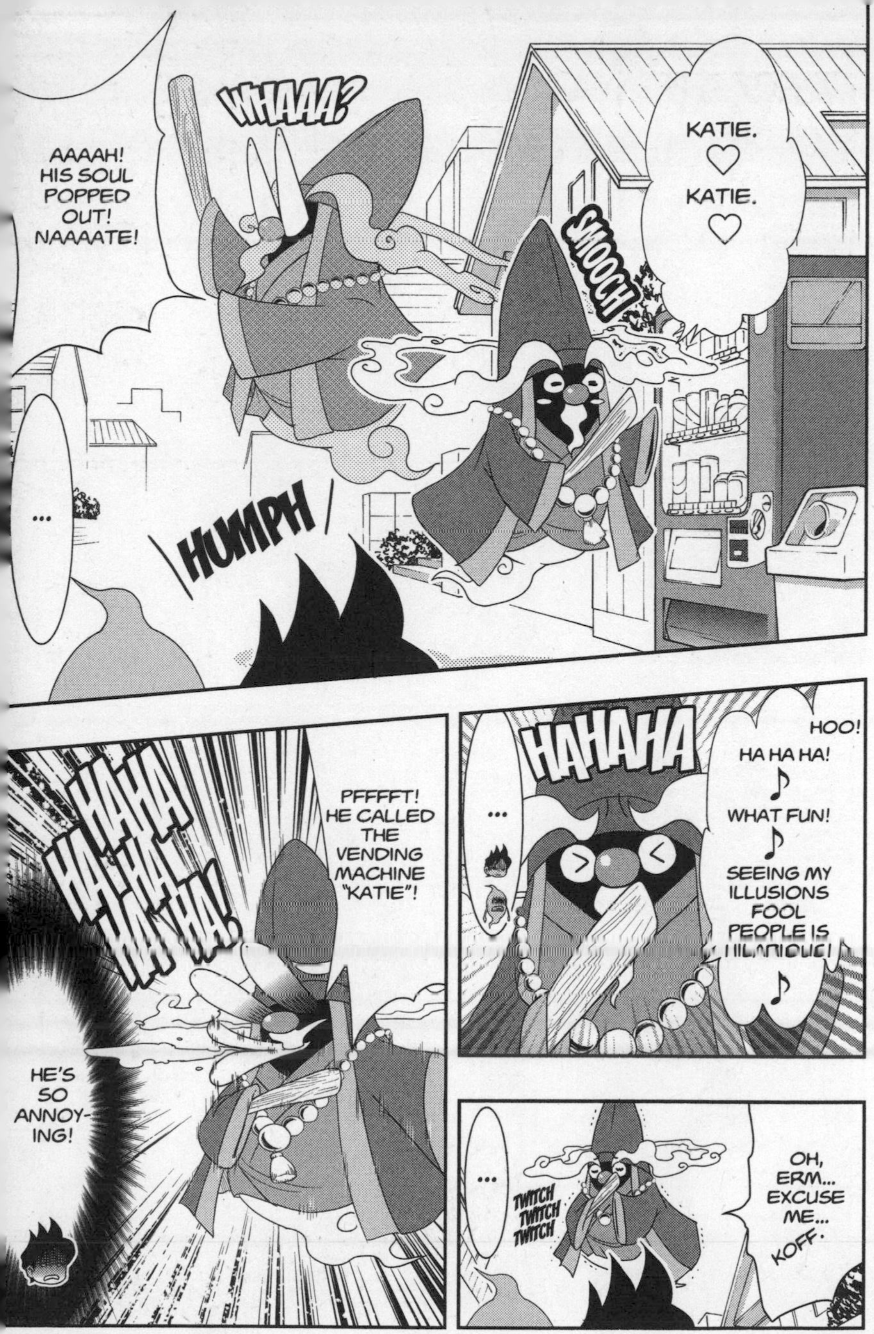
KATIE. ♡ KATIE. ♡
SMOOCH
WHAAAA?
AAAAH! HIS SOUL POPPED OUT! NAAAATE!
...
HUMPH
HAHAHA
HOO! HA HA HA! ♪ WHAT FUN! ♪ SEEING MY ILLUSIONS FOOL PEOPLE IS HILARIOUS! ♪
...
OH, ERM... EXCUSE ME... KOFF.
TWITCH TWITCH TWITCH
...
PFFFFT! HE CALLED THE VENDING MACHINE "KATIE"!
HAHAHA HAHAHA HAHAHA!
HE'S SO ANNOYING!

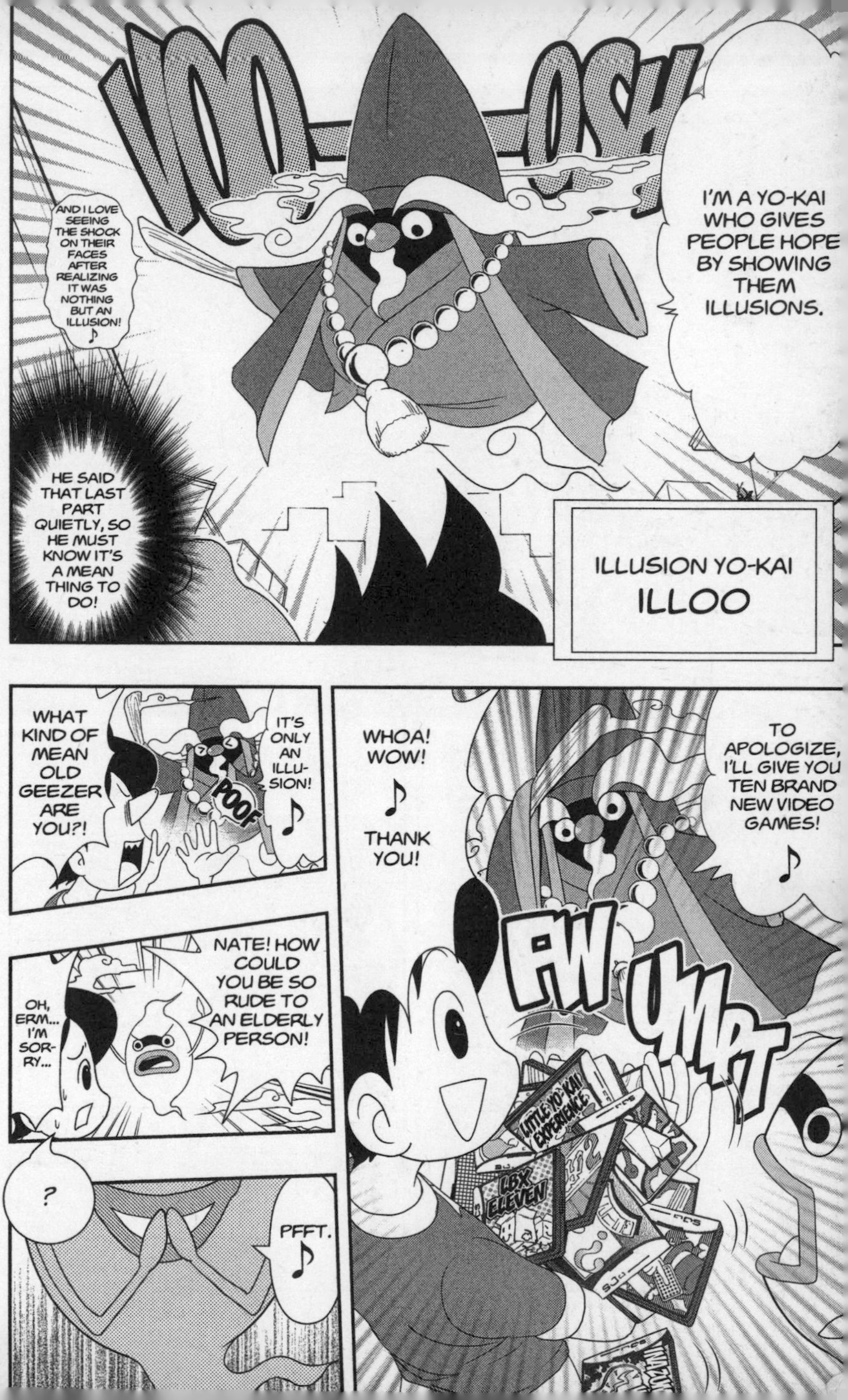
I'M A YO-KAI WHO GIVES PEOPLE HOPE BY SHOWING THEM ILLUSIONS.
AND I LOVE SEEING THE SHOCK ON THEIR FACES AFTER REALIZING IT WAS NOTHING BUT AN ILLUSION! ♪
ILLUSION YO-KAI
ILLOO
HE SAID THAT LAST PART QUIETLY, SO HE MUST KNOW IT'S A MEAN THING TO DO!
TO APOLOGIZE, I'LL GIVE YOU TEN BRAND NEW VIDEO GAMES! ♪
WHOA! WOW! ♪ THANK YOU!
LITTLE YO-KAI EXPERIENCE
LBX ELEVEN
IT'S ONLY AN ILLU-SION! ♪
WHAT KIND OF MEAN OLD GEEZER ARE YOU?!
POOF
NATE! HOW COULD YOU BE SO RUDE TO AN ELDERLY PERSON!
OH, ERM... I'M SOR-RY...
PFFT. ♪
?

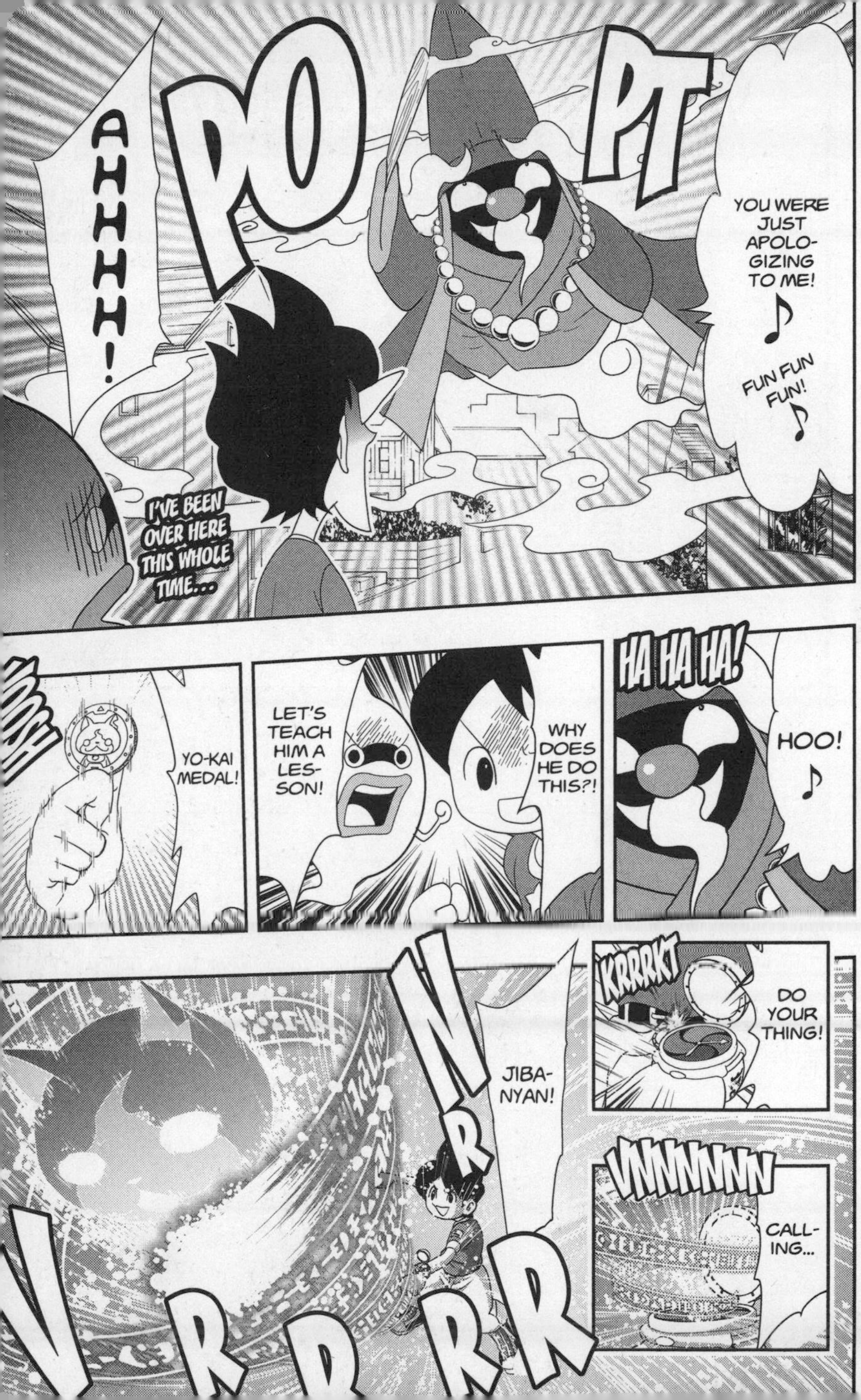
POPT
YOU WERE JUST APOLO-GIZING TO ME! ♪
FUN FUN FUN! ♪
AHHHH!
I'VE BEEN OVER HERE THIS WHOLE TIME...
HA HA HA!
HOO! ♪
WHY DOES HE DO THIS?!
LET'S TEACH HIM A LES-SON!
YO-KAI MEDAL!
KRRRKT
DO YOUR THING!
VNNNNNN
CALL-ING...
JIBA-NYAN!

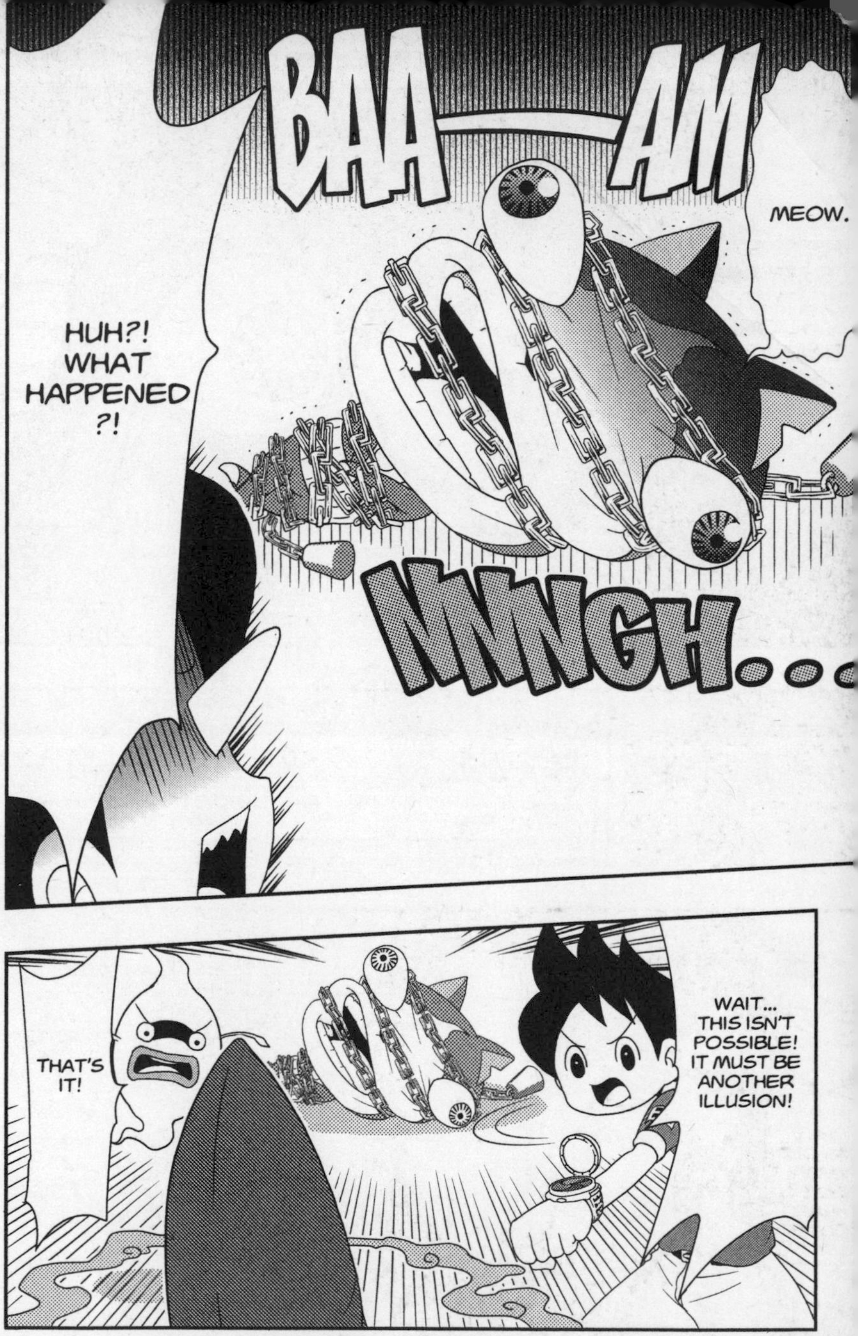
BAA—AM
MEOW.
HUH?! WHAT HAPPENED ?!
MNNNGH...
WAIT... THIS ISN'T POSSIBLE! IT MUST BE ANOTHER ILLUSION!
THAT'S IT!

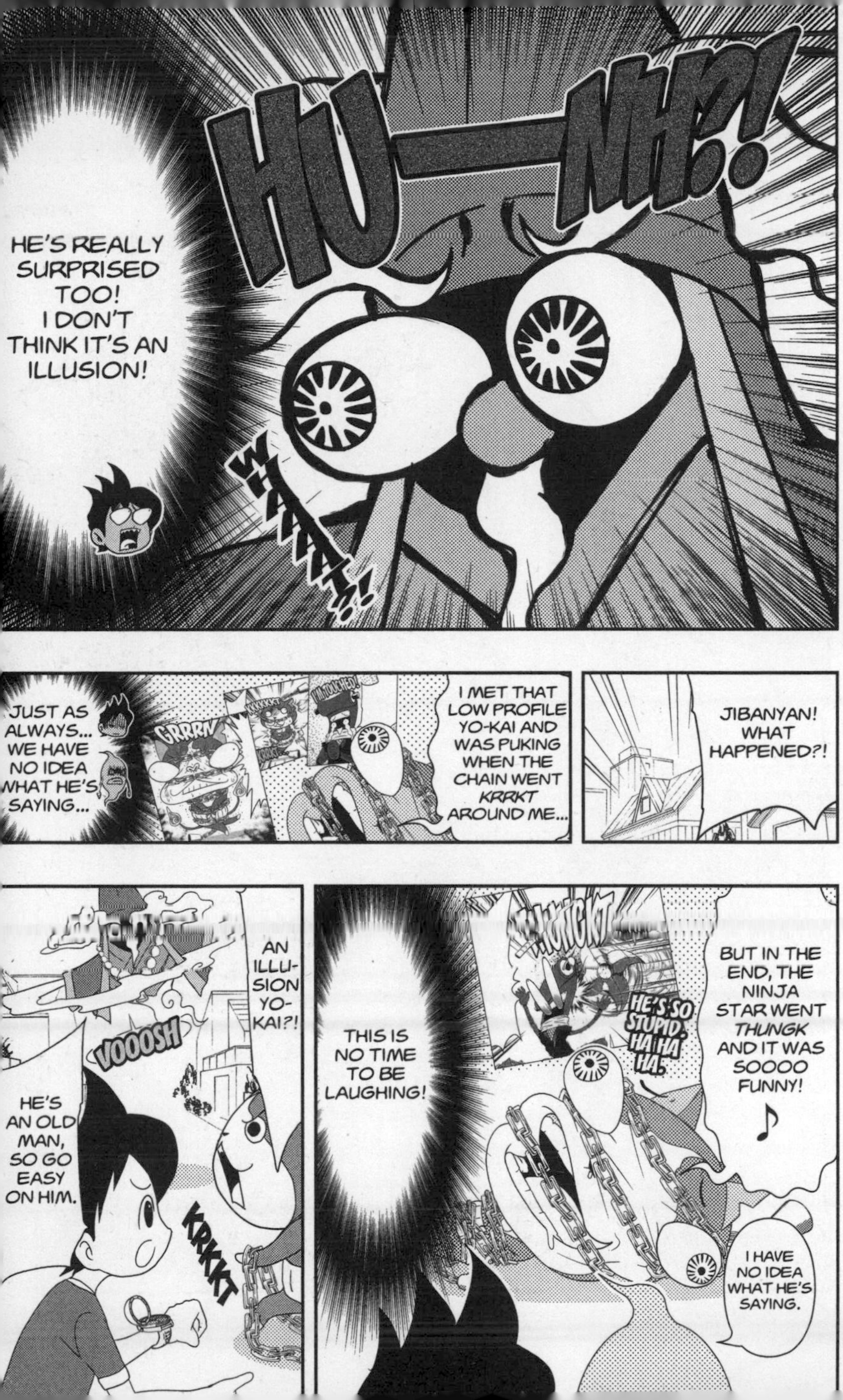
HU—NH?!
HE'S REALLY SURPRISED TOO! I DON'T THINK IT'S AN ILLUSION!
WHAAAT?!
JIBANYAN! WHAT HAPPENED?!
I MET THAT LOW PROFILE YO-KAI AND WAS PUKING WHEN THE CHAIN WENT *KRRKT* AROUND ME...
I'M TOUCHED!
KRRKT
GRRRN
JUST AS ALWAYS... WE HAVE NO IDEA WHAT HE'S SAYING...
BUT IN THE END, THE NINJA STAR WENT *THUNGK* AND IT WAS SOOOO FUNNY! ♪
HE'S SO STUPID. HA HA HA.
THIS IS NO TIME TO BE LAUGHING!
I HAVE NO IDEA WHAT HE'S SAYING.
AN ILLUSION YO-KAI?!
VOOOSH
KRKKT
HE'S AN OLD MAN, SO GO EASY ON HIM.

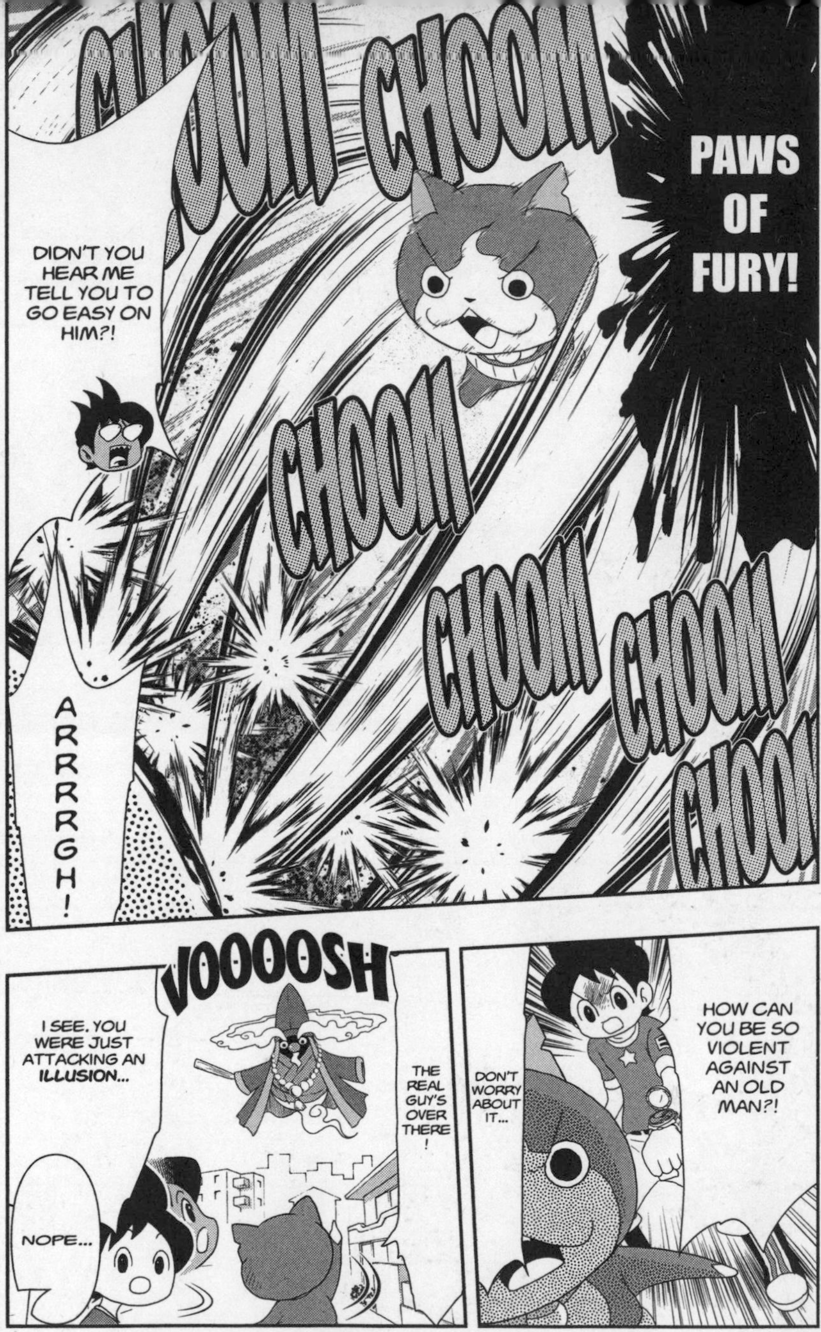
PAWS OF FURY!
CHOOM CHOOM
CHOOM
DIDN'T YOU HEAR ME TELL YOU TO GO EASY ON HIM?!
CHOOM
CHOOM
CHOOM
ARRRRGH!
HOW CAN YOU BE SO VIOLENT AGAINST AN OLD MAN?!
DON'T WORRY ABOUT IT...
VOOOOSH
THE REAL GUY'S OVER THERE!
I SEE. YOU WERE JUST ATTACKING AN **ILLUSION**...
NOPE...

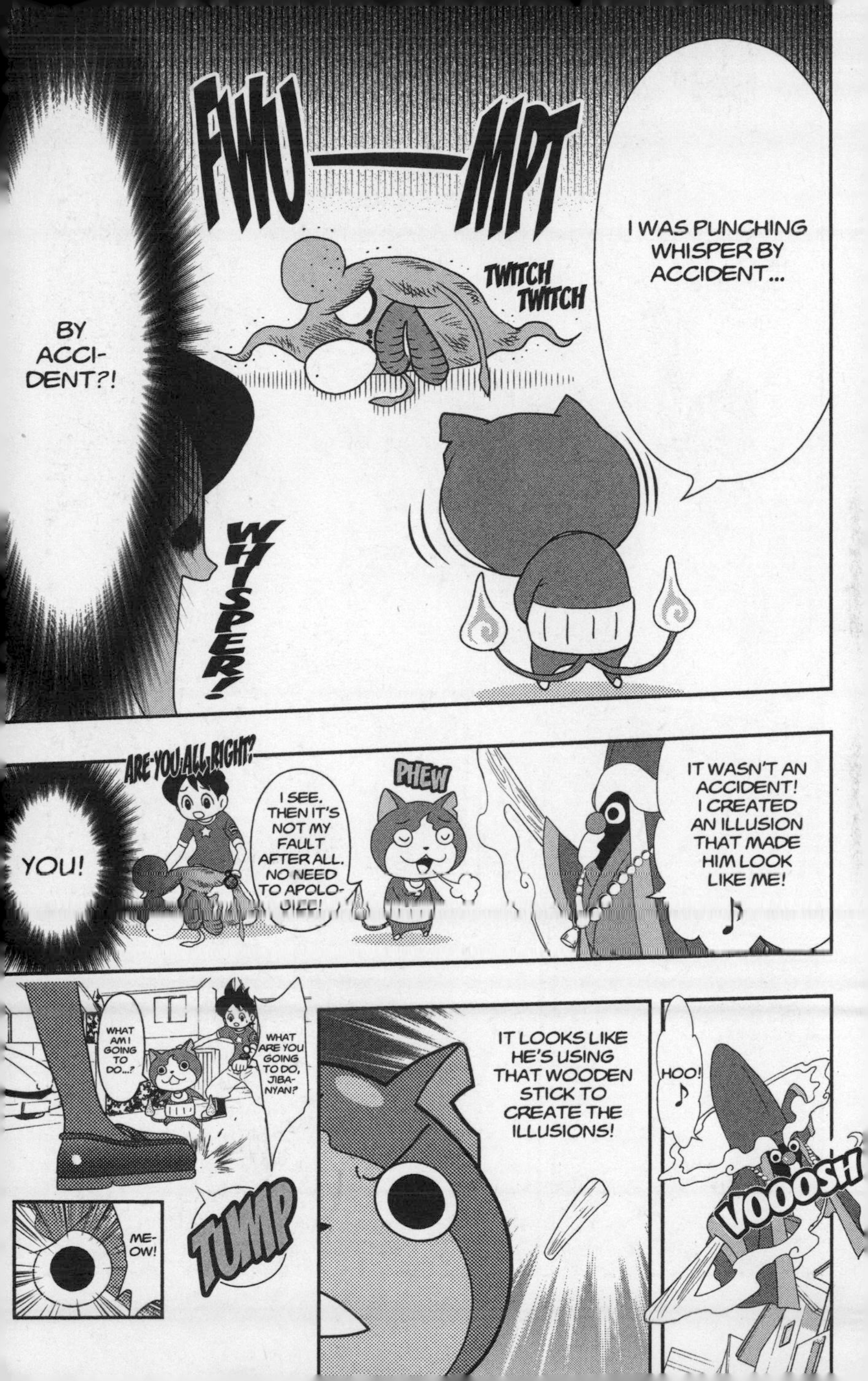
I WAS PUNCHING WHISPER BY ACCIDENT...
FWU—MPT
TWITCH TWITCH
BY ACCI-DENT?!
WHISPER!
IT WASN'T AN ACCIDENT! I CREATED AN ILLUSION THAT MADE HIM LOOK LIKE ME! ♪
PHEW
I SEE. THEN IT'S NOT MY FAULT AFTER ALL. NO NEED TO APOLO-GIZE!
ARE YOU ALL RIGHT?
YOU!
HOO! ♪
VOOOSH
IT LOOKS LIKE HE'S USING THAT WOODEN STICK TO CREATE THE ILLUSIONS!
WHAT ARE YOU GOING TO DO, JIBA-NYAN?
WHAT AM I GOING TO DO...?
TUMP
ME-OW!

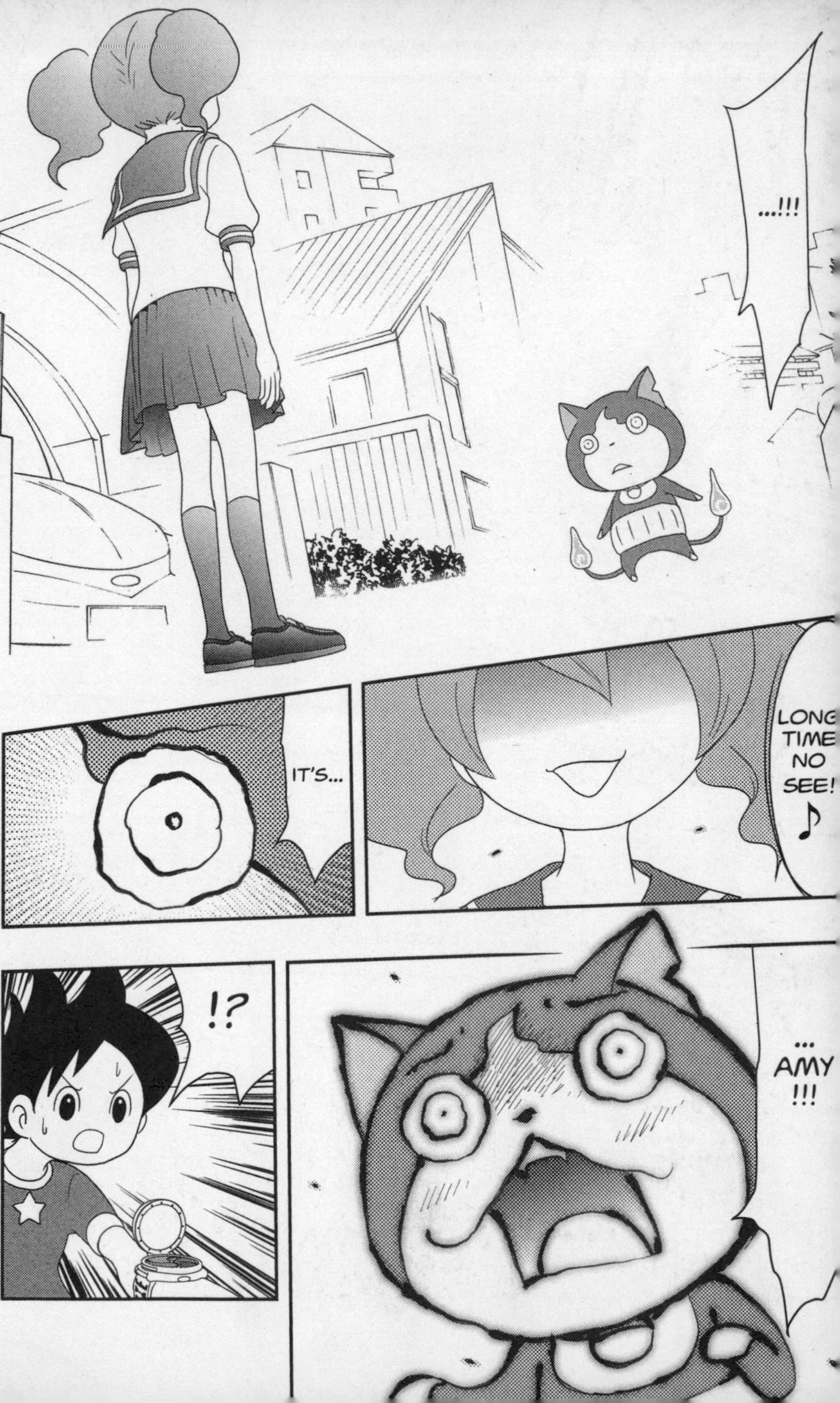
...!!!
LONG TIME NO SEE! ♪
IT'S...
...AMY!!!
!?

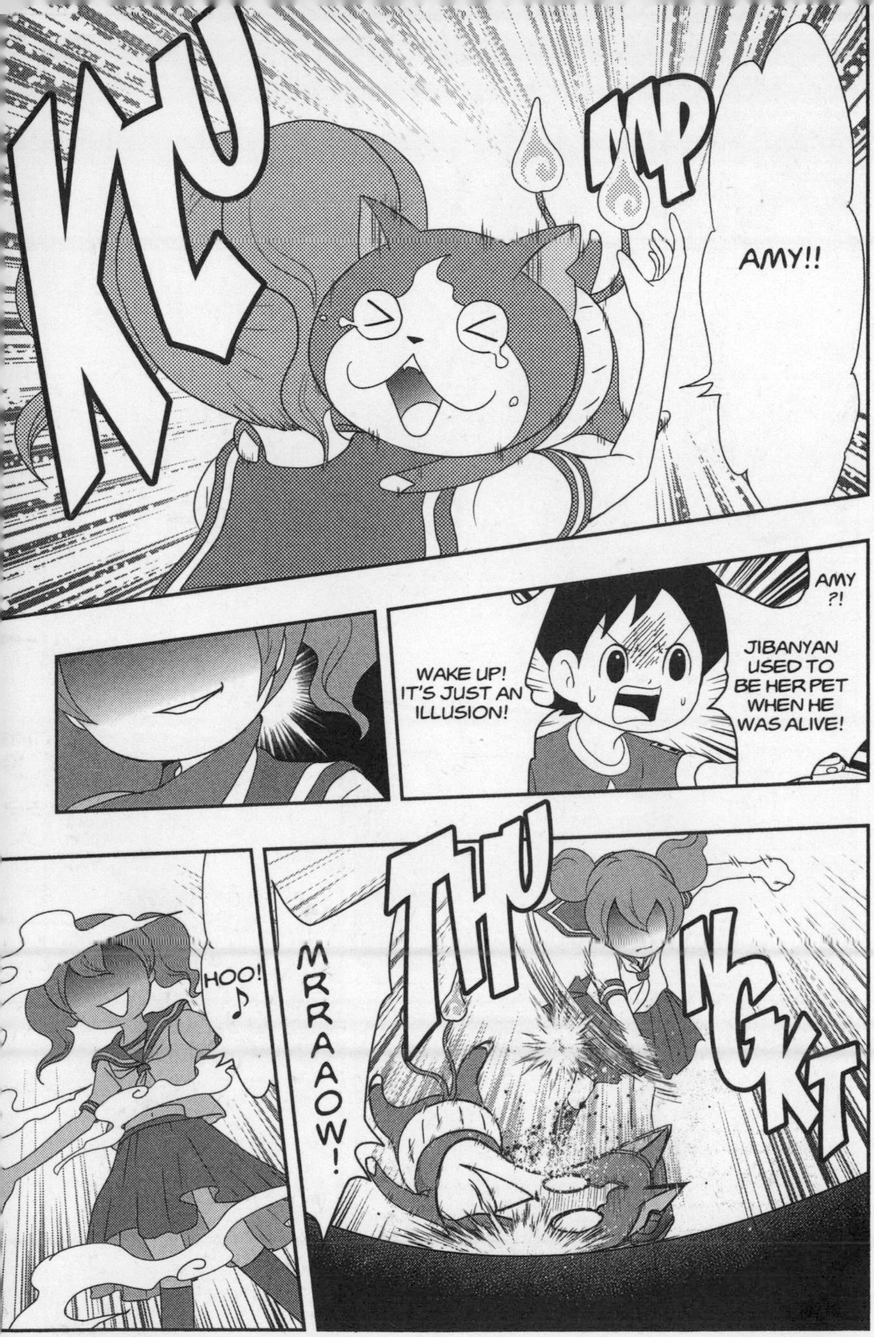
AMY!!
KLUMP
AMY ?!
JIBANYAN USED TO BE HER PET WHEN HE WAS ALIVE!
WAKE UP! IT'S JUST AN ILLUSION!
THUNGKT
MRRAAOW!
HOO! ♪

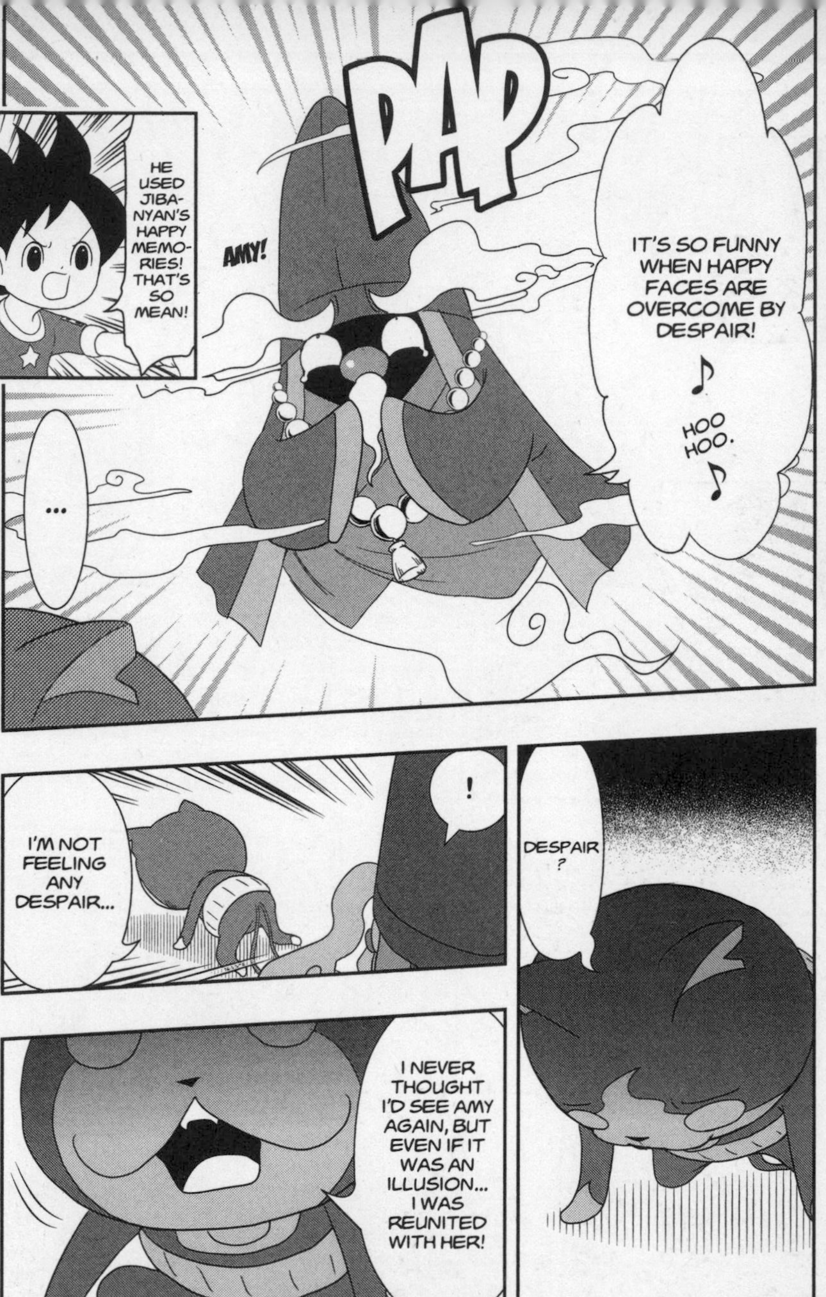
PAP
IT'S SO FUNNY WHEN HAPPY FACES ARE OVERCOME BY DESPAIR! ♪ HOO HOO. ♪
AMY!
HE USED JIBA-NYAN'S HAPPY MEMO-RIES! THAT'S SO MEAN!
...
DESPAIR?
!
I'M NOT FEELING ANY DESPAIR...
I NEVER THOUGHT I'D SEE AMY AGAIN, BUT EVEN IF IT WAS AN ILLUSION... I WAS REUNITED WITH HER!

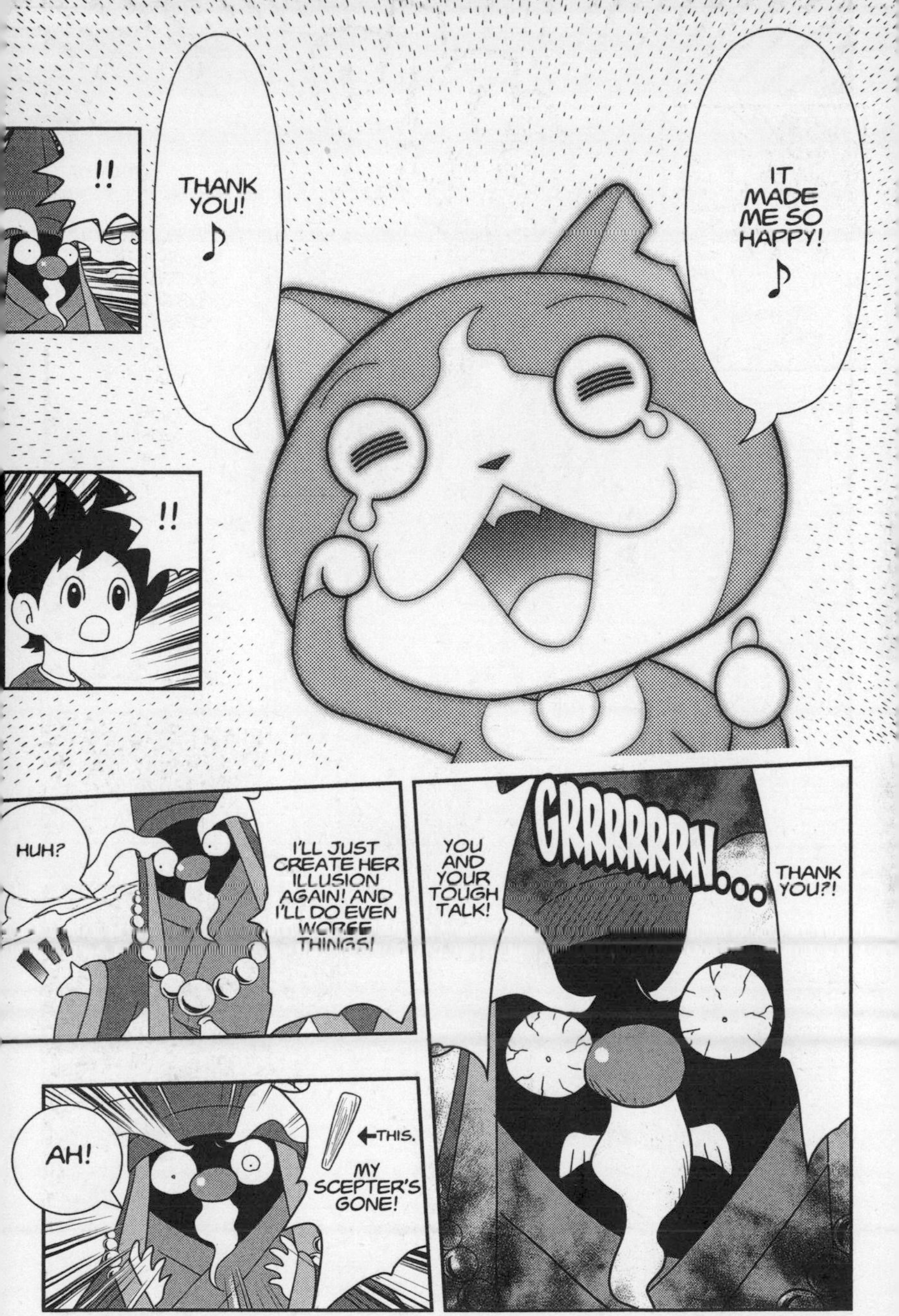
IT MADE ME SO HAPPY! ♪
THANK YOU! ♪
!!
!!
GRRRRRRNOOO
THANK YOU?!
YOU AND YOUR TOUGH TALK!
I'LL JUST CREATE HER ILLUSION AGAIN! AND I'LL DO EVEN WORSE THINGS!
HUH?
←THIS.
MY SCEPTER'S GONE!
AH!

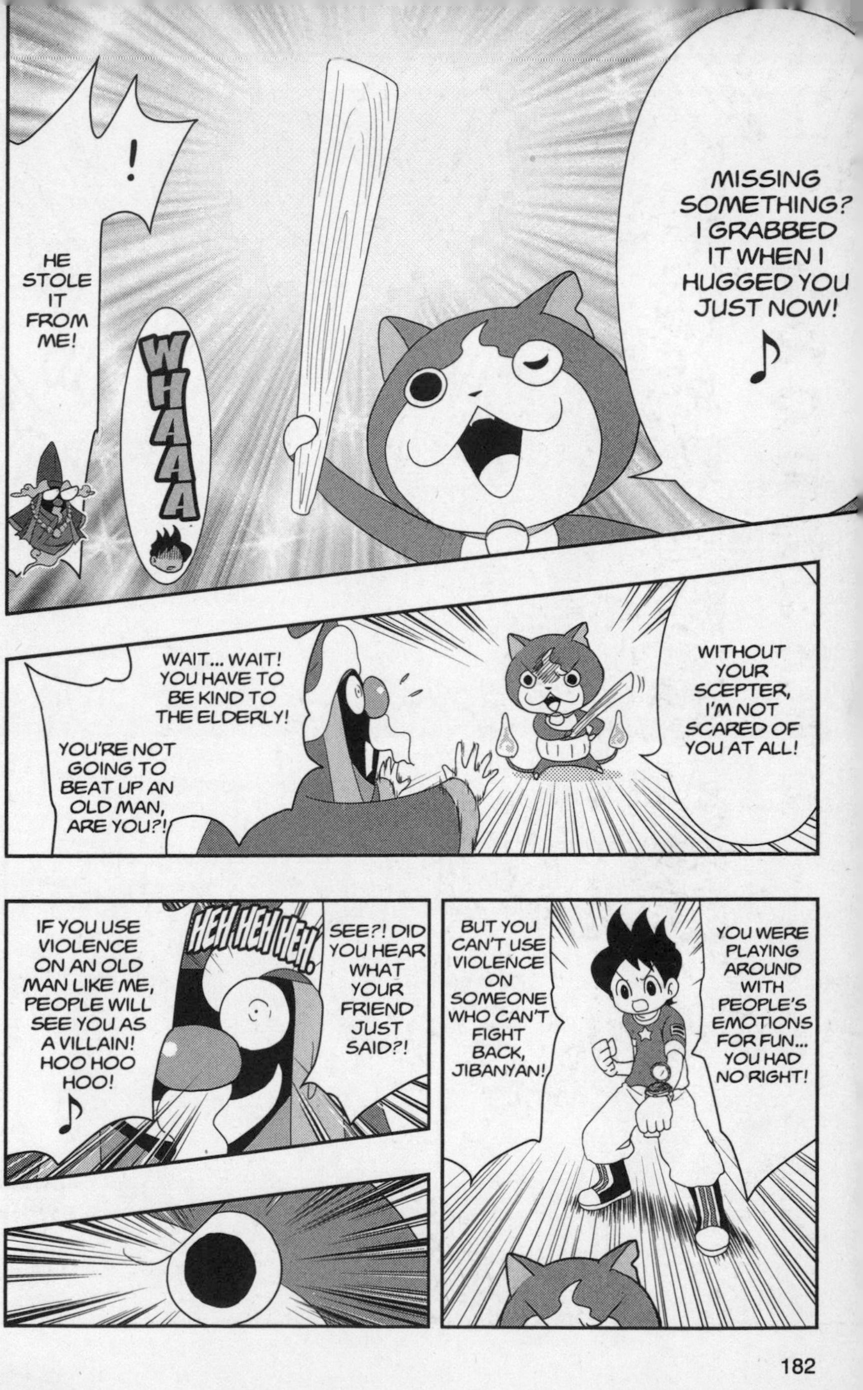
MISSING SOMETHING? I GRABBED IT WHEN I HUGGED YOU JUST NOW! ♪
WHAAAA
!
HE STOLE IT FROM ME!
WITHOUT YOUR SCEPTER, I'M NOT SCARED OF YOU AT ALL!
WAIT... WAIT! YOU HAVE TO BE KIND TO THE ELDERLY!
YOU'RE NOT GOING TO BEAT UP AN OLD MAN, ARE YOU?!
YOU WERE PLAYING AROUND WITH PEOPLE'S EMOTIONS FOR FUN... YOU HAD NO RIGHT!
BUT YOU CAN'T USE VIOLENCE ON SOMEONE WHO CAN'T FIGHT BACK, JIBANYAN!
SEE?! DID YOU HEAR WHAT YOUR FRIEND JUST SAID?!
HEH HEH HEH
IF YOU USE VIOLENCE ON AN OLD MAN LIKE ME, PEOPLE WILL SEE YOU AS A VILLAIN! HOO HOO HOO! ♪

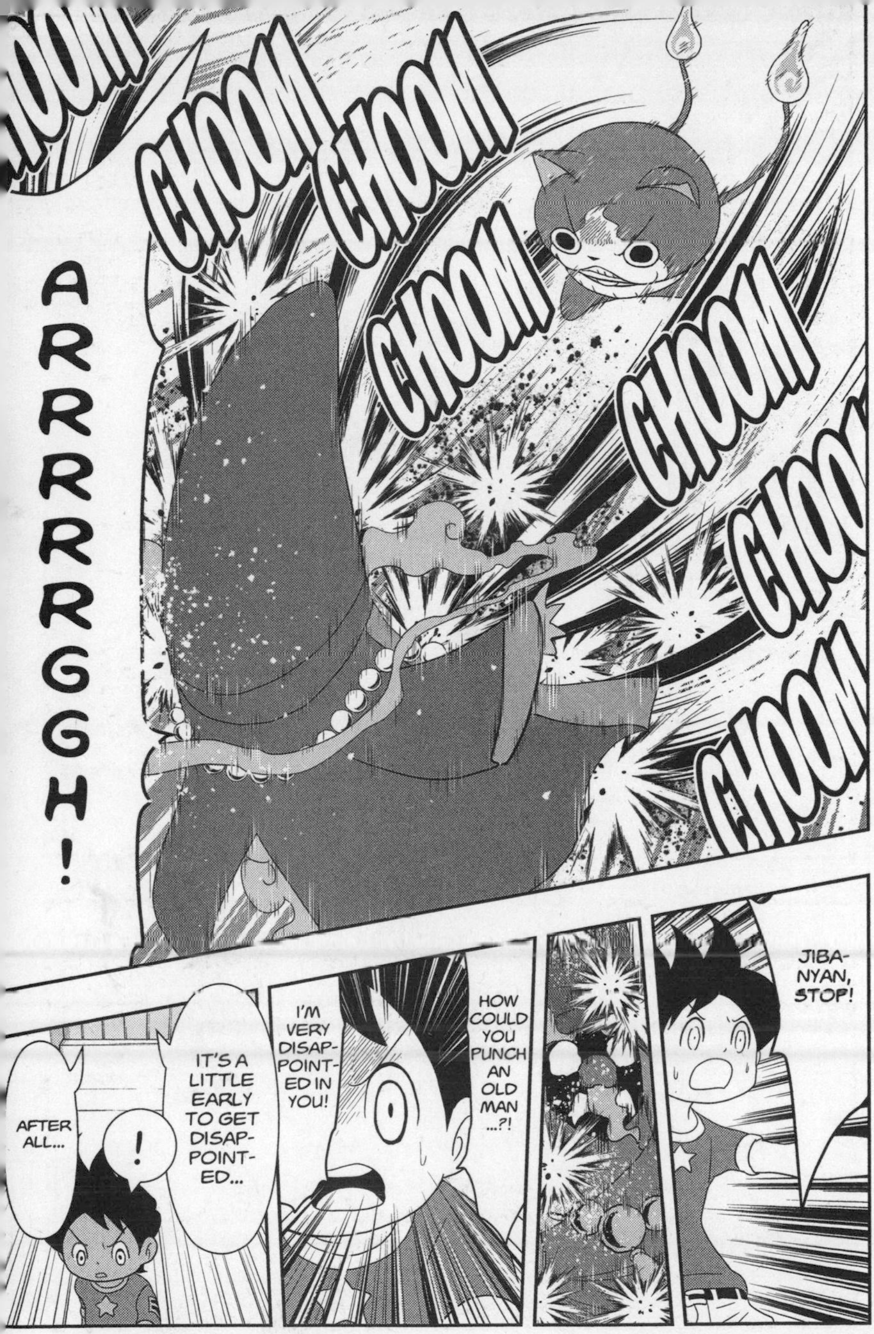
CHOOM CHOOM CHOOM CHOOM CHOOM CHOOM CHOOM CHOOM
ARRRRRGGH!
JIBA-NYAN, STOP!
HOW COULD YOU PUNCH AN OLD MAN ...?!
I'M VERY DISAPPOINTED IN YOU!
IT'S A LITTLE EARLY TO GET DISAPPOINTED...
!
AFTER ALL...

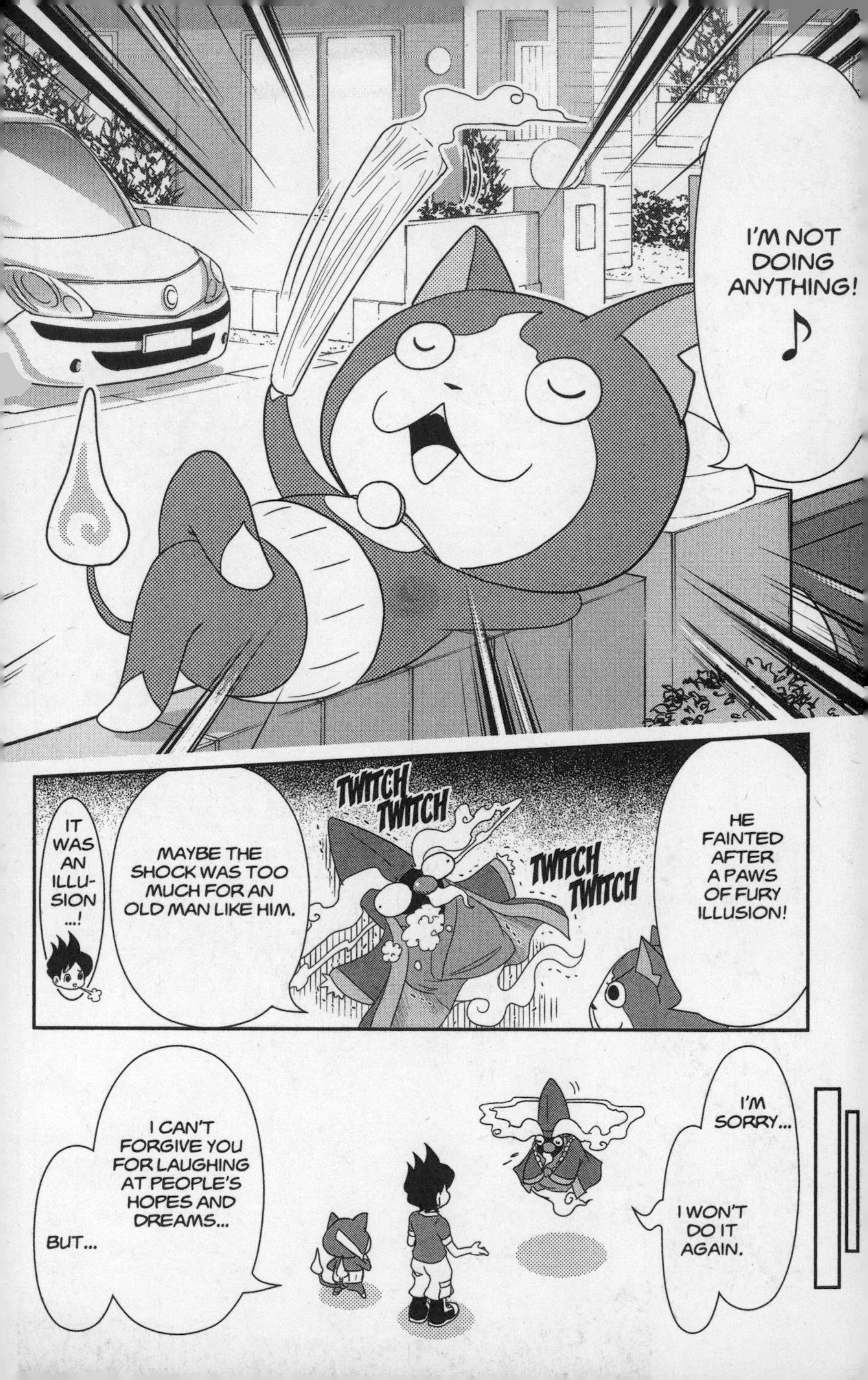
I'M NOT DOING ANYTHING! ♪
HE FAINTED AFTER A PAWS OF FURY ILLUSION!
TWITCH TWITCH
TWITCH TWITCH
MAYBE THE SHOCK WAS TOO MUCH FOR AN OLD MAN LIKE HIM.
IT WAS AN ILLU-SION ...!
I'M SORRY...
I WON'T DO IT AGAIN.
I CAN'T FORGIVE YOU FOR LAUGHING AT PEOPLE'S HOPES AND DREAMS...
BUT...

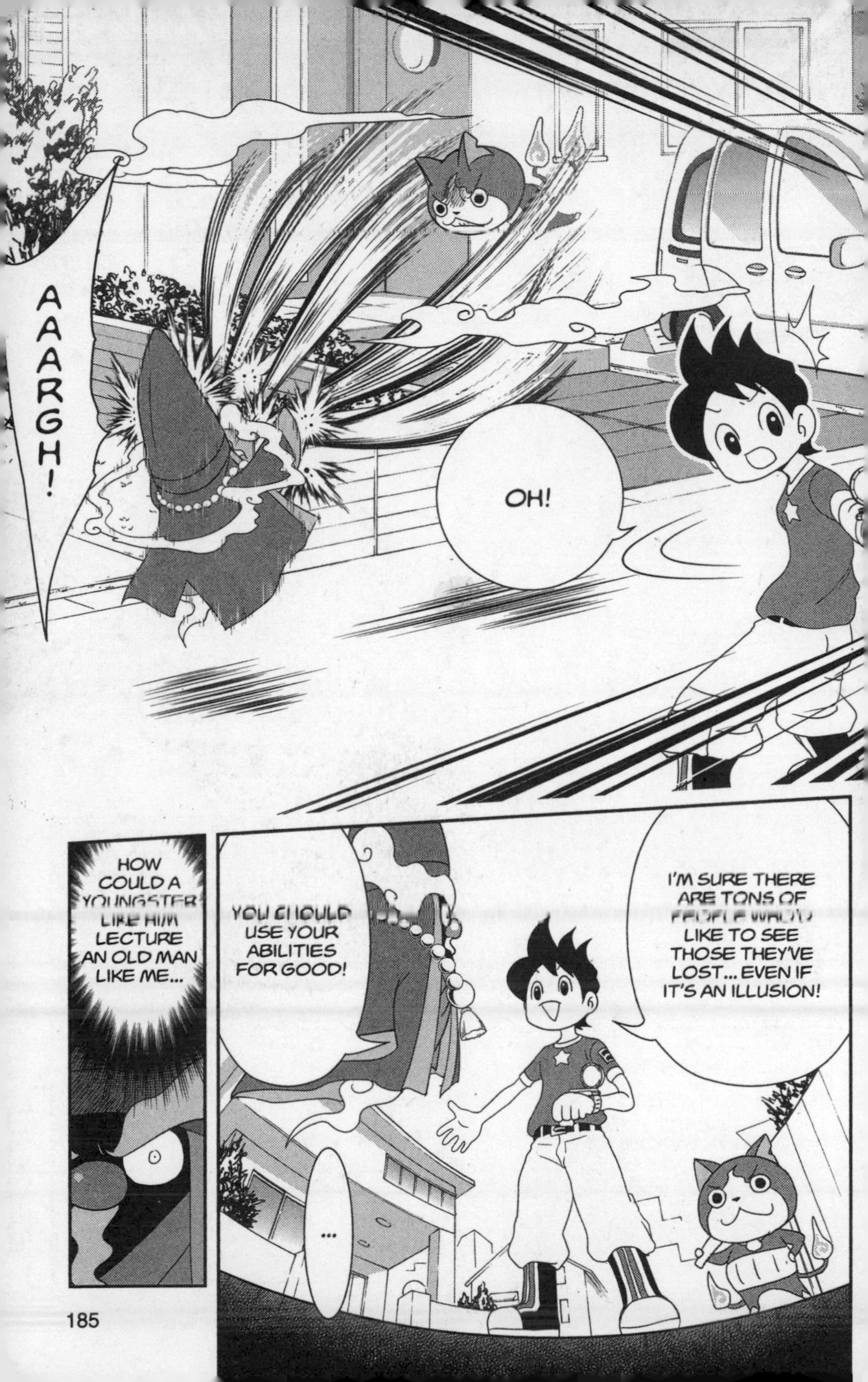
OH!
AAAARGH!
I'M SURE THERE ARE TONS OF PEOPLE WHO'D LIKE TO SEE THOSE THEY'VE LOST... EVEN IF IT'S AN ILLUSION!
YOU SHOULD USE YOUR ABILITIES FOR GOOD!
...
HOW COULD A YOUNGSTER LIKE HIM LECTURE AN OLD MAN LIKE ME...

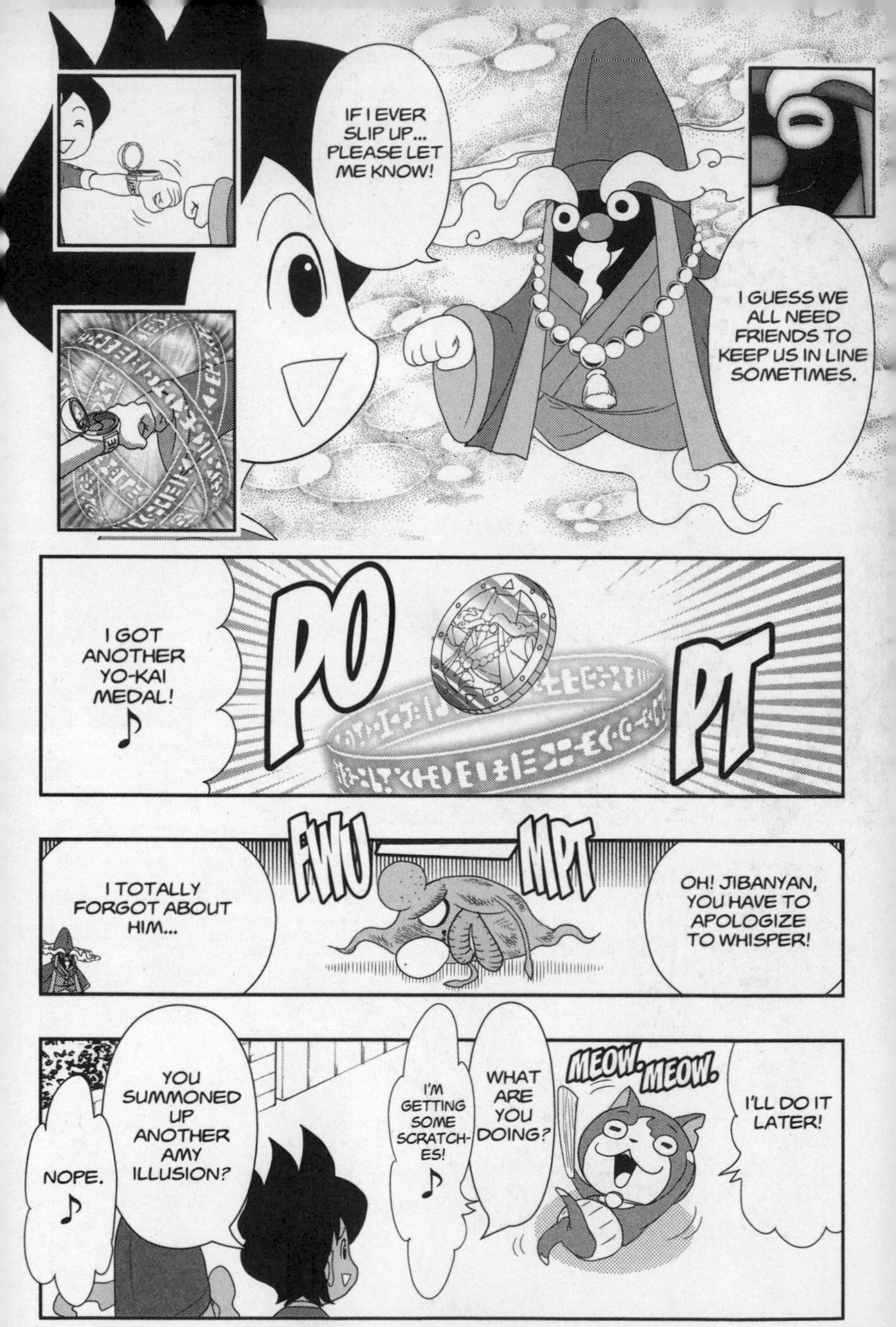
I GUESS WE ALL NEED FRIENDS TO KEEP US IN LINE SOMETIMES.
IF I EVER SLIP UP... PLEASE LET ME KNOW!
PO PT
I GOT ANOTHER YO-KAI MEDAL! ♪
OH! JIBANYAN, YOU HAVE TO APOLOGIZE TO WHISPER!
FWU—MPT
I TOTALLY FORGOT ABOUT HIM...
I'LL DO IT LATER!
MEOW. MEOW.
WHAT ARE YOU DOING?
I'M GETTING SOME SCRATCH-ES! ♪
YOU SUMMONED UP ANOTHER AMY ILLUSION?
NOPE. ♪

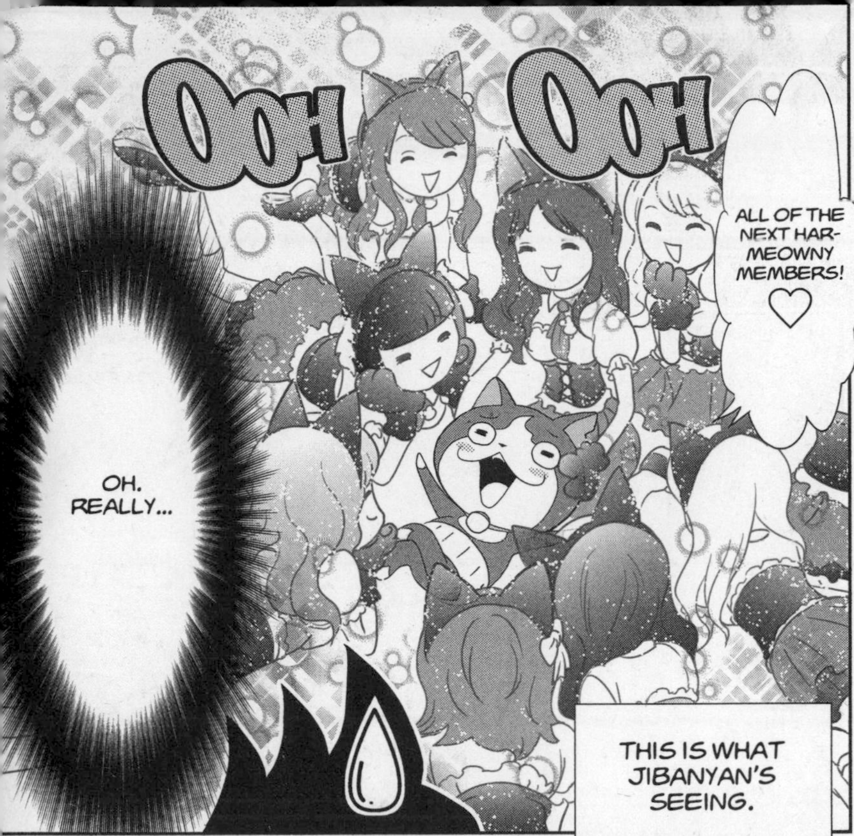
ALL OF THE NEXT HAR-MEOWNY MEMBERS! ♡
OOH
OOH
OH. REALLY...
THIS IS WHAT JIBANYAN'S SEEING.

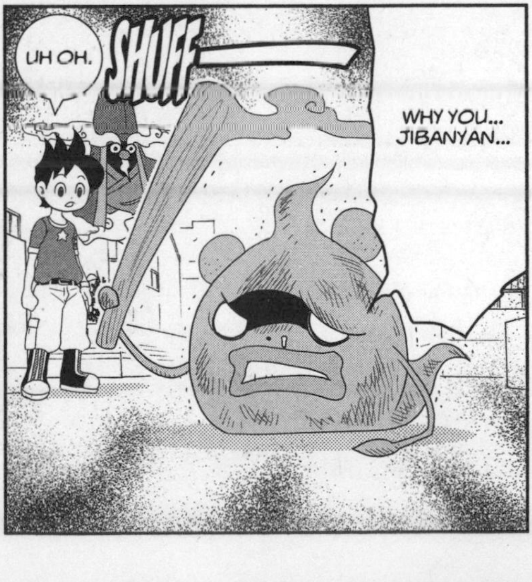
WHY YOU... JIBANYAN...
SHUFF
UH OH.

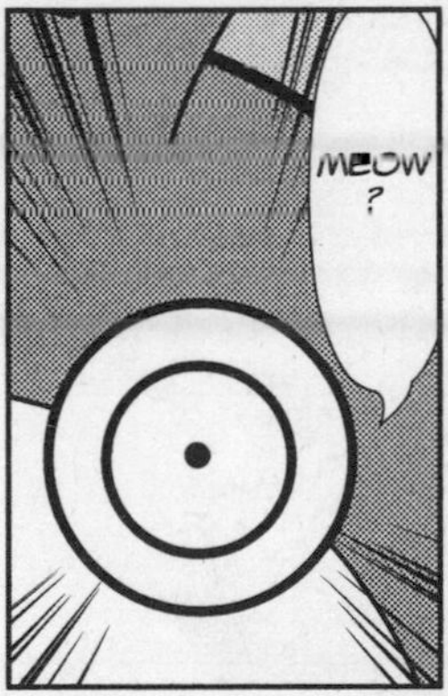
MEOW?

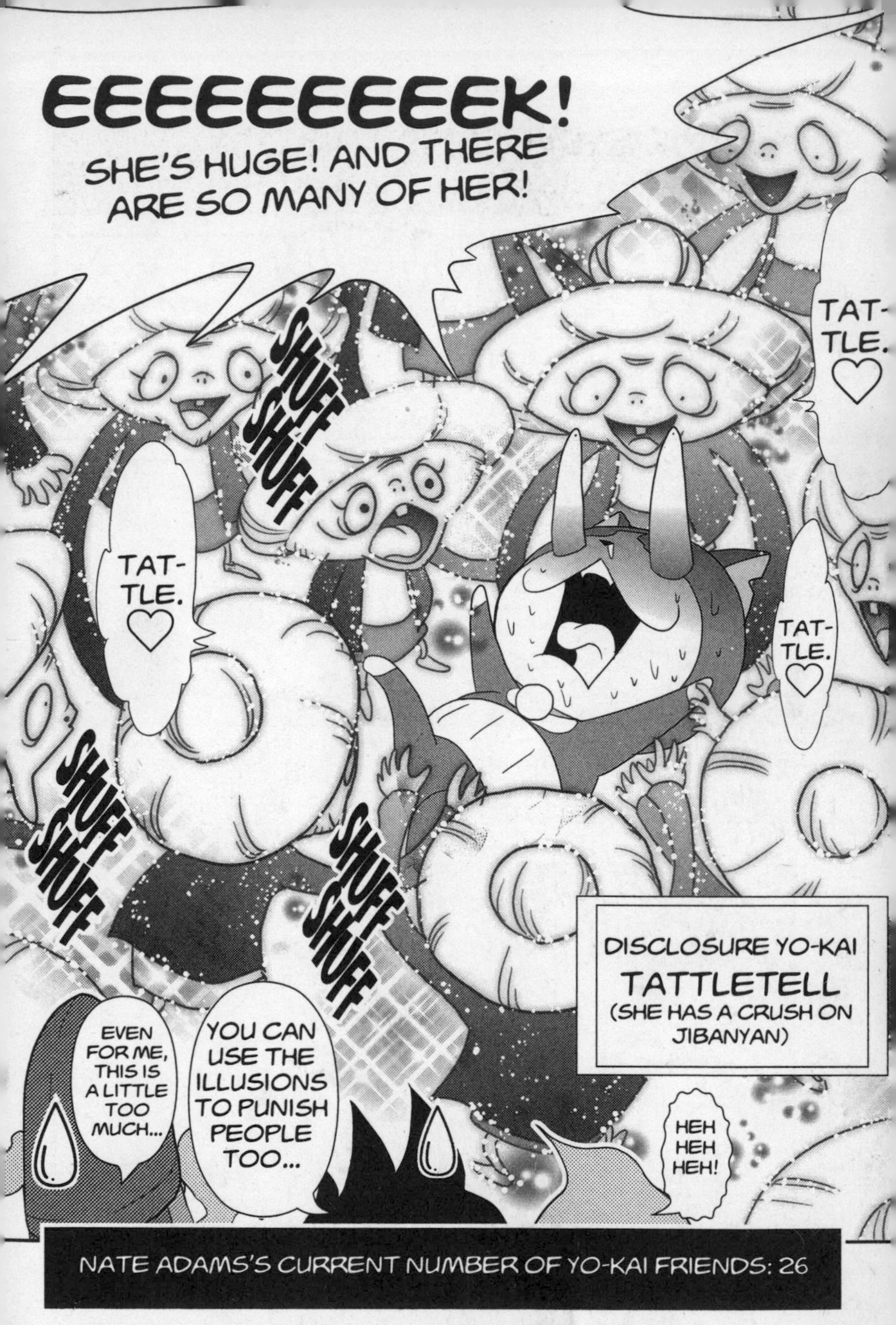
EEEEEEEEEEK!
SHE'S HUGE! AND THERE ARE SO MANY OF HER!
TAT-TLE. ♡
SHUFF SHUFF
TAT-TLE. ♡
TAT-TLE. ♡
SHUFF SHUFF
SHUFF SHUFF
DISCLOSURE YO-KAI TATTLETELL (SHE HAS A CRUSH ON JIBANYAN)
HEH HEH HEH!
YOU CAN USE THE ILLUSIONS TO PUNISH PEOPLE TOO...
EVEN FOR ME, THIS IS A LITTLE TOO MUCH...
NATE ADAMS'S CURRENT NUMBER OF YO-KAI FRIENDS: 26

EPILOGUE: THE TRUTH BEHIND THE ILLUSIONS

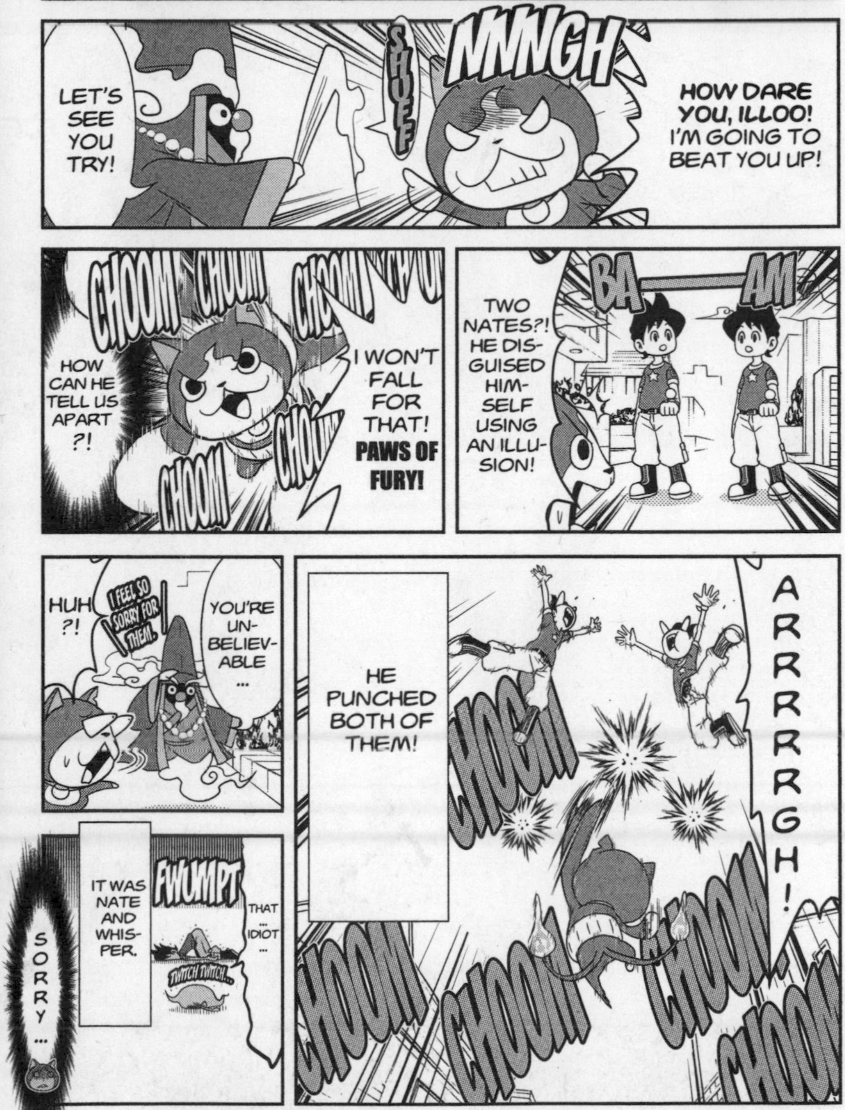

HOW DARE YOU, ILLOO! I'M GOING TO BEAT YOU UP!
NNNGH
SHUFF
LET'S SEE YOU TRY!
BA
AM
TWO NATES?! HE DISGUISED HIMSELF USING AN ILLUSION!
CHOOM CHOOM CHOOM
I WON'T FALL FOR THAT! PAWS OF FURY!
HOW CAN HE TELL US APART ?!
CHOOM
ARRRRRGH!
HE PUNCHED BOTH OF THEM!
CHOOM CHOOM CHOOM CHOOM CHOOM
YOU'RE UNBELIEVABLE ...
I FEEL SO SORRY FOR THEM.
HUH ?!
THAT ... IDIOT ...
FWUMPT
IT WAS NATE AND WHISPER.
TWITCH TWITCH...
SORRY ...

(YO-KAI WATCH VOLUME 4 END / CONTINUED IN VOLUME 5)